Cla

CLARE

John MacKenna

MODERN IRISH CLASSICS

NEW ISLAND

CLARE
First published in 1994 by
The Blackstaff Press Limited
This Edition published 2014
by New Island
2 Brookside
Dundrum Road
Dublin 14

www.newisland.ie

PRINT ISBN: 978-1-84840-323-9
EPUB ISBN: 978-1-84840-324-6
MOBI ISBN: 978-1-84840-325-3

British Library Cataloguing Data. A CIP catalogue record for this book is
available from the British Library

Typeset by JVR Creative India
Cover design by New Island books
Printed by SPRINT-print Ltd.

New Island received financial assistance from
The Arts Council (An Comhairle Ealaíon), Dublin, Ireland

10 9 8 7 6 5 4 3 2 1

About the Author

John MacKenna is the author of fifteen books – novels, short-story collections, memoir, poetry and biography - and a number of radio and stage plays. He is a winner of The Irish Times; Hennessy and Cecil Day Lewis Awards. He is also a winner of a Jacobs Radio award for his documentary series on Leonard Cohen and a Worldplay Silver Medal (New York) for his radio play *The Woman at the Window* (RTE Radio 1) . He lives in Co Carlow and lectures in Creative Writing at NUIM.

Praise for Clare

For Dolores and Peter with
love and deepest admiration.

Contents

HISTORICAL NOTE

John Clare was born in the Northamptonshire village of Helpston on 13 July 1793. He was the son of Parker Clare and Ann Stimson; his twin sister died within a fortnight. Two more girls were born into the family, of whom only one, Sophy, reached adulthood.

When Clare was at school he formed a friendship with Mary Joyce, the daughter of a local farmer. She remained his lifelong obsession, even after her death in 1838.

Having worked as a gardener, a gang labourer, a lime-burner and a harvester, Clare had his first collection of poetry, *Poems Descriptive of Rural Life and Scenery*, published in 1820 — the same year in which he married Martha 'Patty' Turner. The wedding took place on 16 March and their first daughter, Anna, was born on 1 June. Another daughter, Eliza, was born on 16 June 1822. He continued to publish poetry: *The Village Minstrel* (1821); *The Shepherd's Calendar* (1827); and *The Rural Muse* (1835). In 1832, Clare and his family moved to a cottage in Northborough, a village near Helpston.

During his lifetime Clare was befriended by a number of patrons, some more generous and undemanding than others. In this book Lady Kettering is a composite of these various individuals. From childhood Clare had suffered what appear to have been epileptic attacks: by 1837 the severity of these fits, combined with the delusions he was experiencing, led to him being admitted to High Beach asylum in Essex. In July 1841 he escaped and walked the eighty miles to Northborough. He remained there until December of that year, when he was committed to St Andrew's asylum in Northampton. This was to be his home until his death on 20 May 1864.

I AM

1

I am — yet what I am, none cares or knows;
My friends forsake me like a memory lost: —
I am the self-consumer of my woes; —
They rise and vanish in oblivion's host,
Like shadows in love's frenzied stifled throes: —
And yet I am, and live — like vapours tost

2

Into the nothingness of scorn and noise, —
Into the living sea of waking dreams,
Where there is neither sense of life or joys,
But the vast shipwreck of my lifes esteems;
Even the dearest, that I love the best
Are strange — nay, rather stranger than the rest.

3

I long for scenes, where man hath never trod
A place where woman never smiled or wept
There to abide with my Creator, God;
And sleep as I in childhood, sweetly slept,
Untroubling, and untroubled where I lie,
The grass below — above the vaulted sky.

I Sophy Clare

I WAS A WITNESS AT THEIR WEDDING, you know. Him and Patty. Martha was her proper name but the only time I ever heard it used was that day in the church when they exchanged their promises and I stood by as witness. I got married myself, but at a later time. I remember that day of mine but no better than his day. Me beside Patty, and her uncle John beside him. And I remember the rain and wind that day. A March wind whipping in off the fens and rattling the door of the church while we shivered at the altar.

If you asked me to say what kind of life that might make for, I'd say the day was all wrong — and the circumstances too — but it was not the way things turned out at all. It was as good a marriage as most and if there was a failing, it was his. But still. Afterwards there was little enough of celebration. Had it been the summer, we might have danced a little or had some songs, but, as I told you, it wasn't a day for dancing or the like. Not a day for doing more than getting on with it.

Now my day, my wedding day, that was a different day. The year of the Lord eighteen hundred and twenty-four. I was twenty-six years old and not unhandsome. And I'll say no more than that about myself. That day, and I walking to the church, a sheep came out across the road and made right towards me, straight as a hawk's fall, until it nuzzled my dress.

'That's for luck,' John said.

I wasn't so sure but I took his word on it. He was always a one for the lore and the stories. And he played his fiddle for my dance, and he sang one of his songs. He wrote songs, you know, and not just verses. It's the songs I remember best and love the best. I could sing twenty of them if you asked me to. He wrote the most tender songs. Such warming words and singing tunes. I was so proud of him. So proud of everything he did.

I never bury my face in a lilac flower without thinking of him. That smell, that heavy scent of being lost inside the summer, is his smell. And the willow falling to the river's edge, that is where I see him still. Sat there under the arch of the leaves with the Round Oak Waters humming. I still expect, when I pass a lilac hedge, to meet him walking in the lane, to hear him singing some rude verse and laughing to himself.

Not that it was always so. If I tell you the truth, there were days when he was the bane of my life. And I courting, he was forever getting up to his tricks and laying in wait until I'd be settled with some boy and then I'd hear him singing from the branches of a tree above our heads. Singing, you know, quiet, but not so quiet that he couldn't be heard. I never forget one summer evening and a boy kissing me in the churchyard. It was dusk and I was kissing him as much as he was kissing me and then this low voice started singing from beneath a table stone above one of the graves near where we were sat. I knew that voice and I knew those lewd words. Had our mother not forbidden John to sing them in the house?

A maiden head, the virgins trouble, Is well compared to a bubble On a navigable river

— Soon as touch'd 'tis gone for ever.

That boy sat there a minute, petrified, and then he fled before I had the time to tell him who it was. Not that I could have. How could I say, oh, it's only my brother lying under the stone?

And then I heard John laughing and he crept out, swung me by the arms, hugged me, and said: 'He ran and left you. Anyone who would run and leave you is not worth having.'

I told him, I said it to him, 'If I want to run him off,' I said, 'let me be the one to decide that. I don't need you deciding for me.' I told him straight to his face. I was angry with him.

But it wasn't always a tale of jesting. There was a strangeness about John. It went back – or so my mother said – to his delivery. He was a weak thing, she always said, one of a pair. The other was a bonny, ruddy sister, healthy as a parson, but there's the peculiar thing, she was dead within a two week? Faded away like light after the sun has gone. Our other sister, Elizabeth, she died too. But John struggled on. And even when he was as hardy as the other children, he was still the pet lamb in our house.

My mother could neither read nor write herself but her hopes and plans were always high for John. One time he could be a schoolmaster, the next a clerk, and the next again something grander. Oh, how she fussed over that boy, fussed and cockered him. I'd see her in church, singing out above the rest, singing 'Lo, He comes with clouds descending', her voice shaking in the rafters, and suddenly she'd leave off in the middle of the 'hallelujah' and turn to John and see if he was warm enough or well enough. Or close enough. She was always keeping him close to her. In church or at home or in the fields. Not that he was one for hanging about her but she seemed to need reminding every so often that he was alive and well and wasn't going to slip away like his twin sister.

And there's another thing. I'd overhear her talk of learning as 'the blackest art' and yet she had us set on learning, him and me, trotting us off to Master Seaton's school in Glinton church.

You know, I think sometimes my fear of the night and the dead came of playing among the gravestones at our recreation time. John was forever jumping at me from behind the stones. He seemed to find great ease among the dead. Him and Richard Turnill and Mary Joyce would sit among the farthest stones as though they were at home. The rest of us would stay as close to the vestry door as our games would allow. But not those three.

My mother said that he had come as near to death in childhood as he could and it held no fear for him. 'More of it,' I'd say, 'more of the pet lamb.' I'd say it to his face. I'd run along the lane and shout at him like a sheep. 'You're the pet lamb,' I'd say. 'Baa,' I'd say. If he was with his friends, with the Turnill boys or Mary Joyce, he'd be most annoyed and that would please me all the more. 'The pet lamb, John Clare,' I'd shout. 'Baa, our John, and baa again.'

Oh, he would be enraged, you know, and threaten all kinds of torture on me, but I would laugh. I knew him well enough not to fear what he said. Not that he was always the lamb himself. Sometimes, even he would be overcome by the weight of my mother's concern and he would ask her to let him be. And sometimes he would slip her lead in church and sit with the boys at the back and sing bawdy words to the hymns. 'Away with our sorrow and our care' was one they had a liking for. And when I say a liking, it was not for singing that as Wesley intended.

I think my mother caught him between the weakly child he was and the man our father wanted him to be. I think her expectations and our father's expectations were like two crosses laid across John's shoulders.

'An open hand is no lure for a hawk,' my mother would say. 'You must hope to rise if rise you will.'

'Rise?' our father would laugh. 'The lad can hardly rise from bed without your lending him a hand.'

And then they'd be off about his future and his worth and his prospects. Not that our father stopped John or me, you know. He never stopped us out of school beyond the times when we were needed in the fields. At harvest and the like. He saw some sense in schooling but he never had the hopes our mother had.

'That,' she would say, when he was not about, 'is because of his past. He likes nothing better than to set people together by the ears.'

What she meant was that our father was a bastard, though I never heard her say as much. She believed all his sourness stemmed from that. Not that he was continually sour. I would not be the one to say that. His sourness grew with his age and so did his illness, and I think the two grew of one root and my mother, being ill herself and not complaining, could not see that fact. But there, I have gone off down a lane of my own making and left you no nearer the place you were going.

John. He was not like our father or our mother. Neither one in particular. And not like me. He had some of my wildness, or I had some of his, but he was darker than me. I think he carried some of his sister's passing with him through his life. When things were good for him, he missed something of her, and when he missed her, he seemed to find a passion to make up for her loss. He was close to me, you know, but always there was a shadow walking between us. The shadow of our sister or of Richard Turnill or of Mary Joyce, and it made my flesh creep. I tell you, this is truth.

Still, that was only part of it. There were other, better, parts. Let me tell you those. How he'd swing me in his arms, up into the apple tree. Our apple tree. That tree. I must explain to you.

We lived in a cottage that had four apartments and in each apartment was a family. The garden was divided too, and in our division was an apple tree. In winter it would sparkle like a gewgaw and we would watch it in the winter sun, the branches flashing like swimmers in standing water. And in spring the flowers weighed it almost to the grass and then the flowers fell and the leaves were lifted for a while before the apples, small as stones at first, began to lower themselves and grow. That tree paid our rent for years. And it gave us children a place to play. John would swing me high into that tree and I would close my eyes and jump out into the air and always know that he would catch me in his arms. He wasn't strong but he was strong enough. Oh, such games! Just him and me. Just John and me and I screaming in the garden, my dress flying like a wash in the air and John's sure arms catching me and holding me and my feet touching the grass as soft as a leaf. I was a leaf that fell and fell and never once got trodden on.

That tree was everything then. To climb in, to swing in, to pick fruit from. Every morning in the autumn time we would collect the windfalls from the grass and my mother would walk round and round the tree and point to the apples that were ready for picking. And John and me would scramble through the branches, following her orders.

He would make a game of it, naming the apples for the planets and the stars. 'We cannot take that one, Mother, for that would leave us without sun.' Or moon or some other planet of his liking and my mother would laugh and tell him to pass on and then, and we walking to school, he would produce the sun-apple for Mary Joyce, without a word.

And other times John and me would watch our father digging in the garden. His great back bent and the huge clods that he lifted like dead grass. Tossed above his head and caught and shook on their way down. He would worry the clay from a clod and leave it lifeless at the side of a drill. Then he'd call to us to come and gather up the grasses and burn them. And sometimes he would throw the fork to John and say: 'You turn a sod, lad, time is coming for you to do it.'

John would struggle, you know, struggle to lift the heavy clay and our father would take the fork and fling a clod up into the morning sky and catch it and shake it and laugh at John.

'Weak as water,' he'd say. 'And your mother is steady as time.'

'And what am I?' I'd ask.

'You, Sophy, are lovely as a lily,' our father would say.

For the most part, days were good then. I never remember any great trouble and certainly none that could compare with what come afterwards. Days of work or days of schooling. Nights at the fire or in visiting, or nights in dancing as the season set. And John at his fiddling in our house or another house or, sometimes, at James Merrishaw's night school. Even when he was a boy, I recall him fiddling and reading and making up his verses and songs. Whatever troubles there were, they were little as dust. Nothing like what they became. Nothing.

For fun, our mother would ask John, and he nine or ten, to recite by heart from the Bible, and he would always say from Job. He had a fondness for Job. There was one verse, I recall, that frightened me: 'And the Lord said unto Satan, Whence comest thou? Then Satan answered the Lord, and said, From going to and fro in the earth, and from walking up and down in it.'

I would think of that and I walking to and fro myself and when I used to be sitting in the churchyard during school and I'd expect to meet the devil face to face. I daren't tell that to John. He would have reminded me of it in the nighttime or on evenings when I was setting out to walk alone. He was forever doing that but sometimes I thought it was odd, this peace he had among the dead and yet how he was fearful of the demons that lurked in sunless, haunted places.

All these things. I keep returning to these things without meaning to. I can only make sense of it as that shadow that forever fell between us. Always cast by someone or other and not always the same source but always that same coldness. Not that I didn't love him. I loved him with the thickness of blood and the closeness of a sister. But a shadow has a way of coming between things.

I could tell you a hundred things we did in our childhood. We climbed, we sang, we stole birds' eggs, we swam, we hunted snails, we worked with our father, we sat in the same school room, we laughed, we talked and we slept in the same bed and I cannot say in which circumstances that shadowy mist fell. It was not in everyone but it came, and finally it stayed, though by then it was a heavier and more sorrowful affair. But I will not try to explain it away as just my nature. It was more than that. Much more.

John was always following some road: mathematics; poems; fiddling; songs; the thought of schoolmastering; scribbling on sugar bags. But I never believed he would reach a destination. I was proud of him but that darkness fell between us and then fell thicker and thicker on him. And when the crosses our mother and father laid on him were gone at last, he had found his own slow sadness. As though he needed it, as though he could not make his way without a pain inside himself, as though he felt less full without this suffering. Does that make any sense at all?

I'm not always given to this kind of thinking but when I look back, you know, at times like this, these are the things that come to mind and come without my being able to stop them or without my asking them. Good things and darker things, and often the darker things hang a gauze across the brighter. Or hang there just at the edge. Like As if they were waiting. Now I know that sounds odd, or worse, but every time I look back or think back that strangeness, that blackness, is there between us or around us.

I remember, and I a girl out courting, I would dread the sight of a crowd along the roadway. Any crowd anywhere scared me because I never knew until I came upon it whether our John would be in the midst of it. It might not matter now – although I cannot say, not for certain – but then, and I a girl of sixteen and seventeen, it put a fright on me. I'd be walking with some lad and we'd see people huddled on the road and I'd think at once that John must be lying there among them in one of his terrible attacks. He would be taken by these attacks and fall down speechless but not soundless. He would scream and cry and kick and claw until he lost the energy to continue.

Our father said these fits went back to a day at harvesting. He told me John was team-leading the horses for the Turnills and one of the loaders, I think Thomas Drake, fell from the top of a wagon and was killed. His neck was broke and John saw it all. He was standing at the horse's head and Drake fell forward. Our father said everyone in the team heard the crack of his neck when it broke and John heard it most of all, he being the nearest. He went into a weakness straight away with fright, and then these fits and turns began. He told me once, lying in his bed at home, that he always knew when he was about to fall because a coldness would start in his feet and move through his body and he would lose all feeling. But whatever the cause, it would always occupy my fears when I saw a crowd in the lane. Sometimes, and I don't mind confessing this, I would walk on and hope that no one would call out to me that my brother was taken so. I would count to twenty and five, the sum of the figures in my birth year and always my number, and think if none had called me by then that it were not our John that had drawn the crowd together.

But oftentimes the call came. 'Sophy Clare,' they'd call, 'your brother is taken mad again.'

I might try to walk on, hoping his friends would come to his assistance, but more oftentimes than not I was left to tend him and bring him back home when he came to himself. Always, after his madnesses, he would be weak as water. Even in winter days he would sweat and sweat and we would have to dawdle on the roadway and stop every twenty yards or thereabouts.

I saw him once one January after he had taken a turn and fallen into a whitethorn hedge. His face and neck were cut and I had the skin torn from my hands in trying to help him out and he a leaden weight. In the end Morgan the carpenter came by and lifted him clear and laid him on the grass. It was hoary and hard but he lay there a long time without stirring. So long I thought he was dead. So long that when I got him to his feet the shape of his body was left on the frost – the very shape of his body through the frost.

At other times when we were walking from school, John and the Turnills and Mary Joyce and me, he would stop and sit by the road and try to let the madness pass by staying very still, but that never worked. He would go into a weakness and we would wait until he came out it again, and then walk on, carrying him between us. But one thing I must say, and I have always said this, I never heard the Turnills or Mary Joyce laugh or call after him as the others did, about his madness, you know. Never.

My mother's greatest fear was that he should be taken with a turn somewhere out on the fens and fall into the water and be drowned. One day in spring, and John fifteen or so, Richard Turnill told me he was walking a lane and saw a flock of crows grazing close to the woods and a dark patch in their midst, out near Wormstalls' farm this was, and he was about to pass on when something turned his path. He might as easily have walked on, he told me, might not even have seen the form had he been looking the other way, but when the crows scattered into the trees he saw clearly that it was our John sprawled senseless in the grass. He might have lain there for all the day and nigh had Richard not come upon him. That time he was without speech for all of the day and night and some of the next day too. Lying up on his bed with his eyes open but not speaking. I brought him up a cup of broth and his eyes were staring at the roof and there was not a movement in them. This time, I thought, he is dead and I turned to go back down and tell my mother, but he sighed and I knew he was still there.

That was his worst time of all, knowing none of us. The doctor came and looked at him and muttered and sighed, but could do nothing until John found the way back for himself. My mother told me not to ask him about what had happened, not to talk of it to him.

The Turnills came and sat with him that day and the next and Richard said he believed John would mend or die. He said that to me in the garden out our front. 'If he gets worse he will die,' he said. 'But I think the worst is over.'

That was Richard's way, to face the worst and then to find a better hope. I loved him dearly. Of all John's friends he was the truest and kindest. Once, one Christmas time, and we dancing in his house, he took my hand and held it for an hour or more and kissed me, and we leaving and he told me he thought of me all the time. That was the Christmas before he fell ill himself. If he was about, and John in his madnesses, I would never fear. He would stay with John and talk to him and take him home.

But so often there was only me, you know, and all I could do was tell whomever had gathered to stand back and leave him be, that he would come better himself, if only they would leave him be. It got to a time when people knew this and once he had finished his yelling and kicking they left him to me and went their way.

I would sit by him and chatter. Not for his sake but for my own. To keep myself from thinking of what was happening and the things that might yet happen. I would remind him of the games we played as children. Snail-hunting in the fields. That was a favourite of ours.

But it wasn't always so. These mists grow with remembering. There were other times and other days that were happier, brighter. Times when the mists were distant from us or fell so weakly that we didn't see them or feel their icy breath on our necks. Days in the sun when we brought our father's dinner up to him in the fields. Me carrying the bread and cheese, John swinging a can of beer round and round and the beer staying inside, even when it was upside down.

'If it spills our father will kill you,' I'd say.

'It cannot spill,' John would say, shaking his head. 'It cannot spill out if I twirl it fast enough.'

And sure enough, it never did.

Sometimes John would race across the grass and hide among the elms and I would shout at him to wait and he would spring out to frighten me and laugh at my fear. Other days, and we all at school, we would leapfrog home together. Five of us in a line down the long lane. The Turnills and John and Mary Joyce and me. Leapfrogging all that way. Five children laughing so that our voices sent a new warmth through the hedges and the fens. And hopscotching. John made us a rhyme for hopscotch. A rhyme of our own, known only to the five of us. The first rhyme of his that I recall. 'And one is sticks and two is stones and three is hope and four is bones and five is living and six is dying and seven is walking and eight is flying.' That was how it went.

'Say it soft if there's anyone about,' John would tell me. 'This is ours and we must keep it.'

And we did. I never heard another soul say that rhyme.

'Always dying and bones and the like,' Mary Joyce said, when John spoke the rhyme over to us. 'You always talk of that.'

Curious that she should have been the one to mention it. But all that was to come much later. And John was always going on at me, you know, with stories of weird happenings. Not that he was alone in that. My mother was forever telling strange stories and the lower the wick grew, the more frightening the stories grew. Stories about witches and goblins and fairies. Fairies that slipped through the keyholes at night and stole children away. Bold children. I thought then that they had stolen our sisters away from us. I said it once to my mother and she stopped that story ever afterwards.

When we were abed, I'd lie and listen to the mice scratching in the eaves and hear John's steady breathing beside me and imagine all the witches flying by in the blackness outside. From Deeping Gate to Southorpe, from Newborough to Bainton, and all of them swishing over Helpston and scraping the twigs of their brooms on the window of our room. John asleep and me saying over and over the prayers we had said together at our bedside: 'Bless us, Lord, and bless our home. Bless our father, bless our mother. Keep us pure and watch and guard us through the night.' And still the witches flicked our window and still he slept and still I could not find a place to sleep.

But then the summer would come and I'd think no more of witches or fairies or dying in the darkness. I'd think only of games to play and freedom to run and sun to light the evenings and our father singing in the fields. There was one song he sang that my mother chastised him for (she would never hear it sung within the house), but our father sang it anyway, outside in the garden or in the fields or on the lane and he walking.

As I and Molly Baily went along the greenwood side, with some soft words we did concert that she should be my bride.

My instrument was well in tune and she in tune would keep and frankly we did then presume to find a happy sleep.

If our father was intent on making my mother rage he would sing that song softly in her hearing but change the name to Annie Stimson, my mother's name before marrying. And she would tell him to hold his mouth and he would walk outside and go on singing in the garden, louder and louder as the song went on.

Each part did well in concert move, the whisper I did heed and oh such melting strains of love that she cried out with me.

Our music was such charming sweet, we played it three times o'er but when I could no more repeat, she laughed and cried encore.

There, I remember it as well as when I knew it first. I sang it once to my own husband and he scolded me.

'No woman should be heard singing that kind of song,' he said.

'My father sang it,' I said back, as sharp as a needle. He nodded and coughed and said he was not surprised, knowing that would anger me. For I had made the mistake of telling my husband that my father was a bastard and ever since he has taken it upon himself to treat my father's memory as though every failing was to be expected and every virtue was an accident. If someone, in conversation, refers to my father's singing or his drinking or his wrestling, my husband will cough his little cough, the same cough he gives in church when he is passing out the plate for collection, and smile a smile that is neither warm nor sweet. Some day I will find a word about his churchgoing and put it in where it will halt his gallop. Not yet, but some day.

Richard Turnill would not have been like that. He would have remembered the better things about our father. His music and his great laugh that was like thunder. And his storytelling. Our father could hold us silent for an hour, silent on our form in the winter, silent under the apple tree in the summer. Silent as a fly in the web of his stories. Or walking home on harvest nights, down the lanes, he would start up a story, sometimes that same story that has come back to darken my own dark days. The story about Jane the barmaid in Barholm.

Jane was always searching for a lover, for a man who would love her the whole life through. Anyone who wanted her would come to the inn where she worked and when she got some notion that this might be the one, she would take them up to her room and lie with them. Sometimes two in a night, our father said, and always in the hope that this might be the one who would stay. But they all left her afore morning, he said, took her and left. Men came from as far distant as Upton and Glinton to lie with her and leave her. He had met with men himself, our father said, and he a young boy walking to work in the summer mornings, and he would stop to talk with them in the road and they would tell him how they were returning from a night with Jane.

But there was one young farmer who frequented the inn and Jane fell in love with him and he with her, or so it seemed, and she stopped lying with the other men and lay only with him. They walked out together and she lived for him. Then he got her with child and when she told him, he denied her, denied her there in the inn, before all the other men.

The next night she was found hanging in her room, with her face to the window, our father said, and her eyes burning like the deepest coals in hell. They couldn't be closed, he said. And where to bury her? Church gates were closed to her and none would hear of her being buried in or near Barholm. So the landlord of the inn had her body taken by night and buried on the waste patch at the crossroads in Helpston, where the Upton and Barnack roads meet. The same crossroads me and John would pass in going for the milk.

It was a story told in the light and with our father beside us but a story that came back to haunt us on darksome evenings when the wind spoke through the throat of that barmaid and the few leaves and battered trees managed to twist themselves into the shape of a woman and her unborn infant.

Our father's stories and his way in telling them were that good that they went on long after they had been told. My husband could snap all he liked but there was no story he could tell that had the power of our father's tales.

But there were other things too, you know, that I would never tell my husband for fear of him casting them up to me. I loved my father very much and I loved the way that his laughter could make a summer evening seem brighter than it was. I never feared for us when he had his strength. Watching him dig our garden or fell a tree or carry its trunk home on his shoulders and split it for our fire gave me courage. But there was a chillier side – not that I believe that he meant to cause John pain. He was intent only on trying to make him sturdy, to give him the toughness to get on with his life and to come out of the sickness and weakness that cursed him.

Our father would take John into the garden on summer evenings and show him how to hold and wrestle. And each lesson would end in a match between our father and John. They would face up to each other in the grass and my mother would come and stand at the gable's end and sometimes people passing in the road would stop to watch. Round and round they'd go, eyeing each other, rushing, backing, testing, and then suddenly our father would have John in his grip and then flat upon his back, his shoulders hard against the clay. Then he'd back away, you know, to let John up and they would face to each other once again. Sometimes our father would fall and John would leap on him but in a twist our father would be out from under him like a fish and John would be pinned again. Our father would give a great hearty laugh and pull him to his feet and square to him again. It might go on for an hour like that until our father grew weary of always winning and shouted at John and told him to fight like a man.

'Last fight,' our father would shout. 'Last fight, put all your strength in this.' And he would run at John and have him on his back in a blink.

'Mind that boy's head,' my mother would shout and my father would swear quietly and turn John with one last throw and leave him face down in the warm grass.

'You'll never be a fighter, boy,' he'd say, 'unless you learn to fight.'

Then he'd walk away. Often as not John would be up and after him, launching himself onto our father's back like a hawk on a mouse, and laughing. But not always. There were times, after our father had gone into the house, when I heard John sobbing with pain and frustration and anger. He never cried aloud and our father never knew he cried, but I did. I never told our father for he would have said something to John and that would have been worse. But he should have known when to stop. Or so I've always thought. But I would never mention that to my husband, you know, for he would store it and use it when he thought it most hurtful to me. That is the pass we've come to in our lives.

There I go again, shadows again. I mustn't let you think it was all, or even mostly, like that. We threshed with him, my mother and us and our father. Working in the fields together. And all of us seated in farmers' kitchens eating together and my mother laughing because she did not have to cook the food and could enjoy it all the more.

Best of all was the threshing up at Turnills'. I would get to work side by side with Richard and the work never seemed as hard for that. Much more of laughing and playing than at any other farm. I know now that was because of my fondness for Richard and his company but then, and I a girl, it seemed the Turnill harvest was always easier and quicker and the food laid out was always better and we worked more as a team together. Our father and mother in the field, John at the horse's head and me racing about at all kinds of doings and all the while trying to keep Richard in my eyes. There! Not one shadow or finger of coldness in that.

But there were times, too, when our father would show great kindness to John. I recall a time when John went on and on at our father about a book he wanted, a book of verse, for one shilling and six pennies, and in the end our father gave him the money and John walked to Stamford to buy his book but the shop was closed, it being a Sunday. And the following Tuesday he walked there again and came back home carrying his possession proudly. Or so I recollect it, though once, and John and me talking about it, he said it was not so. He told me I remembered it wrong. He told me he sneaked back through the village, climbing into the fields and waiting until dusk, for fear of being seen and called a crazy boy.

They did call him a crazy boy when he went walking with a book in his hand. Not all of them, not the Turnills or Mary Joyce, but there were many that did. Richard Turnill was a true friend to John. And to me. But in a particular way to John.

I may be mistaken on that recollection of John walking home with the book. It may be that he remembered it more correctly but I have my own memory of an evening in January – and this I can swear upon the Bible – and I out the lane. It was dusk. A muslin of snow was hanging on the pastures and there was more in the sky, blowing in from Peakirk and Newborough. I was making for home and the snow behind me and for some reason I cannot recall, or there may have been no reason at all, I turned to search the road behind me for company and there, coming out of the falling darkness and confusion of snow, were three figures walking carelessly in my footsteps. Our John and Mary Joyce and Richard Turnill. Two of them with coats pulled up about their faces, all but Mary Joyce, whose shawl was wrapped about her, leaving her hair free in the chill wind. I stopped in the shelter of a bush and waited for them to come on. They had not noticed me. The three of them linked arm in arm and laughing, as I heard when they came near enough for me to hear above the whistle of the wind and the damping of the snow. Their faces were white with snow and their hands would sweep, from time to time, wiping the frozen blizzard from their skins.

How strange to think of that occasion. There must be a thousand others when John walked with them or with others, or when I myself walked with Richard and Mary, and yet that is the picture I return to, in waking and in sleep, time and time. Three pale figures on the snowy road from Glinton. I can only think that they had gone to call on Mary Joyce and she was coming with them to the Turnills' when the snow came after them, and they carried on their laughing way without a thought for it. She cannot have been coming to our cottage for I have no remembrance of any time in all our lives when she stood on our kitchen floor, not even as a child. But this time that I recall was when Richard was seventeen or so. None of us was still a child.

There is another night I call to mind, when Richard and John and me were walking late. We had gone out into the fen to watch the stars and we were returning home. It was a late night and there was a full moon imprinted on the sky. We came down by the church. It had just been slated at that time and the moon was skating down its grey back. We stopped to look at this and John sighed and said: 'There is no other good in that place than the sight of the moon on its roof.'

He was always against the church and clergy. Always railing and ranting at home about them and then disappearing of a Sunday, out across the fens or deep into the woods, when it was church time. Yet he knew his hymns and said his prayers but he would not go inside the church. It drowned his light, he said, as no river could.

Our father would bang the table of a Saturday night and tell John he must go.

'And listen to them bend the word of God to fit their fences and their rights?' John would say.

'You will be there,' our father would say, very quietly but very sternly, after he had finished slapping his fist upon the wood. 'You will be there.'

But there was never an hour early enough for our father to catch John before he was gone into the woods. In summertime I fancy he stole out in the night and slept in the fields. He was always a great one for sleeping out was John. I think our father went through this ritual to satisfy himself that he had done his duty by the Lord and John went through his to satisfy his own stubbornness. Perhaps it was our father he was besting and not the clergymen at all. Or both.

But still. Let me tell you something that may make you think me crazy too. Some nights, in the pitchy days of the turning of the year, when I am sitting at my fireside and my husband is well asleep and the wind is blowing in hard against the windowpane, carrying a bonnet of snow, I pull back the curtain and press my face against the glass, feeling the draught upon my cheek, and slowly come to recognise the furniture of our yard in the white covering. The pump, the hedges, the fencing, the gateposts, and beyond them the roadway. And I wait there, fancying I see the three figures walking from the storm. Even in the blackness I see Mary Joyce's shawl, red about her shoulders, growing paler by the moment, until she shakes it, and suddenly it is red again. John with his head thrown sidewards, laughing. His drab, thin coat wrapped about him like a sheet, taking his shape in its wetness. And Richard Turnill, whose clothing I can never recall, his bright eyes in the dull day as they came close to where I was standing, sheltered.

It was he who saw me first and he did not say a word to them but walked straight towards me and smiled and said my name. 'Sophy.'

That was enough. I think it is he I miss the most of all. His voice. His face.

I know the life I had as far as John was concerned. It was as good or as bad as it was meant to be. It was beyond my power to change. And as for Mary Joyce, we all of us should have seen what would happen there. That was beyond all our powers to change. We might as well have tried to keep the pastures unfenced for the hope we should have had.

But for Richard, there might have been something as far as my existence was concerned. I feel there was, you know. And when the others walk on past our gate, on nights like that, I wish them well but I fancy Richard comes and stands in recognition of what might have been between us. I think my fancy in this matter is a great degree less than John's was in his expectations of Mary Joyce. But then, perhaps, we are all inclined to see what we would. We forgive those who forgive us. We do unto others as we would have them do to us. Or so my husband prays at church.

I will speak no more about my imaginings for Richard but I must relate the last time he and I were together. It was Eastertide and we went walking in search of John and found him seated, fishing, beneath a willow. The tree was flaming with catkins and John was soon telling us about goat willows and grey willows and eared willows and I was anxious that Richard and I might go on walking together. But we did not. Instead we sat with John, and thereafter I always thought of willows as a curse, you know, but not in a great way. Not like sickness or death or ruin but as a cause of frustration to me.

That is one tale I did relate to my husband and he said nothing, but an hour later he came back to me and said: 'We never called them willows. They were sallows in my parish.'

It was one of the last surprises in our life. Since then I have not been surprised by anything he might say or any road he might take from something I have said. But still, enough of him and this.

Richard Turnill died when he was nineteen years. Of the typhus. He was buried of a May morning and it was the only time I saw John go near the church without complaining, and the least happy time of all.

The whitethorn was hanging out across the path through the churchyard, brushing our faces as we followed after his coffin. John told me afterwards he heard it brush against the side of the coffin. Weeks afterwards one day in June when we were sitting in our garden. I was sewing and John was noting his plants in a book. He would take each flower and hold it up against the sky and say its name and then write that in his book. I recall some of those names even yet: Solomon's seal; a late-flowering yellow star-of-Bethlehem; the columbine; monkshood; and the creeping buttercup. These I remember, perhaps not from that day but from another. Or perhaps I remember them from that day too.

When all his plants were listed and put into his book he closed it and said very quietly to me: 'I heard the whitethorn scrape against the side of Richard's coffin.'

I said nothing because I might have heard it too, but I had no memory of anything beyond my own sorrow from that day. No recollection of any sense but dread.

'I heard the whitethorn scrape along the side of the coffinwood,' he said, 'and I thought it was his fingers scratching to be free, to walk out across the fens with me. To walk into the night and watch the great plough that ploughs the skies. I all but called out to his father to lift the coffin lid.'

And still I was silent. Half-frightened at the thought that Richard might have gone to his grave still breathing, though I knew the typhus had swept him from our lives. But I was frightened, too; at the thought of what my brother's screaming in the churchyard might have done to those of us about. Madness mixed with grief is a terrifying thought.

I was at a loss for words but then I said: 'Tell me the other plants you have in your book, John.'

And he did. Carefully he turned his pages and I pretended an interest in the pale flowers pressed flat upon the paper. Cowslips and false oxlips, whose delicate yellow had yellowed the pages into which they had been pressed. The tall and ghostly poet's narcissus, a flower born for my brother if ever one was born for one man. Salsify with its twisted leaves. Spotted medick and black medick with their three-cornered leaves. The bold forget-me-not, cold there in its page, a reminder of the words my brother had just spoken.

'What next?' I urged, turning the page for him. 'What else is there that you have not shown me? Show me more.'

I wanted him to go on turning his pages, I wanted those dead flowers to continue in procession and stop out all need for words and all thought of the dead boy, the only one who might have helped us both. The only one to hold John and listen to his gibbering and keep him close when the shaking came and his senses were gone. The only one to take him home and see him into his bed and sit with him until his mind returned. The only one to shake him out of his terrible despair. The only one whose face made mine a mirror of delight.

I cannot say that Richard Turnill's death cast that shadow between John and me. It might have been cast by the other dead children or by our own lives and the people that we were but I do believe his light might have kept the desolation at bay. When his light went out, the shadow seemed to settle more firmly on our hopes.

But a thing more frightening still was to come of that. One evening in the harvest time, and we walking home together, John went back to our talk of Richard's burial.

'Do you recall the day of Richard's burying?' he asked me.

As if it was something I could forget, as if it was something a hundred years before. 'I remember,' I said.

'By God but it was hot. And all that mass of people and yet the quietness. So quiet I heard the whitethorn scrape against his coffin. I thought for a long time afterwards he was scraping the wood.'

'I know that, John,' I said.

'It was the whitethorn,' he said, very slowly and very simply and I was terrified by that slowness, that way in which he spoke. Terrified because I knew he had been wrestling with this for all the summer and had only now, perhaps even this day, come to an answer in his own mind. I think I realised then, there, how bleak his future was.

I tried, at once, to take his mind off that talk (and my own, too). I made myself to smile and spoke lightly: 'Do you remember a game we played as children, John, rolling stones in our yard? Do you remember that?'

He said nothing, not one word, and we walked home in silence.

One evening, not long after that time, John was about something in the garden and our father came out and watched and then shouted across the grass.

'You haven't wrestled me in a long time, John,' he said.

John went on with whatever he was doing.

'I fancy a turn,' our father said. He threw his coat into the branches of the apple tree and squared to John. 'Come on, lad, there's many would put a shilling down to face me yet.'

John left down whatever was in his hand and put his own coat on the grass and faced our father and they eyed each other. Our father slapped his hands against his legs a time or two and moved to one side and then the other. All the while John went on circling him and then, as quick as sticks, he had our father on the ground, his knees pressed into our father's arms, his hands upon his chest. I saw our father draw a deep breath and I waited for him to push John back. I saw his muscles strain and his face begin to purple, but there was nothing he could do. John had him pinned and he was pinned for good.

Our father lay there, with John astride him, for a good long time and then John stood and stepped back. I waited for him to offer his hand, to pull our father from the ground, but instead he walked away and picked his coat from the grass and walked out of the garden.

I went inside the house and I knew, as I should have known but had not taken notice of, that our father was broken with work. He was good for nothing but to fill in the stones on the turnpike.

All that winter he sat beside the fire and watched John writing at the table. Once I heard him say as how the table had been used for nothing but to eat from before John started at his poems and I told this to him.

'He laughs at me,' John said. 'He laughs and asks how I could ever hope to be a poet.'

'He's proud of you,' I said. 'We all are.'

John said nothing at all to that.

It seemed to me then that whatever life they should have together, under that roof, must either be brief or bitter but it was not so. They never wrestled again and there was no reply to our father whenever he commented upon John's verse-making.

And I was proud of him, proud to have him there on my wedding day, to hear him sing and play his fiddle. The vicar that married us had said somewhere that John had took his poems from other books and tried to pass them off as his own. But it was not till some months later that the word got back to John concerning this. By that time I was safely married. I shudder to think what might have fallen out on that day if he had known.

As it was, I was pleased and proud to say to my husband's people: 'This is my brother, John Clare, as has had poems published, as has been to London and knows writers and other famous people.'

That was something my husband's family could not contest. His father nodded and said, 'Soft words butter no parsnips', and went about his dull and sullen way but he could not counter John with anything of like nature on his own side.

Not that I wish you to think it was a day full of bitterness, you know. Not at all. No one, not even a queen, would have been fit partner for my husband in his family's eyes. It was not especially me that was wanting, it was but the whole world as had failed them.

I ignored that part of the day and sang, though I was careful in the choosing of what I sang. I called on John to sing and he was not so careful, and I smiled at that, and had him fiddle for our dancing. I danced with him myself and minded him of how our mother was forever finding his verses in our room and using them to scour her pots. At the year's end, what should have been enough to make a book was but a handful left on the window ledge. I gave him my clothes chest after that, the one with the lock, and our mother never knew. I took that chest with me on marrying and John left some verses in it and I have kept them still.

Oh, we laughed and danced and sang that day as we had rarely done before and have never since and never will again. I like to keep that day close to my heart. It was a day of failure in my life. I had hoped to dance my wedding dance with someone else. I had long imagined Sophy Turnill to be the fairest name I could have dreamed of but in spite of all, I made it a day of enjoyment, if not of happiness.

The fiddlers played 'Moss Roses' and I danced with John and smiled at all about me. And for that reason I like to keep its certain warmth where I can draw upon it. I remember his laughter and we dancing, his legs high flying as we brushed the walls about the room, and my husband's people uncertain as to whether he was mad or drunk or both. And my mother crying in the corner, as though she had suffered a loss of life. He minded me how she had cried, too, when he left us for a soldier. Swearing she would never see him again. And all the neighbours waving him away.

'Three hundred men from the county,' he told me afterwards, 'and I one of the shortest.'

And he told me how he hated the other men more than he could ever hope to hate the French, no matter what their crime. And in the end he struck his corporal, and came marching home, disgraced but free. Our father were proud of that, of John striking a corporal. He might have done the same himself. He smiled to hear John tell of that and got him to tell the story over and over and loved it every time. I knew he felt his wrestling had been worthwhile. But John would never nod to that. He told the story and allowed our father some satisfaction but never the satisfaction of knowing he had trained his son that well.

I never spoke of that to John, as I never spoke of many things, and still I do not speak of much that concerns me to those I should confide in but that, you know, is not the same as not caring and not feeling. Perhaps I should not have been able to talk plainly to Richard if he had lived and I had remained his friend or something closer, but I feel we would have had an openness because he was without pretence. My husband does not believe in parading his inner thoughts and therefore does not welcome others doing it to him.

John was open in certain things but the distance he kept between our father and himself – rightly or wrongly – contributed a degree or two to the darkness of that shadow between us. So many things increased its weight. So many factors contrived to bring us where we are. And so few of late have made any light in the darkness.

Those verses I kept I never read any more, not because I do not think them good but because they are all written in a time when we were much younger and there was still a hope that things would improve. Now I see no place where improvement might come, in his life or mine.

The last thing I read from John was this letter which arrived unexpected from Northampton asylum at the start of the springtime. I had reckoned, as I opened it, a letter like the others that had come at intervals, where John had signed himself in the name of Lord Byron. Letters full of fancy and rantings. Not letters at all, really, more the demented ramblings of a man who had forgotten who he was. But when I read this letter I felt grateful for the respite that had been his in writing it and was mine in reading it. Then, I understand, he returned to his state of removal from reality but I try not to think of that but rather of the day when he wrote this letter to me.

It was a day in April. And occasionally, when I take the letter from the box where I have stored it, I close my eyes and recall another day in April, a stormy day full of sunshine and great gusts of wind, and we walking from Northborough. We came through Etton and a mile from home John climbed into a tree, a young tree that swayed ever from east to west in the tongue of the storm. He climbed up into the highest, softest branches and swayed with it. His face towards Peakirk and into the storm coming off the fens. I stood on the road and shouted up to him to have a care but he just shouted back that I should climb into the tree and stand with him.

'I cannot,' I said. 'The storm is too strong; it is too dangerous to stand up there. I will not take the chance.'

'Then you'll never know what it feels like here,' he said and he turned his face into the wind and the look in his eyes, the smile on his mouth! He was like a child with his face buried in the strength of his mother's bosom. He had no fear of anything, he was living for that roar of the surging wind and the sun that was blown across his hair, and the uncertainty of the waving, buoyant branch that was all that kept him from the hardness of the ground thirty feet below.

I could never have stood in that tree in circumstances such as that. John could not resist the possibility. I would never fall to the ground because I would never leave it. He was certain to fall, and each time he climbed, he climbed higher so that the fall, when it came, was one from which there will never be a recovery.

But I was not always anchored to the earth. I can only hope that you see some sign in what I say, I can only hope that you guess at the things I wish to say but cannot.

But there, I was talking about the letter that came last springtime. In that letter there was hope, there was the same smile that I saw in his face that day when he climbed into the tree and embraced the storm from the east. And when I read that letter I imagine John's face as it was all those years ago, alive and eager and alert. 'Little sister', he wrote (that was his endearment for me): 'I write this with an easy heart. I am seated in the open yard and the sun is upon me. I am thinking of a place I was used to walk with Richard Turnill, a place where we twisted sallies until they grew into a knot. I am thinking of this because I still have in my writing drawer a rule that Morgan the carpenter made for me from that tree when he felled it a good many years after. I should have been a carpenter that would have been a trade to put my hand to. What was I — mason painter gardener.

Do you recall they would have made a clerk of me, our mother and father. Do you recall from this distance as how they sent me to Peterborough, that long journey that I was not prepared for in a coat that was too small and gloves that was too big and I had nothing to say for myself and did not want to be there in the first. I would not have made a clerk not locked in some dull office where the sun had not the courage to send even the weakest of its light. I was only happy out there on the fens. I could watch the skylarks there, I would stand with my head thrown back and my eyes fixed directly above me and must have looked a poor thing in that manner and you would ask me what I was looking for and I would say skylark the word gurgling in my throat for I would not look away for fear of losing sight of the bird that was a pebble out in the great celestial sea. Do you recall me always as a child wishing to walk to the end of the world out there across the fens and I did as far as childhood would allow, to the worlds end. That day I walked and walked and walked and stopt to eat some sorrel and went on walking till the sun had dropt behind the elms and the men from the Bluebell came in search of me and I was all of four mile from home and when I was home again and we in bed you askt me little sister what the worlds end were like and I started to tell you but you were asleep by then more worn out with worry than I with my walking. You never see me here, little sister, none of you. Not you nor Mary Joyce none of you.

I have been thinking that there was a time when I could see the whitethorn, touch it taste it smell it and not think on Richard Turnhill's coffin. There was a time when it was all I needed to think on Mary Joyce. I could think of her, I could smell the smell of May and think of her. Always when I was walking from market or out on the fens or rhyming my rhymes or working in a garden I would think of her. I hated the sameness of gardens. It cloyed me but I were away from it inside my head and thinking of Mary Joyce. Why do you not come and see me and bring her with you.

John Clare

You may think parts of his letter strange but I do not and you would not if you read the other letters that have come in the years of late. There is light in this letter, more light than there had been in anything for a long, long time. Too little light, perhaps, and now too late, but something to brighten the memory. And, you know, his thinking of Richard again and expressing those thoughts to me is something I treasure. I cannot deny that to you.

This letter is the last I shall receive from him, his last of all, I think, and is so much happier than anything else that I associate with him in the seven years since we met face to face the final time. I had travelled to Northampton with my husband to visit John and we sat together, the three of us, on a bench in the yard of the asylum there. John talked a great deal, sometimes of things I understood and sometimes as though he were a bare-fist fighter awaiting a match, in a coarse tongue. The visit was drawing to a close and I was content that there was some sense, perhaps a greater deal than I had hoped for, yet in his head. We were saying our farewells when he spoke very tenderly and said: 'I have always had a great love for you, little sister, you have always been the one to whom I was closest. Let me kiss you.'

I waited for the touch of his lips on my cheek but he walked past me towards an inmate, a tall and red-haired man who had been loitering about while we had sat and talked, and kissed this man most delicately upon the cheek and walked off in his company, the man following slightly behind John, subserviently, it seemed to me.

My husband, who had sat throughout the interview in silence, became most insistent that we should leave immediately. 'This visit was a mistake,' he said. 'The man is demented in his insanity.'

I never showed my husband the occasional letters that came for me from John in the time since then. They would merely have confirmed him in his opinion. And I have never shown him that last letter. To me it is a clear flow of remembrance and peace. My husband would demean the letter and its importance to me by pointing out the flaws in its construction and logic. He could not see beyond them. He cannot see.

But this letter, these memories, are small comfort and throw little by way of relief on the sombre dusk that lies around my life. For some there is the hope that loved ones whom they have lost will come again, out of that dimness to meet them and be the friends they were. I see nothing of that hope in the darkness I speak of, nothing that promises even the least crack in the black façade. I may dream, on nights when the storms blow outside my home, of Richard Turnill stopping at my gate but I know he will never come inside my door and I know that if I were to walk out there he would be gone – I mean his imagined person, for that, I know, is all he is. There is no hope in the darkness.

And there is no hope, even now, of the darkness that fell between John and me lifting or fraying. It was always there and it will always be there. Perhaps because, like his hardness towards our father, he wanted it there. Perhaps there was nothing I could do to lighten it. I do not know, I can honestly say that to you, and nothing will ever bring an answer to me now.

On days when the shadow seems to cover the whole of my world I think his kissing of the inmate, in my name, was another way of thickening the shade between us. Not that he was aware of that, I am sure, but his mind, even in its demented state, was telling him that I was not the sister he had been born closest to. She was dead. His other breathing half was dead and I could not replace her. But I try, God knows I try, to keep those days and that terrible feeling as distant as death.

II Patty Clare

HE TOLD ME THE FIRST TIME he ever seed me was one Sunday at the Flower Pot. You may believe that or not but it seems a likely thing to me. The Flower Pot were an inn where John would sometimes fiddle and I would sometimes walk to with my father. It were rare enough for me to be there of a Sunday and rarer still for him but that Sunday it fell that we were there together. He could tell me every mite of that day. What I wore and what I said and how I looked and what way my hair were but I have no remembrance at all of how the day went with me and much less and none at all the way John was. I can't recall even the sight of him. He might as well not have been there at all for ought I knew of him.

But there he was and he was completely taken by me. I had no notion of this until a great time afterward. He didn't tell me for months and months what had happened that afternoon. It seems, according to his recollection, that when the dancing and music come to an end, everyone set out for home and he dawdled, waiting to see which way my father and me should walk. But while he was waiting a man from Helpston come and asked him if he knew the tune of some song or other, and when he got himself free again we were gone from the yard. He told me as how he climbed a tree, right up into the topmost branch, and searched the lanes about until he caught sight of the figures of my father and me walking homeward. He stayed in the branch till we were out of sight and he had settled his mind as to which way we had gone. But by the time he had come down to earth again the inn were shut and not a soul about to ask our names of. So he were left as badly fixed, he said, as if he hadn't known the road we took at all. He knew the road but not the name and no one there to ask of.

But that were a start, he said. Knowing, at least, the path I'd took and the one I were likely to be found upon another time. He said he conjured names for me all the way back home that evening. And never once come up with Patty, my true name. Well, not my right true name. My given name were Martha but I never heard it used in my hearing, neither as child or woman, apart from when the vicar called it from the altar and we marrying. But in that I'm jumping over much in all the way of us.

The second time I met with John I do remember rightly. I were out walking the fens one summer evening. It must have been high summer for the flies were clouding out the shelters of the trees and I had on a light dress for the weather. I were walking a path for sport, not thinking of any place I might go but going where the path might take me, when I come face to face with John. He weren't striking to look at, not at first. A short, wild-haired man even then. He were carrying his fiddle and bow under his arm, wrapped in a kerchief. For all I knew this was the first time we had met. I did not recall him playing among the other fiddlers in the Flower Pot. But he remembered me. I would have passed on along my way with a nod or a 'good morrow' had he not set to talking as soon as he were near me.

'I remember you from the Flower Pot,' he said at once.

I were silent.

'You were there a month ago, one Sunday. Dancing.'

I nodded, wondering all the while if I should remember this man for some good reason. He told me then who he was and what he had been about at the Flower Pot and how he had noticed me among the other girls. He didn't tell about his climbing into the tree to watch me go but he did tell me I was the prettiest girl he had met in all his time. Not that I believed him. I'd seen enough of girls and heard enough of men to know it were not true for myself, but still, it were nice to think that he might say it.

He lingered talking. He were on his way to some alehouse or other to play but he took his time in talking. He asked my name and I told him it were Patty. And then he told me how he had tried to find it in his heart, my name in his heart, in walking home from the Flower Pot.

'And did you hit on Patty?' I asked.

'No,' he said, 'not Patty, but almost every other name.'

He stayed to talking so long that his fiddling fell by the wayside. We stood there in that one spot till the flies and midges took their wing in the dusk and there were only we two left there, giggling and gossiping together. Afterwards, I will confess, I wished he had done more than talk but that wasn't a complaint I was to have for very long. When it came to lovemaking, once he had made his bed in that direction, he were happy to lie in it as often as chance would allow. And so was I. But that is not to say we fell to love that first of our evenings together. No indeed, that was a most honest evening with only banter between us.

He left me to the top of my path that night. It were dark as the heart of a blackberry, not a moon from one end of the night to the other, and he walked to the sight of my home. I wouldn't let him come no farther for fear my father should be rambling about. Not that he had anything to say against me walking with boys but at the time I were strong with a shoemaker from Olney and my father thought he would be a good match for me. I knew John would get a poor look in if my father had his way and thought it better to pick a time of my own making to take him into the light. Soon enough, I thought. Let's see what kind of lad he first turns out to be and then we'll see how far he may be took. He were good to talk with and laugh with but I were not about to say no more than that. Not until I could be sure of him.

He told me afterwards that on the night as he first walked me home he could not find his way back to his own house, what with the darkness and not being certain of where he were in the first place, and he wandered about until well into the night and still got no nearer to any path that he might know. In the end he lay down in a dyke and pulled his coat as well about him as he might and fell to sleep as though the earth beneath him were a softer mattress than his own.

He were always a one for sleeping out if the night overtook him on his walks. I didn't find that easy when I first knew him. If he could find a dry spot, be it winter or summer, he would sleep as sound as a black cat in the chimney seat. No wind or rain or snow would disturb him if the place were dry. He seemed wrapped up in his own warmth. I saw him nights with only a shirt to keep out the cold out and he would still be snug within himself.

He wrote a verse for me, the first night we talked. 'Of all the days in memories list' it went, but I were never a one for verses or reading. I could not read then and cannot.

He said the verses over to me and they sounded well enough. There were other verses, too, with my name in them and he would read them to me or say them out of his head. I had never met a man who would risk being laughed at by saying what he had writ. But John did. I will admit it took me time to take him with any seriousness. I knew men and the rambles they will take to get you in the bramble bush and this were just another way, as far as I could see at first. But bit by bit I took to believing he had writ the words and that they had some feeling in them. What woman would not, for few women, or men, want other than to believe the one who talks of love to them? Is that not true? I know it is.

I would get John to go back to that first verse because it held some feeling for me that nothing afterwards, no matter how well it sounded, could hold. 'Of all the days in memories list. . .' Even yet I like to say that over to myself. I suppose there is no great beauty in it. I've heard so many folk talk of this poem and that of John's, I've sat and listened to all kinds of talk in our home about the merits of his work, but I hold that line most closely in my heart.

Not, let me say, that I were the only one in his life. Not even that I thought I were. I knew how to lead a handful of men in the one long dance and I knew just as well when I were one of many dancing on another's hand. I made my own enquiries about John. I knew a good many people out the Helpston way. News and wind travel fast and news is often faster.

He were walking evenings up the woods and standing there, among the trees, gaping down on the house of Mary Joyce. I could see no purpose in doing that, for it were an aimless task. He could never walk down and talk with her, not in her father's yard. There were always a why and a wherefore for his being there in the woods. He were listening for some particular chelp. He could herry there for hours on end without no reason other than the hope that she would pass across the yard or stand for a moment at her door, and most often there was not even that. He told me once she were pretty as a rainbow, though I never seed her myself. Others as did said she was not the beauty that he made her out to be.

But then that were John. I were not the beauty he made me out to be neither.

But it weren't just Mary Joyce. Indeed, she were the least of worries in one way, though the greatest in another. But there were others a plenty. Some I knew of and some I didn't.

There was Betty Sell, across the fen. Her I did know to see and hear. A tossy sort of girl that I never took to. But I know he were lying with her the same time as he were lying with me. When he were with me I wouldn't think of her, but when he were away lime-burning I would know he were with her. It may have been that it were a race between her and me, we both of us running after him or about him and John standing still to see who would reach him the first. And it may have been that I won because I gave myself all the earlier and found I were with child.

But there, I'm running on in saying that. I must go back. To do him fair and tell the truth, I must go back a peg or two.

He told me things as you wouldn't expect a man to say. Some things were not what anyone would want repeated about them but he would tell me straight and fair. He told me of times when his neighbours would gather at the Blue Bell, of a summer evening, and call him as he passed and have him sit and read his verses over, to them, asking him for more and more and leading him along like a blinded cauf. And then they would laugh at him and put new words and twists and meanings into the words he had writ.

But they weren't the worst, he said. The worst were those he knew as pretended to liking what he wrote. Men who told him to his face as how good his writing was and how much they would do to help. I come to know these people myself, or others like them, by and by.

He told me too, a good many years afterwards, as how he had wrote verses for Mary Joyce but had been afeared to read them to her, she being of farm stock and him being what he was. He would stand in the woods, he said, and recite them down like rain upon her roof top. He would carry the verses in his pocket in the hope of meeting her on the road or at Stamford market and would come home downcast because he had not seen her.

It were made all the harder, he said, by the memories of a time when he and she had walked from school together, had played together as children, had been in one another's confidence. Now that he needed it, he said, it was not there. And once or twice when he did meet her face to face in the street of a market day, even if she were alone, he would finger the paper in his pocket and count to a number, telling himself he would give the verses to her, but he never did. He didn't even speak, he said.

I couldn't understand of that. 'If you had something to say,' I'd tell him, 'then why be put off by her standing. You have never been slow in talking with me,' I'd say.

'But that is different,' he'd say and leave it lie at that.

Sometimes, I thought, I ought not to have listened to his talk of her but I were trying to understand and make some sense on it for him as well as me. I believed the best that could be done for all on us was to hear out what he had to say and answer it myself. I'm not sure now that that was so but I'm not sure neither that it wasn't.

The same water can't be drunk twice, so leave it be.

There's many things like that I've left unturned this good long time. There was nothing to be got from turning them but pain and that comes easy enough without us going out to find where it has nested. And he told me other things as well. Things I might be better not to tell you at all.

Still, if the worst were told, then there's as much reason for telling the best as well, no doubt. He'd whisper things to me in the dark or he'd say them out straight, out loud in the evening and we walking. Out as bold as Beauchamp in the white of day, with the sun still shining and nothing to spare his blushes or mine. And we sheltering beneath a tree, he'd say something that set me hot as soon as it were said. We'd be there waiting for the dusk to make our loving respectable and, of a turn, we couldn't wait that long, neither on us. We'd fall to kissing and he'd touch me, his hand beneath my blouse, his fingers like another tongue, licking the skin of my belly and up and down from there.

But there. I were courting a shoemaker when first I met our John. I'll say nothing more than this. He were a right dry stick — it's not the first time I've said that and it won't be the last.

And then I started taking John to home and there were nothing said the first and second time. My father were used to seeing lads about the place. But when he started calling night after night my father were not in the smallest way pleased. Not that he said anything direct, he were too foxy for that.

'Whatever happened with that shoemaker?' he'd say.

'Too busy with his trade,' I'd say and pass him off like that.

But he come back to that, as soon as he got wind that John and me were more than two peas waiting for the pod to burst. The pods were well burst by then, if only he had known. He wouldn't laugh to hear me say that, God rest his soul, but it is true.

'That other lad,' he'd say, 'that lad that come here courting you, he had a trade, he had good prospects. What has this Clare? Nowt.'

I understood my father saying this. He never had a brass farthing himself. He worked hard and long but that brought nothing to his life but another year of work and another year again, as far back and as far forward as he could see. He wanted more than that from lads as might have an eye on me. He were keen to see me wed to a tradesman. He were keen to see me contented, too, but his mind told him contentment come with shillings on the table at the end of a day's working. He would never hear of me saying how dry the shoemaker were. I would never dare to say it to him. It would be breath gone out on the wind when it might as well have been saved for talk of something else. But a dry stick is what he were and John were the one for words and whisperings and feelings. He'd talk and talk about the woods and the flowers and the fens and it were like a river gabbling on, with music coming unexpected from everything he said. He might be talking on about something or other, about the swallow, say, telling me the differ between the male and female, talking quite the same as any time.

'Look,' he'd say, 'the chestnut colour on the male is deeper than the female and his tail is longer – thinner, too.'

And then, without as much as drawing breath, he'd drop his voice and whisper to me and his mouth would slip between my breasts. And other places, if I tell you the truth. He would pleasure me, out there in the lanes or on the fens or in the trees beyond the church, and one thing must be said, the pleasuring did not end on our wedding day. He were never content unless I were.

Let me tell you, I can recall nights, winter and summer, outside our door and me backed up against our wall and John upon his knees before me and — well, all I'll say is this, I'd bite on the end of my petticoat to keep from crying out from the rapture of what John did to me. His tongue would travel down the side of my neck and trace a river between my breasts and then he'd be there upon his knees, his face buried in the folds of my dress and his hands working slowly from the tops of my boots, sliding slowly up my legs, my skirt rising with them until he had found his way to where he was wanting. And then his tongue would work between my thighs, damply, damply finding its way to where I was most content to have it. But contentment isn't what I were feeling, not for long. His tongue would lick and push and lick and push until I bit my petticoat between my teeth to keep from screaming with joy, lest my father come outside.

I tremble to think what he might have made of that sight, me against the wall, John upon his knees, his face buried between my legs and me moaning with the rising heat that was flowing from his tongue.

Even now it makes me warm to think of that and of all the places he would do that, or the like, to me. On gravestones, in our yard, out on the fens, in Burghley Park beneath the trees, in his mother's kitchen, once, when she were expected any time. I were sitting in a chair, a night in winter, and the place were empty as the sky, apart from him and me. He were sitting there across from me, writing, and he dropped his pencil and bent to pick it up, and before I knew it his head were there. And I began to feel myself slipping away and still I was all the time thinking I heard his mother's step outside. Listening and not wanting to hear. And him murmuring into me, telling me how much he loved that part of me, talking and kissing all in one. And then I heard the scrape of his mother's boots but he went on until the latch cracked. He turned and pushed a log into the fire and dropped my skirts about my legs and smiled, all in one instant, the same instant as his mother pushed the door. I sat there, terrified and delighted. Wet with fear and excitement. That were John. He might do that three times in a night before I could get my chance to do the same for him.

And then, they say, in marrying you find your own place and your own quietness. But there were nights when I bit on my nightgown to keep his father and his mother from hearing. And later still I'd do the same for fear the children would be roused from their sleep by my happiness.

It's no lie to say I missed all that for many a year after he were gone. I miss it still, I don't mind saying so. That were the purest pleasure I have ever had. The purest. But there were other things. Other, slower pleasures from our lives.

He'd sit, from time to time, and list his books. I liked to hear him do that. To hear him read the names: *Abercrombies Gardener's Journal*, *The Seasons*; and *Paradise Lost*. That one he were most particular and proud of as he'd bound it himself. He took satisfaction in a thing like that and I took satisfaction in his contentment about that kind of thing.

But all this came later and I'm running on again. And we courting, he would come to see me of an evening whenever he could, and when I'd see him in the lane or across the fen, I'd run and catch my clean gingham and take it from the bush and put it on, dry or not. Oh, the joy of waiting for a glimpse of him in the lane, some flower or branch or other swinging in his hand, his hair blowing back and his head bobbing about to some song he had made. And his smile at seeing me.

And it wasn't that I was waiting for the deeper delights of the night. I were pleased at his coming, pleased to see him in our yard, happy at the sight of him. We'd go walking out across the countryside, his arm about me, his face turning this way and that so that his voice would come from everywhere. Sometimes he'd bury his face in my hair and whisper and I'd think the whisper came from inside my own head and he'd say some words I was longing to hear and I'd wonder whether he had been listening, his ear against my skull, so that he could hear the things I were thinking about him. It often looked that way to me.

We'd walk to the villages or along the fens but he'd never take me into the woods. They were full of mantraps, he'd say, for poachers. He told me as how he was walking back home one night after fiddling in some alehouse and he heard a man in the woods.

'He were screaming and screaming,' John said to me. 'I knew what part of the wood he were in but I were afraid to go in myself. I heard a good time afterwards as he had his leg cut off.'

Another man would make excuses for not going in but John told his fear. 'I were afraid,' he said.

It were the same all over, trees felled, lands enclosed and ploughed. 'The heart torn out of the land,' as John had it. But it weren't just his fear that burned in him.

He were full of anger, too, at the thought of what were happening to the countryside. It weren't that he thought it more his right or anyone else's but only that he had always rambled the fens and gone about the woods as he had liked. Him and all his childhood friends had grown to manhood in the belief that the land were there for all. Some might have their names upon a part of it and some might use a part of it and some might never own a part of it, but it were there for the use of all and the enjoyment of all.

I sometimes thought the pleasure that John gave me were like the pleasure he took from the countryside. He never said as much, and I'm not a one for making out my own ways of taking what our life was or wasn't for, but that one thing I do believe. His pleasure flowed into me and the pleasure of the fens flowed into his lifetime, man and boy. There must be something in that, I believe. And to have that taken from him, to be told and told again where and where not to walk, to wake up one day and find a fence about a wood as you were used to walk through, that is a bitter thing. Just the way it were for me to find myself without the warmth and closeness and pleasure, yes the pleasure, I were used to, that too was a bitter thing.

John were due his ramblings in the fields and I were due him in me when I wanted him but neither on us got our due. They tried to lock up the pastures and the trees, or worse, they pulled them down, and then John locked himself away from me and I were left with nothing, no one in my bed. I know the loss he felt for I felt as much and more in losing him. He could see his woods and his fens and could not go into them. I could see him and not be able to rely on him. The woods were there but out of his reach. He were there, not dead, but out of reach of me and his children.

He had his anger about all that. He were a man who were angered by the hurt of anything. I seed him run at men twice his size as were badger-baiting. Run at them without a care for how he come out of it. But then he were gone from me and there were no one I could run at. I couldn't scream at him and call him the bastard son of a bastard, as I sometimes did when I were angered by his goings-on. He had his angers but he knew who they were intended for and at the least he had the satisfaction of spending them. I had nothing. I couldn't shout at the children. It weren't them as was to blame. I couldn't shout at him, locked up them miles away. And all the people as had sung his praises and told us how great our lives were going to be were long gone once the troubles came to roost. There were no one left but me to turn my anger on, not one, and that was even greater cause for anger in the end. The real bitterness is gone now, or all but. Still I remember it without having to dig too far.

Not that his going was a new thing to me. When we was walking out together he disappeared as well. He thought that I were carrying and he got drunk and went off to enlist in the artillery. To escape. The sergeant laughed at him, told him he were too short and too weak and sent him home again as soon as he'd arrived.

He crept back to Helpston as timid as he ought and he come up about our house a week later and smiled a feeble smile and tried to laugh the whole thing off. But I were having none of it.

'Keep away from me,' I told him. 'See how the artillery keeps you amused at night.'

He tried to tell me it had all been meant for the best, to get some money for him and me and any child that we might have.

'Who said anything of children?' I said.

He weren't sure as to what my circumstances were and I weren't about to tell him until such time as I were sure myself.

'And anyway,' I said, 'you might have told me where you were and what you were about, running off to join the army.'

'I were drunk,' he said. 'I wouldn't have done it otherwise.'

'There was nights when you were drunk with me,' I said, 'but that never stopped you finding your way to where you wanted to be and it never stopped you telling me what it was you wanted to do to me.'

He had nothing to say to that.

'It's the day after the fair,' I said and left him standing where he were and flounced inside and shut our door.

When he come back, three or four days later, he had verses and a ribbon for me and news that he were working. At lime-burning, the far end of the fens. I were happy to see him and happy to hear of his work, though I wouldn't have been had I knowed he would meet Betty Sell through living off across the fen. I know he were lying with her and I can only think that he used some of his charming ways to get inside her thighs, just as he had done with me. I don't blame her or him but it were something I could never prove and something I knew right well, from knowing him. No doubt he had her up against a wall or on her back behind some house or in his bed for all I know. In the end, she were luckier. Or not. Or not.

It were a wet and dreary March and we marrying. He were disinclined to marry me. I knew that, without his having to say as much. I knew he were. You cannot lie with someone, give yourself to them night after night, hear them talk of things you would not dare to mention to yourself and still not know how they feel. That were how I knew of Betty Sell and that were how I knew he did not want to marry me. Oh, he came and listened to me and said he should look after me and the baby but he were disinclined to marrying.

I recall the night he said we should be wed. My father took him into our kitchen and they sat drinking. I went walking to a neighbour's house, as I had been told by my father, and stayed there until close to midnight and when I come back John told me we were going to be wed. He were drunk and my father were half-drunk but my father were smiling and John were not. He were easily made drunk but he weren't happy and neither were I. I did not like to see him so and I had no wish to marry him if it were only for the sake of keeping one name for the child, to call it Clare instead of Turner. I would not do that to John. I were too fond of him for that.

I had been angry with his running off to join the army and I were angry when I thought of Betty Sell and him. But there were others, too, I might have felt a bitterness about. Mary Joyce, who was always on his lips. Elizabeth Newbon. He had been courting her when he met me and I didn't reckon as he had dropped her just to walk with me, not when he could walk with both of us, at least a while. All these angers and doubts but nothing as would make me want to trap him because I were carrying.

To see him there with my father on our kitchen floor, and my father full of loud laughter and slapping John upon the back and saying as how we could sleep easily now and not be worrying about what might come in the way of children, was no joy to me. John were drunk but that had not made him any happier. Even the drink had not dulled his mind to what he had done.

Not that he did not want me, I can say that. It were what he were leaving behind. And what he were bound to once he crossed the church door. Bound to keeping wife and family and knowing family were just begun. I felt for him in spite of all. I knew we should both have liked a better start than this, but there you are. There were nothing we could do. No way to put the fire out.

I recall, as John were leaving that night, my father said as he might stay if he so wished.

'You might as well lie with your wife tonight as any night,' he said. 'There's nothing that can happen now as hasn't happened yet.'

He was laughing and urging him to stay and not to venture out into the darkness and the rain. John were standing near the fireplace and he reached down and I saw him close his hands about a stool as we had there, about the leg, and I were certain he would bring it down upon my father's head or smash it on the floor. The more my father laughed, the more it seemed that John would not contain his anger.

'I think that John wants to tell his father and mother,' I said. 'I think he wants to get back home.'

My father nodded and slapped him on the back again and bade him goodnight.

I walked with John a good part up the lane. It were cold and the rain were falling and we stood under the hedge and I held his face and told him straight.

'You haven't made a pledge to me,' I said. 'You've spoken with my father and I know he got you drunk. Don't think on this as anything you can't go back on.'

And I meant it. I didn't see much good in how he'd been trapped.

John said nothing. I held onto him. Now it were me holding him, he were the baby being held. I didn't want him to say he wouldn't marry me but I didn't want him doing it to please my father's wishes.

'Do you want me to walk back to Helpston?' I asked him. 'I can, you know, and stay in your house by the fire.'

'No,' he said. 'I shall come and talk with you tomorrow night.'

And then he went off into the darkness.

I stayed where I were sheltered for a good time. I thought perhaps I should never see him again and that would have been a terrible thing but I would have taken it in place of John being unhappy all his life.

When I went back inside my father smiled at me and winked.

'You were a good time out there,' he said. 'No harm in that.'

I took the stool in my hands, the stool nearest the fire, and flung it against the wall. It crashed in pieces across our floor but I didn't care. I felt a good deal better for having done it.

When John come back the next evening he had told his mother and his father and his sister. I had expected, if he came, that he would still be angry but it seemed as he had set his heart on this and there were no more to be said.

In spite of all, I think John's expectations were that we should be unhappy. I think, at the start, he saw no hope for us beyond the pleasures of our company and the coming of the baby. That did not stop him going through with the marriage and it did not mean he did it with a bad grace. It meant only that he set himself to live without the certainty of happiness in his marriage.

But we were not unhappy. I don't say life were always like a summer day but we were a good deal, a great deal, more happy than most people as we knew. And a great deal happier than I had hoped we should be. Maybe that come of neither of us having hopes beyond the way things were. We expected little and anything what came were a blessing and little by little we built on that. Don't think I'm saying there was never things that went awry and never times when I felt hard done by, even before he went that final time, but all in all things went as well as might be hoped for.

We lived with his parents. His father were well battered by the time of our wedding. He were worn out with too many long days in the rain and too many hours of work that barely fed him. John always said as there was nothing of his father in him but I think, and I've never said this afore John, that part of what wore out Parker Clare were the same kind of despair and loss that wore out his son, but at least in John we saw it clearer.

On top of that, John's mother were struck with the dropsy, so when we come to live in their home it were less than I might have liked. I hoped, as all brides do, to have our own cottage and our own garden and our own place to be together, to make our own home as we would have it ourselves. Instead of that I were trying to make a home for us and keep a home as John's mother had made it. And I did. I kept the room as clean as a woman could. And when in time we had our own cottage it were cleaner than any house or cottage or manor in the parish.

No matter who were coming or at what hour, our home were clean and tidy. You ask anyone.

And I were there for John in any need. I were there for him to talk with and there for him to spend himself inside and there to hush the children when he were in need of quiet.

One time, a good time after John had been taken, I were walking back from Stamford, and Morgan the carpenter's wife overtook me and we got to talking. She asked as how our John were and I told her what I could.

'I always thought how well you went together,' she said. 'I had no notion, when you come to live here, how you might go but I often think about you and him, in the days when he were here.'

I had never thought she even passed a word on me and I told her so.

'Indeed I did,' she said. 'In the start I would see the two of you at odd hours, out walking the fens or up by the spinney. I recall one morning, at dawn, I saw you come arm in arm out of the fog and both on you looking at nothing but each other, and I thought how happy you seemed. It were the morning of our Ellen's wedding and I were up preparing and I thought, if only she were to be as happy as you two, how lucky she would be and how blessed.'

I smiled at her and she saw the tears in my eyes.

'At least you have that to keep,' she said to me. 'At least you have something to go back on. Some have nothing to remember all their lives.'

And I did. That day I sat in our kitchen and looked at the garden as he had made and across at the pastures he rambled over and the trees he were so fond of all his life.

I saved him for as long as I were able. I gave him as much of me as I could and I gave him as much of himself as I knew how to find. And towards the end, before he were gone, I would sit with him when I could and listen to his talking or just sit with him for companionship. I should like to have had some cure but I had none and so I sat with him. I'd lay down beside him and hug him. What more could I do? I still hug him to me when I can, even at this distance. I stop in the garden or when I'm here in this kitchen alone and try to picture him as he were. Not as a young man but as the man as needed love and holding when last I saw him and I put my arms around that picture and try to keep him warm, whatever he's doing where he is now. I still sit by him when I'm sat here alone. I can only hope he knows that. But I have no way of knowing.

Once, I could turn his head, he would climb a tree to watch me, and I hope my love can turn him round again. I haven't bid hope goodbye, not yet. I've tried to keep my love as true as I can and hope that something will reach him. Though, God knows, I can't imagine how.

I think of us crossing the pastures in the evening, walking through the ghosts of sheep, and him softly singing to me, some love song as he had made for me, some words that were like the west breeze, that soft and that warm. And I'd ask him to lay down beside me and I'd guide him until I were satisfied and then I'd satisfy him. And we'd lie there, looking up through the trees, up through the sycamore keys, at the last of the light in the sky. And then we'd go on walking, arms about one another, close. I loved him that much. I never wanted any of that to end.

Now, when I go back across them ways, changed and all as they be, I keep meeting his ghost and my ghost, arm in arm, my head on his shoulder, his hands in my hair, his kiss on my breast. But now I walk alone.

One time, and he going off to work somewhere, he left me a letter on our table. I could not read it then but years after I asked our Eliza to tell me what it said. And bit by bit, in learning it and going over the letters, I have got to know the words.

I have it here, look. It says:

Dearest Patty,

I have wrote this poem to keep you close by me and I away. You will know it sometime when you need knowing.

How sweet can courting prove
How can I kiss my love
Muffld i' hat and glove
From the chill air
Lay by thy woolen vest
Rap no cloak oer thy breast
There my hand oft hath prest

Pin nothing there
There my head drops to rest
Leave its bed bare.
John Clare

Isn't that what the letter says? I have that and some days it means a great deal to me to have it and some days it seems such a paltry piece of paper to have at the end of all this.

Oh, there were signs and signs. As far back as the autumn after we were wed. That October John's father fell ill and come close to dying. And his apple tree were barren that same year. People laugh at me when I point to that as the worst sign of all but John were forever telling me as how that tree had been their saving many a time and now I seen it barren, the same time as his father was ill, and I thought it all pointed to no good coming. I still say that were the first real sign. And that tree never bore again, as true as I may breathe. We were left to fend for ourselves and for John's father and mother. It didn't seem a laughing matter then to me and it still don't.

And then the thing as should have been a source of gladness and of us being able to live a better life, John's writing, brought its own trouble in its wake. Not that I were not happy to see him rising in the eyes of those who know of these things, but they were not interested in John or me, not in the most part. They were interested in what he wrote for what it might mean to their own lives and fortunes. Not all of them but most.

There were always someone coming to see him. Some patron, some publisher, some poet or enquiring traveller as stopped off at our home. I would send one of the children scurrying to Royce Wood, for John would take to writing there if he thought there were visitors upon their way. It might be half an hour before he come lumbering back, and in the meantime I would be answering to the most impertinent questions from these people. There were nothing they would not ask me to tell them about. Nothing. They all but stood at the foot of our bed in the night and watched to see what we might do. It were always where and when and how and why out of their mouths. As if by stopping in they had the right to own us as they might own a piece of cloth.

And then John would arrive and they would set to questioning him and getting him to read his verses and asking what he meant by this and that and always suggesting how his verses might be bettered. There wasn't one who didn't have a better way of saying things than John. If it weren't the way he had writ, it were what he had said or who he had intended the poems for. It wore me out and it made him bitter.

They took him off to London to meet with people as I had never heard of — poets and painters and writers. And that in itself were a trial. They promised as he could talk with doctors there about his fits and find a cure for them. That would have been a blessing and a thing worth travelling for.

I recall the day afore he left for London. He come back from Stamford with a new suit. A green suit. A green suit as would make him a laughing stock in Helpston and a suit as had cost him more than he were like to earn in a twelve month. And there were nothing I could say.

'This is what they wear in London,' John told me.

But we weren't living in London. He were going there to meet with people, to talk with publishers and the like, but he were coming back and there were little call for green suits in Helpston, winter or summer.

'Good,' I said to him.

He knew himself the madness in what he had done. I could see that. Walking home from Stamford, mile by mile, it must have worked its way through his brain how crazed he'd been. It didn't need my telling him for him to know. And I said nothing.

He were offered a prospectus to get subscribers for his book of verses. I knew that were what he wanted, more than anything in the world, that were the thing he wanted but he were too much in a muddle to ask people to be his support. He could never go to people and ask them for their money towards the printing of a book and so the notion fell through. But the idea would not go away. He wanted it and his publisher knew how bad he wanted it, until his want drove him to approach people and ask them to subscribe. I seen him come back in here, drained of all strength, more drained than if he'd spent the day out working on the road, drained from the fact of having knocked on people's doors — clergymen and gentry and people as had money left from living — offering them his prospectus and reading them his verse and listening to them telling him how he should change things. Some promised and some criticised and some laughed.

'John Clare, ploughboy poet,' they'd say, laughing. 'I think not.'

But in the end the money come and then the book and then he were all things to all people and we were never done with opening our door to all kinds. And the promises! The promises of books and money and a new cottage and clothes. Oh, the promises as were made under our roof that were never once intended for keeping. I could cut through them when I think as what they did to us.

I do believe and believe it rightly that they were as much to blame for putting him away as were any of his sicknesses in his head or his fits and turns in childhood. All the promises made on this very floor and the only one as was kept was to take him off to London and fill his head with thinking he were like the rest of them writers and painters and suchlike, so that he come back here unhappy, wanting to be somewhere else and something else and he were never happy afterwards. Telling me that he knew not how to behave in London but I could see he were not content no more with being with us. Not if the truth were told.

He were always one for wandering but I knew that afore I married him and I were prepared for his goings.

But always I knew where he were. He were never more distant than Barnack or Wittering and that were the farthest he would roam. And I knew he would be back. If he slept out a night he would be back by the end of the next day. But from the time they set his mind on other things he were never rightly here, even and he sitting in the corner there, he were away some other place and in a different set of life than we could hope to live.

And always there were the money. It had a place afore it come to us at all. It were waited on for his mother or his father or the children or books or something.

There were no hope in his writing. The books were there and the knocks on the door and him being paraded from place to place in his green suit and days when he believed in all of that and days when it were all I could do to keep his eyes off the bottom of the pit.

And after all the talking stopped, we were left with nothing and he turned a second time to lime-burning. He were away again, the far end of the fen, staying in a house with other men as were working at the lime-burning too. A coarse lot they were, by John's account.

He would come back when he could and tell me stories. Once, he told me, one night, a traveller come from London and lodged with them under the same roof. They filled the man's head with tales of all the travellers as some of them had killed. They told him that three of them had cut the throats and robbed the purses of travellers on the fens. This unfortunate man were afeared to travel on, being certain as he should be next to die if he ventured outside of the door, certain that he should have his throat sliced and his purse stole and his body thrown in a ditch. And he were afeared to sleep, thinking they should come and cut him where he lay. So he sat by the fire and every time a man snored upstairs he jumped and looked about. He were gone afore dawn, afore they rose for work. They laughed and laughed about him. Thinking of him sitting by the hearth all night long, jumping at every snore, and them sleeping quite content.

He would tell me stories such as that and I would listen and laugh and think that Betty Sell might again be in his head but he never mentioned her and I would not ask.

He worked hard at the lime-burning. He worked and slept and saved. And if he did see Betty Sell it did not stop him thinking of us. He saved all of fifty shillings. And then one night, while he slept, it were took from his coat by the same men as worked and ate and lodged with him. Hail-fellow-well-met and then taking fifty shillings from his coat. What we could have done with that! But we seemed, or John seemed, to meet with folk like that all his life.

In the end, between the work and the company he were forced to keeping and living with, and the loneliness, his loneliness, he come back here. He were a great one for going off with notions about how things would be and what would come of them but he always needed something to come back to. That were one of the pains of his finally going. I thought he should be most unhappy with not having anything of the places and people he loved about him. But he has found some kind of contentment and that is the greatest sickness in him, the greatest change, that he has found a life away from the life that were so important to him. To be out there in a life of his own, without a single trace of anything from here, and yet not to seem to miss it.

But going back. He threw up the lime-burning and come back to working at the Blue Bell. He took in and out the barrels and suchlike and he were treated well enough. But bit by bit the work become a different kind of work and he found himself out at all hours, morning and night, taking care of cattle, running errands, tending to everything as needed tending to. And of course he nodded aye to everything as he were asked to do and then come grumbling here to me.

'Why don't you grumble where you should?' I'd say. 'There's nowt I can do to change the work as has been given. Talk to him as soon as you can.'

But he would not.

There were another fellow working in the Blue Bell as was supposed to help him, Samuel Foot were his name, but he spent his days in talk and John went on with the work. And long after John had left that work Samuel Foot were still there. 'Tis true what they say, creaking doors hang the longest.

'Say something,' I'd tell him.

'No, there's nothing to be gained from that,' he'd say.

I thought it were all of a kindness but I heard it said, and I cannot say from who, and said to me, that there were another reason for his putting up with Samuel Foot. It seems he had a sister, Ann, and she would come and visit him and he working and John and her took a great liking of one another. My informant told me as how him and Ann would go out together at every opportunity and meet in the nights and once, or so I'm told, they were come across together, lying in the woods, and they were not there for looking at the stars or trees. Not in the way as they were found. I did not hear that till a good time afterwards and by then Ann Foot had moved to live in Northampton and were married to a mason there.

And talking of Northampton, John would go there on business for the Blue Bell and stay over a night and he met up with Mary Ludgate and he there. But that come to my ear much quicker and I soon put a bucket on that fire. I were waiting for him and he come back one dull, wet, miserable January day. He come in expecting food and fire and a cosy hearing but I told him straight out as how he could turn about and walk back the way he'd come and try to find some comfort in her as he had spent the night with in Northampton. He could not guess as how I knew and he went on about that, not denying what he'd done but wanting to know where I had heard this from.

'How I heard or what I heard or who from is not what matters,' I told him. 'What matters is what you were at. Tell me you didn't lie with her, tell me you didn't make her moan and groan when she come with you. Tell me that.'

He stood there, the rain dripping off the end of his coat, for all of Christendom like a beaten dog. I left him waiting for his supper and, I can tell you, he waited a good time afore he found my porches open to his knock. And that cured him for a while, as least as far as I were to know. And he going to Northampton he would tell when he would be back and what he had to do. The following time as he went he took Eliza with him and the time after that he walked straight back through the night and there he were at the table when I woke in the morning.

And still, all this time, they'd come in carriages and on horseback. Wanting to see him, dragging him from his work, having him recite for them. How many times did I send for him from work to come and perform for some loud person as had only suggestions for improvement and then went off without as much as a thank you. As if John owed it to them to perform.

'Why do you do it for them?' I'd say.

'There might be something at the end,' John would say. 'When it comes to publishing another book.'

One man, I remember, come back four times and spent above three hours every time. I don't recall his name. He come from Oxford. The first time he listened to John and told him, as they all did, how he could better what he had wrote. The second time he come, one night, and brought his own verse and read it at us above two hours. He come back again the following week with more to read. And when he were going he left a paper wrapped upon the table and we saw him off. I believed it were a guinea or two wrapped up for John's time and trouble and we opened it and he had writ upon the paper.

'What does it say?' I asked John, expecting it were a way of telling him of some good fortune or route as was opening, after all our attention and hospitality.

John laughed but it were not a sweet laugh. 'It says: "God bless you, I shall pray for you."'

The following week the same man come back but this time John got word of his visit and went out and sat in Royce Wood from five o'clock in the evening until after two in the morning and never showed his face. I left our holy friend sitting in his carriage outside our door. He had come in the expectation that John should listen to him perform his greatest work. He did not come again.

But he were only one. The others still came promising. If they had but left us alone I think he might have been content within his mind. But maybe not.

But then our fortune seemed to swing us up into a better place. We was offered a cottage at Northborough. Oh, the joy of moving all our bits to a home of our own. We travelled back and forth the three miles from Helpston to Northborough all that day of our moving, carrying and arranging. Meeting one another at Etton, one coming and one going. And the happiness of the first night under our own roof with no one to think for but us and our children. Our home, our cottage. Oh, how we let our fancy go that night, tired and all as we were. For once I did not think of whether the children might wake. I let my voice cry out with the double ecstasy that I felt, of John in me and us in our own home at last. And yet that were the most blissful of nights and probably the start of all our troubles and our journey down a road as has never seen the true light of day.

In truth, John never settled in Northborough. We were no more than a good walk from Helpston, but it were like another country to him. The same fens were all about us, Deeping fen and Morris fen. The same rivers flowed, the Glen above us, the Welland to our west, the Nene below us.

'Moreton Leam is still in the same place,' I'd say when he were down.

'I know,' he'd say. No more than that.

But we settled in, John and me and all the children. It were a fine house. A good kitchen and a sitting room as John could use for writing and studying, a back kitchen and three bedrooms. It had been built, at John's asking, with the door facing away from the roadway. He could walk unseen into his garden and orchard and across the fens without as much as notice from those walking the roads. I loved that house. I still do. I spent so long between Walkherd Lodge, where I were born and lived as a girl, and here, as I thought I should never see a home of my own. It were nothing of my doing that

John did not settle here. It cannot be that the house were not right. It were the best he had ever lived in and made as much to his order as could have been.

In the years that come after our moving to Northborough we had our better times and less but for John it seemed as though we had moved to the other end of the world. Days and months would go past without anything untoward. His work and writing went apace. He tended his trees and played with the children in the orchard and I kept my garden happy enough and it seemed all were well. But to us, living under one roof with him, there were dykes from which there seemed no escaping for him.

He would take to talking, day after day, as to how he should never have left Helpston, as to how his writing could not prosper away from there. I'd tell him to go back, to stay there a week or two, to write when he were there. Sometimes he would but when he were down, there were no urging as could get him out. He would sit in at his table, looking out across the day and seeing nothing in anything. His food would go untouched. The children would not dare to open his door. Even the small ones learned that fast enough. Not that he would beat them, only that he could not be reached, could not be touched even by their frail voices.

And then the world — at any cost his world — went slowly dark and stayed so.

Nothing in it was right. As I have said, he was always talking of London and of how he would be among people there as could understand his gift. And then, on the other side, he would get letters from his publisher and patrons as were telling him of the changes they wanted in his poems.

'They want to publish books over my name but they're not the poems I've wrote,' he would say to me.

And then he would stand in the road and say this same thing to them as were passing. All on that were one matter but then things come to a different pass. He began to complain as how he could not get his poems put into books and he the queen of England's father. In the start I thought he were saying he couldn't get his poems printed even if he were the king but by and by it come clear in talking to us, and about the village, that he were sure in his head that he were born of royal blood.

People would smile at him and then laugh at him in the inn, and the more as they laughed the more upset and enraged he would become. He were like a strange child and they laughed at him as children would.

To remember that time is most painful to me, even at this distance. He were altered, and every day I woke hoping he would have changed back to the way he were but it were not so. He were not the man I had married.

He would still come to me sometimes at night but only in our bed. Never, as he was used to, in the pastures or on the path when we were walking home at night. It were all done quietly now. Oh, he would still bury his face in me, his tongue would still follow its course from my bosom to my belly and down and down and he would still work to bring me pleasure there between my thighs. But when I took his head in my hands and looked at him, his eyes were stone. Black. Dark and hard. No light there, no love, no feeling.

When he kissed me he weren't with me. His mouth were cold. His tongue were not the same as brought me to pleasure a thousand times afore. His hands were touching but there were no feeling in their touch. I were sure that I were lying with a ghost beside me in the dark.

Even in the dawn, when we were holding tight onto each other, just before he would come into me, I'd look for something as I'd remembered from another time, some spark of life, but there were nothing there. Only him moving and moving down into me and nothing in his face at all.

And still he worked and still he wrote his verse and still he spoke with them as come to call on him and still he chased with the children among the apple trees. But he were gone from me.

It come to a time where there were nothing I could do. No one could. The summer were come but it brought no hope. There were doctors come to us and doctors sent their word from London and they said all things were right but I knew otherwise. John were no longer with us; he were somewhere else, out there.

Eliza would walk him across the pastures and back and forth. I would take him with me to Market Deeping. The children would follow him, at a distance, across the fens, for fear of something happening. His sister come and told me about times, and he a boy, when she would come upon him in one of his convulsions. But it were nothing like that now. No fits or turns. It were as like a changeling in our home.

In the end I left him in Eliza's caring one day and walked back to my childhood home to talk with my father about John's condition. And mine.

'You made yourself a hard bed and must lie in it,' he said.

As if I had not lain there long enough to know as much.

'I did not come to ask for anything,' I told my father. 'I come to know what I must do with John.'

'A woman cannot leave her man,' my father said.

I could not make him see as I was not for leaving or breaking the home. I needed someone to tell me where I should turn to find a place for John. My father were no help at all. It had been a day wasted, beyond the pleasure of walking up the summer lane to Walkherd Lodge and remembering my childhood there. When I come back to Northborough I sent again for the doctor and told him as how I saw the changes rung in John. He in turn sent word to John Taylor, as had published John's books, and he, thinking John should come around in time, arranged to have him taken to the care of Dr Allen at High Beach in the Epping Forest.

I saw him off, that June day. He were sitting in a coach outside our home, in the very corner, pushed up against the window, though there were no one else upon the seat and only the doctor sitting opposite. I could not kiss him for I had had enough of holding onto him and having nothing of him and so I let him go. 'Twere not that I did not care. I could not care. How could I care and not be taken with him? And so I let him go.

His sister told me once, and I remembered it that day, that when he left them to join the militia his mother and all the village waved him off. There were no one there but me that day. The children were safe away and clear of knowing what were happening. I stood in the open gate and stared at him and then I slammed it shut and went inside and sat and remembered him as he were when first we fell in love. When his hands would hold my waist and his smile were like a light and my tongue would ache after a night of kissing him.

There were some as said I never visited him in High Beach. As though I could up and walk the eighty miles without a care for my children. And if there had been no children to leave, how could I visit him there and live with that again? I sent him word, with John Taylor, that I had not forgotten him and that I should like to visit when I could, lest he think I did not care.

When John Taylor come back, I asked him what John had said and he would not tell me for a good long time. He said John had smiled and nodded and then he said John had sent his fondest love but all of this did not sound true. I knew that he were lying for he come back without one letter from John. I would not let him leave our home until he sat and told me what had fallen out on his visit. And in the end he did.

'When I gave John your message,' he told me, 'he laughed and laughed in a delirium and then said: "Visit me! Visit me and I dead."'

I asked John Taylor what this meant.

'He is in a fantasy,' he said. 'He fancies himself to be Lord Byron. He told me he had watched his own funeral pass in London, Lord Byron's funeral, with the hearse and a hundred empty coaches behind and no one there to see it pass but him. That is what he told me when I said that you should like to come and visit him.'

And then one July day, with but a few hours' warning, after years in High Beach asylum, John were home again, coming in at our door as though he had been no more than for a long ramble.

His return brought hope but where hope lives fear is sure to find a home. There were days when our lives and his would be a pair but there were days when he seemed to know nothing of what the world is about. He would return to his talk of being father to the queen of England, at other times he would swear he was Lord Byron. He would wander the house in the night, mumbling and swearing. There was never a peace as could be counted upon.

It were one evening, one evening in the start of December, when he finally stopped living here as husband and father, as himself. I recall each moment.

Eliza had took in a small bunch of wild flowers and put them in a jug on his writing table, knowing how pleased he would be. She were waiting for his coming, to share his happiness. He loved wild flowers always but most especially in the dark days of the year. He often told us how, in several Christmases of his childhood, he had walked up to the high pastures to pick primroses, as out of season as a March apple.

But that December evening he come in and walked through the kitchen without a word and went and sat at his table and shook and shook. I went in after him and pointed the flowers out to him but he didn't seem to see. His eyes were open but he saw nothing and heard nothing. And then he told me that he had been out walking the road when some man, I think he said it were Thomas Brewer, had met him and told him of Mary Joyce's death. In truth, she had been dead above a two year and Eliza had sent the news in writing to John at High Beach but he had never mentioned it in writing back to us.

'But you knew of that. That is done and gone,' I said. He made no sign that he had heard. I left him there and went about my work.

A good time into that night he come out and sat with me and told me as how the Joyces had been cursed once for crossing gypsies, cursed never to have another generation.

'And there she is,' he said. 'Mary Joyce, unmarried, dead.'

The next day he went up through the woods alone and did not come back. I sent the children out to search but they could not find him. I enquired all about and late that night word come that he had been standing about the trees above Glinton Manor, the home of Mary Joyce. He come back some time in the following morning and I sat him down and tried to talk to him. No sense, I thought, in hiding this away.

'Tell me where you were and why?' I said.

And he told me. He started to talk and went on talking in a scramble but bit by bit the tale come out. He told me how her house looked, the high, steep roofs, the chimneys peeping out across the slate, the deep-set porch, the pointed stone. As if he wanted me to see the beauty of the place. And he went on about the windows.

'All the high, fine windows,' he said. 'I stared and stared at them and at the closed curtains of her window and thought of her lying there, her eyes closed as tight as the curtains from the light.'

I listened to all this. I believe he thought she was lying dead in her room that very night. 'But she's long dead,' I said.

He never answered but went on as how her father would never hear of him being with her, the Joyces being farmers. I knew this were not the same as Betty Sell or all the others. This were something I must hear in the hope of talking it out. And then he turned to me after all that time of not knowing if I was there or not and said: 'Did she think on me? Were I the thought behind her eyes?'

It were from that night as things fell all asunder.

He never went to see where she were laid in the churchyard. It would have been as well if he had done. To see her final end. To see her laid under the sod and clay. To know that she were dead. He never truly faced to that. I urged him to go and see her grave but he never crossed the stile into the church. He said there were nothing there for him. But I think it were her lying there that kept him out. She were dead and he knew it but he would not let himself believe.

It went like that above a week and the darkness hung more and more about him and more and more upon us and about the house. I would not have us all lost in that and I had Eliza send a message to Dr Allen about John going back to High Beach. But that were not to be. Instead, he arranged for John to be took to Northampton asylum.

We kept him with us for that Christmas, the blackest Christmas I ever saw or hope to, and then at the year's end he went from us. He were a good step nearer than High Beach but no nearer in the end.

There were some, in Northborough and Helpston and Glinton, as said ill of me for not visiting him.

'She never once visited him,' they said.

That and more.

'Him in that asylum for the mad and her not pretending,' they said.

Widow Clare, they called me, some in good nature and some not. But I know this, in spite of all their chattering, I never once refused him in all our life. Not once.

Not since that first time, that first warm evening, a Sunday, when John and me went walking with nothing more than courting in my mind. We walked away beyond the river into a quiet spot and lay down together and kissed and touched and the like. I don't remember what words he said that day but I do remember things as they fell out. A bright summer evening with a deal of folk out on the fens and us together, lying sheltered from them.

I were not one for saying no but neither were I one for hanging myself out like washing for any breeze that blew past. I wanted to do as he asked but he did not ask as others had and neither did he make himself a nuisance as some did. I only knew when it were done that he had taken off my gingham and my blouse and I felt his face against my skin and I thought I might as well be hanging for a sheep as for a lamb. It were as natural and good as that. And never afterwards did I refuse him, not from then. But he were different at that time. We both of us were.

III Lady Kettering

IT IS NOT SO MUCH that I want to justify myself. Not at all. But I consider it important to say what I feel needs to be said. I have heard you talk about the situation on a number of occasions and I am not at all sure that you grasp the truth of the circumstances. I fear you may have been taken in by the well-meant, but inaccurate, accounts offered by Mr Clare's sister and by his wife. They are kind people, kind but somewhat unreliable. And the scene they paint is, like their views on their own lives, equally unreliable.

His sister's marriage, if the truth were openly spoken, is not the path of roses she and her husband would have us believe. And his wife — she likes to call herself Patty but her name is Martha — is not the affable, amiable individual she would like you to imagine. Even that change of name is an attempt to soften the image. I call her Mrs Clare myself; familiarity has a way of turning on the giver, as I shall point out to you. And, let me add, anyone who tries to persuade you that she spent the last twenty years of her life in lonely waiting for a death that would free her from the burdens of this life is lying. I have it on good authority, indeed the best authority, that her life has been by no means one of celibacy.

When Mr Clare first came to my husband, on the recommendation of some petty clerk or other, it was to seek employment of a clerical nature for himself.

He waited all day in our kitchen while my husband worked away in his library, oblivious to the presence of the wretched scribbler below. He had been told that the miserable fellow was waiting, but he had forgotten. So it was in so many things in our life. I waited years myself and he seemed to have forgotten that too.

Mr Clare returned home that evening, only to reappear the following morning, still in search of a post. None such existed, of course, but my husband, having heard of his literary endeavours, put a guinea in his hand and bade him God speed. And that was where our paths first crossed. He was clomping noisily down our corridor, his nailed boots clattering on the marble flooring, when I met him. I had no idea whatsoever as to his identity. I enquired about his reasons for being in our house, taking him to be a new man in the garden. He seemed confused by my questioning and said my husband had just dismissed him. I took this to mean that he was leaving my husband's employ and told him he had better quit the house if that was the case.

It was some months later that his work came to my attention, through the efforts of Mrs Emmerson, who had taken him under her ample wing. She invited me to a reading she had arranged and while we awaited his arrival she handed me a letter (I have it still) and asked me to peruse it. It was a roughly written affair that ran thus:

My dear Miss Richardson,

You have asked of me a letter of love and I write to you on that subject. It shines with delight from eyes like yours and its light will doubtless come back a thousand times to illumine your own life. There is no love I or anyone can give that will be of greater help and hope than the love you yourself possess. Its going out will be its return. Trust in the love you have and it will not be misplaced.

Yours

John Clare

It was hardly inspiring stuff and I told Mrs Emmerson so. She informed me that Miss Richardson, a governess at General Reynardson's, had accosted Mr Clare in the garden of the house one afternoon and asked him, on hearing he was a poet, to write her love letters. This document was the response to her rather pert request.

As the story was explained, Mr Clare arrived and I recognised him at once as the man I had met in my own home. The verses he read were in some cases merely adequate, but in others they were more stimulating, and the possibilities touched upon in Miss Richardson's request raised an interest in me that might otherwise never have been excited. On my return home I enquired of my husband and he told me of the circumstances of Mr Clare's visit and his petition for a post in our home.

I went again the following week to hear Mr Clare read in Mrs Emmerson's home. On closer observation I could see why Miss Richardson had framed her request to the scribbler. He was not unappealing. He was a short man, without the immediate physical attraction of some of his fellows, but there was that mixture of raw intelligence and the earthiness of one who, otherwise, might never have entered our drawing rooms.

I determined to find more out for myself and one evening I sent word that I should expect Mr Clare at my home the following morning. Not wanting to appear overly eager, I asked that he bring a selection of his verses for my scrutiny.

He did not come. I spent the morning watching the rain-swept avenue for his approach. In the afternoon, as the rain closed into darkness, I reread the letter he had written to Miss Richardson. (I had inadvertently forgotten to return it to Mrs Emmerson.) I began to detect something less than kindness in it, and the evening brought with it a certainty that the letter was one of coldness. And now he had the nerve to ignore my invitation! I could not suffer such ingratitude lightly.

The following morning's sunlight did little to dispel my humour and then suddenly, there he was, in the garden outside. When, finally, I bade him enter, he was full of apologies for his absence on the previous day. He beat so much about the bush that in the end I asked him to give an account, clearly and promptly, as to why he had not come.

'The rain,' he mumbled.

'It was raining rain, Mr Clare, not fire and brimstone,' I said.

He blushed and mumbled again.

'Kindly explain yourself,' I repeated.

'My boots would not keep out the rain,' he said quickly, keeping his eyes upon the ground, 'and I did not dare to come into your house with stockings that were wringing wet.'

For a moment I thought he was being clever but then I realised the truth of the situation. I had but to look at his feet to see the veracity of his claim.

'I would have sent one of the children to inform you but. . .' He left the statement incomplete. There were all the children, he explained, and his wife Martha and himself and his only income at that time was writing.

But I had not brought him into my home to listen to the troubles of his life. 'You must not let this state of affairs come between you and your ambition,' I told him. 'If you become overly concerned with the circumstance of your condition today, you will never raise yourself to a better condition tomorrow.'

He seemed to see the sense in that and his manner became more relaxed. We sat and talked about the genesis of his interest in writing and then I asked him to read me some verses.

'Read me the first piece that comes to hand,' I said. He picked a sheet from the pile by his side and read for me, glancing from the page to my face and back at intervals. When he had concluded, I took the page from his hand and read it for myself.

I sleep with thee and wake with thee, And yet thou
art not there:— I fill my arms, with thoughts of thee,
And press the common air, — Thy eyes are gazing
upon mine, When thou art out of sight;

My lips are always touching thine,

At morning, noon and night.

I finished reading the lines and observed the man
seated opposite. He was staring at me. I felt myself a
little uneasy and yet a little startled, aroused even. It
was not the man and it was not the verse, which had
been written for someone else, or perhaps simply
as an exercise in rhyme, but it was the combination
of the two — words and man — which was so
disconcerting. There was a certain naive sweetness in
the words but there was a deeper, darker side to this
man. And he struck me as one who might supply the
intrigue and stimulation then absent from my life —
the excitement of a flirtation and perhaps something
bolder. And I determined to delve more thoroughly
into his mind.

I saw no merit in waiting until another time and
another opportunity occurred. If one has a question
then one must put that question. 'Tell me, Mr Clare,' I
said, 'when you and Mrs Clare were courting, where did
you do your courting?'

He was quite open and unabashed in his reply.
'Everywhere,' he said.

I pressed onward. 'And your lovemaking? Was that
done everywhere too?' I asked. He blushed at this, to my

surprise, and yet I felt he would, with encouragement, open himself to me.

'Oh come now,' I said, 'you cannot be bashful with me. We are friends, are we not? It is my intention to help you in whatever ways I may. We shall be accomplices in your poetic plans, shall we not?'

He nodded at this but did not speak.

'Today has been, perhaps, less well judged than it might have been. It comes in the shadow of yesterday's disappointment,' I told him. 'Let us begin again next week. You shall come here on Tuesday and we shall walk in the garden and discuss your verse and then we shall decide on what may be best done to enhance your career.'

He stood and mumbled something and bowed.

'You might, perhaps, leave me a selection of your verse so that I may prepare myself to discuss the stronger points and the shortcomings with you,' I added. 'I shall choose a dozen verses at random.'

'I'll happily leave them all to your ladyship,' he said.

'No,' I replied, 'a dozen will suffice.' I did not want to face his expectation of my commenting on every rhyme he had penned.

I counted out the twelve, we set a time for his return on the following Tuesday and our first private audience concluded.

I read his verses that evening. They were ordinary in the extreme, promising in places, but no more than that. I made notes of my suggested alterations. (I did not want him to feel that my interest was simply in him.) Indeed, in a number of instances I fancied the results of my corrections to be quite successful. My improvements in the grammatical constructions made the pieces immediately more pleasant to eye and ear. A number of the verses jarred because of the colloquial nature of the language. This was something I had expected in conversation but had not been prepared for in the written form. Certainly, at the readings in Mrs Emmerson's home there had been none of these expressions. They were distractions and I made notes suggesting new words, or in some instances lines, which would more adequately capture the imagination of the audience which he hoped to attract.

I put a great deal of effort into my reconstruction of his work. But as I remarked earlier, kindness is often ill received by those on whom it is bestowed. But that was still a time away.

On the following Tuesday Mr Clare did arrive at the appointed time and we walked in the garden and I read over the verses in their corrected form and explained the changes to him. In some cases he accepted what I said but in others he was quite adamant that no changes were necessary and that he wished to retain the local expressions which I had amended. I pointed out that he might wish this for his friends and neighbours but a book-buying public in London would not be impressed by such obscurity. In the end he agreed to review his verses and consider my proposals.

'I wish to take you with me to recite for friends of mine,' I told him. 'And they will be appreciative, you know that. Guineas, subscriptions, donations, contributions, books. Guineas. In order to benefit one must conform. And one must listen to one's friends. And we must be friends, must we not?'

He nodded. 'Aye,' he said.

'Come with me,' I said and I led him into the house and up the stairs and into my private sitting room.

'There,' I said, 'do you see this fine writing desk and this chair and these inks and quills and papers?'

He nodded and mumbled.

'I am giving you these to help with your writing,' I told him.

He seemed genuinely grateful for the assistance. More grateful than for any introductions or visits I had suggested to him.

He was taciturn when it came to the question of human contact. I blame that on his peasant background. He could, indeed, deal with things – with desks and chairs and paper and poems – but he could not deal with people of another class. Doubtless he was quite successful with women of his own class. I have heard so many stories of his escapades and from so many sources that they cannot all be concoctions of idle minds. But how many times did I take him to talk in company and found him inebriate beyond description within the hour, having consumed as much wine as quickly as possible? I suspect his manner of lovemaking may have been of a similar short, sharp nature. Or so it seems safe to assume. Certainly, in the matter of drink, he was incapable of controlling his intake or the effects it had on his behaviour. He became, by turns, loud and offensive or dull and forbidding and neither state was particularly pleasant to deal with. On the first occasion I put the matter down to his nervousness but its repetition made me aware of his inability to deal with society beyond his own upbringing. At his worst he resembled a wild animal in an enclosed space, unpredictable, dangerous and a threat to all within his reach.

His tongue, too, would loosen foolishly, becoming either political or coarse and tasteless. Which may have been acceptable in the alehouses where he seemed to think he had an audience but was certainly unacceptable in the houses into which I took him.

His greatest folly of all was the assumption that his own class should be impressed by him. But he was one of their own who had stepped, even temporarily, out of the pit and was no sooner cleaned up and polished than they began the none too difficult task of dragging him back among them. He was more than capable of slipping back himself. They were jealous of his day in the light, and raised to a state of ecstasy by his fall. Not one of them was sufficiently interested in his welfare to make the journey to see him in the madhouse. Not even his wife!

However, to return to the development of our relationship. I was at pains to ensure that he saw me as a friend of his. My gift had been an attempt to remove whatever barriers his lowly station might create for us. I was truly interested in his welfare. I wanted success for him and I wanted to fortify the bond between us. I was making myself available and putting my position at some risk in doing so and in return I sought some commitment from Mr Clare.

After I had made my gift known and after he had examined the desk and papers, I took him back into the garden and we walked together again and I put my initial question to him.

'Will you write verses for me, John?' I asked. 'Will you write love letters, just for me?'

'If you wish,' he said.

'I do wish,' I said.

He nodded his assent.

'And would you wish for anything?' I asked.

He seemed to spend a long time thinking upon this and finally he stopped his walking and turned to me and said, very quietly but with great tenderness, it seemed: 'Perhaps a likeness of your ladyship.'

Such had been the length of the request in coming that I found it almost a disappointment and yet he was requesting something of a personal nature and I agreed at once, promising a locket and likeness within the week.

'You shall have it,' I said. 'And I shall have my love letters.'

That moment promised much, I thought. And one afternoon, perhaps a month afterwards, we drove in my carriage to Mrs Holden's home, where Mr Clare was to read for some ladies who were interested in his progress. In the course of the journey he was more open than hitherto. He told me about his childhood pastimes, the games he played, the music he learned on his violin, the first rude verses he had composed and how he would read them for his father and pretend they were penny ballads he had learned from a passing singer. And he told me of his dancing days. He described to me dances I had never seen performed. He sang me songs that he had collected. He was, altogether, a different man.

When we arrived at Mrs Holden's home he read his verse and spoke with the ladies and then I asked him to show us the dances he had spoken of on our journey. I asked Mrs Holden to send for one of the gardener's boys and have him bring in two sticks from the yard. Then we settled to watch Mr Clare demonstrate his dancing steps with the boy.

He seemed most wary of my request and was slow in making any move to illustrate the dances he had spoken of, so that I began to wonder whether they existed anywhere but in his imagination. I suggested this to him and at once he began to move, not gracefully, but rapidly through a series of passes, clapping his stick against the boy's stick and twirling as he moved, thumping his foot on the floor and at all times fixing the boy with his eyes. And each time their sticks clashed he brought his down with greater force until at length his stick smashed the other and he came to a stop. The boy was holding his hand and blood was flowing from a wound above the knuckles.

Mrs Holden clapped her hands and signalled to the boy that he might go. He left the room and, immediately, Mr Clare followed him and I heard him speaking with the boy in the hallway.

As we drove home he chided me for insisting that he dance. 'I hurt that boy and that should not have happened,' he said.

'I merely requested a demonstration,' I replied. 'Nothing more.'

'You should not have done. You made me angry. I should not have struck him, even without intention.'

I laughed at this and pointed out that my asking him to dance was hardly justification or excuse for his having wounded the boy.

'You should not have put us in that position, him or me,' he said.

And to make matters worse, I discovered later, through a conversation with Mrs Holden, that he had given the boy a crown for his troubles – and this from a man who could barely feed his children. As if the boy had never been wounded before and as if all this led back in some inexplicable way to my little request.

The simple explanation for this incident and for his frequent drunkenness lies in his inability to cope with the things to which he aspired. Aspiration is not enough if one does not possess the gift of acceptance. Mr Clare was forever looking backward and forward and as a result was unable to keep his feet steady or his head clear at times when that was demanded by the company to which he had been introduced. The problem was as easy and as complex as that.

Aware as I was of my own desires, I was also aware of the necessity for keeping appearances and to this end I made a point of visiting his cottage on a number of occasions, to talk with Mrs Clare and the children. I cannot deny being surprised by the cleanliness and warmth of the Clares' cottage. The children were well nourished, well washed and well behaved. The house itself was nothing if not clean. It was a large cottage by the standards of Mr Clare's class, being possessed of three bedrooms, a sitting room, a kitchen and a back kitchen.

It had been made, at Mr Clare's request, with the door to the back, so that he could step straight into his garden.

He was greatly proud of this garden, not for its neatness but rather for the wildness he had cultivated in it. Rarely have I seen him more animated than the first time he walked me through it. He was thoroughly enraptured by it. He had transplanted many flowers from their native grounds, taking them with clumps of their soil, and put them into his own. Many I should have passed off as weeds but these were among the plants he was most enamoured of: horehound, oxlip, basil, bugloss, mullein, were all pointed out to me. I offered him some of the plants from my own garden but these, he said, 'would hardly sit in such a wilderness as this'.

I mentioned to Mrs Clare his inability to hold his drink and she seemed to share my dislike for it.

'But,' she added, 'he cannot be easy in an alehouse unless he is well drunk; he fears the scorn of his neighbours unless he is as drunk as they.'

That hardly seemed an adequate explanation for his behaviour in other company but I saw little point in pursuing this matter with her. It would be of little import to her and would make no difference to him.

As the weather, that first summer of our acquaintance, grew more warming, so his moods seemed greatly to improve and his companionship became more pleasant. My husband spent much of that summer in London and I determined to have Mr Clare for myself.

One afternoon in that July he and I were seated in my sitting room. The windows were thrown open and the sun was heating the soft breeze that carried the scent of the garden to the deepest corners of my home. It was an altogether idyllic afternoon. Mr Clare had read me some of his verse and I had made my reactions known to him and he had not dismissed them. We were speaking of the experiences of childhood. I told him of mine and he told me of his.

He described his perpetual search, as a child, for the land rail – a little-seen bird – among the summer wheat. He recollected evenings when he and his sister would attempt to race the moon on their way back home, flying like clouds in its face and never succeeding in reaching home before it. He laughed a great, deep laugh when he spoke of that. The most sincere laughter I ever heard him take.

Gently, I moved the conversation on to later times and I enquired, finally, of his courtship and whether it had been of only one woman.

He replied that it had not.

'Of many?' I asked.

'Some,' he said.

I feared he was about to become sullen and withdrawn again but I ventured onward with my questioning. 'Was there one you loved especially?'

He was silent but it was not a sullen silence now, instead, he seemed deeply moved.

'I may take it that there was,' I continued.

He nodded.

I recall leaning forward in my chair and reaching across and putting my hands on his and then, very softly, kneeling before him, my face looking up into his, divided between the desire to kiss and the need to know what story might be there to be told, a story never heard, perhaps, by another soul.

'Tell me,' I whispered, 'tell me some intimacy of your courtship. In one courtship. Tell me something you have never told anyone else in your life.'

He was silent for a very long time and I feared he might not respond.

'Please,' I whispered, even more quietly than before.

He began to speak so slowly that it was difficult at first to decide whether there was any connection between the words he was uttering. But gradually the sense of what he was saying began to emerge.

'I were in ... I love ... once, always, with a girl as I met in school.'

I continued staring into his face, into his eyes. Our eyes were staring each into the other's and yet I think he saw nothing of me.

'Tell me her name, tell me this girl's name,' I whispered.

'Mary Joyce.'

He paused again and I moved my hand from where it rested on his, along the sleeve of his shirt and up onto his shoulder and then my fingers touched the strands of his wild hair. I stroked them as though they were the most delicate petals on a prized rose, so softly that he would hardly have sensed my fingers brushing him. And then he began to speak and I went on touching his hair. He spoke quietly but with great sureness, intent on telling his story.

'I were writing poems for her,' he said, 'but I never felt free to tell her this and I would never dare give them to her. All that time I were writing for her ... to her ... and I were afraid to let her see the words I had wrote for her. I could not find the way to tell her and I could never muster the courage to tell her my feelings for her.'

He stopped speaking and I pressed the palm of my hand against the side of his face. His eyes were still unwavering in their gaze and yet he was not seeing me. If he was aware of a presence at all, it was not of mine. And then he returned to his story in that same low, set voice.

'One Sunday evening,' he continued, 'when I knew she was at church, I took a book of love poems as I'd bought for myself and I put flowers in two of the pages, forget-me-nots, and I stood outside the church until people started to leave. It were raining and it were evening, but a warm evening, and she come out with her father. He went away to get their cart and she stood in the shelter of the church doorway and I come out of the shelter I were standing in and I handed her the book, I reached out and put it into her hand.'

His eyes seemed to take on a light, a life, as though he were either seeing me for the first time or he was seeing through me, past me. I remained kneeling and then he went on talking, as though he had never paused at all.

'She never looked at the book, not a glance. She looked at me and spoke not a word and neither did I. We stood there in the rain without speaking a single word between us. And then her father called to her that the cart were ready and she went away.'

I said nothing for some time, thinking there might be more to be told, but at length it was obvious that he had no more to say.

'Did you make love to her? Later?' I asked.

He shook his head.

'I should like to make love to you, John,' I said and I took his hand in mine and pressed it to my face. 'I gave you my likeness. You asked it of me. You found it attractive. Do you find me attractive, John?'

'Aye,' he said.

'Come with me, then, where we shall not be disturbed.'

I led him up to my bedroom. There, too, the windows were thrown wide on the glorious afternoon. I pulled the curtains closed and turned to face him. He was standing, so uneasy, in the centre of the room. I moved towards him and stood, my breasts against his shirt, looking up into his eyes, waiting for him to touch me.

He shook his head several times. At first I thought it was a sign of admiration, but then he spoke.

'I cannot do it,' he said.

'Surely it isn't that you are afraid?' I said.

He said nothing.

'It can hardly be that you have not made love to another woman since your marriage?'

'No,' he said, 'it isn't that. I cannot do it. I cannot be at ease here.'

'Let us go elsewhere, then,' I said.

'It isn't that neither,' he said. 'I do find you attractive but it would not be right with me. I could not be at ease and so it would not be good . . . for you.'

'May I not be the judge of that?' I said.

He went on shaking his head and I knew nothing would come of this. I felt anger, not shame but something like it. The sting of his rejection resembled that of a thistle on the skin. The discourtesy and arrogance of this saucebox was as demeaning as it was unwarranted.

'Wait for me downstairs,' I told him.

And I left him waiting for a long time.

When I went down to my sitting room I took with me a violin that had lain about the house for many years, unused. I handed it to Mr Clare.

'Will you, at least, play for me?' I asked.

He took the violin and began to tune it. I poured myself a glass of wine.

'What shall you play for me?' I asked. 'I should like to know what I am about to hear.'

' "Nancy Dawson",' he said.

'Is this one of your own collecting?' I said.

'No,' he replied.

'Very well,' I said, walking to the window. 'Play for me.'

Something in my tone must have surprised and frightened him for his eyes narrowed and his face was suddenly pipe white.

'Play me the tune,' I repeated.

He began to play and as he did I walked about the room until I came towards him face to face, and in an instant I splashed my glass of wine across his face. The red wine dripped from his hair and face onto his white linen shirt. I stayed but long enough to take the scene in and then I swept from the room and left him to find his own way out and home.

I did not see Mr Clare again that month and was not sure I should ever see him, other than by chance. But he did reappear, unannounced, and spent much time in apology for his behaviour. It crossed my mind that he had come, perhaps, at a time when he was hopeful of the completion of my suggested intimacy but if this was so then he was greatly disappointed for I never mentioned it to him.

I did, however, tell him that I had been apprised, by Mrs Emmerson, of the fact that he had submitted a poem to his publisher which contained lines about 'accursed wealth o'erbounding human laws'. I asked him whether this was true and he replied that it was so.

'He has insisted on the poem's removal,' I told him. 'You know you cannot publish that kind of sedition. You know that.'

He said nothing.

'And you have written verses attacking the hunt,' I went on.

'Aye,' he muttered, 'and badger-baiting.'

This I could not accept, not after what had gone before, and certainly not in my own home.

'I know nothing of that,' I said. 'That is among your own people. But the hunt is part of England, part of its history.'

'A bloody, brutal part,' he said.

Suddenly his boldness was growing. I turned on him in a fury.

'A part,' I reiterated. 'You cannot hope for continued support if you insist on writing this kind of seditious nonsense. You are someone now. You are a writer, a poet, a person of standing who has access to the homes of the highest. Have I not taken you into houses myself, have I not introduced you to influential people, people who will be of assistance to you, people who will open ways that would never have been open to you? Have you not met important people in London because of your position?'

There was no retort. I took the opportunity to drive the point to its conclusion.

'You must see the senselessness, the treason, the danger to your standing and to your family in all this. You must stick to the things you know of, the rhymes of rivers and fields and birds.'

'I have never wrote of fields,' he interrupted.

'Don't talk to me of enclosure,' I sighed. 'I do not want to hear of it. It is done. Done. You must accept the things that are done, John. Just as you must accept the responsibilities that go with your position. You owe it to those of us who have facilitated your position.'

Again, he was silent.

'And you have not used your writing desk,' I said.

'I am waiting to take it home,' he said.

And I believe he meant it.

'Home! Home!' I said when I had recovered. And then I laughed. 'Surely you did not think it was for taking home? No, it is there for your use, as you require it, in my home. That is why I made it available. So that you could come and write in my home. Where you could have peace. Quietness. Where you and I could be close. Where I could be on hand to advise you on the finer points of your work.'

He seemed genuinely deflated.

'And when did you last write me a love letter?' I asked. 'When did you last speak with me? More than a month ago. No love letters. Nothing.'

I stood again, as I had stood a month earlier, my body close to his.

'Undo your britches for me,' I said.

He hesitated. There were so many emotions in that hesitation, not least the awakening of desire and possibility. That thrilled me, it restored my self-belief. But there were other emotions too. Fear loathing, embarrassment, uncertainty.

'Undo your britches,' I repeated.

Slowly he undid them and when he had done I took his hands in mine and held them momentarily, long enough for his britches to slide about his ankles. There he stood, as I had done, like a fool. I saw the pathetic comedy in the figure before me and I laughed and laughed and laughed. The moment was mine.

I do not accept the claim that my encounter with Mr Clare contributed in any way to the decline in his ability to reason and to live a life that might be described as normal. There was a battle raging within his own head and it was not bettered or worsened by anything I or anyone else did for or against him.

I date Mr Clare's deterioration from the failure of his verse to sell. Initially, there had been a fascination with this strange man and his writings. But many of those who would question my involvement with Mr Clare would already have deserted him once he ceased to be a passing fancy. I at least remained involved. He could not, however, cope with the fact that he was not destined for a central place on the London literary stage. His fame there was fleet. And in his own area his fame was nothing. He was a laughing stock. Once the dual nature of his rejection became clear, the sinister collapse of his brain was hastened. That is my analysis and I was well placed to observe it.

Only once did I see his mental state at its most violent. That was one afternoon in autumn when I called unannounced at his cottage. I rounded the corner into the garden, by way of entering the cottage, and was confronted by the sight, through the open door, of Mr Clare smashing his fists and face against the kitchen table while at the same time screaming incomprehensibly. His wife ran past me to the end of their garden and called to their daughter, who came hurriedly from the field beyond and rushed inside.

A moment later all was quiet and then his daughter led Mr Clare out through the doorway, still muttering and cursing, and bleeding from a gash above the bridge of his nose, but calmer than he had been. She led him as you would lead an infant, down the garden path and into the pasture beyond and out across the fens. Mrs Clare explained that this was the only cure for his anger and that their daughter Eliza was the only one with whom he would walk.

'He may walk with her for hours now,' she told me, 'but he will come back quieter and we will have at least seven or eight days of peace afore this happens again.'

I cannot deny that I thought of the afternoons in my own home, only a couple of years earlier – I had even knelt before this same man – and I shivered at the thought of what might have been.

I was not surprised when I heard that he had been incarcerated in an asylum for the deranged. I was, however, taken aback that he had been admitted to High Beach, an asylum in the Epping Forest. The sanity of the man who ran that establishment was, in itself, suspect. Had he not maintained that one part of society was at war with another and that this was one of the reasons for the existence of insanity! It seemed as though he had been reading, and heeding, the rantings of Mr Clare himself. Fate had matched doctor and patient, it seemed to me.

His internment brought many sympathisers. They claimed, among other things, that his state was not one of insanity or delirium but rather of anxiety brought on by poverty and bodily exhaustion. When I heard opinions such as these I was tempted to mention his incessant inebriation, his incessant wenching and his incessant turn of ill-chosen and offensive poetic statements. But I did not. Soon enough these people would find that the hand that feeds is often bitten.

I was, however, astounded to hear of Mr Clare's return to his home. He had been absent for three years and the reports we had received had not suggested the possibility of return. Indeed, we had settled into the expectation of his long-term incarceration and then, suddenly, there was word that he was home again.

It was July when he returned but our paths did not cross until late in that August when, one radiant evening, he appeared on my lawn. I saw him and thought it best to face him down. But he was quite removed from any state of anxiety and smiled when I approached. My own fears were somewhat allayed by the sight of his daughter loitering at the farther end of the lawn. Evidently she had been sent to be his guardian angel in his wanderings.

'I'm pleased to see you back among us, John,' I said.

'I'm pleased to be back,' he said.

'Is your writing going well?' I asked.

'Well indeed,' he said.

He wandered away from me and began to smell, deeply, the roses that provided a shelter along the pathway.

'If you wish to take some flowers with you, for Mrs Clare, please do,' I said.

'No, we have flowers enough in our own garden,' he said. 'Not roses such as these but all kinds of flowers. I have spent the day watching the silver-washed butterflies among them.'

'You have settled back then?' I asked.

'Well settled. And free,' he replied.

'I'm glad to hear that,' I said. 'We shall look forward to hearing you read for us all again in the autumn. You must have a great deal of new verse to choose from.'

'A great deal,' he said.

We walked on, he asking me the names of roses, I asking about the direction his verse was taking. It was a perfectly amicable hour we spent together and it was he who first made his excuses and left.

I was happy for him, for though I still harboured then, and still do now, the bitter memory of an earlier time, I never wished him the awful sickness that had struck him so terribly.

We did not meet again until December and then it was in Stamford one afternoon, when we came face to face in the street. He was carrying a sheaf of papers and again his daughter was following at a distance.

'I see you have been writing,' I said, referring to the papers under his arm.

'I have,' he said.

I was about to make some other remark when he continued: 'Would you like me to read you a new verse?'

'Very much,' I said. 'We must arrange a reading where we can hear a selection.'

'I shall read you one now,' he said.

I assumed it was something freshly written, something of great pride. 'Of course,' I assented.

And then he knelt in the street, and began as if to read from one of the sheets that he carried.

'Our father, which art in heaven . . .' he said.

I thought for an instant that this was an introduction but the lunacy of his kneeling in the public thoroughfare and the words which followed made it clear that it was not.

'. . . hallowed be thy name,' he continued. 'Thy kingdom come, thy will be done on earth as it is in heaven. Give us this day our daily bread, and forgive us our trespasses, as we forgive them that trespass against us and lead us not into temptation but deliver us from evil, for Thine is the kingdom, the power and the glory, for ever and ever. Amen.'

I had stood among the gaping throng while this went on and now I signalled to his daughter to come and take him away. She came and stood by him and waited until he had got to his feet again. So calm was she that the possibility fleetingly crossed my mind that this performance was his way of publicly humiliating me but then he turned his attention from me and began to search the faces of passing girls, at the same time shouting loudly as he went. The words were a mockery of those he had already spoken. I could not but hear them, for his voice rose above the clamour of the street.

'Mary Joyce, who were in my heart,' he shouted, 'bleésed be thy name. Thy loving come, thy will be done in this place as it was in that time. Give me this day thy needed love and forgive me my absence, as I forgive thee thine, and lead me into temptation, deliver me from loneliness, for thine are the eyes, the lips, the breasts, for ever and ever. Amen.'

I was transfixed by this display of madness. The women to whom he addressed his tirade were either terrified or amused. Some laughed, some ran from his effrontery. His daughter merely allowed the harangue to come to its natural conclusion. It seemed, momentarily, that it had, when suddenly Clare threw himself into the roadway and began a series of shrieks that made me weak. These sounds stopped briefly and then recommenced, but as distinguishable words.

'Sweet Jesus, Mary Joyce,' he screamed over and over again until his voice grew hoarse.

Finally, some men of the town succeeded in quietening him and they led him away, past the spot where I stood. He was muttering the opening words of the Lord's Prayer over and over to himself as he went.

I returned to my carriage and travelled homeward, shocked and trembling at what I had seen.

Now I can recall the anticipation, the disappointment, the ennui in trying to deal with a man whose expectations were so narrow, a man who claimed that the enclosure would curb freedom and imagination and yet a man who, even in his sanest moments, was incapable of anything other than profanity.

It is sad, pathetic, to see any human fall to these depths but particularly one whose talents were clear, if limited. One would not wish such a curse on any human being. A struggle regarding the hurt of the heart is one thing, a plague of the mind is another. But this plague, this disease, is nothing to do with the inadequacies which led to my suffering at the hands of Mr Clare. Nothing. He was, then, a different man. I feel pity for the creature he became but I feel rage and loathing for the man he was. I make no connection between the two.

IV Eliza Clare

MY FATHER SPENT the last two dozen years of his life in the asylum for the mad, St Andrew's in Northampton. When I say that, it may sound clean and easy but it was not so. All of us – wife, children, family – were affected by my father's illness. And having him removed from the family was not a simple way of dealing with the problem, just as the removal of a damaged arm or leg from the body cannot be said to be the end of the damage. The limb remains in the mind and the regret at its loss continues for as long as there is life in the body. We did not breathe a sigh of relief when my father was taken away a second and final time to the asylum. We lived in hope that he might return at some period to live with us. Our hope was that he might become better, or at least passive, and be capable of staying with us and doing the things he was happiest in doing – writing, tending to his flowers, walking on the fens, talking with his neighbours, observing the changes in the natural world. These are elementary things and are not beyond the capabilities of most people. To know that is to know the closeness of the possibility of having my father return. And as regret remains, so hope remains and each day brings the chance of return.

We would visit my father in Northampton whenever we could but it was difficult. The four pounds for the journey was not readily come by. As we grew older it became easier but when my father was first taken's into High Beach asylum, in Essex, I was but a girl of fifteen and when he was finally taken's from us I was nineteen and only finding my own way in the world. It is not my place to say but I was, of all his children, the one who seemed most to be in his company. I saw him, in childhood, as a man who knew all that was worth knowing in the way of nature. And he shared this knowledge with all of us.

My Aunt Sophy often remarked that I was as close to him in my childhood as she had been in hers, and so it seems I was, for I cannot recall anything in my youngest days that did not have my father's presence. No journey, no matter how brief, no occasion was complete without his figure in the landscape of my memory. His arms seemed eternally to be about me – holding me, hugging me, swinging me, throwing me into the air and catching me. But as I grew, my father seemed gradually to change and the man I knew became, in ways, a stranger. His reactions were less predictable. His depressions were of greater duration. His laughter and happiness seemed uncustomary. I could not then assess the changes that were taking place but I was caught in situations which I realised, even as a young girl, were not natural. Among my friends I knew of no other father who spent as much time with his children as my father did but neither did I know of any father who could seem so removed from the world about him.

No other father would rant in the street against badger-baiting; no other father would fall to his knees in prayer in the marketplace and then seem not to recall what he had done. And no other daughter seemed constantly charged with the responsibility of watching for these strangenesses. Not that I objected. It merely required my being with my father, or in a position to observe him, much of the time. And this was the case, anyway. He rarely went about his ramblings without one or more of us, and I seemed the one most often chosen. Not that I was oldest or youngest but that I seemed most interested in all he wrote and said.

I set this before you not to claim a special closeness, for I was unaware of it, but because this is how things transpired in our lives. I think his love for reading was most thoroughly observed and copied in my life. I am grateful for that gift, though I am grateful, too, that it did not impinge upon my acquaintance with normality. My father paid that extortionate price in his own life and lived to regret it. I saw that with my own eyes and heard it from his lips on many an occasion.

But I was not the only one affected by the events of his illness. All of us were dealt blows of our own. My mother was left without a husband at a time when she should have been in the prime of her enjoyment of companionship. When he was taken to High Beach she lived in hope that he would recover. His incarceration there was offered as a hopeful thing. He would return as the man she had married. Even his letters to her spoke of this. She never made the journey to see him there, nor did any of us. It was beyond our means. And she was sick with the palsy much of the time. Another burden sent for her to bear. But she did see my father again. For some months. That was in the summer and through to the year's end of eighteen hundred and forty-one.

My father had, at that time, been three years in the asylum in the Epping Forest and we had had letters and calls from a great many people who had been to visit him there. All of them spoke of his comfort and his good temper. His letters came too, and I would read them to my mother. Some of them seemed to augur well; they were full of hope and talk of home. But others were confused and painful. Even in my eighteenth year I began to keep the true contents of some of these letters from my mother. I would read only those passages which seemed appropriate to her capacity to accept the sadness they delivered. Not that I kept his illness from her, merely that I did not always tell her of the references his letters contained to other women. Some of these were known to me and to my mother. Others seemed to be women he had met at High Beach. And still others, I believe, were creatures of his imagination.

One name recurred with terrible regularity. That of Mary Joyce. I was aware from my mother's conversations of her existence in my father's growing years and of her death. Indeed, I had gone once to see her grave. It was in the wake of a series of letters my father had sent, addressed to her. I went to satisfy myself that she was dead. I derived some peace of mind from the sight of her name carved into the stone. I dropped a spray of blooms onto the grave, not from any sense of sorrow, but rather from one of gratitude.

However, to return to my father's reappearance. It was in the month of July of eighteen hundred and forty-one. His life in High Beach had been one of relative freedom. His master, Dr Allen, had allowed him to come and go as he pleased, with only the eyes of his keepers cast irregularly upon him. This was part of Dr Allen's method of encouraging a responsibility which might lead to a return to full health. My father took advantage of this freedom to make the acquaintance of a large number of people – householders, gypsies, children, inmates, shopkeepers – as well as of those writers and patrons who called to visit him.

In a letter sent to us at the Easter of that year he wrote of a visit to Buckhurst church on Easter day and of seeing a child there who reminded him of my brother William. 'A small boy with a serious face', he wrote. Afterwards I saw in that short, sad reference a spur that gave him the reason for wanting to get back to his home and his family.

That freedom had allowed him to make his hasty plans and execute them. He was well clear of High Beach before his absence was reported. And he had the sense to avoid detection, despite lookouts along his journey. In three days he walked the eighty miles from High Beach to our home but he was ill-prepared for the rigours of the journey, taking no food or money in his pocket, intent only on getting back to his home and his family.

He slept, as he had done in his youth, my mother said, in fields and ditches upon the way. He told me afterwards that he slept the first night with his first wife – in that he meant Mary Joyce – upon his left side. When he awoke the next morning she was not there, he said.

'Someone came and took her away from my side,' he told me. 'I searched about the field I were sleeping in and the next field and along the roadway, thinking she might have gone walking without me, but I never discovered her and knew that she would not have left me by her own choosing. Someone came and took her away from me.'

It made me sad to hear him talk of his first wife and sad to hear him say he was alone on waking. I think he was alone for most of his life. He had his family in his own childhood and us in his manhood but he was always alone.

On the second night of his escape he slept in the porch of a doorway. Though it was July, the night was cool and he told me how he gazed through a window of this house and was mesmerised by the glowing of a fire in the grate. He imagined it to be a house he could have lived in with his first wife, he said. But he was afraid to knock and ask for lodging, fearing he would be taken back to High Beach.

Each time he spoke to me of his first wife, it cut me for myself and for our family and most for our mother.

Because she could neither read nor write there are those who make the assumption that she could not feel the pain of always being second to this other woman, this ghost who could do no wrong because she was safe within the grave. It is my mother who could do little in the way of wrong. She accepted all that my father delivered in the way of loyalty and betrayal. Some of that betrayal came from the sickness in his mind but much of it came from his continual dissatisfaction with his life, and that was something my mother was not the cause of. Rather, she did all in her power to make life pleasant for him and us.

I loved my father dearly. I was closer to him than any of his other children but I see, too, the infidelity, the difficulty of living with him as my mother did. One moment she was the object of great affection and gentleness and the next she was his second wife, or worse, she was left while he pursued some other woman who had caught his eye.

The other thing my father told me about those nights spent in the open was that he always slept with his head in the direction he must walk the following day. He was in search of a ghost and taken up with the fantasies of a sick mind and yet he had the wit to sleep with his head in the direction of our home. That, too, is a sadness. So much sickness and yet so much that is clever. So much possibility and so little hope.

On his third day of walking, he told me, he was so hungry that he ate grass from the roadside. He assured me 'it tasted as good as bread'. He told me how he considered his position then.

'There I was, a man whose daughter is the queen of England, seated on a heap of stones, without a farthing to my name. And yet, I thought, if I put fresh speed into my step, then I shall see my family tomorrow, and so I walked on.'

A man from Helpston saw him and he six miles from our home and I took a cart and went out to meet him. He was seated on a stile, three miles from Northborough, when first I saw him. He looked a melancholy sight, his face dirty, his shoes torn, his shirt stained. And yet I was more happy than I could say to see him. Had he not escaped, made his way as true as a stone to the home where his family lived? Had he not been valiant in his efforts to be reunited with us?

I alighted from the cart and walked towards him. He looked at me as he might have looked on any stranger passing the way.

'You know me, Father?' I asked.

He shook his head.

'I am Eliza, your daughter.'

Still his stare was blank.

'You have walked a great way. We were told you were walking and I came to meet you.'

He smiled at this.

'My mother is waiting for you at home. I have brought Morgan's cart so that you may travel the last miles in comfort.'

'You would take me back to the madhouse,' he said.

'No, Father,' I assured him. 'I will take you home.'

He smiled again at this. 'You have devised this to take me to the madhouse,' he said, shaking his head.

'Father, if I were to take you to the madhouse, should I have come out here alone, without strong men to take you with them. I shall bring you home. To your wife.'

He seemed puzzled by this and sat a long time without speaking. I sat by him on the stile. Finally, he seemed to have reached an understanding of what I had said.

'Patty?' he asked.

'Yes, Father, your wife Patty,' I said.

'You will take me to her?' he asked.

'Yes,' I said, as gently as I could.

I took his arm and we walked to the cart and he looked inside several times before he had satisfied himself that this was not a way of capturing him.

'Where is my other wife?' he asked then.

'Who be that, Father?' I asked.

He became indignant at once.

'My first wife,' he shouted. 'Mary Joyce.'

'She is dead, Father,' I said, 'this years. I wrote and told you so.'

'No,' he said quietly, 'I have seen her myself, not two days ago.'

'Perhaps you have,' I said. 'Let us talk about her later. Patty will be waiting for you, and the children.'

He climbed into the cart and we set off for Northborough and our home. My mind in a muddle. My joy at seeing him had been tempered by the talk of Mary Joyce and by his not knowing me. And yet as we travelled towards home, he seemed to ease back into himself. He chatted with me about the places we passed. He seemed, now, to know exactly who I was and he thanked me for the letters I had sent to him at High Beach.

'The gypsies helped me escape,' he told me. 'They left me a change of clothes and a peeled stick that pointed the way I should walk in order to get here.'

'That's good, Father,' I said.

We were journeying slowly onward and homeward and I was putting my nervousness behind me. It was strange to see so many people come and stand at their doors and watch us making our unhurried way home. And not one of them said other than 'Good morrow, John Clare' or 'Tis good to see you, John.' He smiled at them and searched their faces and I knew he was looking for Mary Joyce, and all the old fear, that had but ten minutes earlier been put from my mind, began to return. But I could not tell him again that she was lying buried this good time, unwed.

And then his mind took to another subject. He looked about him from the cart at all the fields around us – not that they were changed since his last seeing them, but he seemed greatly shocked by the sight.

'They've closed in every pasture,' he said.

'Everything, Father. All in fields,' I said.

'Everything,' he mumbled and then he was silent.

I could only imagine how, in his long days in High Beach, he had dreamed this land of his childhood back to the state it had been in forty years earlier, when he ran freely through unenclosed pastures.

My mother was in tears at the sight of him. She hugged him and held his hand and walked him about the garden a dozen times, telling him how fit and healthy he looked. He smiled at her and we stood back and observed them, as you would young lovers who have been parted.

He commented on how well the garden looked. It was a high summer afternoon and the flowers were showing of their best colours. It was as though we were all back in childhood times with our parents happily looking over the garden. To the observer nothing could seem more perfect and ideal than the sight that we saw. A man and wife, arm in arm in their garden, while inside the cottage their children went about the task of preparing a meal for them. And such was the sight in our home on that July afternoon.

In the following three days my father concerned himself with writing an account of his journey home. In that time, too, Dr Allen sent word that he would be happy to have my father back at High Beach if he or my mother desired this. My mother did not mention this contact to my father. She seemed convinced that he was much better and was anxious to try him at home, hoping that the company of his family would be a further source of recovery.

At home my father was quiet and went about his tasks in the garden with the same enjoyment he had always shown. With the onset of the harvest he appeared in the fields with my brothers. He gave what assistance he could and, indeed, his strength seemed to return as the weeks passed.

One morning he and I set out to follow my brothers to where they were harvesting. We walked through Northborough. The village was deserted.

'It is like winter,' my father said. 'Or like a village frightened of some plundering army.'

I thought his mind was becoming uneasy again but he explained himself more clearly as we walked.

'I have always thought it so,' he said. 'When harvest comes there is not a soul's shadow about the villages, not a child at play, not a mother in a garden, every door is closed and every window latched. They are all away at the harvesting. There's a deadness about a village without children.'

Sometimes he would set off alone across the fens and one of us would follow at a distance, never allowing him to know he was being observed. At other times he would walk to visit someone of his acquaintance and I would walk with him and wait outside until his conversation was complete.

On one such day I observed Lady Kettering and my father walking in her garden. I had met her once when she called to our home but I had never before seen her garden. It was full of roses of a thousand shades of red and yellow and purple. The scent carried down the avenue. My father told me she had offered him some roses to take back with him but he had declined.

For the most part, on these journeys, my father's conversations were of an ordinary nature but there were times when they took courses that were not predictable. Sometimes it was simply reminiscence. We would walk across the edge of the fens on September afternoons and sit in the sunlight and I would talk or he would talk and I would listen. Once, he told me very intensely about how he would sit behind a wall in High Beach and imagine himself back in Helpston or Northborough again.

'I would close my eyes and be back here,' he said. 'I could stop out every sound and be walking here and stop on a woodland stile and hear the pigeons clacking in the oaks.'

On one such afternoon we were talking when suddenly, and with great frustration, he produced a letter from his pocket and handed it to me.

'I have writ this to my first wife and I have nowhere to send it,' he said.

I took the letter and put it in my pocket. In a short time he was calm again and seemed completely to have forgotten it. I kept it, as I kept every word he scribbled or wrote. It seemed that the letter had been written in Northborough and carried about by him in his keeping in the weeks he had been with us. It caused me great pain to read that letter and I was sorely tempted to destroy it but I did not. It read:

My dear wife

I would have told you how I got here but not being able to see you I soon began to feel homeless at home and shall, by and by, feel nearly hopeless but not as lonely as I was for here I can see the place we were used to be and know you are safe if not happy. Though my home is no home to me my hopes are not entirely hopeless while even your memory lives so near to me. Believe me as ever I have been and shall be

your affectionate husband

John Clare

Even had he not mentioned for whom this letter was intended, I should have known. It made me feel a dreadful sense of the hopeless. He had, from my reading then and now, accepted Mary Joyce as dead but he had not relinquished the hold she had on him. It seemed the main inspiration for his return to live with us was his intention of being close to the places associated with her. Perhaps I am being overly hard in saying this but it was nothing to the bitterness that rested in my mind for several days thereafter. I could not see my father without wondering what twisted sense was in his head and what thoughts of this dead woman were always swimming there. I did, in time, come to think of that letter as another unplanned piece of scribbling that was forgotten in the hour after it was written and forgotten for ever in the hour after it was given to me. But I have never been quite certain.

There were occasions when his rantings were of a more difficult nature. Occasions when he shouted about the house, shouted at my mother and at me. I recall times when his violence of speech seemed destined to become a violence of act, though it never did.

The worst of these was the first. It was an afternoon in September. We had been quietly about our business when my father came in from the garden where he had been seated in writing. Without a word, he swept what dishes there were from the table. He accused my mother of being 'false' to him.

'I left thee,' he screamed, 'because of thy faults. Untruth is what I left for. Untruth in you. Falseness and untruth. I would never have been away from here were it not for falseness. I was born a poet and you a whore.'

I shouted at him to stop this slander but my mother hushed me.

'Let him have his say; he will be all the quieter,' she said.

'He cannot say the like of that,' I said.

'I can say as I wish,' my father said. 'I was locked away so that she might carry on with other men, sneaking about the place and thinking I did not know. I knew. I heard in people's conversations. It was the talk all over Essex, as far away as that. I should never have married. I was trapped into madness the day I married Patty Turner. When I could, for the asking, have married Betty Sell or Mary Joyce or anyone who was there to be asked.'

I had heard enough at this. There was no reason why my mother should have this thrown in her face after all she had been through and I told my father so. It seemed to stop his onslaught but it was my mother who intervened. She went and got his coat and my cape and asked us to walk together to the fens and settle our differences for she had none with either of us.

And we did walk and it did seem to quiet my father a great deal for he spoke not a word on the outward walk. Returning homeward, he began to talk about the warmth the family gave to his life.

'I could not go out from the cottage if I did not have it to come back to, and it has ever been so,' he said. 'I have always had Patty's love on which to build my life. But I have a fault in that every friendship has grown into a warm attachment and I have believed in all who came to me and put more energy into them that should otherwise, and to better account, have been expended in my own home.'

He left the matter there and so did I. He was not changed, I knew, but he had tried to explain the man he was and that, for then, was as much as might be expected of him.

About this time, too, letters came to our home offering assistance but giving none. They came from my father's acquaintances in London, saying how they had heard of his difficulties and would be happy to assist. He wrote back to them all immediately.

'I do not wish my hardships to be trumpeted by all and sundry. I have never sought praise or reward and I do not seek it now. I wish only to live an independent life. I am not fallen upon charity.'

We might have done with help but I could not but be pleased at what he had written.

But such incidents as this were solitary among the more alarming occasions on which his anger or his complete loss of recognition of the places and times in which he found himself created embarrassment and then danger. This culminated in a display of piety in Stamford, in the presence of a great number of people. My father lost all sense of time and place and seemed to be further away from the day-to-day living we were in than at any other time.

I sent word of this to Dr Allen at High Beach and he advised us to watch my father carefully, for he feared this might lead to something more dangerous. The delusions continued, with imaginings and rantings and weaknesses, and in the end, with my father's admission, or half-admission, that Mary Joyce was dead, it became impossible that my mother should live a normal life in such abnormal circumstances. It was settled that he should be taken to Northampton asylum. He had stayed with us a good time and now it was apparent that he could stay no longer.

For a number of days before leaving us he talked of little else but hellfire and damnation. He seemed convinced that only these rewards awaited him after his life was over. At every turn he would talk of the sinfulness of his life and then of the horrible pains that awaited him in eternity. He seemed to have lost all faith in the goodness of himself and in the beauty of the world, a beauty he had so long suckled from and the sense of which he had instilled in all his children. Nothing could shake him from the terror of death and hell.

He would sit in our kitchen decrying his life and when my mother would say 'God is good', he would shout about his loss of faith in God. Or he would murmur on about the loves of his life and conclude with something such as 'I have loved much but there is none left to love, I have done with it'.

He stayed with us that Christmas of eighteen hundred and forty-one. It was a sombre time, overshadowed by the knowledge that two doctors had certified my father fit only for admission to St Andrew's Hospital for Mental Diseases. My brother and I had had this certification done, for my mother would not and yet she could not carry on. And so we celebrated our Christmas as a family, all of us knowing, except for my father, that he would be leaving us within the week. Two days after Christmas and two days before he left us, my mother told him that he must go back to the asylum for treatment.

'To High Beach?' he asked.

'No,' my mother said, 'to Northampton. It is not such a great way off.'

'No,' he said. 'I shall be close for coming home.'

She nodded to him and he seemed satisfied in that.

The following day I walked with him to the edge of the fen and he asked me to wait while he crossed to the four oaks that grew on the pasture's limit. He had a great fondness for them and he went and spoke quietly and hugged each of them in turn. I think, when he was hugging farewell to the oaks, he was saying farewell to all of us 'and to his life in Helpston and Northborough.

And so he left us on the twenty-ninth day of December of that year, the year's end, for Northampton and the asylum there. The doctor who came to accompany him on his journey told me that he blamed my father's illness on years 'addicted to poetical prosings'. I could not think of any right reply to this.

We stood outside and my mother walked with him from the house to the coach. I could not help but think of the joy of his coming home six months earlier. Just before he climbed into the carriage with the doctor, he turned to me and he spoke.

'Do the primroses still grow in the churchyard?' he asked.

'Yes, Father,' I said. 'In their season.'

He nodded and said 'Good', and then climbed inside.

My father was never to see his wife again, or his village.

I would go and visit with him when I could. That was not often but I tried to see him once in every two years.

Sometimes he would sit, during my visit, saying nothing and I would sit with him, knowing there was no word I could say to break him out of where he was. If the weather was at all clement he would sit in the garden of the asylum. It was strange to see him among the flowers and trees, seeming so peaceful, when he might have sat among his own flowers in his own garden, with his own people. But each time I thought of enquiring, and the few occasions that I did, I was told it was not possible for him to come back home. Yet. And yet became two years and then four and then a decade. Twenty-three years in all.

But sometimes he would be talkative. His conversation would always be of the past and the freedom it had given him. Once, he talked of nothing but his times in London. Nothing else seemed to exist in his head but those weeks when he had visited the city and had been introduced to the great writers and painters. And yet at the end of it all, his speech became deeper and more quiet.

'I were walking past St Paul's Cathedral,' he told me. 'I saw an African, a black man, sitting in the street asking for alms. He were more lost than I was. So far from home, like me, but I leastways could go back home. I passed him by and all that night I thought as how I should have given him a shilling. I went back the next day and the next and the next but I never saw him again.'

And those were the last words he spoke to me that day. Always, I came away with a feeling of terrible sadness. And now that he could no longer do my mother direct hurt by going off with other women or stabbing her with his words and the sharpness of his spoken memories, I felt more and more for him. He never waved me goodbye when I left. I seemed to drift out of his mind before I had gone and he seemed as though he was cutting my presence off before I could do it myself.

Sometimes when I visited he would think he was someone else. A wrestler or a bare-fist fighter or even Lord Byron, the poet. And another time he told me as how he saw Lord Byron's funeral and he in London, with empty carriages behind the hearse. 'Ne'er a person in any carriage,' he said. And he told me how he stood and watched it pass.

On the times when he would talk with me, I would ask him how his writing went and he would tell me the poems he had written. Even at his worst times he could read and recite his verses to me and it was a joy to hear them flow. He had a gift of memory when it came to verse. It dated back, I believe, to days when he would find verses while he was out walking the fens, without a paper on which to write. He would memorise the words and come back home, perhaps half a day later or even the next day, with the words still clear within his head.

I was not the only visitor to my father's place of detention. There were several in each year but they were people who knew nothing of him as a man and came only because of what they had heard or read. And they were strangers to him. They did nothing to allay his fears or warm his loneliness. He was merely a spectator at their spectating and he knew it.

In most of his days he would sit on the roadside, watching the children at play, observing the passing carts, and scribble in one of his pocketbooks, but at other times he would stand in the garden of the asylum, gazing, as a child would, into the sky, entranced for hours by something inside his head. Imagining what might follow on a better day? The thought has crossed my mind, though I have no reason for thinking so.

There were times when I brought bad news to my father. And there were times when it seemed the only news I brought. Two years after he entered Northampton asylum it was I who brought him word of my brother Frederick's death. He was twenty years old and my grief was compounded by having to speak of it to my father. He sent a letter to the family which I carried on my return, urging us 'to behave well to your mother'. A year later I was back in his company to tell him of my sister Anna's death. She was twenty-four years old and her death brought back a torrent of memories, for my mother had been pregnant with Anna when she and my father married. In one afternoon, he relived again the tempestuous days of their marrying, his doubts and his fleeing the village for a time. Those memories seemed to occupy his mind more than Anna's death. It was, I imagine, his way of painting the present over with the colours of the past. Finally, in that twisting trickle of sadness, I travelled in the March of eighteen hundred and forty-six to tell my father of his own father's death.

He sat a long time on hearing the news from me and then he said: 'I had thought him dead this good many years.'

'He lived a good long life,' I said.

'Love cannot be made to grow where no love is,' my father replied and left his comments at that.

My mother, all this time, dealt with the living and the dead in our home. She it was who laid out my brother and my sister and my grandfather in their turns. She it was who looked to their burying. She it was who accepted the sympathies of the village and she it was who despatched me, finding the fare from God knew what place, to tell my father of the news.

My other brothers did what little was to be done in helping. John went about his life and became an inspector of bridges. William worked our land and hired himself to farmers in Northborough and Helpston. Charles took upon himself many of our debts, paid from his clerk's wage, until he too died, in the year of eighteen hundred and fifty-two. I did not bring that news to my father. I could not, for I had not seen him in three years and to arrive with another tale of loss was more than I could bear. Instead, I wrote to his doctor and asked that he should tell the news.

Letters would come to us at the oddest intervals, some quite sane, some quite beyond our reckoning, some at peace and some complaining that we had not sent him books he had asked of us. He would give most detailed instructions as to where the volumes might be found upon such and such a shelf, but in the greater part these were volumes he had long ago lost or given to someone.

In telling all this I know I bring my own memories, as they are, to bear upon the facts but these are the memories which surface first. There are others. I have memories of my father heartily laughing; of his love of laughter; of his clever way with words; of the warmth of his greeting; of the beauty of his verses; of the closeness of his arm about my waist as we went walking through the grounds of Northampton asylum. But these are not the first things I think of. They come only with an effort because they are not how I imagine my father to have been in that dark, misty uncertainty that was his mind for all my adult life.

Of course I do not know how he truly felt or what the real thought was that kept his other thoughts together. I can only surmise and in doing so I find myself drawn again and again to a darkness in his life. What man, even the heartiest and most open to the ways of nature, could be content with a life that ended so slowly and in such lonely circumstances? When I look from side to side, from my father to my mother, I see them both in isolation, battling against the vagaries of a life that had been cruel in weaving a rope of hope and then using it to tie them separately to illness and poverty and the heartbreak of death upon death in a time when their lives might have been easier.

When I saw him among the other men at Northampton I could not but think, as I knew he did constantly, of his times in London and of the company he had treasured and of the days he had spent in the company of people who encouraged him and treated him as his talent deserved. But the kindnesses of his patrons were never without the expectation of some return. They never possessed the unselfish devotion of which my father was capable. Each small generosity had a purpose and, indeed, many took more than will ever be known. They stripped my father of everything – even the respect that gave resolve to his life.

And then my mother, labelled 'the widow Clare', although her husband was hale and hearty in his body, going about her life as though there was a purpose to it, when all the purpose had been ground out of her by her own sickness and the loss of her family.

All this comes easily to my mind. The brighter days are deep, too deep to find with ease. Too deep.

And yet, at times when I felt most lost, most hopeless in his company, he might utter one sentence and set me thinking. Such a time came at the end of a long day I had spent with my father in the summer of eighteen hundred and fifty-nine. I had sat with him while he finished his evening meal. It was a day of great heat and even at that late hour we went and sat in the garden and watched the sky for all the signs of another warm day to come. We had sat a great time in silence when my father spoke.

'Genesis is a paltry piece of work. Now John's gospel is where the real tale is told,' he said.

I had heard him say that once before, another summer's evening, in the days before he had been sent away in the first place. My mother had sent me to fetch him from the Blue Bell and when I went in he was talking with some men and he was saying that very same thing. And here he was saying it again, so many years later.

'The clergy preach Genesis as if there were no other book,' he said that evening, from the doorway. And then he walked home with me, leaning upon my arm and telling me I was a good girl.

Other evenings he'd return from walking the fens, with a long scrawl of lines, and while he ate his supper I'd read them back to him. There was one I was always most fond of and still am. I think of it when I am troubled about the life he lived and I think of it, without an effort, when I remember his happiest times. Up this green woodland ride lets softly rove And list the nightingale — she dwelleth here. Hush let the wood gate softly clap — for fear The noise may drive her from her home of love.

I think of that and I see my father, his finger to his lips to quiet my chattering, listening for the birds of the wood; I see him gently closing the gate behind us, the timbered latch deadened by his fingers.

But for every such memory there is another that comes to undermine it. The times when my father would slip away to see some woman. All that pretence of no one knowing when my mother knew right well and when, in time, those of us old enough to know knew what was happening. But our mother went on with her life and ours, knowing my father would return. But why should she have had to go through that? And why should we?

I recall one event from the year of Anna's death. That autumn a young man came calling on me, frequently, and walked with me and was at my beck and call. He was in love with me and I with him, I think. And that Christmas he called to take me dancing to a house dance in Market Deeping. I was in a state of despair at that time. It had been a year of loss and illness in our family, and he had called every evening in that month to sit with my mother and me and had arranged to have someone sit with my mother while we were away. I was happy to go with him and I had resewn an old white dress of Anna's and made of it a dress of my own for that night. He had brought a trap and we sped the miles to Market Deeping, under a bright quartered moon.

As we were entering the house where the party was being held, he handed me a sheet of paper and bade me read it at my leisure. This I did once the opportunity came. It was a verse he had written for me. I thanked him for it, as we danced, and later, at supper, he told me he had a great deal of verse written.

'I should like to have it published in books,' he said. 'I should like to be a poet such as your father.'

I knew then that he meant what he said; it was not to impress me, it was his intention. And I knew too that he had spoken the epitaph on our love without knowing it. I could not face the thought of another writer in my life, I could no longer trust him despite his kindness. I could never tell him why I had begun at once to grow cold in my affections, for he would not have understood, the reason being inexplicable to any but myself. My mother would have understood in some way but I did not explain to her. Perhaps, of all, my father would most clearly have understood my fears but he was not to know of my predicament. I recall the journey home that night as one might recall a funeral of a loved one or as a soul might recall its own separation and observation of the body left behind. The moon was as bright and the night as sharp as when we had journeyed outward but now there was a terrible coldness within.

Of course, life might have gone sweetly and one man may not be like another, but I had had my fill of poems and poets. I had my father still to think of and in doing so I could not escape the shadow his darkness cast.

But enough of that. To return to my father's life. In his last years he was afflicted with a great many illnesses. His sight was poorly and I was sent for at one time because his delusions had grown more stubborn. He would no longer answer to his own name but only to that of Lord Byron. It was hoped that the sight of my face might bring some recognition of his true self. I stayed in Northampton two days at that time and sat with him a great deal. In private I would ask him if he knew who he was and he would nod.

'You are John Clare, Father,' I would say. 'You are not Lord Byron.'

'Aye,' he would agree, 'but I was Byron. Now I am John Clare.'

But this delusion, too, seemed to dissolve in the months that followed my visit.

At the Christmastide of eighteen hundred and sixty-two I wrote my father a long letter, reminding him of a Christmastide years before when he and I had walked home from market together, me prattling on about all we had seen, and he had stopped in the roadway and held my attention with the straight look of his blue eyes and said one sentence to me: 'Anticipation is the sweetest of earthly pleasures.'

I reminded him of that in writing, for it had occupied my own mind greatly in all that month. He replied in the early days of the following month, calling me his 'dear daughter' and telling me how much he missed me and my mother and recalling the happier days when he had worked with his hands and felt the better and clearer for it.

I have thought a great deal of late about that phrase which came back to me and inspired my letter to him. I think that dedication to anticipation of pleasure made him much the way he was. A man always waiting for Mary Joyce and never being quite fulfilled by anything within his life. In seeing that, I have seen, beyond doubt, that none of us failed him in any way. Nothing we could have done within the family could have made his life in any way better or sweeter. Nothing that his closest friends and patrons could have done would truly have softened his life.

The last occasion on which I went to visit him was in the October of eighteen hundred and sixty-three, a seven month before he died. He had been confined for more than two years to the gardens of the asylum but in the February of that year he had lost the use of his legs and been committed to bed. At the summer's end he seemed to regain his strength and when I visited him I wheeled him in a chair into the garden. I had been warned of his growing coarseness of tongue but I heard nothing of it in my two days with him.

As we sat in the garden on my last afternoon with him he was, for the most of our time, quiet but he talked occasionally. It was not a pleasant conversation but rather one in which his failures seemed to rise like demons about him.

'There were a time when I thought as I should never fail,' he said to me. 'I failed. How could I fail?'

'You did not fail, Father,' I said.

'Writing has ruined me,' he said quietly and then he became agitated in the extreme. 'They have cut the top off my head and taken out all the vowels so I cannot write.' He was shouting by then and I calmed him by easing my fingers through his hair, as you would a child. When he had settled himself once more, I tried to reassure him.

'Oh, Father,' I said, 'you will write again.'

My only thought then was that he should not become disillusioned beyond hope. I had no thought of the hardness he had brought into our lives but only of the softness I might instil in his old mind.

'I have lost the language,' he said. 'I spoke it once and one other spoke it but I cannot speak it alone.'

And with that he seemed to have withdrawn again into himself but suddenly, and with a great degree of strength in his voice and with a light in his eyes, he went on speaking, urgently, looking straight into my eyes as he did.

'The last time I saw her it were a russet evening this time of year and the apples hung in bunches from the trees.'

And then his eyes seemed to cloud and he squinted and looked about him and searched the sky for something before returning his gaze, questioningly, to me.

'Or were there flowers on the whitethorn?' he asked.

I made no answer and immediately he went on.

'We were two children, yet when I touched her hand my heart would turn chill for fear of rejection. But oftentimes I fancied I saw her brush a tear from her face. Her heart were as tender as a bird's, yet she grew to think her station above mine. Her parents were farmers and had pretensions, something my passion could not match.'

His voice faded as he spoke. In a way I was pleased with what I had heard for it brought, at last but not too late, a recognition that Mary Joyce had not been the warm creature he had imagined in his earlier years. That much had been recognised.

I was lost in such thoughts when he spoke again.

'Take me inside,' he whispered. 'I am tired. I should like to sleep now.'

I had some feeling, some premonition, as I prepared to leave the asylum that evening that I might not see my father again. I went back to watch him sleep and thought he was still awake and spoke to him.

'Did you ever write to her or speak to her, to Mary Joyce, in her last years, Father?'

His breathing was soft and settled and he made no answer. I left with uncertain emotions. I knew he was ill in the extreme but I could not but be pleased that this other delusion had at last been laid to rest with her corpse.

The month of May of eighteen hundred and sixty-four was a dry, hot month before its time. On the tenth day of that month my father had another seizure and we were notified. But none of us could go to be with him. He died in the late afternoon of the twentieth day of May, a Friday. They sent word to us on the next day.

My mother was poorly herself at that time but she set about preparing for my father's return.

He had passed away on a day when the hedges were alive with the confetti of the whitethorn and the primroses and cowslips were heavy in the dykes. It was as hot as a day in June.

My father's coffin arrived before our preparations were complete and it lay in the Blue Bell before his burying. We followed it to the churchyard and saw him safe at last in the earth he had walked, and written and spoken and sung of, all his life. There was a final comfort in that but it was a sadness to me that none of us was there to see him off on his last journey into death.

I was left on that day, the day of his burying, with sorrow and with satisfaction. Sorrow on his lost life, satisfaction on his return among us. But I was left with a great tiredness too. All my life had been a part of his. I seemed to feel the need to be his support from when first I learned to walk. This, perhaps, is something my brothers and sisters felt in turn. I never spoke of it with them, but until the day of my father's death I seemed constantly to search for an answer to so many of the griefs his life created in mine. And then when he was dead I felt only regret and satisfaction but not serenity.

And now that feeling of tiredness persists so that I do not want to talk or think again of the vicissitudes of our lives with my father. I need never talk of him again.

I have told you all that I can recall. But to dismiss him from my thoughts would be as unnatural as it would be impossible. I can only hope that the pictures which appear uninvited are as pleasant as those I choose to recall.

V John Clare

MY DEAREST LOVE, this is the fifth day of the Maytime and of my seventy-first summer to the world. These last nights of spring, like many of the nights of this winter and of all the winters since childhood, I have lay here in my bed and felt the form of your body next to mine and held it in my arms. But there be nights when I long for more, for kissing you in the places of secrecy, for the shape of your body and the touch of your hand. I long for the particular scent which I may drink in as apple scent in the autumn. I long, too, for the rarer, deeper scent.

Do you recall a day and us walking together, you and me and Richard Turnill, tramping the road from your home to Helpston? I recall it more and more now. A day deep in the folds of winter and us on the road without a thought for the weathers about us and you bright as sunshine despite the day. We walked in that snowy day, the snow come down on us and we cared nothing for it, trudging on, no doubt, though our feet seemed hardly to notice the miles and we were so lost we never noticed my sister in wait for us beneath a tree, sheltering from the snow. Us three walking. What I would give for us to be back there walking again, wind or snow, I would care not. Walking. Thought of that often concerns me. I thought of it and I walking from High Beach to you or to the hope of you. I felt you there with me as I feel your presence these many nights but when I turned for your comfort there was nothing.

But still there are other memories I have that come to me and you are not seen in them but you are there. Most at this time of the year I remember the great tossing shoulders of whitethorn in the hedges of Helpston, though they were not so great at Northborough. At Glinton they were white as sheets for you and you passed among them with the blueness of bird eggs that were your eyes and the ease of a girl who is free of sin.

As you were and are, unlike John Clare.

Was it not Maytime, too, when we last spoke together face to face without the need for darkness or spirit between us? At Langley Bush before it was destroyed. The whitethorn was a wedding dress about you, though I did not say as much for fear of hurting you, even as you were intent on hurting me and bidding farewell with all our lives still before us, and for what? To satisfy the family circumstance and your father's expectations? I would have dropped all expectations tied to a stone into Round Oak Waters if I had thought you might have been for me and without a hesitation, without as much as a glance at where they sank and how and yet you talked of circumstance as if that should satisfy my mind. It never did. And nor yours, I think.

I had much to say to you then and much that was said but no answer to you when you said I must find someone else who would support me in what I had laid out for myself, for you could not and would not. You spoke it as though my need was something new and unknown to you when all the time till then my need was matched only by the need of one other and that was you. To throw my need in my face was a great cut to me among all the cuts we each inflicted that evening. That most beautiful of evenings. A time we had often been together and I had always looked to, that time between work and sleep, a time when dreams are sowed. Now and since I think of evenings as a time when others are left wandering without a home and must look in on the windows in passing and never share the comfort and companionship within. And if I needed what you could not give, have I not in the time since then been careful not to burden you with my need? In the nights when my need has been greatest my loss has been greatest, and I have only your memory to mesmerise and harry me. To think of you sleeping in that distant bed is no consolation and no source of joy but only of pain. When I close my arms with longing, the longing is increased. I have talked to you, slept with you, dreamed of you, walked with you, kissed you, touched you and imagined your touch in my own but I have not gone back on what in the end you demanded of me. Instead, I set myself to quietness again. When the storm of your absence and my longing blows harshly against itself, I set myself to quiet whisperings of your name, your tender name, to the slightest touch of my lips against your phantom skin.

I am no longer afeared of spectres as I was in my childhood, wishing only that yours would come even for a moment to my side, that I might touch and taste you. We have lay in darkness and I thought no word could bring us closer and no word could keep us apart. I looked to death as a welcome state, as a place and time where you already were and where we could be without the circumstances that kept us so long apart in this mad world. And then, of late, I dreamed that I woke in paradise and you were there as you promised and I spoke with you, I spoke the warmest whisperings of love and passion and you looked at me with your soft blue eyes, as you were used to, and asked my name and did not remember me at all. And I awoke in tears and called to you, my beloved, in the terror of the grey morning and none came but another prisoner in this madhouse and he stroked my head and stared at me and stroked my head again, most gently, and then went away. None came but him.

And I still call to you, my love, and am calling to you still. I recall you as a girl singing that song you did so sweetly, swinging about the deathstones and singing to me.

Will you go to the rolling of the stones, the tossing of the ball,

or will you go and see pretty Susie dance among them all,

will you drink of the blood, the white wine and the red

or will you go and see pretty Susie when that I am dead?

Susie charmed the birds from the sky, the fish from out the waves

and there she'd lie in her true love's arms and there was content to stay.

I have never lain with Susie or no one since seeing you. Lie with me now.

The Evolution of Christie Harris

Kathleen Clunan

The Evolution of Christie Harris
Kathleen Clunan

First published in the UK by Eagle Eye Books

Revision 1 2 3 4 5 6 7 8 9

Printed and bound by PrintDomain Ltd, UK

ISBN: 978-0-9931860-5-9
A CIP catalogue record for this title is available from the
British Library

Dedicated to my family and best friends.

Acknowledgements

A debt of gratitude, is offered to everyone who has supported me with my writing. I would like to thank specifically, my good friend, Margaret Leak, who gave me the confidence to keep on writing, many times over. Without her support, I doubt this book would have even reached the half way mark.

I would like also to thank my cover girl, Julie Mitchell, who patiently gave up many hours, to poise in less than perfect weather conditions! Very much appreciated.

And finally, Dr Greg Hall, who has worked tirelessly in helping get this book to publication. Again, without his expertise and dedication, I would not have the pleasure of seeing my novel in print. Thank you.

Follow me on Facebook

 Kathleen Clunan

Developments

- **Double Trouble**
- **Home Truths**
- **Monty Mitten Presents**
- **Evolution**
- **Brunch**
- **Key Critics**
- **Busted or Not**
- **Designated Driver**
- **Pottering Tuesday**
- **Happy Families**
- **Close Encounter**
- **Out of the Frying Pan**
- **Escape?**
- **Commando**
- **Reviews**
- **Fraya-Froo**
- **Meet and Greet**
- **Not a Date**
- **Paint Away the Heartache**
- **Glow White Knickers**
- **Pluck Required**
- **Tied Up**
- **Shifting Grains of Sand**
- **Flowers**
- **Shadows**
- **Compromised**
- **All for One**
- **Deadly Serious**
- **Dawn**

Double Trouble

"Five-inch heels here, remember."

My parents did a moonlight flit after Dad jacked his job. Little Upton is now abuzz with speculation as to where they've gone. And why.

I know the answer to one of those questions, and I've a feeling I'll soon find out the answer to the other. I've been summoned to a family meeting, it's all very cloak and dagger, not really Dad's style.

I park Trudy's car a few doors away from their new house. Don't want to risk my parents spotting me sloping off to the pub. Well, yes, I know I'm hardly a teenager, but still... My housemates, Trudy and Suzi, offered a lazy couple of hours out, and since I'm putting off the family pow-wow as long as pos, why not?

Suzi leans forward. 'So, Christie, where's the lovely country pub you promised us?'

Tonight, I feel no guilt in making the pair of them walk a few hundred metres, since my designated driver duties have apparently developed into full-on chauffeur. 'It's about five minutes down the lane. After the day I've had, Suzi, I need a brisk walk to clear the lingering misery of Mr Sloan.'

Suzi rolls her eyes. 'That man, what's he been up to now?'

'Oh, the usual. Trying to keep education as dull and predictable as it was last century. Unfortunately, my style of teaching is a tad too radical for his mindset.'

Suzi shrugs. 'He probably just wants an easy life, you know, plod on to early retirement.'

Oh, if only that were true... I keep longing the man will develop a long-term mystery illness... I'd settle for him getting raging impetigo... That would keep him off school for a week or two. I sigh. 'Suzi, he goes out of his way to dissect my teaching... I don't know what his problem is.'

'Threatened!' Trudy tosses the word in disgust. 'Middle-aged man syndrome!'

'Not sure I threaten him! The way the vein in his temple throbs when he challenges me... It's a bit on the freaky side.' I shudder.

'Miss Harris, there have been complaints. Again. Rowdy behaviour by your pupils at the end of every lesson. High fives and fist bumps. You are their teacher!'

'Mr Sloan, with respect, my classes work in near silence throughout their lessons... It's just as they are leaving, they—'

'Yes! It's unacceptable.'

'At teacher training, we were taught to think outside the box.'

'Well, Miss Harris, you are firmly within the box of St. Stephens Academy now. So please act accordingly.'

I scrub out the memory of our latest skirmish as best I can. Not going to let him ruin my half-term break.

Trudy swings her legs out of the car. 'Forget about him, Christie. Come on, let's get going.'

Suzi dutifully follows, though not quite so elegantly.

Setting off, I take giant strides in the direction of *The Rose and Crown*. I glance back at Trudy tottering behind me.

She points down the length of her long-toned legs towards her beautifully painted toenails. 'Five-inch heels here, remember.'

'Sorry, Trudy, just eager to get the weekend started.'

'Anyway, Christie...' says Suzi. 'Back to your dad, what do you really think?'

'I know what I think,' whispers Trudy. 'Eyes right, and look at that gorgeous scenery.'

I let my eyes drift right, and they instantly lock with those of mysterious Miles. I was hoping I'd bump into him again... But not now! I should have parked at the pub! Heat sears through my body. A tell-tale prickle of a blush rises up from my chest. Please, please don't speak to me, just get in your car and drive away. Fast. Go on. Scram.

Yet again, my telepathy isn't working, because here he comes, wearing his hello smile. A quiver of anticipation shoots through me.

Any other time, I'd be relishing the chance of five minutes of frivolous banter with Miles. But now, really? Come on! I try my best glare. Then purse my lips and shake my head slightly.

Nothing!

He's still sauntering towards us, oblivious! I put my head down as he draws closer. Risking a glance up I note his look of confusion. Not surprising, usually I'm grinning like a love-struck teen when we meet.

His step slows.

Mine speeds.

He skilfully intercepts me by stepping between me and my friends. 'Well, hello.'

'Shh... Not now!' I hiss under my breath. 'Pretend you don't know me!'

He frowns momentarily. 'Your mum said you'd be seeing her tonight, so—'

'I'm going later!' I hiss. 'Shh!'

Miles turns slightly as Trudy totters towards us. 'Good evening, ladies,' he says, eyes alight with mischief.

I close my eyes while my stomach does its usual flip...

Trudy angles her shoulder in front of mine and thrusts one hip forward, thus giving Miles the full benefit of her minimal outfit. 'Just got better for me,' she oozes, brazenly looking him up and down. 'Didn't know country boys look so fine.'

Miles laughs. 'They don't, I'm only visiting.'

Dragging my bottom lip between my teeth an involuntary groan rumbles. I look directly into his eyes. His easy smile has been replaced by a wolfish grin. I'm conscious every part of my body is fizzing with adolescent desire.

'What a coincidence, so are we.' Trudy eyes him like a lioness about to devour her prey. 'You do know you're going in the wrong direction... The pub is this way.' She points a well-manicured finger in the general direction we're heading.

'Bit pushed for time tonight, need to get back home.' He doesn't take his eyes off me.

Trudy angles her chin up and wags her finger playfully. 'You, have just missed a once in a lifetime offer. Come on, ladies, prosecco awaits.'

And we're off, without a backwards glance, but I know Miles has turned around to watch us. I can feel the heat of his eyes on me.

'Another time, perhaps…' he calls out.

I can hear the laughter in his tone. Honestly, I could just die!

Suzi starts her tutting. 'I wish you wouldn't do that, Trudy. It's really embarrassing.'

'How many times, Suzi? When an opportunity presents itself, go for it, especially when it looks like that!'

Suzi shakes her head. 'He could have been married!'

'Well, it won't last if he is. I'm sure even you noticed the way he was looking at Christie.'

'Leave me out of it,' I say. 'I just want to get to the pub.'

'I was only trying to do you a favour. It must be months since your last date…'

Six months, and I'm certain Nigel will get over it. 'I've given up on men. Thanks for reminding me.' Not entirely true…

Trudy sighs dramatically. 'When you fall off a horse, the best thing to do is get right back in the saddle.'

'Well, I'm sick of being bucked off! And let's be honest, Trudy, I'm not likely to get a look in, with all you've got to offer on display!'

'Whatevs.' Trudy flicks her hair over her shoulder, and juts her chin up. 'Nothing wrong with having a bit of fun!'

Suzi shrugs. 'So, about your dad, Christie, any news?'

I shake my head. Hopefully she'll take the hint.

Not very likely.

She tucks her hair behind her ears, the slight crinkling of her brow, and tilt of her head complete her concerned look. 'He could have cast off his cassock and cardigan, then started a mad passionate fling with one of the Women's Institute.'

'Suzi!' I scowl. 'This is my dad you're talking about, remember, the one who wears socks with his sandals.' I cross my arms. I'm just going to leave them to it. I am not going to say another word, I wonder how long will it take them to notice?

Trudy grins. 'And be honest, would any man in their right mind? They're not known as "The Little Upton Mafia" for nothing!'

'True. How about a midlife crisis?' offers Suzi.

Trudy grimaces. 'Nope, he's a tad too old for that.'

'He could have been sacked. Some of those churchy lot have some very strange rules. Look, otherwise we're back to my favourite, a lottery win,' says Suzi for the twenty-seventh time.

I roll my eyes, and continue to resist the urge to throttle her.

'Given his views on gambling, he'd be just too ashamed to admit it,' she continues.

I stride ahead, my two best friends continue chortling about the latest scandal to hit the village. Okay, so Dad's created a bit of a stir. Nobody, least of all me, expected him to up and leave. I mean, abandoning his flock, it's just not the thing for a vicar to do. But I've had this ongoing interrogation for a week now.

A whole week!

Suzi's like a dog with a bone. 'And nobody knows where he's gone. Christie, your mum and dad could be anywhere. Anywhere! And my mum is beside herself.'

Trudy smiles. 'Your mum knows everyone's business before it even happens.'

'Well, she does usually know what's going on,' admits Suzi, with a wry smile.

'Christie, slow down! Where is this pub? We must have been walking for ten minutes. These shoes, are not made for trekking down country lanes!'

I turn as Trudy stops and looks down at her Jimmy Choo's. 'Seriously, Christie, I should have worn hiking boots.'

'Not with that excuse for a skirt,' I say. 'Anyway, it's just round the next corner, and the thing is, it's only going to be the two of you, I'll pick you up later.'

'Really?' drawls Trudy. 'Planning on kidnapping that hunk for yourself, are you?'

'Err, no, Trudy! Actually, I'm going back to Mum and Dad's. I parked outside their new home!'

'Nooo!' splutters Suzi. 'That big house! So… So, you know who that bloke is!'

'Ish.'

Suzi scowls. 'No wonder you went a funny colour. Well, come on, details.'

'He works for a charity or something. I've only met him a few times.' And my heart nearly bounded out of my chest every time, not that I'll admit it to these two yet. He has the kind of face I could gaze at for hours. And his body, well. There are only so many times you can get away with being a born-again virgin, even if you are a vicar's daughter. Obviously, I'm not going to let Trudy linger anywhere near, she who has the attributes of a goddess.

Suzi looks ready to stamp her feet. 'And you've known where your parents have been all along!'

'Well, of course, I have. It's only actually five miles away from the bothered busybodies in Little Upton, but feels like a world away.'

'Very true, and nicely done.' Trudy smiles. 'And look, isn't that quaint?'

The Rose and Crown nestles between two giant oaks, hazy evening sunlight bathes the courtyard as patrons relax. A shriek of laughter rises above the low hum of conversation drifting on the breeze.

Trudy turns to look at me. 'Children. You know I don't do children, especially at the weekend. This is supposed to be a civilised grown up weekend, just the three of us, chilling out... Remember, civilised? We've got that art exhibition in a couple of days, the one your Auntie Maddie sent us the tickets for?'

'Yes, yes, I remember. And sorry about the children, but it's the nearest pub. I might need rescuing later...'

'What's going on then?' asks Suzi, eyes wide, eager for any drama.

I sigh. 'I don't know, but Dad asked me to come round for a chat, could be anything.' I catch my bottom lip between my teeth. 'Whatever it is, Suzi, you'll be the first to know.'

Suzi flushes. 'I didn't mean—'

'I know. It's probably nothing.'

Trudy examines her talons. 'Right then, come on, Suzi. You find a quiet table away from the brats, and I'll get the drinks in.' She stalks off, her caramelised body inviting the usual attention, and gives me a half wave over her shoulder. 'See you later, Christie. Good luck.'

Suzi turns to me, and catches my hand. 'Just have a quick one, you look like you need it, after the week you've had.'

'I'm driving, remember, seeing as your car needs a new thingy what's it... Again!'

'Yeah, sorry about that, can't help my car being poorly... Having a bloke round to look at it tomorrow. Come on, just have a coke.' Suzi pouts, and makes her puppy-dog eyes.

'Okay, one condition.'

'Anything.'

'Don't go on about Mum and Dad.'

Suzi links her arm through mine. 'Okay, you've got a deal.'

At the bar, Trudy adds my coke to her order, then follows us out into the beer garden. 'Suzi twist your arm then?'

'She simply pointed out I've had a stressful week, and need a chillax.'

'Mine's not been much better.' Trudy brushes an imaginary speck of dust from her fingernail. 'One of the prehistoric rottweilers in accounts has been questioning my expenses. Apparently, prosecco isn't VAT deductible... Honestly! I was entertaining a potential client—'

'Good-looking?' I ask.

'Incredibly...' Trudy nods.

Suzi smirks. 'Rich?'

'Rolex says yes!' Trudy grins. 'Ha-ha... Making a follow up next week.' Her eyes sparkle with mischief.

I shake my head. 'Only you, Trudy, can get away with charging a date to expenses. My only perk is my two-week half-term—'

'Ha!' barks Trudy. 'Knowing you, Christie, you'll be waffling on about how you're missing the brats by Tuesday, followed by ten days of prep for when you get back.'

Suzi pouts. 'All I've got to look forward to, is stool samples and swabs. Christie does get to influence all those young minds.'

'Yep, and I've got some very talented kids in my classes.'

'Okay, class, remember our first day.' I hold up a stick-man picture. 'Dexter's first attempt at impressing me.' I show the class Dexter's latest work, an intricate sketch of five bodies entwined on a sofa. 'Now, Dexter, this does impress... Not just me, look around the class... This level of detail allows each of us to connect with those tangled souls. Each face and body oozes individual personality, yet combined, they are family. A united collective. Well done, Dexter.'

'Thank you, Miss.'

The classroom fills with the sound of hands drumming on desks. Faces split by grinning mouths; eyes lit by the glow of achievement. I give them a moment to savour the feeling. They'd earned it. We'd earned it.

'Remember your hard work. Remember your failures and your successes, you can learn from both. But, mostly, remember the only limitations you have, are the ones you impose on yourselves.' I present both the pictures. 'Your choices are your future. Class dismissed.'

I place the two pieces of artwork back on my desk. Catch the high fives and fist bumps as the class file out of the room. From the corner of my eye, I spot Mr Sloan hovering in the doorway.

I finish my coke. 'I'm going to have to get going now, Suzi. Mum and Dad are going to think I'm not coming.

And please, try and rescue that poor bloke from Trudy. He looks terrified.'

'Will do. See you later.'

I leave my friends and make my way back down the lane. Trudy's right, these are not lanes for Jimmy Choo's. The road gives way to lush grass verges, flanked by hawthorn hedges. The fields beyond, are green with neat rows of shoots, well on their way to providing a bumper harvest. From somewhere in the distance, I can hear the bleating of lambs. Perfect.

I'm sure Dad knows what chaos and rumour he's left behind…

In Little Upton, you can only actually be classed as a local in the village, if you are a third-generation resident. The exception to this rule, is if you are the local vicar, and have been for more than twenty years. Lucky for Dad, he's done twenty-three. Mum and I are therefore locals by default.

I'm not sure how deserters are punished.

Home Truths

Rolling down Buttercup Hill.

Well, their new house is like something out of *Hello* but without the fabulous celebrities. Every time I look at it, I get the urge to sketch.

Nobody could ever accuse my parents of being anything like stylish, yet here they are, living in the desirably chic village of Clover Beck. And honestly, this house and grounds are amazing. Eight tall elegant windows frame a huge solid oak door, and a portico adds grandeur to the already substantial Georgian house. The ageing red bricks add character, the clinging wisteria romance, and the symmetry assures confidence. The gardens boast generations of maturity, evidence of elaborate planning and years of meticulous tending.

If I didn't know better, I really would put it down to a lottery win. Whatever is going on, I think I'm about to find out. Taking a deep, steadying breath, I knock at the door and wait.

'Come in, don't loiter on the doorstep like a stranger.' Dad half drags me into the hallway, and envelops me in his usual bear hug. For a moment I relish his unique smell of shaving cream, fabric conditioner and Dad.

'Hi, Dad,' I muffle into his worn pullover. 'I was half expecting a butler to open the door!'

'Honestly, Christie, what are you talking about? It's our home, just walk in.'

'Okay, I will in future. It still feels a bit odd.'

'I'm sure you'll get used to it. Mum's in the sitting room.'

Sitting room!

I follow Dad into the beautifully decorated room. Propped up on the marble mantlepiece is a framed ink-sketch I did of them in my final year at uni.

'Really, Dad? Come on, this room's too elegant for any of my work.'

'Christie, we love it. Everyone who's seen it, loves it. And we are very proud of you, so, it's going up—'

'When your father remembers where he's hid the spirit level. Hello, Christie.' Mum gets up and gives me a little squeeze. 'I'll go and put the kettle on before we start.'

Dad sits down. 'How's school? Those pesky year seven children still trying to get under your skin?'

'Nope, they've settled down since spring half-term. Mr Sloan is being his usual self, trying to undermine me at every opportunity.'

'Then don't give him the opportunity.'

'I knew you'd say that.'

'And need I ask, how's your painting going?'

I smile, Dad knows I spend every spare minute up in the attic, painting, sketching or daydreaming. My own private world, away from the demands of teaching and reality. Suzi and Trudy are usually very understanding about me prowling about in the middle of the night. Though Suzi has an irritating habit of snooping round my makeshift studio... She calls it cleaning. I've started setting boobytraps as a deterrent...

'It's going well, I've just sent another to Auntie Maddie. I've called it *The Long Farewell*. It's how I last remember seeing her, all smartly dressed with a flowing red scarf. I hope she likes it, but I know as soon as she gets it, she'll be after the next!'

'Keeps you focused, what's her motto?'

'Again, Dad? You ask me every time! "Effort and achievement go hand in hand".'

'So, it does.' He chuckles to himself, and years of chuckling crinkles round his eyes.

'Anyway, Dad, get you, it's all a bit mysterious. First the three-minute retirement, and now "We've something you need to know".' I try to impersonate his gruff voice. 'So, what's it all about?'

His eyes lose their chuckle. 'I'll go and give your mother a hand in the kitchen.'

I try brushing aside another slither of worry.

And fail.

The house is beautiful, more beautiful than the rambling old rectory at Little Upton. I'm going to miss the old place, so many of my memories are entwined with the house and village. I suppose Mum and Dad are ready for some peace and quiet, after the demands of running a rural parish church. Everyone assumes it's quaint and cosy. Believe me, it's anything but. The Flower Ladies are as subtle as secateurs.

Mum brings in the tea tray, and Dad follows behind with a plate of evenly sliced Battenberg. They set them down on the table, and sit down together on the sofa opposite me. Always together, in everything. I resist the urge to roll my eyes.

'You're in your usual cup,' says Mum.

'Thanks.' I pick it up, it always makes me smile. "I'm a teacher, what's your superpower?" it asks. I take a sip of the familiar sweet brew. I'm aware that neither of them take their eyes off me. I place the cup back down.

The last time they sat me down like this, was after I accidentally set the church on fire. It *was* an accident, and I *was* only six. Back then, all Dad said, after giving me a long hard look was, "Christie, we could have lost you". Mum had hugged me, and I cried. I didn't know why I cried, I just did, for what seemed like ages. Then I went to bed, and they never mentioned it again.

'So…' I swallow the lump down in my throat. 'What's going on?'

Dad steeples his fingers. 'There is something we need to tell you,' he draws his words out slowly. 'But before we do, we want you to know…' He looks at Mum, who pulls a hankie from up her sleeve. 'We want you to know, that you will always be our little Christie, and we love you very much. We couldn't love you more.'

Okay, here we go, I'm probably going to get a lecture on concentrating on my career, and stop pandering to Auntie Maddie's demands for more sketches and paintings. Or maybe I should reconsider dating Nigel again... "A polite young man with a ready smile and a healthy career ahead of him." Mum often said... Sadly, he's about as exciting as a Pot Noodle in the middle of a heat wave… Or, it could be because I keep moaning about Mr Sloan, because apart from him, my job is perfect. Whatever it is, it surely can't be that bad.

'As you know, your mother and I were married very young, we couldn't wait.'

So now I roll my eyes.

'As a curate, I was moved about rather a lot. Your mother was happy to follow me. Most of my postings were inner city parishes, and I became passionate about working with what were commonly referred to, as "down and outs". Eventually we got our own parish.'

'Dad, I already know all this.' They've told me the stories over and over again.

'Just listen, please,' says Mum.

'We set up help and self-help groups, and community commitment programmes, and mother and toddler hubs, and all sorts of things. The response was almost unbelievable. The Bishop earmarked other struggling parishes. I became a sort of trouble shooting vicar, which was all very well, but it meant we moved about such a lot.'

Mum tilts her head to one side. 'We did a terrible thing, Christie.'

'Come on Mum, you're scaring me. You two are practically saints.'

'No.' Dad shakes his head, his voice is hushed, measured. 'You're wrong, just listen.'

'We had a daughter…' says Mum, her eyes heavy with unshed tears.

'I have a sister?'

'Hush, just listen, please.' Dad rests his hand on top of Mum's hand. She closes her eyes, tears escape, tracing a path down her cheeks, Dad brushes them away with his thumbs. Such a simple thing, but so intimate I have to look away.

I try swallowing back my own tears, as my throat tightens. I'm back to being six years old, needing to cry and not fully knowing why.

'We had a daughter.' Dad clears the frog from his throat. 'And she was beautiful and clever and she always had a smile on her face. One of those rare gems, who infect everyone with joy, by simply being who they are. She used to say the funniest things, she was the perfect daughter, just like you. You're so alike, in very many ways. When she was younger, she just followed us round. The moving about didn't seem to bother her, she made friends wherever we went, with anyone.'

'So, I do have a sister… Right?' I look from one, to the other of them. My mouth is dry, my heart pounding, and I'm in a haze. How could they keep her from me? I've never even seen a photo! She must be dead. An accident? What did they do that was so terrible? I look at my parents through eyes that no longer know them, not sure I want to hear what they have to say. 'Just tell me!'

Dad shakes his head. 'Just listen. Not only was she moved from school to school, and new house to new house, but she was exposed to the most desperate of people. We always ran an open house policy. Anyone who had a problem could just turn up, eat with us, join our family. We were too busy being good Samaritans, we forgot that our family, was her family too. More importantly, she was our child. We let her sit with alcoholics, drug addicts, prostitutes, the desperate and those who had no shame. You name it. We exposed our lovely girl, to the most appalling, and potentially volatile situations, and expected her to smile through them… And she did…'

Mum nods. 'She always did.'

'I am ashamed…' Dad's voice is thick with emotion. '… Ashamed of what we put her through. We shouldn't have been surprised, when we had a full-on rebellion on our hands. She joined the ranks of troubled souls we left our door open for, except we saw more of them, than we did of her. How could we blame her? She'd seen the love and support we gave to others, and she'd been left with the scraps of our time and energy.'

'We are all equal in God's sight; I think she was testing the theory,' says Mum.

'We are all equal, but—'

'No.' Mum shakes her head. 'There is no but. We try our best, we do our best, and when we fail, hopefully we are wise enough to learn from our mistakes. We reap what we sow.'

'She pushed and pushed us, almost to breaking point. She needed to know if the unconditional love we preached, was true.'

'Your dad had been approached, short listed for a new appointment. It would have fast tracked him to become a Bishop.'

Dad tuts and shakes his head. 'It doesn't matter about that… She was out all night, sometimes missing for days on end, doing God only knows what. We had nobody to turn to. The two of us who'd thought we were the answer to everyone's prayers, found ourselves in need of rescuing. All we could do was pray for a miracle.'

Mum's face looks haunted. 'Sometimes we don't recognise them, miracles. But they are miracles, life changing, and made just for us. It's only when we look back at the full picture, can we see all the different elements coming together.'

Dad sighs. 'One night she came in, chin in the air, hands on hips, and announced she was pregnant… Despite her defiant stance, she was just a frightened kid, needing help. I just looked at your mother, saw the grief in her eyes, and knew that she was seeing all the possibilities for our little girl to get a good start in life, vanish. No matter what people say, once you have a baby, your choices have to be made around them. We wanted her to realise this baby was another life, not some point to score against us. We'd heard she'd been seeing a lad who'd been part of one of our programmes. He'd always seemed a bit of a loner, whether it was him…' Dad shrugs. 'We did try and talk to her about who she was involved with, she wouldn't tell. And we were too conscious of not wanting her to run away again, to push too hard.'

I swallow back the tears, do the maths. I look from one to another, these people I call Mum and Dad. I can see the hurt in their eyes.

They lost their daughter, but got me. It must have broken their hearts. 'I'm not your little girl, I'm hers, aren't I?'

Together they nod.

'What was her name?' The difficulty saying the words out loud, causes a spasm of grief to twist in my gut. Grief for a mother I lost before I knew her. I draw a sharp breath and hold it, as if I can make time stand still so they can't tell me what I already know.

'Madeline,' says Dad.

'I don't remember her at all.' Madeline, like Auntie Maddie. Must be a family name, so pretty. Madeline, it swirls through my brain like a multi-coloured cloud, touching every memory I have. I feel a tear uncurl down my face. I try to picture a younger looking version of Mum, maybe at the park twirling the roundabout for me, or pushing me on the swings. Or in jeans and a T-shirt, instead of the skirts and blouses Mum always wore. Rolling down Buttercup Hill with flowers in her hair, instead of striding purposefully down. Paddling in the brook at Fairy Meadow with me, instead of urging me to be careful. Climbing up trees to rescue me, instead of talking me down. Until ten minutes ago, I could never have even thought of imagining a better Mum, than the one I have.

Madeline, my mum.

Mum tilts her head; she looks so sad. 'It took a little baby called Christina Anne, to set her free.'

'I must have been very young when she died,' I rasp.

'Oh no!' gasps Mum, covering her mouth with her hand. 'No, Christie, Madeline isn't... No, she didn't die. She is very much alive!'

'So?' A brief burst of joy, is instantly swamped by a stab of realisation. This Madeline can't possibly love me, or she'd be here, now. 'Where is she? Where has she been for the last twenty-four years?' The taint of anger I hear in my voice, takes me by surprise.

'Christie, listen before you judge,' says Dad. He fixes me with serious eyes. Reluctantly, I nod. 'After you were born, we sat her down, just like we have with you, now. We asked her what she wanted to do. She was a frightened kid, honestly, only sixteen. She was beginning to understand how tough being a mum is. What the rest of her life was going to be like. She thought we wanted to have you adopted, but we promised her that would never happen. By that time of course, we'd realised God was giving us a second chance, with you, and with Madeline too.'

'Where is she?' I looked straight at Dad, demanding answers with my eyes.

'We'll get to that soon enough... More than anything, Madeline wanted to go to drama school, become a famous actress, the whole fairy-tale dream. So, we came to an understanding, if she could get into drama school, we would take care of you while she was

20

away in London. She went to quite a few auditions, and eventually a school accepted her.'

Dad covers his ashen face with his hand for a moment before continuing. 'Before she left, she made us promise no more urban parishes. She made us promise to find a village church, with lots of fields for you to explore. She made us promise to stay in one place, and give you the stability she'd missed out on. She wanted you to make friends, who would last a lifetime. She wanted you to belong, and to know you belonged. It hit home how much she had missed out… How she'd craved to belong somewhere.'

'She could have belonged to me!' I splutter.

Dad raises his eyebrows. 'We did as she asked, expecting her to come back home during holidays, and to be back permanently in a couple of years. We thought she'd be older and wiser, and with our support, ready to take on the responsibility of being a mum to you. Maybe go to college and university, she could still catch up. Most of all, we wanted to give her time to grow up. But as well as that, we wanted her to have the freedom to make her own choices. By our moving around, she'd missed out on a stable upbringing, we'd spoilt her childhood.'

Dad sighs deeply, and glances at Mum. 'By the time we'd found Little Upton for our home, everything had changed. Madeline had been so sure of her future success, that she, with our permission changed her surname. To protect you, she said. Off she went to London, and within five weeks…' Dad shakes his head. 'Within five weeks she'd landed the lead role in the TV drama *The Fallen*. Madeline played her role as a child prostitute, with such sensitivity and insight that the country wept at her plight. She was so believable; it was as if she'd lived it herself.'

He shakes his head. 'The critics could hardly believe she was only sixteen, tried to pry into her past. She went from the restrictions of being a clergy child, to the restrictions of guarding her privacy and public image. Ironically, her upbringing was a good preparation for her new lifestyle. She managed to keep herself to herself much of the time. She thrived and blossomed into a confident young woman. She had, still has, a certain mystique. She soaked up the attention, and was adored by everyone. She didn't put a foot wrong, and the camera loved her. Her work ethic and charm made it inevitable she'd become successful. She was spotted by an American talent scout; she just couldn't miss a chance at Hollywood fame. Our daughter is very famous.'

I look from one of them to the other. 'Well, who is she then? This woman who chose to leave me.'

Mum shrugs. 'Our little Madeline, is Madeline De-Muir.'

'Come on! You must be joking!'

'It's the truth, Christie,' says Dad

The truth?

I keep swallowing back the bitter taste in my mouth. The knot in my stomach tightens. Looking away from my parents, down to my hands clasped on my knees, still they're shaking. I'm suddenly cold. I swallow again. The faint smell of cut grass drifts in through an open window. I don't want to throw up in this elegant room, everything just so, after years of making do in a draughty old-fashioned rectory.

I manage to raise my chin, look across at the two people who've devoted their lives to others.

Sometimes it made me so angry. It made me angry how much they did for all those villagers, who often didn't appreciate the work my parents put in to make everything happen. They made it look so easy you see, but I knew. I know.

And still they always had time for me, another imposter, it seems.

The only time Dad ever shut the study door, was when he wrote his sermons, even then, he'd let me creep in. Once I built a *Jenga Tower*, as tall as myself out of Dad's theology books while he scribbled away at his desk. When he'd finished, we played the game, tumbling his precious books in all directions. While we were sorting all the books back into the bookcase, he'd given me a mini sermon about how it doesn't matter how messy things get, we can always sort them out.

Oh, the irony!

And, no matter who was at the house, whenever I came home, Mum always said, "Excuse me a moment, this is really important, I want to see how my daughter is". I was always first, first before everything and everyone. I always knew I was special. Probably why I sometimes resented other people taking up their time.

So, how can it be? How can I be someone else's child? How can I be anything to do with the elusive Madeline De-Muir?

'I can't be, she's just so…' What is she? Perfect? I shake my head, almost snort out loud. 'So together. The whole movie star package.'

'She's a very good actress, she plays the part well.' Dad sits with his hands clasped, elbows resting on his knees, half out of the sofa leaning towards me. He looks suddenly older, less sure of himself than he did minutes ago.

'We're sorry it's like this, Christie.' Mum's eyes betray the myriad of contrasting emotions assaulting her, as her words seep out, barely a whisper.

I try to swallow down the knot of anguish in my throat. Covering my mouth with my hand, I turn away from them. It's not the end of the world, just a new one for me. 'So, why now?' I force the question. 'Why are you telling me all this now?'

Dad nods. 'Madeline wants to get to know you properly… It's time to—'

'So, she wants to swan back into my life after twenty-four years.' Every nerve in my body prickles, screams with resentment. 'I don't think so.'

I can't even look at them. How can they even think I would want anything to do with her? She left me behind, like an unwanted gift.

'It's our fault,' whispers Mum. She's beside me, her hand on my arm. 'It's our fault. She'd been gone too long, you were settled, had started school. We were happy in Little Upton, after all the moving about, it was nice to be settled, not looking to the next challenge. She wanted to be your Mum, but I… I already was… I couldn't let you go.'

Dad shakes his head. 'When she came back, she'd changed. And while the rest of the world clamoured for news of Madeline De-Muir's next blockbuster, we saw a fragile young woman close to breaking point. Photographers followed her every move, her agent phoned practically daily with offers of work. Madeline discovered the fame and celebrity she'd craved, was brittle, hollow and demanding. The people around her only saw the veneer of Madeline De-Muir, none of them saw the shadows of sadness threatening to engulf her. Until it was too late.'

'She shut herself away from everyone, we thought we were going to lose her again…' Mum purses her lips. A gesture marking her stubborn resilience I know only too well. '…We couldn't let that happen. We came up with a plan, it worked, of a fashion, until now.'

Dad nods. 'As I've already said, she is a very good actress. Your mum came up with an idea which would allow Madeline to meet up with you, and get to know you, without exposing her, or exposing you.'

Mum fiddles with the edge of her hankie. 'I thought, if Madeline dressed up, and made-up as someone much older, played the part, she could meet you without anyone suspecting. Not even you. It worked for three wonderful years—'

'But, Mum, the only person who used to visit was Auntie Maddie…'

'… She came to see you whenever she could; but as you got older, you started to ask her too many questions. She said she couldn't keep pretending, it wasn't fair to risk exposing you to the media. So, she decided to stay away to protect you, but first she made you promise to send her pictures and write to her.'

'So, Auntie Maddie, really, is actually my Mum?'

Mum nods. 'She is.

I remember that last time she visited. The smell of cut grass hung in the air then too. We were outside in the garden. She cupped my face in her hands, and planted a kiss on the top of my head. She told me she was going away for a while. She told me to follow my dreams and work hard to make them happen. I remember a solemn pinkie promise to send her sketches, and paintings and doodles. She told me I was the most special girl she had ever met, and it made me feel like a secret princess.

Whenever I've felt sad about anything, I've always remembered that moment, the look in her eyes promising it was the truth. Then she gave me a tight hug and left, her scarlet head scarf slung over her arm, dancing behind her as she strode away; it almost begged me to follow.

I went to play on the climbing frame instead. I'd shouted "Bye" as I dangled upside down, swinging by my knees from the monkey bars.

She hadn't turned around.

And I hadn't followed.

I know Auntie Maddie. I've known her, loved her all my life. I've told her all my secrets, poured my heart out to her in my art. Always clamoured for her praise. Always got it. Always been encouraged to challenge myself, step out of my comfort zone.

I shake my head, try to wake up from this nightmare. 'Auntie Maddie.' I say, not sure if I can believe it still.

Dad rubs his hands over his face, and then clasps them again. 'I know it must seem like a terrible betrayal, but we were all trying to protect you.'

'And now? What's going to happen now? I presume one of you has come up with a plan.'

Dad lowers his gaze from mine. 'It's up to Maddie now. She's been watching from a distance as you've grown up. She thinks it's now or never; she chose now…'

I would have chosen never.

'… And I think…' He looks at Mum. 'We think, the time is right.'

'Really? Well right now, I have no idea if I will *ever* want to meet her… Again… I need time to sort this all out in my own mind. I hope *she'll* understand that.' I try to keep my tone level; pretend I'm talking to an errant

Year seven. My cheeks hurt, and my eyes. This must be tearing their hearts out, and I know I'm going to spill tears as soon as I say the words out loud. But still, I need to know. 'Are you still my mum and dad?'

They are one, either side of me on the sofa, hugging me as tears flood down my face. Mum dabs a hankie under my eyes. She's stroking my hair, her forehead is resting on my temple, muttering God only knows what. Dad's arms bind the three of us together, his chin rests on top of my head. I'm surrounded with love, pure and simple. I always have been.

But now I know the truth of how precious it is.

Monty Mitten Presents

"That skirt is now officially a belt!"

Back at home, Trudy eases off her skyscraper sandals. 'So, you drag us out of a pub, on a Friday night at eight o'clock, because?'

I look at Trudy, not one to miss out on a night out for just any old reason. Yet here she is, putting her social life on hold for me. Wringing my hands, I fiddle with my stack rings. 'The thing is, I need you both to watch something with me. It's an interview Madeline De-Muir did a while ago. Mum gave it to me.' I bite the inside of my lip, and offer a wonky smile.

Suzi grins. 'My mum loves her!'

'Mine too,' I mutter.

'Why would you want...' starts Trudy, then scrunches her forehead. She flicks her hand dismissively. 'Forget it, forget it.' Wedging herself on the sofa between me and Suzi as usual, she hauls her legs up, and sits cross-legged, her otherwise dainty toes jabbing into each of us.

Suzi tuts. 'Honestly, Trudy, your toes get bonier by the day, and that skirt is now officially a belt!'

Trudy shrugs and grins, she stretches her arms back and slings one over each of our shoulders. 'I know you guys love me anyway. Come on, Christie, let's get this over with.'

I press play on the remote. My stomach churning.

Monty Mitten beams from our screen. 'Thank you, everyone, and welcome to the show. Tonight's gorgeous special guest, is a lady, who really needs no introduction at all. She shot to fame at the tender age of sixteen in *The Fallen*. Later, Hollywood success in a string of films including, *An English Rose* and *Here and Now*, has marked her as one of our best loved actresses of all time. More recently, she is known for her work with young people. Madeline De-Muir, everybody.'

I can feel Suzi grinning, I don't even need to look. I cross my arms and push myself further back into the sofa. With any luck it'll eat me.

Monty swings out his arm towards the sweeping staircase, the band strike up the theme tune to *An English Rose*. Madeline De-Muir gracefully steps into the limelight. She is wearing a shimmering silver jumpsuit, tall strappy sandals and a Mona Lisa smile. Her skin appears translucent beneath the studio lighting, and her frame, as fragile as a sparrow.

Suzi rests forward. 'She looks fabulous.'

'Probably Botox,' says Trudy.

'Don't be so cynical,' says Suzi. 'She has such a natural grace, your mum is like that too, Christie. Come to think of it, she looks a bit like your mum.'

'Oh,' is all I manage. I swallow back bile, and pray I'm not going to throw up.

Madeline glides towards Monty Mitten, and leans forward to accept the air kisses he offers. She smiles, and settles gracefully on the offered chair.

'Thank you for joining us this evening.'

Madeline inclines her head a little. 'My pleasure, Monty.'

'Now, d-harling, I know you are eager to talk about your charity work. But first though, I'd like to go back in time, because not many people rise to fame so meteorically. It must have been quite an adventure.'

'Oh, absolutely! I was nineteen, and being told I was the next Grace Kelly. I loved almost every second.'

Trudy tuts and shakes her head. 'Not in the same league, darling.'

Suzi pokes her in the ribs and gives her a death stare.

Trudy shrugs. 'What? I'm just saying, Grace Kelly married a prince.'

'Tell us, what was it like, the parties and the jetting around the world?' Monty leans forward in his chair.

'At nineteen it was fun. Hectic. Tiring. But fun. I met people I never thought I'd ever get chance to meet, it was an exciting time. But what the public don't see, is this huge publicity machine. Everything, for me anyway, was so well organised and planned out, that I didn't need to think. All I did, was either turn up and act, or turn up and party.'

Whoa! Back then, while she was partying, I would have just been starting nursery school. Meeting these two. I glance at Suzi, my first ever friend. She'd led me by the hand into the playhouse, and cooked me a pretend meal of apples, eggs and cauliflower. And Trudy, she was always aloof with newbies, not keen on sharing the limelight... Or her toys. Our friendship was cemented when one of the boys tipped sand over my head. She walloped him with his bucket, and has continued to look out for me ever since.

'Well, your films were successful, and the partying always in all the tabloids. But amazingly, d-harling, never any scandal. So why did you give it all up?'

Madeline clasps her hands, looks down, then back up at Monty. 'Because, it wasn't the real me.' She flutters her hand dismissively. 'Sure, it was who I'd wanted to be. But I missed my family. I missed them very much. One day it just dawned on me… I'd traded who I was, for what I thought I wanted to be. And it wasn't worth the trade.'

A stabbing pain in my chest is making it painful to even breathe. I'm trying to take deep steadying breaths, but every gulp of fresh air is like a sword to my soul. I rest my hand on my chest.

Trudy leans forward, and angles her head to look at me, frowning. 'Are you okay?'

'Indigestion.' I grimace. That's what having a heart attack is often mistaken for. It feels like my heart is actually imploding.

Madeline's honeyed voice trickles from the television. 'Even while I was having this wonderful time.' She touches her rib cage. 'Inside, I felt something was missing. What was missing, was me. My purpose in life.'

Actually, Madeline, I think it was me! Remember, the baby you left behind?

'So, you gave up the acting, and did what?'

'I did nothing, almost became a hermit I suppose.' She shrugs. 'I got back to basics. Down to the bare bones of existence. I stripped out all the frivolity. And yes, I was very low, as down as I've ever been. I couldn't go back and be the girl I was at nineteen or sixteen. The only way out, was to take responsibility, and become the woman I was always intended to be.' Her wide eyes search for Monty's reassurance.

He nods for her to go on.

'My parents were always out there helping people, and I discovered that I'd inherited this, I don't know what you'd call it, desire, vocation, need to help others. If anyone, had ever asked me, if I had anything in common with my parents, I would always have answered "No". So, it was a revelation, because, in a way, I'd always thought they were foolish to waste their time.'

Trudy untangles her legs and stretches them out in front of her, wiggling her toes. 'Pins and needles.'

Suzi shuffles. 'Well you shouldn't sit like that then, should you! You always get them, and I've missed what he's said now!'

'… is what your charity does. Would you like to tell us a bit about it?'

'Sounds like there's a plug,' says Trudy.

'Shh!'

'I started the *Keep-a-Key* campaign a couple of years ago. Basically, we ask people if they are willing to trust a young person to share their home, or even garden shed. Maybe give them the option to just turn up when they need a bed, or a meal, or both. A lot of the young adults we help have been in care, some are having problems at home, and others have perhaps been in trouble with the police, or are struggling with mental health problems.'

'And people what? Foster them?'

'People trust them. Obviously, all the carers have been police vetted. But they just say "Here you are, this is my door key. If you need a chat, somewhere to stay, or something to eat, help yourself". And it seems to work.'

'Well, Madeline, I wish you and your key sharers good luck. It certainly is a novel endeavour.'

'Thank you, Monty.'

'Now just before you go, I know you won't like this, but I must ask about your PA. There have been rumours about the two of you for years.'

'My Personal Assistant is my very best friend. Nothing more, nothing less.'

'He is your only companion. People are bound to jump to their own conclusions.'

'Monty! Well, of course he is a very attractive young man, why wouldn't I want to be seen out with him.' Madeline laughs. 'But seriously, I'm forty years old, he's much younger, and let's face it, a hunk. Our relationship is purely platonic.' A coy smile plays on her lips, as she dips her gaze.

'Well, thank you. Ladies and gentlemen, the resplendent, Madeline De-Muir.'

I press stop on the remote control. Agitation spikes through me. She was so absolutely composed throughout, while galloping panic is still coursing through me. Surely, she must know what she's doing to me. I look down at my shaking hands. How can she be my mother? I don't even know if I'm brave enough to tell my best friends, never mind face the world. I turn to Suzi. 'So, what do you think of her, Suzi?'

'She's just lovely,' gushes Suzi.

Trudy leans forward. 'Too good to be true, if you ask me.'

'No, Trudy, you're just a cynic,' replies Suzi. 'She always comes across as honest and fresh. Just the perfect English rose, like in the film.'

Trudy looks heavenwards. 'Suzi, you're such a pushover! I'll admit she's a good actress, okay, but I think she's got her own agenda. Why thrust yourself into the limelight, after fifteen or twenty years? I think this is all a big PR stunt. She's either going to relaunch her abandoned career, or, this is a smoke screen, and she's trying to hide something. I can't really see your mum being starstruck by her, Christie. Why on earth did she bother downloading this?'

Suzi grins. 'Madeline De-Muir isn't her long-lost daughter, is she?'

I can feel the blood draining from my face.

Suzi laughs at her own joke, then stops short when she looks at me.

'Close, Suzi,' I mutter. 'Madeline De-Muir is my parent's only daughter... And my birth mother.' I clamp my hands over my mouth, trapping the howl of despair. Closing my eyes, I squeeze back the tears.

'Nooo! She's your mum?' splutters Suzi. 'Is it some kind of joke?'

'If only.'

Trudy looks as shaken as I feel. 'Oh, Christie, how awful for you. I mean, what I've been saying about her. Obviously, I didn't mean to upset you.'

'It's only a fraction of what I've been thinking,' I say honestly.

Trudy sits back close beside me, and pulls me into an embrace, resting my head on her shoulder. The salt of my tears on my lips proves I'm still alive.

Suzi tuts. 'I knew something was behind this retirement.'

'Give it a rest, Suzi!' Trudy strokes my hair out of my soggy face.

Suzi makes it a group hug. 'I knew it had been more than a chat about old times with your mum and dad. You poor thing.'

'The elusive Auntie Maddie, by any chance?'

Typical Trudy, nobody's fool. 'The one and only.' I shudder. 'She used to dress up as an old lady to visit me; it was the only way she could avoid being followed by the paparazzi... Apparently... I should have known something wasn't right, she was always wearing pretty clothes, stylish... According to Mum and Dad, Madeline has wanted to go public for years, but they made her wait. They said they'd wanted me to have a secure childhood,' I croak.

'Well, I don't suppose childhoods come much more secure than yours,' says Suzi.

Trudy stands and folds her arms over her chest. 'Well, I managed to survive childhood unscathed by the high-profile antics of my parents. And let's face it, Mummy's still a bit of a goer.'

'Trudy!' Suzi splutters. 'You used to hate it! I remember when your daddy dearest, used a family holiday pic to promote some gadget or other, you wouldn't show your face at school for days and—'

'That was different, Suzi!' Trudy plants her hands firmly on her waist, and raises her chin. 'Daddy should have asked us first. And Mummy's dress was practically transparent... Anyway, when I realised being Lord Drummond's daughter had benefits, I fully embraced it!'

'I'll say!' Suzi snorts.

I feel the energy drain from my body. 'But I'm not like that, I just want to get on with my life... No fuss.'

'Christie, this is a fab excuse for letting your hair down, and having some full-on adventures. Grab it by the throat and enjoy!'

'Trudy, this is me. Seriously, what about my teaching? I'm not risking losing my career over this.'

Suzi's eyes widen. 'I know! People always love to gossip—'

And she should know with her mother!

'… but if you play it cool, and shrug it off as if it's really boring, and you've known for years—'

'But, Suzi, how can I walk back into school with everybody knowing I'm the daughter of the famous Madeline De-Muir?'

Suzi shrugs. 'You could sneak in early—'

'But I've still got to stand up at the front of my class and teach.'

Trudy flicks her head tossing her hair over her shoulders, legs astride, hands on hips and pout in place. 'Well, if it were me, I'd own it… Slimy Sloan might cut you a break if he's got the hots for Madeline.'

My stomach turns. 'Thanks for that, Trudy! Now I really do feel sick.'

'Christie! There's nothing wrong with taking advantage of the situation any way you can. I'm just trying to point out the potential positives.'

'Oh, having him… I can't even say the words!' I close my eyes. 'I just want to teach the kids. I want to go to work, come home, maybe go out for a drink with you guys… I want to be normal.'

Trudy moves directly in front of me, and sits on the floor. She has a thing about looking directly at people while she speaks to them. 'So, if that's what you want, call a meeting, take control of the situation. That's absolutely what I'd do.'

'You know I'm no good at taking control. And that's another thing, what am I supposed to call her? I can hardly call her Mum.'

Trudy curls her lips. 'I can think of a few names.' Disgust drips from every word.

'Call her Maddie. That's what you've always called her,' says Suzi.

'It doesn't exactly go with her image, does it?' I say.

'Not your problem,' dismisses Trudy, waving her arm. 'She's the one who's been pretending to live like a saint, for how long? Going by the interview we've just seen I'd say Madeline De-Muir is one tough cookie.'

'She's not as tough as she makes out. She's had a difficult childhood,' I say.

Trudy looks heavenward. 'Yeah, right. With your mum and dad!'

I explain about Dad being a sort of roving troubleshooting vicar. The moving about, and the unsavoury characters. As I'm telling the story of Madeline's childhood, I find myself trying to imagine how it must have been for her. Mum and Dad too busy with everyone else, to make time for her. Too busy opening their home to strangers, to make a safe environment for the little Madeline. Too busy making everyone else feel loved and precious, to make Madeline feel loved and precious. Too busy searching for their next mission, to see the mission right in front of them. Madeline. Maddie. A lost little girl. I wonder how I would have turned out, if I'd had that kind of childhood. I don't want to know. 'So, you see, things are not always as they seem.'

Trudy frowns. 'You feel sorry for her, don't you?'

'Wouldn't you, Trudy?' I ask.

'I don't know. I know I'd be furious she left me to go and play at being a film star.'

'Well, I can't seem to separate the little girl Madeline, from Madeline De-Muir, from Auntie Maddie. That woman on TV is terrifyingly confident. Not at all how I think of Auntie Maddie. So, if it was just Madeline who was my mother, I would be furious. But it's not, it's Auntie Maddie, and she's been a really big influence in my life.'

Suzi splutters, 'Excuse me, you haven't seen her for years.'

'Okay, but I wrote to her all the time while I was growing up. Trudy, you have brothers, and, Suzi, you have a sister…' Suzi screws up her face. '… I know you don't get on with Chloe, but she's still your sister. And I'm sure you've confided in her over the years. Am I right?'

'Suppose.'

'Well, I don't have brothers or a sister. I have always confided in Auntie Maddie. She has a wicked sense of humour, lots of down to earth advice, and she has always lifted my expectations of me. Built my confidence, and coaxed away my insecurities. She knows things about me, that I haven't even told you two. That's how close I've always felt to her.'

'Like what?' I can see Suzi is clearly miffed she doesn't know all my secrets.

'Okay, let me think…'

Obviously, I'm not going to tell them things that'll hurt them, like the fact that I've been sending them both Valentines cards for the past ten years. Dad always sends me one, and the first time I got one, Trudy and Suzi got none; at thirteen that's almost as bad as discovering your mum's growing facial hair.

'Number one. Dad sends me a Valentine card every year, and that means, on average, I've never had any admirers. Number two. The reason I was sent home that day in our last year at primary school, was *not* because I had suspected small pox, but because I sneezed and wet my knickers. Number three. The

38

revision cards I wrote out for private study at school before our GCSEs, didn't have any useful data on them, I just used them to write out nasty things about the teachers. Actually, I still do that one in my head. When Mr Sloan has a go at me, I just imagine him in a chicken outfit doing the Birdie Song, you know. "With a little bit of this, and a little bit of that, now shake your ass. Na na na na". Oh, and this one is really embarrassing—'

'Like the others weren't?' Trudy wiggles her fingers while examining her talons.

Not sure I'm brave enough to admit my crush on Trudy's brother, Simon. A couple of years older than us, he's always possessed natural leadership skills, and enough confidence to strip to his waist through the summer months. As a serious artist, I had to study how muscles moved under the taut bronzing skin, of a potentially perfect male form. I close my eyes briefly to summon the image. Yep, that'll do it for me, any day of the week. I continue, 'Number four. I had a crush on your brother Simon for years.' There, I've said it, sometimes confession can be liberating...

Trudy sits bolt upright. 'What! Spotty Simon!'

And sometimes not. 'He was hardly spotty! And he can be quite charming.' I try to defend my teenage plus crush.

'And he can be a complete pain in the ass,' says Trudy.

Suzi tuts. 'That's two "asses" in the last two minutes!'

Trudy sighs. 'Well honestly, having a crush on Simon. He's not even human. More a cross between ET and Tin Tin.'

'ET is quite cute...' says Suzi.

'And Tin Tin has high morals,' I add.

'And they're both fictional characters, devised to appeal to eight-year-olds,' scoffs Trudy.

'Anyway, let's forget about Simon, pretend I never told you,' I say, wishing I hadn't.

'How can I?' asks Trudy. 'I'm probably going to have nightmares.' She raises her hands in mock surrender. 'Okay, I'll try, but no promises.'

'Thank you.' Like I've not got enough problems. Give a girl a break!

'So, Auntie Maddie knows all your secrets?' says Suzi.

Trudy wags her immaculate forefinger. 'Ah, ah, ah, just call her Maddie now!'

'Yes, *Maddie* knows all about me. It's making me feel exposed. I mean, she knows everything about me, and all I know about her are the bits Mum and Dad told me, and what she said in the interview.'

And I can admit, at least to myself, she's got Mum's easy grace.

I got Dad's hairy legs...

He's not my dad...

Fresh tears well up in my eyes.

Trudy taps her lips with her finger. 'You don't think she'll turn up at the art exhibition, do you? She does come across as liking to hold all the cards. Maybe she's planning to bump into you casually.'

Suzi frowns. 'That's only a couple of days away.'

Trudy leaps to her feet. 'I'll go and get the tickets.' Marching out of the room, she returns seconds later clutching an envelope. She reads aloud, 'You are invited to the opening of *Evolution*. An exhibition with a difference. Champagne reception at 2pm.' Trudy waves the accompanying note from Auntie Maddie, and continues, 'There is an informal brunch at 11am to meet the exhibition organisers to which you are also requested to attend.'

Suzi raises her eyebrows. '*Requested to attend,*' she repeats.

'Sounds more like an order,' says Trudy.

Looking at their expectant faces makes the decision for me. I'd been looking forward to a relaxing stroll round a gallery. I like to study how other artists perceive things, and if I'm honest, I'm always in awe of their courage, allowing all and sundry to pass judgement on their work. 'Sounds like a request we can't refuse.' Why should I be the one to miss out because of *Maddie's* interference?

Trudy throws up a high five, which neither me or Suzi catch, she shakes her head wandering off muttering under her breath. Seconds later she's back with a bottle of prosecco and three glasses.

When nobody else speaks, I decide they must be waiting for me to utter some words of wisdom. Not very likely, but still, I feel I should fill the silence. 'You think she'll be there?'

Trudy tilts her head to one side. 'I honestly don't know.'

Suzi shrugs. 'She might go as Auntie Maddie, so the press don't recognise her.'

'Well…' I say. 'I don't think she'll be there. I think it's too open. After all, she doesn't know how I'll react to seeing her. I don't know how I'll react to seeing her.'

Trudy points at Suzi. 'Ah, but what if she goes as Auntie Maddie, like Suzi said?'

'I'd still know who she is, and it would be worse for her to be outed in that way. Madeline De-Muir, dressed as a granny, all the press would go wild.'

Suzi nods. 'So, it might just be what it looks like, a nice day out at an art gallery for three friends. Or it could be a test, to see if you're up to life mingling with celebs.'

Trudy grins. 'There are hardly likely to be celebs at a minor art exhibition in Chippington. Christie would be more likely to meet celebs while she's stalking Simon.'

'I have never stalked him!' Well, only a couple of times anyway 'And I don't have a crush on him now!'

Much!

Ha.

'Okay, keep your hair on.'

'So, Trudy,' I say, swiftly changing the subject. 'Do we take the invitation at face value, or do we expect the unexpected?'

'I think, when Maddie decides to meet you, she'll want the backing of your parents. Think about it, at any time she could have revealed the truth. But she hasn't. She hasn't because she wants their support.' Trudy closes her eyes, and rubs her temples. 'She's in a very tricky situation.'

'Go on,' I urge.

'For years she's been the darling of the British film industry. She has always appeared to be above reproach. Excellent career, no scandal, no affairs, no public slanging matches, no enemies. In fact, everyone loves her. So, to tell the world that, not only does she have a twenty-four-year-old daughter, but also that she abandoned her in favour of her acting career, might just kill her image.'

'And not just her image,' chirps in Suzi. 'Her charity too. There she's been, encouraging people to open their homes to teenagers, while she didn't even bother to keep her beautiful, adorable, helpless little baba. She'll be branded a fraud. Trudy, you tell her...'

'She is going to have to play this very carefully. I guarantee she won't be there. Cheers, girls.' Trudy raises her glass to us.

Suzi grins. 'So, we're definitely going then!'

Trudy nods. 'You bet, free brunch and a champagne reception. Wild horses couldn't keep me away, I want to know what she's up to.'

Suzi pats her tummy. 'I'm glad I've lost a bit of weight.'

'Girls, we look fan-bloody-tastic,' confirms Trudy.

'Well I do feel much healthier,' says Suzi.

Trudy winks. 'So, do you feel up to jogging into the kitchen and grabbing another bottle? Go on, you know you want to.'

'Okay, but no more after that one.'

'Guides honour,' says Trudy, holding up three fingers. 'Dib dib dib.'

I shake my head. 'You weren't in the Guides.'

'*Ahh*, but I've held many a Scouts woggle to ransom.'

'I bet you have,' snorts Suzi, and stalks of out the room.

Hopefully for more prosecco.

Evolution

... her legs in the air ...

I'm not sure what exactly I'd been expecting, but I know it wasn't this. I suppose I'd thought the art exhibition would be held in one of those new glass buildings, airy and bright, oozing sophistication. I did think Trudy's Satnav must be wrong, because rather than heading for a city centre gallery, we've ended up in an entirely less desirable part of town.

Trudy deemed to drive us to the gallery, I'll drive us home. So, here we are, sitting in Trudy's flash car, outside an apparently derelict mill. My eyes follow the huge brick funnel chimney reaching skyward, random greenery sprouting from between the bricks. I close my eyes briefly in disbelief.

I wonder if Madeline knew this place was such a dive when she got the tickets?

Trudy taps the screen of her Satnav. 'This is definitely the place.'

'I can see that,' I reply, pointing at a huge banner with *Evolution* sprawled down it.

Suzi unclips her rear seatbelt, and leans forward between me and Trudy. 'Do you think Madeline's made some kind of mistake?'

I shake my head. 'I don't think she would have gone to the trouble of involving you and me in this day out, to go and make a mistake.'

'I hope she's not planning to kidnap us!' squeaks Suzi.

Trudy pokes her arm. 'Su-zi!'

A gang of youths walk round from the back of the building. It doesn't take them long to spot us, they huddle in a group, heads in, clearly talking tactics.

'I don't like this,' says Trudy. 'Call me shallow, but they look like trouble to me. They don't look like they've a tenner between them, but they're all wearing brand-new trainers.'

She's right! Not only brand-new trainers, but the latest must haves. One of the gang ambles over to the car, hands stuffed deep in baggy jeans pockets.

Trudy runs her finger over the automatic door lock button on the dashboard. 'Safe.'

The youth peers into the car, and nods. Trudy opens her window about two inches.

'Are you 'ere for the art exhibition?' asks the lad. Close up he looks nearer fourteen than eighteen.

Trudy nods. 'Yes, that's right, but there doesn't appear to be anyone about.'

'They're all round the back. What do ya think of it?' he asks, gesturing towards the awning where *Evolution* is splattered in multi coloured letters. 'We did that.' He sounds rather proud of the fact. The awning sways defiantly in the breeze.

Unclipping my seatbelt, I lean my whole body across Trudy, open the window fully and stick my head out. 'It looks great. Whose idea was it to use those bold colours?'

Trudy squirms under me.

'That was Mickey. Mickey get over here.'

A beanpole kid stashes an E-cig in his pocket, and they all scuff their way over.

'She did most of it. But it was my idea to use mixed up big an' little letters all different sizes though.'

Mickey, who on closer inspection, really is a girl, grunts an acknowledgement.

'Hi,' I say, doing my best to ignore Trudy poking my ribs. 'What great use of colour, shape and sizes. You must be very proud of your work.'

Mickey shrugs. 'Suppose.'

I notice the barest inkling of pride. 'Well I think it's fantastic. If the work inside is anywhere near as bold as that, then we're in for a treat.' I sport my beamiest beam.

'We ain't seen it. It's supposed to be top secret. We just did that banner, and tidied up the mill,' says the lad.

Mickey shrugs. 'Somethin' to do.'

'Well, you've done a good job. Well done.' Both of them shrug again and flush. 'So, where do you think we should park the car?'

'All the others are round the back. It'll probably get nicked if you leave it here.'

'Very reassuring,' mutters Trudy.

'Shh...' I hiss at Trudy. But to the kids, I say, 'Hope to see you all later.'

'You'll have to ring the bell at the back door to be let in, cos they always keep it locked.'

I drag myself back into the passenger seat, and Trudy closes the window. 'Take a good look,' she mutters. 'We'll probably have to identify them all at the police station later.'

'I've been memorising their clothes...' says Suzi, after being remarkably quiet for so long.

'I don't believe you two! They're just a bunch of kids, give them a break.'

'Which arm?' asks Trudy.

'Look, they've probably been involved in a youth programme or something. At least they aren't prowling the streets.'

Neither of them answers, but exchange looks. Trudy drives to the back of the mill. There are four cars parked along the back wall of the building, including a black sporty Porsche.

'I think it'll be safe here,' concedes Trudy.

We get out, and make our way over to the back door of the mill.

Suzi links her arm in mine. 'Are you okay?' she asks.

'Fine,' I say. 'It doesn't look like there are many people here for the informal brunch, does it?'

'Do you think it's a trick to get you to meet her?' says Suzi.

'Only one way to find out.' I reach to press the bell next to the door. My hand looks steady, but my whole body feels like electricity is buzzing through my veins, wouldn't be surprised if my hair is fizzed and standing on end. I can hear movement inside, the clink of a lock. A woman in a dated tweed suit and sensible flats opens the door. Relief floods through me. It isn't Madeline.

'Can I help you?' she asks.

I try for a confident stance, and take a steadying breath. 'I hope so, we've been invited to the opening of *Evolution*, and to an informal brunch at 11 o'clock.'

'Lovely. Names please.'

'Christie Harris, Tru—'

'Oh, I am sorry, Miss Harris, come in please.' The lady opens the door fully. 'I'm Annabel Price, do call me Annabel. Pleased to meet you. If you'll follow me?'

I exchange looks with Trudy and Suzi, as we are led through a bright reception lounge, then on into a large and surprisingly plush office.

'If you would like to make yourselves comfortable, Mr Hepworth will be with you shortly.'

I exchange a nervous smile with my friends before I sit down on the oversized leather sofa. Suzi plonks herself down next to me while Annabel Price closes the door as she leaves.

Trudy casts her sharp eyes over the immaculate expanse of office, as she perches on the edge of a desk. 'All very mysterious, even my office isn't this lush, and why, actually, are we in an office? Not quite the informal brunch we were led to believe.'

The door ebbs open, and Annabel's head appears. 'He's on his way. Don't let his brusque manner put you off, it's just his way, he can sometimes be a little—'

'Mrs Price, spare me the character assassination,' says an oddly familiar growl from outside the room.

An unexpected flutter builds in my stomach.

Surely not! It can't be…

Annabel grimaces, and mouths "sorry" to us.

I exchange looks first with Suzi, and next Trudy, who remains casually adorning the desk like a lavish accessory. What have I got them into? Mr Hepworth strides into the room.

It is him!

Miles, all six foot two of him in the flesh, and so much more…

Trudy raises an eyebrow, stretches her legs out and crosses one ankle over the other before looking speculatively in my direction. Suzi starts to examine her hands. I sit like an open-mouthed gawp. Surely there can't be this many coincidences in anyone's life.

The easy smile, and relaxed attitude he wears for my parents, has been replaced by a crisp business-like stance. A cool, confident smile has tamed the wolfish grin of Friday night. His angular face is softened only by the jet-black flop of hair that dares to fall forward over his broad forehead. Dark eyes give away not one clue as to what he's thinking. Those eyes, which rest steadfastly on me, strip away my shaky composure. A buzz of awareness flares through my body, disregarding the countless reasons my head is screaming to control my wayward reactions. I squirm at the realisation, that just one look can turn me to mush.

'Welcome, ladies. I hope you don't mind the unconventional circumstances of this meeting.' He reaches out to shake my hand. 'Christie, we meet again.'

Okay, now he smiles and leans forward, brushing a completely inappropriate kiss on my cheek. My heart practically leaps from my chest! I can feel Trudy and Suzi's eyes on me.

'And of course, Trudy and Suzi.' He shakes their hands in turn.

No kisses for them I note, Trudy looks slightly putout, hides it well with a head flick.

'I'm Miles Hepworth.'

'So, what's going on here, Miles?'

'I'm here on behalf of Madeline De-Muir. I'm her Personal Assistant—'

Unbelievable!

'… With help from some of her friends, Madeline has arranged a little surprise for you, Christie. But first, before I tell you about that, I'd like to explain why.'

I remember back to all my flirty little exchanges with him in the safety of Mum's kitchen. I feel like a complete fool. The heat in my chest is crawling upwards, and soon my ears will be glowing red with embarrassment. Once again, I feel outmanoeuvred. 'I've changed my mind. I don't want to be here. I do not want to be here!' I resist the urge to stamp my feet like a three-year-old, but I stand up ready to leave.

So do Trudy and Suzi.

'Please, Christie…' says Miles, placing his hand on my arm.

A jolt of awareness shoots though me. I just stare at him.

'Christie, give me five minutes. If you want to leave then, by all means do. Five minutes.'

I drag my eyes from him and look from Trudy to Suzi. United we stand, but still I raise my brows to silently question them.

Trudy tilts her head to look at me. 'If you leave now, you might regret it, Christie.'

'She's right,' says Suzi.

'But he works for Madeline!' I turn to him, clenching my teeth. 'You should have told me when we first met.' I'm impressed with myself for not actually hissing.

'We met by chance.'

'In my mum's kitchen!' Now I hiss.

'If she'd told me you were coming, I would have left before you arrived.'

'I just turned up, so she didn't know!'

'There you go then.' He shrugs, as if this excuses his omission.

'You could have told me who you were.'

'Your mum introduced me as a charity worker; she just neglected to say it was Madeline's charity. And of course, when we met, you knew nothing about Madeline.' His smile is infuriatingly self-righteous.

Irritation flits through my entire body. I'd look churlish to walk away without even hearing him out. He knows it, has used it to gain the edge.

'Five minutes,' I say.

'Thank you, Christie,' says Miles politely. He loses the smile, and glances at Trudy and Suzi. 'Should we be alone, perhaps?'

'Whatever you've got to say, just say it! These two know all about *Madeline*!'

'Okay... As you now know, I *do* work for Madeline. I spoke to your parents last night, so I know you are aware Madeline wants to go public with your identity. I also assume you know Madeline has wanted to do this for some time...'

I nod, can't speak, catch the fleshy bit inside my cheeks between my teeth.

'One of the reasons your parents have been against this, is because they felt it would interfere with your career as a teacher. Madeline agrees, but also feels your talent for art is very much overlooked. Madeline thinks, and I happen to agree with her—'

'You've seen my work!' I catch my breath; this is too much!

'... That you are talented enough to exhibit your art professionally,' continues Miles.

'I can't believe she showed you my work!'

'Please, just listen... If you are ever going to get the credit you are entitled to as a serious artist, it cannot be as Madeline De-Muir's illegitimate daughter. It has to be as Christie Harris.'

I can feel the blood pulsing round my brain and scrunch my eyes shut. How did I get to this?

'Is there a point to all this,' demands Trudy, stepping forward. 'Or are you just trying to upset Christie for the fun of it?'

'Yes, there is a point. As you know Madeline set up the *Keep-a-Key* charity, working with, let's say, challenging youths. You probably met a couple of them out there. Madeline bought this old mill to convert into small flats for some of the older teens, to have a warden or caretaker to oversee the complex. Then she had this crazy idea, to help you get the credibility your artwork deserves...' Miles' eyes rest solely on me.

The penny drops. She's displaying some of the paintings I've sent her. I feel the blood drain from my face, as panic grips me. 'So, some of my art is on display in *Evolution*?' I feel suddenly faint, nauseous. I flop back into the chair. How could she be so insensitive? Oh, that's right, she's Madeline De-Muir, she can do whatever she wants.

Suzi rests her hand on my shoulder, Trudy takes another hostile step towards Miles.

Miles raises his hands in a gesture of surrender. 'Okay, let's just stay calm. I need Christie to hear me out...' Trudy steps back, shrugs one shoulder, giving Miles minimal permission to continue. 'Christie, it's entirely all your work in there... So far, the only name anyone can the exhibition is Christie. It's up to you if you want to claim it as your own. The decision is yours. But think about it. The exhibition will open at 2pm today, with or without your approval. Remember, all those pictures *belong* to Madeline. If you want to put your name to them, it would serve you both well.'

I hug my arms tight around my body, holding myself together. I'm shocked to the core. How could she do this to me? How could she betray me so callously?

'I know this is a huge shock. Why don't you go and look at the exhibition with your friends before you decide? I think you'll be pleasantly surprised… Follow me.'

Suzi squeezes my shoulder.

Trudy gestures for me to get up. 'You can do this, Christie.'

Mindlessly I get up and follow Miles, Suzi to my left, Trudy to my right. He leads us back outside and round to the front of the mill. I notice the group of youths are still standing chatting together.

'Can you believe them?' Miles nods towards the group. 'They were each given a hundred and fifty pounds to get themselves kitted out for today's opening, and what did they do? They all bought trainers.' He shakes his head.

Trudy nods. 'We did notice the trainers.'

'Hey,' I shout. 'Sick trainers.' I give them an imaginary high five and fist bump. 'Bo-om.'

I'm rewarded with a "Deep" from Mickey, and a look of disgust from Miles. Good, I'm glad he doesn't approve. The need to contradict Miles, gives me a flicker of energy I desperately need.

My strength feels like it's been drained away, because… That's right, I've been betrayed…

Over and over again…

And Miles is part of that betrayal. The need to rebel gives me some relief from reality.

'We've been trying to encourage them to prioritise with their money,' explains Miles.

'I think they've done well,' I say. 'It's really important to wear comfortable shoes. It's hard to smile if your feet hurt.'

'But they could have bought a smart outfit for the same amount of money, including shoes,' counters Miles.

'And how often would they have worn their smart outfit, including shoes? Today? Once? They'll wear those trainers until they drop off their feet. Looks to me like they've got their heads screwed on the right way.'

Miles unlocks the main entrance to the mill. Sunlight streams in through tall windows, flooding the open foyer with light. Trestles laden with empty wine glasses and canapés stand to attention, waiting for the expected guests.

'I'm bringing you in this way, so you'll see the exhibition as the public will.'

Suzi points at the tables. 'Those canapés should be refrigerated.'

'Actually, they've been frozen; they're supposed to be defrosted at room temperature for four hours.' Miles looks at his watch. 'Two and a half to go.'

There is something about this man, actually making me want to scream.

'Like I said, we could have entered via the back of the mill, but I want you to see it the first time as the public will see it. The staircase to your left, leads to the main viewing area, although you may have noticed the odd sketching in the cabinet to your right. Madeline has had the vast majority of your work framed or re-framed, but some of your earlier pieces she felt were too naive to burden with frames.'

'Naive?' I question.

'Some of your very early pictures are so innocent and simple, a frame would look ridiculous. I'll leave you to it.' Miles turns to leave. 'By the way, Mrs Price has organised an informal brunch. Please join us when you've finished your viewing.'

I watch him walk up the stairs and through a door, presumably back to where we came from.

Suzi practically strains her neck watching him leave the gallery. 'No wonder you are off men if you've had him to drool over.'

'I've only met him a few times at Mum's!' I hiss.

'Okay, okay!' says Trudy. 'So, what do you think?'

'Arrogant, self-centred, totally un—'

'Not about him, Christie! About this?'

'I don't know; he's got me rattled!'

'So I see.'

'He is a little unnerving,' says Suzi. 'He nearly bit my head off when I said those canapés should be refrigerated.'

'Madeline's personal assistant, jumped-up lackey more like,' I say.

'Christie, it's not like you to be so judgmental. What happened to live and let live?'

'Oh, you know, too innocent, simple and naive, I guess.'

Trudy gestures towards the cabinets. 'He wasn't talking about you. He was talking about some of your early artwork.'

'Trudy, don't you get it. My artwork *is* me. It's the me, I don't let anyone see.'

'Until now,' says Suzi.

'Thanks.'

Trudy heads off towards the main viewing area. 'Come on, we might as well have a look. After all, it'll be open in a couple of hours.'

Suzi looks longingly at the trestle of food. 'I could just eat one of those, I'm starving. I only had toast for breakfast.'

'Suzi! How can you think about food at a time like this? All my emotions poured out on canvas, exposed to the world, and all you can think about is food.'

'They're still frozen,' says Trudy. 'You'd give yourself food poisoning. Anyway, let's look round the gallery, and then we can go and join the others for brunch.'

'Call yourselves friends.'

Trudy inclines her head. 'Christie, either way, people are going to be looking round in a couple of hours. We may as well look at the exhibition first.'

I follow them up the stairs. The distressed red brick walls are lit by natural light from huge skylights, and complimented by subtle up-lighting from the uneven wooden floorboards.

Each of my pictures, has a beautifully handwritten explanation of the scene or event on a small chalk board beneath it. Madeline's handwriting.

The first picture, *Suzi on Skates*, is a picture of, you guessed it, Suzi on skates. By Christie, age eight and three quarters. She looks rather cute, I think. With her long black pigtails flying in the breeze, her arms akimbo, a look of horror on her face, as she heads for the school's industrial-size dustbins. It could have been worse; I could have painted her after the collision.

'Christie, why have you painted me in such a ridiculous situation? You know I hated those roller skates.'

'It was your face. I just remember seeing the look of horror on your face, it looked so comical… Sorry.'

'You have captured her expression. How old were you?'

'Eight and three quarters, see, it says so there,' I say proudly.

Trudy grins. 'Don't be so miffed Suzi, you're going to be famous.'

'What as?'

'The very first portrait by Christie Harris,' replies Trudy.

But not the last.

The second painting is *Trudy takes a Tumble*. Quite. Which is, you guessed it... Typically, Trudy, even back then, managed to make falling off a horse look stylish! With her arms swinging franticly, riding hat slightly skewwhiff and her legs in the air, (somethings never change). The horse doesn't look bad either.

'Okay, Christie, why does the horse look better than me?' she demands.

'Probably because he's the right way up. See, this is what I mean! You two are my best friends, and you hate me already.'

Trudy shakes her head. 'We don't hate you; it's just a shock recognising ourselves in an art gallery.'

'So how do you think I feel. All my work. What did you think I painted all these years? Buttercups? Mountains? Bowls of fruit?'

'Fine, we get the idea,' says Suzi. 'But how many more are there of us two?'

'Not many,' I say, crossing my fingers behind my back.

'Good!' says Trudy. 'Can we move along now?'

Next up is *Last Again*. A painting showing the backs of all the kids in front of me, in the one hundred metre sprint on sports day. Again, this features Trudy and

Suzi, Trudy way out front, Suzi much closer. Neither of them looks their best from behind. Neither of them comments. There are a few natural world sketches next, including a classic called *Trees in the Breeze*. I went through a kitten stage at eleven; *Sooky on a Skateboard*, is my finest kitty in motion painting.

Suzi hauls me over to *Summer Sun*. 'Hey, Christie, now this one is lovely.'

It's a portrait of Mum and Dad sat on a bench in the back garden of the rectory. Just looking at it makes me smile. I remember making them sit there all afternoon. If it hadn't been for the partial shade of the apple tree, I'm sure they would both have had sunstroke. I, being the grand artist, had the advantage of a huge parasol. Poor Mum and Dad.

Trudy gasps. 'Oh Christie, how could you sink so low?'

'What?'

'Does *Score* ring any bells?'

Oh dear! 'I was only fourteen!'

'And that would put Simon at, what? Sixteen. You hussy!' says Trudy.

Score is a superb – okay I'm biased – action painting of an impromptu football match on the village green. The main subject of the painting is Trudy's brother, Simon, who just happens to be stripped to the waist, and wearing skin-tight Levi's. Bless him. What can I say? Hormones are a terrible thing, especially at fourteen. I manage to drag the pair of them past the most embarrassing of the paintings, without too much comment. Though, there is an avalanche of eye fluttering going on.

The Long Farewell, is greeted with knowing looks. It seems even more poignant now I know she's my mother. 'Life just gets better and better,' I groan.

Suzi places her hand on my arm, and tilting her head to one side offers a sad smile.

We continue to weave our way through images of my childhood in silence. Occasionally we exchange knowing glances. Between true friends, sometimes words are simply not needed.

Finally, Trudy reverently breaks the tranquillity. 'For what it's worth, I think they've done a splendid job.'

Her hushed tone caresses my soul.

She places her hand on my arm, and waits for me to raise my eyes to hers. 'All your work is in order, the lighting is just right, and the rustic feel of this mill is hauntingly evocative. It seems they've involved some of those teenager creatures in the preparation of this event, so, that should please you, Christie. And, they have organised an entire event without you, the artist, suffering a single doubt or headache.'

'But I am suffering doubts! Every time I look at any one of these pictures. And just walking around this place, it's like re-living my entire childhood, except worse, because in about an hour's time, a whole bunch of art critics, are going to prowl round this beautiful exhibition with their little notepads, scribbling horrid comments to print in the local papers.'

Trudy grins. 'Ah, you said beautiful.'

'Sorry?'

'You said, "Beautiful exhibition", that means you like it.'

'Trudy's right,' says Suzi smugly.

'Girls, let me explain. *Any* exhibition would look beautiful in this building.'

'Disagree,' says Trudy raising a pointed finger. 'A whole load of that blobby art would look stupid.'

'Why?'

'Because, it would, it looks stupid at the best of times, but here, in this old mill, the atmosphere is so mellow and achingly serene, it would look doubly stupid.'

Suzi groans dramatically. 'Really, now? Let's not get into this argument again, please.' She is well aware that it could go on for hours, if not days.

I tut. 'Okay, truce.'

'So, are you pleased with it?' asks Trudy.

Am I pleased with it? How should I answer that? I am not pleased that the all-knowing Madeline, has taken it upon herself to exhibit *my* work. Granted work that I've given her. But that was when I thought she was a lonely old lady. And, if I'd been asked last week if I thought any of my work was good enough to be exhibited, the answer would have been an emphatic no.

But here, it does seem in keeping with the environment. Okay, the building looks like a wreck from the outside... Inside, the floors aren't exactly level, the bricks haven't been pointed in years, and some of the skirting boards have buckled away from the walls, but it has real charm and character.

It feels comfortable, like a pair of old slippers. It doesn't feel like some of those modern art galleries, harsh and uninviting. It feels friendly and warm, almost as if the building is hugging you. Maybe it's just me, mellowed by all these reminders from my childhood.

Suzi runs her fingers along the brickwork. 'I've never understood people when they've said buildings have personalities. I've always preferred new, clean, easy to maintain buildings. But this place is awesome. I love it.'

'So, Christie, are you pleased with it?' asks Trudy again.

'Yes. Yes I am.'

'Good. Can we go and get that brunch now?' says Suzi. 'I'm starving!'

Brunch

"Go strut your stuff."

We wander round to the back of the building, and Mrs Price leads us into a small conference room. Miles doesn't notice us coming in, he's too engrossed in his telephone conversation. 'Well there's nothing I can do about it... Not at the moment. I'm all tied up here... Yes, Maddie, it's going as well as you'd expect. You're just going to have to manage Terry as best you can, and you know what Pixy is like, she'll be out on the streets terrorising the other neighbourhood cats. If you're that worried, I'll look for her when I get back. That cat will outlive both of us, Maddie, she's tough as old boots... Okay, I'll speak to you later. And don't worry.'

Annabel makes a small sound, so as to draw attention to us.

Miles turns. 'Sorry about that. Mrs Price, would you let the caterers know we're ready to eat...' She turns to leave the room. 'Oh, hold on, you'd better round up all the Key kids, they've been invited to join us.' Miles gestures for us to sit down. 'Christie, I hope you like your exhibition, it has a certain charm, don't you think?'

'I think this building adds to its appeal. I'm not sure I'm going to enjoy it being metaphorically ripped to shreds by the critics,' I say.

'It won't be,' he says. His mouth curls into a smile, which again doesn't reach his eyes.

I suppose it's meant to reassure me. It doesn't, in fact, I find it rather patronising. The toad, wheedling his way into my affections, and then this. 'How do you know?' I say, trying to keep the irritation out of my voice. 'Are you an art critic as well as a PA?'

Trudy stands up, and waits for Miles to look at her, knowing no man can resist. She taps her foot impatiently as he takes a heartbeat too long. 'What Christie is trying to say, is, do you have any assurances you can offer her. You understand, most artists have months, years, to psych up for their work to be exhibited. Christie has come here today, completely unaware of all of this, and she's slightly unnerved.'

'I am *not* unnerved,' I snap. 'I am just *very* concerned about how this exhibition is going to affect *me*. If it's a complete flop, how am I going to live it down?'

'It won't be a flop,' says Miles.

'I'd lose the respect of the kids I teach... Be a laughing stock with the other teachers... Worse still, *Mr Sloan* would have another reason to undermine my abilities, such as they are. I'm a good teacher!'

Miles guides me back to a chair. 'Christie, come and sit down. Listen to me. Forget about school, for now. The appeal of this exhibition is unique. Think about it, a selection of an artist's work, starting from the age of eight. It has never been done before. Not consistent work of an entire development. Even the name of the exhibition, *Evolution*, requests patience.'

'I don't want patience, I want acceptance.' And if I'm honest, respect.

'You'll get it.'

'How can you be sure?'

'Do you think Madeline would have organised this exhibition, without asking a couple of her arty friends their opinion of your work?'

'I don't know! Remember, I don't know her.'

'Well, let me assure you, she has connections with some of the top experts in the art world. And, there aren't many artists, who'd have the nerve to exhibit their earlier efforts—'

Like I do have the nerve?

'… *Nobody* is going to rubbish your work.'

'Why?'

'Just because,' he says, with forced patience. His brow crumples into a frown. 'Can't you see? It's just too good, Christie.'

The complement takes me by surprise. 'Fine,' I say flatly.

The Key kids form an inquisitive circle round us. The caterers lay out the food. Trudy secures us a table. And Suzi starts queuing at the end of the serving table. What a team.

Mickey edges forward. 'So, are you the artist?'

'I haven't decided yet. It's a secret. I don't want everyone gawping at me. I know I can trust you, and your friends to keep a secret,' I say, smiling, hoping the gamble pays off.

The one who acts like the head honcho, pats his heart with his hand, and thrusts it forward to shake mine. I mimic his actions, and shake his hand.

The lad smiles, and is transformed from a scowling teenager, into a sweet-faced cherub. Remarkable.

'I'm Frank, but my crew calls me "Baby Face". Don't know why.'

Oh, I do. 'So, what would you like *me* to call you, then?' I ask.

He thinks about it, clearly not used to being asked the question. 'Dunno.' He shrugs. 'Authorities all call me Frank, mates call me Baby Face.' He leans in close to me, and whispers, 'It's a bit childish init?'

'How about I call you Frankie?' I whisper. 'It's kind of in-between.'

'Done.'

We move apart.

'Okay, Frankie, how about you and your crew joining me for a light brunch?'

'Yeah, Frank-ie,' one of his friends says. 'Come on, man! We're starvin'.'

Frankie grins his baby face grin, and leads the way. The others follow.

I ask Annabel to point me in the direction of the loos, and make a discreet exit. The toilets are rather swanky. No expense spared. I examine my face in the lavish baroque style mirror. I look flustered and flushed, not at all like a successful artist.

After a few minutes I amble back into the conference room. People are in groups, chatting away; plates balanced in one hand, glasses in the other. How they manage to eat anything is beyond me. Trudy, Suzi and the Key kids are the sensible exception. Remarkably, they are sitting at a table together, all making short work of the contents of their plates. Trudy beckons me to join them. I select a couple of topped bagels from the buffet, a glass of orange juice, and join them.

Trudy points about the room. 'Everyone here already knows who you are. I don't think you're going to be able to keep your identity secret.'

'Oh, I think I will, just for today. I don't mind people knowing my name, but I don't want people coming up to me asking me all sorts of personal questions.'

Suzi eyes the Key kids, then whispers in my ear, 'What if one of these kids tells?'

'They won't. They promised,' I say. I'm sure they won't, I'm one of them now. 'So, as long as you two keep quiet about my ID, I'll be fine.'

Suzi nods towards the kids. 'If you can trust them… You can trust us.'

Trudy nods.

'Mind if I join you?' asks Miles. He sits down without waiting for an answer. 'There are one or two things we need to sort out before the exhibition opens. First, are you going to acknowledge this work as belonging to you, as in Christie Harris?'

'Yes, I am.' Phew, how brave am I?

'Good. Secondly, are you going to meet and greet?'

'No.' Not very brave, then!

'Okay, will you meet and greet later in the week? When you've got used to the idea of being an exhibiting artist.'

'That would depend on whether or not I've had good reviews.'

'Right, so what day is best for you?'

'It depends on the reviews.'

'Yes, but as I've already explained, *you will* have good reviews. So what day is best? I need to organise press presence. It would have been easier today of course, since they are already going to be here.'

'Any day. If the reviews are good.'

'Great, I'll get on to the press office,' says Miles, giving us the benefit of his first genuine smile of the day. 'There are a couple of posters that could do with your endorsement, would you mind signing them?'

'Lead the way,' I say, abandoning my untouched bagels. They don't look very appetising anyway.

'Mrs Price,' says Miles, gesturing for the long-suffering Annabel to join us. 'Would you take Christie through to the workroom to sign those posters? You could get a couple of the kids to give you a lift taking them out to the front of the building.'

'Yes, Mr Hepworth,' she says turning towards me. 'Would you like to follow me?' She leads the way to a medium-sized workroom.

Tools are stacked neatly in storage trolleys, and paints sit to attention on shelving. Sturdy work surfaces look out over a small walled garden, and stretch the length of one wall. The room has been well planned.

'This was going to be the caretaker's work and store room, but the Key kids have been using it to do projects for Madeline,' reveals Annabel. 'Miles insists they keep the room immaculate, as you can see… If the council wants to be awkward, they could say that this is still a working mill, and then there would be no chance of getting the place converted into flats.'

'I assumed they'd already been given planning permission.'

'They had, but that was before Madeline started your exhibition, and Miles has a feeling the council would prefer it to remain an art gallery. Possibly with an attached working craft centre—'

Really?

'… I'm sure you've noticed the rundown state of this area?'

'We did think we'd taken a wrong turning, until we saw the *Evolution* sign outside the mill.'

'If this were to remain a gallery, with the added attraction of a craft centre, it would bring in much needed investment to the area. Push up the prices of the other derelict buildings and wasteland about. It would be a good thing for the people round here.'

'Am I right in thinking, Miles doesn't want that?'

Annabel glances towards the open door. 'I couldn't say... Are you going to sign these posters? Here's a permanent marker.'

'Oh, right.' Quick change of subject; methinks Annabel has said too much. Very interesting. The posters are the same design as the large *Evolution* sign outside.

'The idea is, we clip these up in the reception area, so people don't forget the name of the exhibition.'

I sign several posters. There's a knock on the door, and Frankie's head appears. 'Do you need a hand?'

'Yes please, Frank,' says Annabel.

'It's Frankie now, Mrs Price.'

'Okay, Frank-ie, come in.' Mickey, like a shadow, follows Frankie into the room.

Frankie gathers up the posters. 'Do you want us to take them round the front?'

'Please.'

We all traipse round again... Annabel unlocks the doors at the front of the building, and Frankie and Mickey clip the posters up around the reception area. Mickey walks over to the cabinet which holds some of my sketching, and looks in.

Frankie does a 360-degree turn, and lets out a low whistle. 'We've not been in here since they put your pictures up. It's been like *Fort Knox*.'

'Would you like to have a look at my other work?' I ask. Annabel takes a sharp intake of breath.

'Yeah, can we?' says Mickey, spinning round to face us.

Annabel looks at her watch. 'I'm not sure if there'll be time, it's quarter past one already.'

Mickey turns back round, and carries on looking at the sketches in the cabinet. Frankie scuffs one of his new trainers on the floor and looks down at his feet.

'Okay then...' I say, clapping my hands together in a, let's make a deal kind of way. 'It does seem very unfair that you've not had a chance to have a good nosy round. How about I give you, say, ten minutes to look? The deal is, you give me your honest opinion of the pictures. And I mean *honest*.'

'Done!' says Frankie.

'Even if we don't like them?' asks Mickey.

'Especially if you don't like them. That's the whole point, if they're rubbish, I'd rather hear it from my friends.'

Mickey nods, and they both bound up the open staircase to the exhibition.

'I really don't think it was a good idea to let those two loose up there,' says Annabel.

'Why not?'

'Why not? Because you don't know what they'll do.'

'They'll give me their honest opinion of my pictures, that's what they'll do.'

Annabel gives me a look implying I'm rather simple. 'Mr Hepworth isn't going to like this.'

'Well, we'll just have to make sure *Mr Hepworth* doesn't find out then, won't we?' My eyes are drawn back towards the entrance. Miles is resting on the doorframe.

Great! Just what I need!

'Make sure I don't find out about what?'

Really? What is this man? And where did he come from?

'Oh, Mr Hepworth,' simpers Annabel. 'Christie has let Mickey and Frank go and take a look at the exhibition, *on their own*. I told her it wasn't a good idea.'

'It's Mickey and Frankie, actually,' I say.

Miles raises his eyebrows, and is clearly not amused. 'That will be all, Mrs Price.' Annabel's shoes shuffle on the wooden flooring as she leaves the reception area. 'We'd better go and see what they're up to then, hadn't we?'

'I told them they could have ten minutes.'

'How long have they had?'

'About two.'

'I suppose we might as well wait then.'

Ahh, so he does trust them. 'I think I'll just have a look in the cabinet over there. I didn't get a proper chance earlier,' I say.

Anything to get away from him.

It doesn't work.

He follows me.

'Madeline is keen for this exhibition to be a success. We've put a lot of work into it,' says Miles.

I continue staring into the cabinet.

What does he expect me to say?

'You do know she has been wanting to meet with you for some time?'

I nod, not prepared to even turn to glance at him.

'She wants this to be a success for *you*. She wants you to have your own identity.'

I clench my fists by my side. 'How lovely, an identity of my own. Guess what? I already have my own identity, had it for years, thank you very much. I have family, friends and even a career. Wow! In fact, I was very happy with my life, until Madeline decided to interfere.'

'Madeline has waited years—'

'Well I wish she'd waited a few more!' I snap.

Miles steps between me and the cabinet, completely blocking my view; and entirely too close for comfort. His subtle aftershave fills my nostrils. His presence fills my space. I step back, his closeness making me uneasy.

He leans forward, so his eyes are level with mine. 'Listen, Christie, and listen well, I don't like this any more than you do. But this is what Madeline wants, and I will do anything in my power, to get Madeline what she wants. Anything; I'd walk over hot coals for her—'

'Madeline's little lap dog, are you?' As soon as the words are out of my mouth, I regret them.

Miles stands to his full height, his face unreadable. 'Hardly! But believe me when I say I'd do anything for her, I mean it. Just be careful.'

He starts to walk away from me.

'Sounds like a threat.' It's like my mouth just won't stop! Usually when these barbed little comments flirt into my head, I manage to keep them to myself. Not with Miles, it's like he deserves to know my inner thoughts.

'Whatever.' Miles unlocks an internal door at the far end of the reception area. 'You can get back to the conference room this way, when Frank-ie and Mickey have completed their viewing.'

Okay, the man's a complete control freak. And scary. And I don't like him. He obviously doesn't like me. And what is this with Madeline? What has she got over him? I'm still standing staring at the cabinet when Frankie and Mickey return.

Mickey's face is glowing. 'It's wicked. I wish I could paint like that.'

'Yeah, an' those two women who come with you today, they're the kids on the pictures, aren't they?'

'Yes, Trudy and Suzi, though I'd rather you didn't mention to either of them that you recognised them in the paintings. They're a bit sensitive.' The trouble is; if these two can recognise Trudy and Suzi, so will everyone else who visits the gallery.

'Who's that lad in *Score*?' asks Mickey casually.

'She's only askin', cos she fancies 'im.'

'Do not!'

'He's a family friend.'

'Told me he looked hot,' Frankie persists. 'Can't see it mysel'. Looks a bit of a wimp.'

'No, he doesn't,' I say, defending the object of my adolescent crush perhaps a little too forcefully.

'So, you've got the hots for 'im too,' says Frankie, rubbing salt in the wound.

'Don't be ridiculous, he's just a friend. Trudy's brother actually. And considering he's only sixteen in that picture, I think his muscle definition is rather good.' There I go, digging my own grave. 'He just happened to be playing football on the village green.' Without his shirt on. 'And I just happened to be watching.' Stalking.

'So, he's sixteen then, is he?' asks Mickey hopefully.

'Nooo, he'll be about... I'd say twenty-seven-ish.'

'Oh.'

'Out of your league anyway, Mickey. If he's her brother. She's dead stuck up.'

'Frankie, she's not stuck up at all. She's just not very good with anyone under the age of twenty. You'd be surprised at what she gets up to.'

'Go on, tell us then,' says Frankie.

'I could, but then I'd have to kill you.'

'So, she's a spy then?' He half-heartedly rolls his eyes.

'Something like that,' I say.

'What is she really?' asks Frankie.

'She's a senior technical sales executive.' I try to sound upbeat, but really, even I struggle. I suppose if you're naturally sassy, and smart with it, a fab job. How all those intricate thingy whatsits work, is a complete mystery, and I've always been short on sassy.

'Bor-ring,' says Frankie.

'She seems to like it, and she earns more than me and Suzi put together.'

'So, what do you do, beside painting I mean?' Mickey asks the question I've been dreading, and I pretty much talked myself into it.

'Can't you tell?' I ask, playing for time. They both shrug and shake their heads. Oh well, here goes. 'I teach art.'

'I hate teachers,' says Frankie. 'They're only interested in rules 'n stuff.'

'To be honest, I'm a bit of a rebel,' I say, trying to win back their confidence. 'I'm always in trouble with the deputy head, and spend most of my break times hiding from him.' Well it's the truth.

'Why's that then?' asks Mickey.

'Mainly because I don't stick to all the ridiculous rules, or, I just bend them to suit my situation.' They don't seem impressed. 'And also, because some of my Year 10 and 11 students are like you and your crew. They've got personality and spark, and a need to be recognised as wholly unique. I encourage my kids to embrace their individuality… Unfortunately, schools and most teachers like conformity. It makes life easy.'

'I've never fit in. Nobody ever listened,' says Frankie. 'Not until I got involved with the Key project.'

'I can see you're a valued member of this team, Frankie.' Ah yes, back to safe ground.

'I know. Doin' stuff like this makes me feel like I've done somethin' good for a change.'

'And you've both got a talent for it. In fact, I'd call you ambassadors for the project.'

'That's what Miles says,' mutters Mickey. ''Cept he says it more like a threat—'

I bet he does, trumped-up toad.

'… He's not that bad when you get to know 'im though.'

I raise an eyebrow. 'Really?'

Frankie shrugs. 'He just puts on that tough guy image to impress people—'

It doesn't impress me.

'… An' Madeline's got him wrapped round 'er little finger.'

'You've met Madeline?' I say, trying to keep the surprise from sounding in my voice.

'Ye-ah, loads of times. She's dead famous you know. She always makes cakes when any of us go round. Really good cakes an' all. An' she's always tellin' us 'bout things she used to get up to when she was a film star. Not in a showy off way, just kind of mischief, an' people she's met, an' what they're like 'n stuff.'

'Sounds like fun.' Please stop! You're breaking my heart!

'Yeah, mostly. But even she gives us a load of crap about not lettin' ourselves down,' says Frankie.

'Crap?' I raise an eyebrow again; it's taken me years of practice to perfect it.

'Sorry, I mean pressure 'n stuff. Real bad.'

'It's only because she wants us to do well,' says Mickey.

'Yeah, I know.'

I tap an imaginary watch on my wrist. 'Oh well, suppose we'd better make our way back to the others,' I say. As much as I like chatting with the two of them, I'd rather not hear too much about the wonders of Madeline. I lead the way back to the conference room, and make a beeline for Trudy and Suzi. From the look of them they've been having a good time with the complimentary champagne.

Unfortunately, I'm intercepted by Miles, who skilfully leads me to a quiet corner of the room. 'We open in fifteen minutes. I've already spoken to Trudy and Suzi, and they agree with me. So, to keep your identity under wraps, you're going to have to be my partner for the day.'

I nearly choke. 'Can't I just be on my own? You know, like a freelance art critic or something.'

'Not a chance. You'd soon be rumbled; they all know each other. Anyway, this way I can at least keep an eye on what you're up to.'

'Exactly what does that mean?'

'I've been having a little chat with your friends over there, and they've been telling me some more of the things you've got up to—'

Oh, I can do much worse.

'…So, I think you'd be better with me as your chaperone—'

'Chaperone!'

'Escort, then—'

'Escort! I have no idea what those two have been saying—'

'You know, just in case.'

'Just in case what?' I hiss.

'Just in case you talk yourself into trouble. Oh, don't worry, I'll not introduce you as my date... I'll say you're a family friend. After all, that's what you are.'

I turn on my heel and walk away. The man is a complete... Arrrrg, words fail me. I can't wait to get my hands on Trudy and Suzi! They should have known better than to tell Miles anything about me. Now it's looking like me having to spend all afternoon with *him*.

My so-called best buddies are sat with their heads together, sniggering away about something when I get to the table. 'Having a good time, girls?' I mutter.

They both have the grace to look bashful. Not easy I suppose, when you've consumed the quantity of champagne, the two of them look like they've guzzled.

'We're not drunk,' says Suzi, shaking her head vigorously.

'Had a couple to help loosen up,' confirms Trudy with a nod.

'The champagne is very nice, have you tried some?' Suzi asks.

'I'm driving us home, remember! As per usual. And besides that, I just happen to be at the opening of my own art exhibition.'

'Oh yes,' says Trudy. 'How's it going? We've been chatting to Miles, he's keen to keep you close, you lucky, lucky girl!'

'You think, Trudy? Really?' I huff.

'I wouldn't say no—'

Well, that wouldn't surprise anybody!

'… But, anyway, he seems to think that you'd be better sticking with him today. Away from us two, in case we are recognised from your paintings.'

'Not very likely,' slurs Suzi. 'We have changed since we were kids.'

'What would you say if someone *did* recognise you?' I ask.

Trudy grins. 'I'd just say, you're a bit of hot totty, and you couldn't make it today because you've had a better offer!'

'Trudy!'

'Jo-king… Don't worry, kiddo. I'd think of something.'

'That, Trudy, is exactly what I'm worried about!'

She offers a beauteous smile, and blows me a kiss. Is it any wonder it feels like an Argentine Tango competition is taking place inside my stomach?

Miles is luring people towards the gallery.

'Looks like this is it, Christie,' says Trudy. 'Go strut your stuff.

'Yeah, Christie. Go strut your stuff,' echoes Suzi.

'Thanks for your support!'

'Nooo prob-lem-o,' says Suzi, making the "okay" sign with her fingers.

Unbelievable.

She is so embarrassing when she's drunk *and* happy.

'Right then, ladies, show time,' says Miles. 'I think it would be a good idea if Trudy and Suzi make a late entrance to the opening. All the critics will be eyeing up who's there while I'm doing my introductory speech, so it'll be best for you to stay out of sight.'

'I think I'd be better out of sight too,' I say hopefully.

Miles smiles his tight little smile. 'I don't think so.'

'I'll stand out like a sore thumb,' I say.

'I thought, since you're getting along so well with Frank and Mickey—'

'Frankie,' I correct.

'I thought you could stand with the Key kids. Frankie is going to say a few words about how the project has changed his life. Madeline thought it was a good opportunity. The programme needs positive publicity and community support—'

She doesn't miss a trick.

'… So, you'll be able to blend in with the group.'

Suzi hiccups. 'Not without a pair of new trainers, she won't.'

'I'm sure she'll cope. I've arranged for Mrs Price to bring the two of you a drink while you're waiting to come through to the exhibition.'

'Ah… Lovely… More champagne,' says Suzi.

'Coffee, actually,' says Miles. 'We need to keep our wits about us. I'm sure we all want this to be a successful venture.'

'Perhaps it would be better if they stayed in here all afternoon,' I say.

'When, have I, *ever* missed a party?' says Trudy indignantly.

'Today!' If you don't sober up!'

'I'm not drunk! It's "Little Miss Environmental Health" here, who's necked all the bubbly, not me.'

'Well why didn't you stop her?'

'Because, I thought we'd come out for a nice, relaxing day out, not a sit up straight, knees together tea party.'

'Well, just try to keep an eye on her, will you?'

'Obviously... I'm going to pour three litres of black coffee down her throat, before I let her anywhere near the gallery. I am a responsible adult, you know.'

'Thanks for reminding me, never would have guessed.'

Miles turns towards me and tilts his head to one side. 'So, Christie, are you ready?'

Key Critics

"... her first lover."

Miles holds out his arm for me to link.

I hope he's joking.

Unfortunately, not. Raising a brow, he waits, until I oblige. The fabric of his jacket feels reassuringly soft beneath my hand, and my fingers betray me by curling around the crook of his arm.

Miles opens the connecting door. As we enter the foyer, a hush settles over the room. All eyes turn toward us. Frankie and his crew stand uneasily on the dais by the side of the main entrance. Wide-eyed and twitchy, they look ready to bolt at any moment. I feel, rather than see Miles tilting his head to gesture them over to us. In the hushed room, five pairs of new trainers squeak across the wooden floor. Miles releases my hand. I escape and stand behind Frankie and his friends.

'Ladies and gentlemen,' begins Miles. 'It is such a pleasure to welcome you to *Evolution*.' A shimmer of applause ripples around the foyer. Miles bows his head slightly in acceptance. 'I know most of you have been bristling for a preview since you heard about *Evolution* several weeks ago, but once you've seen it, you'll understand the need for secrecy... Madeline has been privileged to view from a distance, the development of a fine young artist, Christie Harris. And I'm sure, Christie herself would be the first to admit, that without the intervention of Madeline De-Muir, this collection of art would never have been seen by the public—'

Too right!

'… Unfortunately, Christie is unable to be with us today, but I do believe she will be available soon—'

Pending good reviews.

'… Now just before you all go into the main gallery; I'd like to introduce you to Frankie. Frankie is one of the young people, who have been involved in getting this exhibition set up. For example, the *Evolution* poster design was developed by Frankie and his team… Frankie.' Miles extends his arm in Frankie's direction.

There's another ripple of applause as Frankie shuffles his way forward, chin slumped to his chest. He rolls his head up, and stands up straight, leaving his head on a slight angle as he looks round the room. 'Hi, my name is Frankie. I don't think any of ya will remember me tomorrow, but that don't matter. What matters is that I'm here today, 'n' without Madeline, I'd probably 'ave been locked up. Ya see, I'm one of the people Madeline 'as helped through the *Keep-a-Key* project. I'm not very old, but I'm old enough to know that I've seen 'n' done things that *nobody* should 'ave to see, or do…'

The foyer is still, every eye fixed on Frankie, every ear, eager to hear more.

'…My mam was sick of me. The 'thorities was sick of me. The police was sick of me. The neighbours was well sick of me. Probably even the man in the moon was sick of me an' all.'

A collective nervous laugh titters between his spellbound audience. 'Then one night, I met this woman. She was walkin' her dog, 'n' it was chuckin' it down. It was late, 'n' I was wet through cos my mam' ad locked me out, again. This woman, she asked me if I wanted a coffee. I thought she was takin' the pi... Thought she was jokin'. But she weren't.

She took me to 'er 'ouse, she made me a brew, 'n' a bacon butty, the best bacon butty I've ever 'ad, with all butter drippin' through my fingers...'

Every face smiles at Frankie's memory.

'...Then she asked me if I'd anywhere to stay, 'n' when I said my mam 'ad locked me out, she got me a sleepin' bag, 'n' told me to sleep on her sofa. I didn't want to, cos it looked dead posh. But then I thought there might be somethin' worth nickin'. So, I stopped. But I couldn't do it, this woman 'ad been dead kind to me. Most people didn't bother to look at me anymore, not even me, I wasn't even worth lookin' at, not even in a mirror or a shop window. I was just rubbish. But this woman, she'd made me a drink, 'n' a bacon butty, 'n' let me stop in her posh 'ouse. It was like, *Are you crazy woman?*' Frankie swirls his hands round his head. 'But she wasn't, cos I didn't nick anythin', see.'

Frankie stuffs his hands into his jean's pockets. 'Next day, she fed me some more. She likes feedin' people. Then she give me a key, 'n' said if my mam locks me out again I can stop at hers. That's the first time I've ever been given a key.'

Frankie reaches down the neck of his sweatshirt, and pulls out a key on a chain. 'This is it, the key what changed my life. Without this key, without this project, my life was worth nothin'. *Nothin'.* But now I know that I am worth somethin', 'n' I just want you all to know what Madeline did for me.'

Frankie shrugs and shuffles back to his place. I clap my hands together so hard they hurt. Pretty much everyone else settles for polite applause.

'Well, thank you, Frankie,' says Miles. 'I don't think I can add anything more to that, to support the *Keep-a-Key* project. Frankie and his friends are proof that trust breeds trust. I'm sure you have all had a look in the cabinet over there, and have had a taster for what lies ahead. So, I declare *Evolution* open, and trust you'll be fair with your reviews. Enjoy.'

People make their way up the gallery steps, chatting to each other along the way. As the foyer empties, Miles turns to face Frankie, he places a hand on his shoulder. 'Well done, Frankie. I think they'll remember your name, so just be careful if any of them become too friendly.'

'What do ya mean?'

'It's like this, they may be art critics, but any one of them would love a tasty scandal to fill their coffers. It's all very well when they write nice things, but more often than not, they'd rather dish the dirt.'

Reassuring for me then.

Mickey shuffles her feet. 'Like when they say you're Madeline's toy boy?' Everyone sniggers bar Miles and myself.

'Exactly,' says Miles, and silences them with a glare. 'So be careful what you say, and to whom. Better to keep quiet and look cool in your new trainers.'

Nobody moves.

'Go on, Frankie, you lead the way. Christie, you stay with me for now, until we've got your identity established.' Frankie, Mickey and the others leave me alone with Miles. 'I thought I'd introduce you as Anne, since it's your middle name.'

Is there any point objecting? 'Whatever.'

'If we go up into the gallery together, and chat with some of the more influential critics together, then maybe you could mingle alone. Get a feel for what they are saying about *Evolution*. They might be a little more honest about what they think with you. After all, they're not likely to confide in me, being Madeline's toy boy!'

'Quite.'

'People can believe what they want, but just for the record, Madeline and I are just good friends.'

'Whatever. It makes no difference to me either way… Unless of course, you're planning to become my stepdad.'

'What a charming thought… Although… I'd rather have a different kind of relationship with you—'

Not a chance!

His eyes twinkle as they did the first time we met. '… A far pleasanter thought, don't you think?'

'Errrr… No! 'I squeak sarcastically.

'Oh, you think!' He grins. Grins! 'Come on, like I said "showtime".' Again, he offers his arm, reluctantly I link my hand through. He smiles a wolfish smile and my heart bounces in my chest.

Oh, why him!

'Atta girl.'

I actually feel like strangling him, but offer a tight smile instead. He rewards me with a chuckle. We join the small throng of people in the upper gallery. He guides me in his desired direction.

'Just smile, Anne. Look like you're enjoying yourself.'

'How can I not enjoy myself, with such a charming companion?' I mutter.

Again, he chuckles. 'Well I'm enjoying it enough for both of us! Okay, first, I'd like you to meet Timothy Grey. He's the one over there wearing the Dr Who scarf. Don't let his quiet voice and gentle manner fool you, he's probably the most savage critic here, so let's try and put him in a good mood, shall we?'

Miles leads me to where Timothy is stood. He's looking at *Score* – the painting of sexy Simon at sixteen.

'Well, Miles, I'll say this for your mystery artist, she certainly knows her way around the male anatomy.'

'You're probably right,' says Miles. 'Most artists do. May I introduce you to Anne?'

'Mr Grey.' I smile. 'I've heard such a lot about you. What a pleasure it is to meet you.'

'Anne, my dear, the pleasure is all mine.' He lifts both my hands, turns them over and honours the insides of my wrists with a kiss. Very forward!

What a creep.

'What, pray tell, are you doing with this old rogue?' Timothy asks in a sly manner.

'Anne's a family friend.'

'Really?' says Timothy. 'I didn't know you had family. Or friends.'

'You'd be surprised,' says Miles.

I notice a flare of red creeping up his neck. Obviously, Timothy's comment has hit a nerve.

'He's only a very distant family friend. I don't want you to get the wrong idea, Mr Grey. And I'm sure I wouldn't be here today but for my great aunt. Bit of a matchmaker, she's been trying to marry me off since I was eight.'

Timothy and Miles laugh indulgently.

'Never mind, my dear, you'll meet lots of new people here, you should be able to give Miles the push before the afternoon is over.'

'What a lovely idea!' I enthuse with as much charm as I can muster.

'Here's my card, next time you want to preview an exhibition, call. Nothing is worth having to endure an afternoon with Miles. Ciao.'

Oh dear, poor Miles is not amused. We leave Timothy to continue his way round the gallery.

'You are supposed to be keeping a low profile, not flirting with the most notorious womaniser in the art world.'

'You told me he was the most savage art critic, not the most notorious womaniser.'

'It doesn't take a degree to work it out. He is called Mr Grey…'

'I was trying to put him in a good mood, not an easy task when he clearly dislikes you intensely.'

'He doesn't dislike me. He was just playing, and I'm an easy target. He knew I wouldn't cause a scene, not today. Right, next I think Sarah McBride. Sarah you'll get on with.'

Sarah is looking at one of my earlier paintings, *Trudy takes a Tumble*.

'Sarah.'

'Miles, sweetie, haven't seen you in donkeys'. I do know Madeline keeps you on a short rein, even so, what have you been doing? And who is this adorable creature? Something you've been keeping from me, you naughty boy.'

'Let me introduce Anne, she's a friend of the family.'

'And you expect me to believe that?' Sarah sighs, and takes me to one side. 'Now, don't be shy, tell me everything you know about Miles. He's never even taken me out for lunch, let alone to an exhibition.'

'That's not true, I took you out the other week,' says Miles.

'Doesn't count sweetie, not when you've got your chaperone.' Sarah winks at me. 'Of course, Madeline doesn't let him out of her sight, unless he's working, that is.'

Interesting, very interesting.

Now how can I describe Sarah kindly? Clearly, she's developed her large personality to disguise her size, though underneath the layers of caftans, she's probably not as huge as she looks to be. But multi-layers of lilacs, pinks and purples don't do much for anyone. And what is it with Dr Who scarves? Granted, Sarah's are probably silk, but still, the way they're draped over her ample bosom, it only serves as a colourful frame for her double chins.

Okay, I'm being bitchy, but if anyone is in need of one of Trudy's makeovers, it's Sarah. In fact, I'm tempted to introduce them to each other.

Sarah formally shakes my hand. 'You look like you're in a world of your own. You don't need to be shy with me. Goodness, I'm one of the nicest people here, aren't I Miles?'

'Sarah, you are the nicest lady I know, at least until you pick up a pen.'

'But, Miles, sweetie, it's my job. I'm an art critic I've got to be critical,' purrs Sarah.

'Well I hope you're not going to be too critical of *Evolution*,' says Miles.

Sarah shrugs. 'You'll have to wait and see, sweetie.'

'Mr Hepworth,' interrupts Frankie. 'Mrs Price would like a word with you in the conference room. Bit of a problem with—'

'Yes, yes, Frankie, I'm on my way. Excuse me please, ladies. Sarah, you will take care of Anne won't you, she's new to all this?'

'She's safe with me. Now then, Anne, what shall we look at next? I've heard a whisper about a topless schoolboy, shall we look for him?' Sarah edges her way past the sketches and paintings until she reaches *Score*. There are already others stood round the painting, making notes and passing comments.

'So, I think this would have been her first lover—'

Really?

'But don't you think he's rather too perfect?'

Oh yes, definitely.

'What do you mean?' says the first.

'If he'd already been her lover, surely, she'd have been tempted to show his vulnerability, and this boy is resplendent, so confident and completely unaffected by her presence. It's almost as if he's unaware she's painting him.'

Well, I was up a tree at the time.

'True, but teenage boys are an arrogant breed.'

'What do you think, Anne?' whispers Sarah. 'Do you think they were lovers?'

Simon is going to kill me!

'I don't know. It just looks like a lad playing football to me. But you're the expert, what do you think?'

'I think she fancied the pants off him, and he didn't even know she existed.' Sarah chuckles. 'I think this young man is in for a bit of a surprise, don't you?'

I just nod.

It's safer not to speak.

Or cry.

And it's too late to run away.

'See that skinny woman over there?' asks Sarah.

I nod.

'Well that's Bunty Hargreaves. She's never lived up to her jolly hockey sticks name. The woman's a witch. If she takes a disliking to someone, they may as well hang themselves, and be done with it.'

'Miles said you were lovely, until you picked up a pen,' I remind Sarah.

'Bunty Hargreaves has never been lovely in her life! I may make the odd barbed comment in my column, but it is generally well placed, and done with no malice. Bunty does a hatchet job if she doesn't like someone, or their work.'

'Where are you taking me?'

'To meet the wicked witch, of course. May as well have a listen to what she thinks of this Christie Harris gal.'

'Bunty, nice to see you. Have you met Anne, she's a friend of Miles Hepworth?'

Bunty looks me up and down, sucks in her thin lips, and narrows her eyes. 'Can't say that I have.' She holds out her hand, I obligingly shake her cold fingers. 'Young lady,' is her only greeting.

'What do you make of *Evolution*, Bunty? Quite something to have the early efforts of an artist on display like this. Must have taken some pluck don't you think?'

Bunty sniffs. 'Sarah, don't you think it's a little too naive? A little too sentimental and cute?'

'I suppose…' Sarah's eyes twinkle.

'It's like this, everything is too well stage-managed. The age of the artist neatly written beneath each picture, the speed at which this exhibition has *allegedly* been set up. I think someone is playing with us. I think it's fake.'

'Fake!' I gasp.

'It's not unknown for an established artist to try and pull the wool over our eyes, and make us critics out to be bumbling fools. Especially one who has been recently rebuked.' Bunty taps the side of her nose with her forefinger. 'I think there might be tears before bedtime.'

I think she's probably right.

Mine.

Sarah leads me away. 'Oh dear, it sounds like Christie Harris is in for a rough ride with Bunty. I do hope the gal's got her head screwed on.'

Strange, something I've never been described as having. 'But what if Bunty's wrong? What if Christie Harris is just a normal kind of—'

Sarah shakes her head and her bosom; though that was probably just a natural progression. 'Dear me, no. There's nothing normal about Christie Harris.'

You don't say? 'Nothing normal?'

'Nothing at all, sweetie. First of all, Bunty does have a point about the meticulous detail to age. "Christie, age eight and three quarters", it's almost like a doting mother proudly announcing her baby's cut its first tooth. And of course, again, the speed this exhibition got off the ground. Most young artists tout their work around for ages before they're spotted, so to speak.'

'So, you think she's a fake too.' Just rip my heart out and throw it to the lions. Go on... We Christie Anne's know all about lions.

'No, she's not a fake. Don't worry, we've not been bamboozled. My guess is…' Sarah looks about herself.

'You won't pass it on, will you? Don't like being upstaged.'

'Not a word. Promise.'

'Not even to Miles?'

'Not even to Miles.'

JUST TELL ME.

NOW!

'That's my gal. Liked you as soon as we met. My guess is, this Christie Harris is either someone already famous for some other reason, and doesn't want to be accused of exploiting her real name. Or, she could be the sibling or child of someone famous. Whoever she is, what I can say with certainty, is, she is one mighty fine artist.'

'Wow, really?'

'Oh yes, my dear, she's got talent by the spadesful.'

Oh, Thank You Thank You Thank You Thank You.

'Of course, the poor thing has probably been pushed by her overbearing parents. She's probably a complete basket case; that would explain her not being here.'

That's the way to do it, build 'em up to knock 'em down, the higher you build, the farther they'll fall.

But still, I, Christie Harris, have got talent by the spadesful.

I, Christie Harris, *am* one mighty fine artist.

As we wander silently round the gallery, I inwardly fluff my own feathers, preening myself, because, let's face it, I'm the next big thing.

Until I fall.

No, no, no, I shan't think of that.

Sarah takes out a small notebook from her oversized carpet bag, and begins to jot down notes as we stop at each picture. Her pencil is chewed from the top, and worn from the bottom. The three and a half inches which remain, have clearly seen some action. She holds her head to one side while looking at each picture, then her head rocks from side to side, as if she's summing up her opinion of the picture, then she writes.

The speed of her pencil causes a ripple effect all through her body. Especially her bosom. I haven't a fetish for big bosoms, but honestly, they've a whole life of their own. Throughout she doesn't utter a word; she saves those for her notebook. We reach *The Long Farewell.*

'What do you think of this?' asks Sarah. She taps her lips with the stubby pencil.

It'd been Suzi's idea, to paint my snapshot memory of my last meeting with Auntie Maddie. Looking at the painting now, leaves a hole in my stomach. A hole in my life. Auntie Maddie only remains in my mind's eye, and this painting. The pain of her deception is too raw to hide. I can feel Sarah watching me. I was the little girl, with years ahead of her, trying to please a woman who doesn't exist.

'It makes me profoundly sad,' I manage to say at last.

'Really? I think the old lady wants the little girl to follow her. She's tempting her with the gay red scarf, and tall heels. A promise of excitement.'

'Maybe the little girl is too young to understand.'

'Or maybe she doesn't want to follow, guess we'll never know. Unless Christie Harris cares to enlighten us.' Sarah starts making more notes.

'Excuse me, I think I'll go and find out what Miles is up to,' I say.

Sarah hardly seems to notice me leave, so intent are her scribblings.

I do hope she is kind.

Busted or Not

... her right boob threatening to liberate itself ...

'Right, I've a few things to tie up here, but I'll be with you as soon as I can.' Back in the conference room, Miles is on his mobile. 'No, there's nothing here that Mrs Price can't handle, so don't worry, Christie's fine. It's her two friends who need babysitting. I'm going now, and I'll be with you soon.' Miles turns to me, his expression grim.

'Problems?' I ask, trying to keep the gleam of hope from clearly shining through.

'Complications we could have done without, but it could have been much worse. Very much worse.' Miles rubs both hands over his face. 'I'm sorry, I'm afraid I'll have to leave.'

Yay!!! Free at last! 'I suppose I'd better leave as well, since you're my escort,' I say solemnly.

'Probably would be wise. I'll speak to you later, just don't let those two friends of yours anywhere near the gallery... Or the critics. The only thing I want to read about is *Evolution*.'

The cheek of the man. Suzi and Trudy aren't that bad. Maybe a little high-spirited... Now I'm free to escape, I am feeling more magnanimous towards my best buddies...

'Coo-eee. Any chance of some...' Suzi staggers towards us. 'Christie? Is that you, Christie—'

Really?

'… Course it is. Sil-ly me. Silly-silly-silly-silly-silly meee. Do I usually wear glassseesss, cos everything's all swishy-wishy-wishy-wishy-wOOOO.' Suzi makes two peep holes with her forefingers and thumbs, and holds pretend binoculars to her eyes.

Miles raises his eyebrows.

I cringe.

Suzi pouts. 'Christie-wisty, I really-really don't feel very-very-very well. I think I'm gonna be sick.'

'Come on, let's get you to the loos.' I put my arm round her and lead her back out of the room.

Why me? What did I do to deserve this? I mean, it's not as if Suzi's an out and out drunk, so why did she choose today, of all days. Oh yes, that's right, free champers. The main culprit for Suzi's alcohol induced illness, is muttering his excuses and making his escape. The toad.

That's right, leave me to sort out poor Suzi. I mentally give Miles a kick in the shin. It makes me feel better for about ten seconds, then I remember Dad saying that it's as bad to think of doing something, as to actually do it. The glow of satisfaction doesn't last long. Still, it's a shame Miles doesn't feel the pain in his shin I mentally inflicted.

We make it just in time. Suzi starts heaving her guts up. I, being a true friend, hold her hair out of the line of fire, and make suitably soothing sounds and gestures. The door creaks open.

'Having fun girls?' asks Trudy.

'Not really. I thought you were supposed to be looking after this one,' I say, nodding towards a dishevelled Suzi.

'She gave me the slip. I've been looking all over for her.'

'Well, I think she went in search of more alcohol, and found it, by the looks of her.'

Suzi gives us a soulful glance. 'It was lovely bubbly…'

Trudy shakes her head. 'Surely you've not been drinking again! She's already thrown up once.'

'I don't get out much,' says Suzi, from her half slumped, half kneeling position over the toilet. 'Anyway, it was free, and Annadel, Annadu, Mrs Price said I could.'

'Mrs Price should have known better,' says Trudy in disgust. 'Wait until I see her. She doesn't have to get you cleaned up and home. You'd better not be sick in my car! I'm serious! Come on. Christie, we'll have to get her home before she starts again. We can't stay here with her like this, if that Bunty Hargreaves gets her hands on her, all our names will be in the papers tomorrow.'

'Have you been in the gallery?' Please don't say yes. Please say you just peeped through a crack in the door. Please say Bunty Hargreaves is a family friend, a dear sweet lady despite what others say.

'I had to! Suzi was on the loose, and the last time I'd seen her she was singing *I've got a lovely bunch of coconuts*. Can you imagine what that lot in there would have made of her—'

Unfortunately, yes.

I nod.

'Hard-nuts Hargreaves, made a beeline for me.'

'Does she know who you are?'

Trudy shrugs. 'Ish'

'Ish. ISH. What do you mean, ISH. She either knows you, or she doesn't,' I hiss. My innards quiver, and tell-tale heat starts it's crawl up towards my ears.

'We've met at a few charity events. Always creeping up to Mum and Dad. Loves to schmooze with the crowd.' Trudy holds her arms out at full length, and examines her talons; a sure sign of hostility.

'Great. That's all I need. Did she pummel you for information?'

'She tried, but I didn't tell her anything about you. When I walked into the gallery, she looked at me, and a very smug expression came over her, as if she'd just worked something out. Not very likely, in my opinion.'

'That's it, my cover's blown!' I huff. How will I be able to show my face in school again?

'I don't think so, she seems to think I'm Christie Harris, and since I'm Lord Drummond's daughter…'

'You wouldn't want to be accused of using your connection,' I finish for her.

'Exactly.'

Okay, that makes sense.

'I think I'm going to be sick again,' whines Suzi.

I hold Suzi's hair out of her face, again, and Trudy rubs her back. I need to go back into the gallery and find out what Bunty Hargreaves thinks she knows. I also want to make sure Sarah hasn't made the same assumption. I don't want Sarah to think I've been deliberately dishonest with her. Although, I suppose I have.

Suzi staggers to her feet, and looks at her gaunt reflection in the mirror. She turns on the cold tap and starts splashing her face. She turns the tap off, bends double and holds her face under the hand dryer. This helps, now she's red of face, and green of gills. Her hands are white and her feet unsteady, but somehow, with the help of her two nearest and dearest, she makes it to the car, and promptly falls asleep on the back seat.

Friends, who'd have them?

'Trudy, I've just got to pop back inside for a couple of minutes. You'll be okay with the sleeping beauty, won't you?'

'Sure, but don't be long, or I might join her.'

I make my way back into the gallery, and go over to Sarah. She's chatting to Dr Who. As soon as she spots me, she excuses herself, and takes me to one side.

'Bunty has left. She told me she'd just been talking to Christie Harris, and is going to let the rest of us keep guessing until we read her review.' Sarah smiles.

'Oh.'

'Yes, "Oh" indeed. Now Anne, or should I call you Christie—'

'Shh! Don't let anybody hear you. How do you know it's me?'

'Just an inkling at first, my dear. And then your reaction to *The Long Farewell*. But what really clinched it was when Trudy came in. *Trudy takes a tumble*. Bunty is convinced that Trudy is you... Now Trudy wouldn't have painted herself, now would she? Silly Bunty, sometimes she can't see past the end of her own nose. I'm afraid it's going to be *Bunty makes a blunder* next.'

I smile, it has a nice ring to it. 'What are you going to do?' Even though Sarah seems to like me, I know that she'd be a fool not to exploit the situation. And Sarah is nobody's fool.

She tilts her head to one side. 'We need to talk, but not here with everyone about.'

'You could meet me at the back of the building, and we could go into the conference room.' I need to make this right before it gets anymore out of control. Madeline and Miles have a lot to answer for, leaving me to mop up the mess.

'Lovely, I'll meet you in five minutes, my dear. Off you go.'

'Poor dear,' Sarah booms to Dr Who, and anybody else in the room who cares. 'Miles, the cad, has gone off and left her. She's been looking for him all over the place. He's probably been summoned by Madeline.'

Everyone laughs. I don't know why, it's probably true.

Dashing outside, I briefly explain to Trudy what's going on. She decides she might as well try and get some sleep in the car with Suzi. I wait at the back of the mill for Sarah. When she arrives, she's breathing heavily.

'Didn't want to give the game up,' she huffs. 'I waited a few minutes before I left. I'm out of puff; I didn't want anyone seeing me come around here, so I ran. I can't remember the last time I did that. Come on, let's get inside.'

The place seems deserted. We sit down at a table in the corner of the conference room. Sarah takes out her notepad and three-inch pencil, and looks at me expectantly.

'Now then, my dear, where would you like to start?'

The truth, the whole truth, up until mother Madeline interrupted my life. I'm just plain old Christie Harris, spinster of this parish. It's only in the last few days I've developed a mysterious past.

'What would you like to know?' I ask.

'Well, first off, who did you paint your pictures for, and why?'

Good question. Here goes. 'When I was a little girl, an Aunt of my mother's visited us. She asked me what I wanted to be when I grew up. I told her I wanted to be an artist, so she set me the task of sending her my pictures. It was supposed to make me disciplined.'

'Did it make you disciplined?'

'Yes, I think it probably did. I didn't want to let her down. She'd made it sound very important for me to chase my dream.'

'I like that, a dream chaser. What about your family, any brothers or sisters?'

'No, it was just me and my parents, though I have two close friends.'

'Trudy and Suzi?'

'Yes, they're still my best friends. We share a house.' Maybe that's too much information.

'Oh, what fun, so all night parties, and boyfriends galore.'

'Hardly.' I laugh. 'It's more cleaning rotas, who ate the last Snicker, and which bin needs to go out this week.'

'No boyfriends then?'

'Not that I've noticed. Trudy tends to get the most, Suzi and I don't do too badly, but no one special for any of us, yet.'

'Never mind, plenty of fish in the sea.'

'Sharks too!' Now why did I say that? And why am I thinking of Miles? And why am I *still* thinking of Miles? And still!

'So, Christie, what do you do when you're not eavesdropping at the opening of your own exhibition?'

'You mean in the real world? I'm an art teacher. And I love it, but I'd rather not mention the name of the school. I'm always getting into trouble with the deputy head, and I don't want to give him any more reasons to pick on me than he already has.'

'You intend to carry on teaching?' Sarah raises an eyebrow.

'Of course, it's what I do. I'm a teacher. I have the best kids, the ones who try the hardest. Some of them have hardly ever been praised before in their lives, so with a bit of encouragement, and a lot of hard work, their portfolios are just as good, if not better than the "A" sets. I love watching the kids grow in confidence. It just kind of bubbles inside them, under the surface, then all of a sudden, it explodes! With a bit of luck, the explosion is impressive enough to affect their whole outlook on life.'

'Wow, you really do love teaching; I can tell you're driven.'

'Oh, Sarah, I love teaching. It's what I was born for, and but for my love of art, I may never have realised it. I suppose I've a lot to thank Auntie…'

'Auntie?'

'Sorry.' I bow my head. 'She's no longer with us.'

'I'm sorry to hear that. Were you *very* close?'

'Always, we wrote often.' And then she betrayed me.

'And you kept all the letters?'

'As it happens, yes.'

'Any chance of sharing them?'

'Not in a million years.' Spot remedies, yuk. First disco, arrrh. My crush on Simon, too embarrassing for words. 'No, not ever.'

'Shame. Now, Christie, if there was one thing you could change about your life, what would it be?'

Oh, you know, just the last few days. 'What I'd really like is double glazing. The house is really draughty.'

Sarah looks crestfallen, I think she expected me to say money, fame or happily ever after. Oh well, never mind.

'Last question, do you have any splendidly sensational secrets you'd like to share with me?'

'None...' Ha! 'That I'd like to share with you.'

'But you do have secrets?'

'Sarah, everyone has secrets.'

'Well, thank you very much for your time, Christie.' Sarah closes her notebook. 'I'm sure you're going to be very successful in the future. Just promise me one thing.'

'What?'

'When you want people to know your secrets, tell them to me first!' Sarah winks and hands me her business card. Then off she glides like an oversized belly dancer. From behind, she looked disturbingly like the headmistress from the old St. Trinian's films; I'm sure she was played by a man. Oh well.

By the time I get back to the car, both Suzi and Trudy are asleep on the back seat. I rummage in the boot, find a picnic blanket and cover them both up. They look like two tired-out children after a day of excitement.

Suzi snores and dribbles, while Trudy truly does look like a sleeping beauty. There is no justice in the world. Sadly, I snore and dribble, so I can say this with conviction.

Key in the ignition and off we go. Oh no! Where did Bunty Hargreaves spring from? What's that she's pointing at the car? No, no, no, it's her mobile.

'I think that's your first brush with the paparazzi, a` la Bunty,' drawls Trudy, not dribbles.

'I'm well aware of that! But you do realise the mobile was pointing at you and Suzi in the back, and not me driving.'

'How very rude!' yelps Trudy.

'Indeed.'

Suzi belches. 'What's all the noise about? Trying to rest here.'

Trudy lunges forward, and makes a grab for the steering wheel. 'Stop the car!'

I start to break.

'NOW, Christie! I'm not going to let that sour-faced battle-axe get away with intruding in *our* privacy. Who does she think she is?'

The car scrunches to a halt, and Trudy launches herself out of the car, and marches across to where Bunty Hargreaves stands still happily tapping away. Trudy is barefoot, and the gravel must be cutting into her feet. Unbelievably, Bunty Hargreaves is *still* blatantly taking pictures. Clearly, she's never encountered anyone like Trudy before. Trudy does not take prisoners, "seek and destroy", is her motto.

'Hey, you, who do you think you are? How dare you take pictures of me, give me that mobile!'

Bunty staggers backwards as Trudy surges forward. Trudy snatches the phone and starts swiping her finger over the screen.

Bunty makes a grab for her mobile. 'How dare you! That is private property.'

Trudy continues swiping. 'So is my face and theirs.' She thrust the phone back towards Bunty. 'Have it! Put it away! Believe me, if you *dare* point it in our direction again, I'll crush the bloody thing!' Trudy stamps her unshod foot on the ground, and grinds it into the gravel.

I need to get to her before she really loses it. Getting out of the car, I snag my ankle on the trailing seatbelt, landing flat on my face in the gravel and a conveniently placed puddle. My hands, knees, elbows, chin and nose smart as tiny stones cut into then.

Muddy water gurgles into my mouth and nose. I gasp in pain and shock, raising my head in time to avoid sucking up the yucky water. Suzi swings open her door, pain sears the back of my head… I plunged right back into the muddy water…

Full frontal impact. Face fully submerged. Head throbbing. Hair dripping. Eyes stinging.

Fab.

Suzi plonks herself down in the wet gravel beside me, skirt up round her waist, cranberry knickers exposed for all to see, and her right boob threatening to liberate itself from the confines of her bustier. She yanks my head onto her lap, and starts RUBBING the gravel and mud from my face, whilst rocking forward and back, and humming *Is this the way to Amarillo*.

I try grappling Suzi's hands from my face… She's having none of it.

I can still hear Trudy and Bunty going at each other. A small group of onlookers appear, gawping from Trudy and Bunty's verbal assault on each other, to the two damsels in distress, or dis-dress, apparently mud wrestling. Finally, Trudy becomes aware of my plight, stalks across the car park and rescues me from Suzi's ministrations.

A woman on a mission.

'Oi, you! Frank or Frankie, whatever your name is. Get here now!' hollers Trudy, using exaggerated arm movements.

Frankie ambles towards us.

'Ever driven a car?' demands Trudy.

Eyes wide, Frankie nods.

'Then get your backside in that car, and park where it was parked before.'

Frankie gets in the car, and drives it ever so slowly away... Clearly to not cause me any more upset. Speeding up dramatically, he does a handbrake turn at the end of the car park... Slows back down to park the car, and gives a fuming Trudy a salute.

Cheeky moose.

'You lot, Mickey, Goofy, Donald...' shouts Trudy.

I cringe and shiver at the same time. One of my many talents, multitasking. Mickey and the other Key kids look at each other, and shuffle their way over to us.

'Is there anywhere we can take these two, to get cleaned up?'

'There's a posh bathroom 'n' shower next to the office. Mrs Price 'ill 'ave the key,' says Mickey.

'Okay, you help me with Christie. You three, see if you can manage Suzi. Good luck!'

Suzi sulks as she's hoisted to her feet, slithering back down again seconds later. 'Maybe, I just be a little teeny-weeny, itsy-bitsy, bitsy, bitsy bit, bit tipsy,' admits Suzi, her eyes squinting at the miniature gap she's conjured between her thumb and forefinger.

After three attempts, we're on our way back to the rear entrance of the mill.

Suzi makes a bid for freedom. 'Is this the way to Amarillo, ev'ry night I've bin huggin' my pillow. Come on you lot, join in. I'll be Peter Kay. Dreamin' dreams of Amarillo, and sweet Marie who waits for me. Sha la la la la la la la, come on clap. Sha la la la la la la la.'

The day, it seems, just gets better and better. Ah well.

A horrified looking Mrs Price leads the way to the bathroom; though I think she's secretly enjoying the spectacle. And because Trudy won't leave me on my own, I shower with my underwear on. Not that she hasn't seen it all before, but I doubt very much that I'd be able to bend my knees to get my knickers back on. And, I'd rather not stand butt naked in front of Trudy, whose body is sculpted to perfection.

I'll just have to go commando later.

'You're not going to like this,' announces Trudy, once I'm safely under the steaming water, wincing with pain. 'But I've arranged for Dr Pilkington to meet us back at the house in about an hour.'

'Gee, thanks,' I gurgle. Not sure if I manage to pull off the sarcasm. 'But I doubt I'm in a financial position to meet his professional fees.'

'It'll be covered by Daddy's expenses; Dr P. is always on hand for company emergencies.' Trudy flicks her hand. 'You know, you could have a concussion, and I refuse to sit in A&E for hours with Suzi in tow. Dr P is a real sweetie, it'll make his day! I'll call us a taxi when you get out of there, since none of us are in any fit state to drive.'

Trudy helps me out of the shower and dabs me with a pristine white towel which feels like sandpaper. Has nobody heard of Comfort?

Mrs Price has kindly found me some clean clothes "A spare set, just in case I have an accident while I'm here". The tweed skirt, smooth knit turtleneck and matching cardigan all threaten me from hangers. The colour, cow pat green, is not my shade to be honest. And really, would anyone believe that Mrs Price *hadn't* had an accident if she wore that ensemble? I think not. But beggars can't be choosers, so they say. Trudy helps me dress.

'Not really your colour,' states Trudy.

'Or shape, or size either,' I add, pulling at the gaping waistband of the itchy tweed skirt.

'It'll all come together when you put the headscarf on, dearie.' Trudy holds up her hands in self-defence. 'Joking, I'd better go and book the taxi now.'

'Couldn't Frankie drive us home?' I ask innocently.

'Only when pigs fly backwards through the valleys of Wales, but maybe Mrs Price could. Good thinking.'

Mrs Price jumps at the chance to drive us home. As we traipse to the car, I realise Suzi has been even less fortunate than I, in the clean dry clothing department.

The orange boiler suit, I surmise, wouldn't fit over her boobs, hence it's tied at the waist by its sleeves. The extra bulk caused by the boiler suit, under the "R U UP 4 IT?" black hoody, makes Suzi look like a delinquent *Teletubby.* Her scowl only adds to the effect.

Looking on the bright side, Frankie and crew are positively beaming. The sight of me and Suzi has cheered them up no end. Let's face it, it's not every day you get to see people at their behavioural and visual extremes.

AM (About Midday), absolutely stunning, well dressed, perfectly made-up, uptight, upstanding and sober.

PM (Post Mud-wrestle), completely uninhibited, battered, bruised, and suffering from severe, almost fatal, no dress sense syndrome.

So, you see, it's quite understandable why they all look so sodding cheerful.

Designated Driver

Trudy practically drags her out of the car ...

Mrs Price, once again, "call me Annabel", seems to have taken on the persona of an F1 Racing driver, as she gleefully revs Trudy's car.

'It's quite powerful,' says Trudy. 'It can be a little jumpy.'

'Oh, I'll soon get the hang of this baby!'

'Ahem, Mrs Price, Annabel. Are you sure you don't mind driving us home? It will mean you having to get a taxi back here, taking up your time, and I'm sure you're a very busy lady,' says Trudy nervously.

'Don't mind at all. I've always wanted to drive one of these beauties. I used to do a bit of off-road rally driving when I was younger. That's where I met my husband.'

'Oh.' Trudy's voice is uncharacteristically weak.

'So, you see, nothing to worry about. I'll have you home in a jiffy.'

Now, that's what worries me.

Trudy shrugs her shoulders, and mouths to me, 'How bad can she be?'

I wonder.

Mrs Price shuffles herself lower into the driving seat, rolls her shoulders, stretches her arms out before her, takes a firm grip on the steering wheel and revs the engine. Again. Slinging her arm over the back of the passenger seat, she swivels to look out of the back window. Swinging the car in a wide reversing arc, she sends a spray of gravel across the car park, splattering the Key kids who jump away in dismay. The car then jerks forward, scrunching to a shuddering halt at the road edge.

'Sit back, and relax, ladies. I'll have you home in no time.'

Mrs Price's promise to get us home in a jiffy, suddenly seems not such a good offer. As the car bumps off the pavement, it becomes clear Mrs Price has no concerns about the mental and physical state of us passengers.

At speed, we're off, the flash of a speed camera catches my eye as we swerve to the middle of the road.

'Watch out for that—' gasps Trudy.

'Cyclists!' hisses Mrs Price. 'They all think they're Bradley Wiggins! Shouldn't be on the road!'

It soon becomes clear Mrs Price has no concerns about other motorists, pedestrians either. She has no worries about mini roundabouts, or speed bumps as she calls them, traffic lights, or curbs. She certainly has no worries about speed limits, speed cameras, or any other aspect of the Highway Code.

And to be honest, none of that would matter if we were all inebriated, heavily sedated, or better still, completely unconscious.

But me and Trudy aren't, so we witness the shock and horror of other motorists and cyclists, see their hand gestures and mouthed verbal abuse. We see the wide-eyed fear of pedestrians, even hear some of them scream. Our stomachs lurch as the car mounts the series of mini roundabouts, and bounces over to the other side.

As we cruise towards the oncoming traffic after going through another red light, I can say quite honestly, I actually taste fear. The grind and jolt of *catching* the odd curb or two, sets my teeth on edge.

The *Mind your speed*, and *Please drive carefully through our village* signs are merely a blur at the roadside, while speed cameras flash happily at us as we rush over their fining white lines.

Trudy yanks out her mobile and phones for a taxi to meet us at home, ready to return the demon driver back to where she came from.

I don't know what she offered the taxi driver by way of an incentive, but bless his little heart, as we screech round the final bend, and I plunge for the last time into Trudy's lap, I see him ready and waiting at Rose Lodge.

'Just on the left here!' shouts Trudy.

The car skids to a halt, inches behind the taxi.

'Home sweet home, ladies. I enjoyed that.'

Trudy practically drags her out of the car and thrusts her into the back of the waiting taxi. The taxi is brisk to whisk the dice-with-our-life Mrs Price away. Gone. Vamoose. Vanished and banished, and never ever to be permitted to terrorize this trio again.

After Trudy explains the whole sorry story to him, dear old Dr Pilkington has the pleasure of examining three badly shaken young ladies. He jovially jabs my ass with a sedative, and tipples a handful of pink painkillers (two) into my shaking white hands.

'No concussion,' he decides, as he blinds me with a torch. 'Just a few bruises,' he announces as he prods my battered body. 'And abrasions,' he declares, as he swabs my face with an antiseptic wipe. 'A couple of days R&R and you'll be good as new,' he says, as he accepts a cup of tea rattling on a saucer from Trudy.

Suzi sits, silent. Her body slumps, eyes wide. Her dishevelled bob hangs about her face. The orange boiler suit creases around her middle, while the "R U UP 4 IT?" hoodie wisely disguises its challenge. Now it's more a statement, "UP IT", which in my drug induced state, I think rather appropriate.

'Somehow,' says Trudy, 'I don't think "Little Miss Environmental Health" is going to be up to stool samples and swabs tomorrow. I'll phone her department now and let them know she won't be in.'

'Bank holiday. Shut,' says Suzi without emotion.

'I'll talk to the answering machine,' says Trudy patiently.

I can tell she's at least trying to keep the sarcasm from her voice, in deference to Suzi's weakened state. Suzi nods oblivious.

'I'll tell them we've been in a road accident.'

I nod my head; a shooting pain makes me instantly regret it. 'We have. The accident was letting that woman drive, we might need counselling.'

'Don't worry, Christie, I've learned my lesson. The only person I will ever let drive my car from now on, is you. Anyway, I don't think I'll be up to going to work tomorrow either. So, I'll let them know. *And,* I'm going to get someone round to look at that poor car. I'm sure it must have suffered as much as we have.'

I'm not sure about that, but I nod anyway.

'Going to bed now,' says Suzi, but she makes no attempt to move.

'Come on, Suzi, I'll give you a hand.' Trudy leans towards her, and offers her two. She hoists Suzi up, puts her arm round her and guides her out of the room. I hear their slow progress up the stairs. Some shuffling, voices, more shuffling, and then stomping down the stairs.

Trudy doesn't stomp, ever, at least not until today.

'Made an executive decision,' declares Trudy. 'I hope you don't mind. Can't put myself through all that again, so you'll have to sleep on the sofa. I've brought your quilt down.' Trudy tucks me in and makes me quite comfy. 'Okay, can I get you anything before I go and sort myself out?'

'I just want my mum,' I say, feeling like sobbing. 'And my dad.'

'It's been a long day, Christie. Sleep now, we'll get you home tomorrow.'

Pottering Tuesday

I was awestruck.

It has been years, since I've woken up uncomfortable and in pain on a sofa. In my youthful, early university days, it was like an initiation into the real world of an undergraduate. I'd stagger, sloshed and singing back to my digs, waking up bleary-eyed and uncomfortable in the morning. A small price to pay for a night of partying, or so I'd thought, foolishly, at first.

It hadn't taken me too long to figure out, that actually I was there for more than a good time. Hangovers, hallucinations and hedonism weren't for me. Hard work, honest friends and the occasional hot date were more my scene. I left the partying to Trudy.

So, why does my head feel like I've drunk a barrel of beer? Why do my eyes feel puffy and sore? And why is Trudy sat *in her dressing gown* watching me like I'm a scientific experiment gone wrong.

Trudy doesn't do in her dressing gown. Trudy does, dressed immaculately, at all times, and in all places, regardless. I'm trying to figure out why. I squint my eyes, turn my head, and wince.

Trudy nods at me. 'How are you feeling? Bit of an eventful day we had.'

It could have sounded patronising, but it didn't. Instead, slowly, dizzying images trickle into my head. The gallery, Miles, the *Keep-a-Key* kids, Mrs Price,

Miles, Bunty Hargreaves, Sarah McBride, the car, the gravel, Mrs Price, terror, Dr Pilkington, Miles.

'I feel—' How do I feel? Sore. Tired. Confused. 'Why are you wearing your dressing gown?'

'Oh, I've just been pottering round, that's all'

'Trudy, you *never* potter around. And what about your poor feet?' I remember the gravel grinding.

'They're fine, years of ballet and surgical spirits has made them tough as old boots. But I think today we all need to do a bit of pottering. It can be pottering Tuesday.'

'Don't think I'm up to pottering.' I haul myself up into a semi sit. 'I might just be up to a coffee though.'

'Could you manage toast as well?' asks Trudy, shuffling herself into the kitchen.

'No thanks, just coffee would be great.'

'I'll take one up for Suzi too, I heard her pottering earlier.'

'Suzi always potters.'

The room hasn't changed. My head hurts. Rummaging, I find a Snickers wrapper stuffed down the side of the cushion. I smile. Everything is the same, but different. Not so long ago my only real problem was Mr Sloan. Now I have a head full.

I sit up as Trudy hands me my coffee, it tastes good. Just what I need to wake me up. After all, I could be a world-famous artist by now. I hear Trudy go up the stairs, probably taking Suzi her coffee. I wonder how she is this morning. Probably mortified by her behaviour yesterday. Probably suffering for it too. Suzi the saint, drunk as a skunk.

Balancing my cup on the arm of the sofa, I run my fingers down over my face. My skin feels tight and rough over the scratched skin. I feel round the back of my head to the painful lump under my tangled hair. I'm still trying to untangle my hair when Trudy comes back into the room.

She's still in her dressing gown.

'How bad do I look?' I'm brave enough to ask.

Trudy tilts her head to one side, scrutinizes me. 'Do I compare thee to a—'

'No, seriously.'

'Dr P cleaned the cuts on your face thoroughly last night, there's no sign of infection, but they look quite raw. They're more like little scratches really, I'm sure they'll heal fine. All easily covered by the miracle of foundation.'

I nod, can't quite manage to speak, but attempt a smile. A tight smile. I can feel the pressure building as I hold my lips together valiantly. My chin begins to crumple, my nostrils flare and tears squeeze out of my swollen eyes.

'I'm not vain,' I profess, as Trudy dabs snot from my streaming nose. I know I'm not the prettiest, but I do try to keep myself looking okay-ish, most of the time. I go blotchy when I'm hot, so I try to stay cool. I burn in the sun, so I stay in the shade. My eyes are my best feature, so I always wear mascara. The last few days I've had panda eyes.

'I know you're not vain, you daft Muppet,' agrees Trudy. 'You just have a healthy interest in your appearance. Nothing wrong with that.'

'Nothing at all. I just don't want to frighten any children when I go out,' I add.

'Exactly.'

'So how bad do I look, really?'

'I'll go and bring a mirror.'

In the unforgiving sunlight, the mirror isn't as kind as I would have liked it to be. The grazes aren't too deep, just the odd one or two have started to scab over, but the skin around them is shiny and red raw, proof that Dr Pilkington has indeed done his job well. As Trudy promised, they aren't too bad. Suzi would be horrified if she ever found out she was responsible for some of them. But it's my eyes that give away my true state. Swollen and red.

Proof of my self-pity.

Sarah's words come back to me, "I do hope the gal's got some pluck". If she could see me now, she'd be heartily disappointed. Maybe it's time to find it. All I need to do is find my pluck.

Suzi ambles into the room. She doesn't look like she's borrowed my pluck, she looks like she could do with some too. 'My head is sore,' she says, and flops down into a chair without even looking at me. 'I can't remember much of yesterday, just being at that gallery. Was Tony Christie there?' She turns to look at me, her eyes widen. 'What happened to you?'

'Just a bit of a tumble. I'll be okay in a few days.'

'You look like you've been in a fight!' She stands up, and makes her way gingerly across the room, then starts to examine me like one of her specimens. 'You've got gravel in your hair. You've been attacked!'

'No, honestly, I just fell over, that's all.'

'Was it one of those unruly teenagers?'

'No!'

'I know you, pretending it didn't happen, just so they won't get in trouble with the police. Wake up, Christie, they're nothing but a bunch of hoodlums.'

Oh, the irony! 'Suzi, let it drop, it was nothing to do with them. If you don't believe me, then go and ask Trudy.'

I feel for Suzi. Her mum is such a busybody know-it-all, who judges *everybody*. Sometimes, in times of stress, Suzi's default button makes her just the same. She tries not to, I think.

'How would Trudy know? She was drunk!'

I shake my head in disbelief and immediately wish I hadn't. 'Not as drunk as you, do you remember your solo rendition of *Amarillo*?' A pained expression flashes over Suzi's face. 'Thought not. At least Trudy was in control of all her faculties, have you noticed what you're wearing?'

The way the crumpled hoody is now hanging, it reads "R U IT?", I doubt Suzi can figure that out at the moment though.

She half-heartedly pulls at the offending garment and shrugs. 'Whatever.'

"Whatever" isn't really a Suzi word, and Trudy just does not do dressing gowns during the day. And me, I don't do bumped and bruised on the sofa, not unless I have Mum looking after me.

'I need my mum,' I mumble and snuggle down under my duvet. I try to sleep. I hear Suzi shuffling slowly out of the room.

It's amazing how much can happen while we are sleeping. Homemade broth, care of Trudy.

I know, totally amazing! She can cook!

Travel arrangements, are also care of Trudy, but why she had to ask Nigel I have no idea. Yes, he's good-looking in a geeky kind of way, is the perfect gentleman at all times, and so reliable he could be classed as boring except for his mischievously twinkling eyes. He is also sweet, kind and an incredibly humble genius. He's the head of the science faculty at St. Stephen's at only twenty-nine, and has a natural affinity with the kids. I first met him when I started at St. Stephen's. I was awestruck. It didn't take me long to figure out everybody loves Nigel. He's just great at making everyone feel great.

Didn't take long for the two of us to hook up, but, after only a handful of disastrous dates, he's now my ex.

I'm sure he'll be impressed with my new Quasimodo image.

Thanks, Trudy!

Happy Families

A truth.

Well this is awkward! Nigel marches up to the front door. He's insisted on carrying my proficiently packed, (care of Suzi), overnight bag.

'This looks very nice,' he says, twinkle in action. 'Clover Beck, how long have your parents been here, then?

'Not long.' I shrug. 'And yes, it is very nice... So... Thanks for the lift... I'm sure you've lots to do... So, thanks again... Enjoy the rest of the break.' I smile my big bright OTT smile and grab my bag.

Honestly! I could throttle Trudy.

This is excruciatingly embarrassing. Poor Nigel has been trying his best to impress me all the way here. I feel like I'm kicking a puppy... But really, it's kinder to be a bitch with him now, than to let him think there's any lingering chance.

I walk into Mum and Dad's new house without looking back. How rude. And without knocking. Again, how rude. I slump with my back against the door. Listen for the scrunch of Nigel's footsteps back to the car.

Phew, and relax. I can hear low voices coming from the kitchen. 'Hello, anybody home?' No reply, oh well. I shuffle through the hallway. The kitchen door is ajar.

'I know it's not ideal Anne, but I'm not sure what other options there are.'

Miles!

Suddenly I'm ultra-alert. What is he doing here? I edge closer to the door, can't quite catch what Mum's saying. I'm not eavesdropping, just listening in.

'She needs someone to look after her. I've got double the workload now,' reasons Miles.

'But... Christie?'

'But Christie what? Christie is a grown woman, Anne. Don't you think it's about time she started living in the real world? Madeline had been practically fending for herself for five years by the time she was twenty-four!'

'Madeline and Christie are two entirely different people, Miles! Maddie chose her own path.'

'That maybe so, but Madeline has taken a back seat for a long time now. Sometimes she needs her mum, too.' He speaks the words softly, not an accusation, just a truth...

A truth.

He loves Madeline. He really does love her! I slump against the wall. A knot of resentment tightens in my chest.

'But what about the press? You know we can't cope with all that kind of carry-on. Not at our age, Miles.'

'I'll deal with it, I promise. So, can she come here, at least until she's more mobile?'

Mum sighs. 'Like you said, what other options are there.'

'Thank you.'

Giving the kitchen door a push, it swings silently open, just in time for me to see Miles stoop to kiss Mum on her cheek.

For a nanosecond I'm transfixed by their closeness. 'What's going on?' I hardly recognise my own voice.

They spring apart.

'Christie! What are you doing here?' Mum flushes. 'What's happened to your face?'

She steps forward, and reaches up, her fingers butterfly over my grazes.

'I'm okay.' I can feel tears forming. 'Just tripped up, that's all. You know how clumsy I am.' She holds me close. I squeeze the tears back and swallow. I will not cry in front of him. I can feel him watching me. 'Anyway, I didn't want to worry you by 'phoning, and you did say I could stay, if I ever needed a bolthole...' I loosen out of her embrace.

'Yes, of course,' says Mum.

'But it seems you have other... Commitments.' I shrug her hand from my arm.

'Madeline has broken her ankle,' the words dripped from Miles. 'She needs somewhere out of the glare of publicity to rest.'

'Miles has just popped round to see if she can stay here.' Mum shuffles in her slippers on the tiled floor.

'I heard. How very thoughtful of him,' I try to keep the sarcasm from my tone.

Fail.

'Yes, Anne has very kindly offered to let Madeline stay,' says Miles pleasantly. 'Until she's able to get about herself.'

'I'd best start sorting out bedrooms, looks like we're going to have a full house. Will Maddie need to sleep downstairs?'

'That would be the easiest for her,' says Miles. 'Thank you, Anne. It really is appreciated.'

'Okay, Christie, you sit yourself down.' She leads me to the table and plants a kiss on my head as I sit. 'Miles will make you a nice cup of tea. She takes two sugars, and set a plate of biscuits out, there's a good boy.'

There's a good boy!

Am I hearing properly? Sure enough, as Mum leaves the kitchen, Miles clicks the kettle on, and starts rummaging for biscuits.

'It hasn't taken you long to cosy up to my mum,' I all but hiss.

'Which would you prefer, Hobnobs or Chocolate Digestives?' Miles turns to look at me. I can tell he's trying not to stare at my grazes, because his gaze burrows into mine, flint to flint.

'Neither,' I say, holding each of my hands in tight fists, so as not to wrap them round his conceited throat. I do not want to commit murder in my parent's home. Just who does he think he is?

'Okay, I think I'll have Hobnobs.'

'Just help yourself, why don't you?'

'It seems you have a problem with me being here, Christie,' he states reasonably.

Dah. 'You think?'

'I'm here on behalf of Madeline.'

'Like I said, I heard.'

'Who, unlike you, does not presume to just turn up, and expect to be taken care of.'

'Excuse me! Just who the *hell* do you think you are? This is *my* parent's home, but here you are, barging into our lives and passing judgement.'

'I've barged into no one's life. I've known your parents for over ten years—'

I snort, if he thinks I'll believe that!

'... Maddie and I have met up with your parents on holiday many times over the last few years. Believe it or not, we all get along very well.'

'I can't stay in here, with you, and listen to this tosh.'

I stalk out of the house. My whole body quivers with pent up anger waiting to explode. It's like a bad dream, except I don't wake up, and it keeps getting worse.

And I'm sure I could have found a more appropriate word than "tosh"! Let me see, bullshit, that would have been better. Please God, give me the patience to not kill this man, and not to say bullshit in front of my mother.

The grass is squidgy as I make my way across the lawn to the end of the garden. Daisies and dandelions make a colourful carpet at my feet. Weeds, very pretty, but still weeds. I've always liked weeds.

I need to put as much distance as I can between me and Miles. I pull out my mobile, I suppose I could phone Nigel to come back… But then I'd need an excuse for not staying… And I *was* rude when he dropped me off earlier… I'm sure he'd come back for me… If I ask… I'm not telling him about Madeline, or Miles, and I'm rubbish at telling lies.

Arrrh. I slip my mobile back into my pocket, carefully sit on the garden bench. I cover my face with my hands. When I was little, I used to cover my face up all the time. I'd thought, if I couldn't see anyone, then no one could see me. If only it were true, life would be so much easier.

I shiver as a shadow falls over me. I know it's Miles. Can feel his presence. The hairs on my arms bristle. I keep my face covered.

'You know, Christie,' his words are smooth, and sweet as honey. 'Lots of things happen in our lives over which we have no control. I've always found, in the long run, things turn out fine. You might not be able to see it yet, but only good will come of this. I'll put your cup of tea by the side of the bench.'

Get lost.

I drop my hands from my face in time to see him striding across the lawn towards the house. I resist, just, hurling the hot tea after him. *Things turn out fine.* How naïve does he think I am? How can anything good come out of this mess?

Oh, and here comes the cavalry. Mum in her beige pants, cream blouse and ditsy print apron with patchwork pockets. She always used to be the cavalry. I wonder whose side she's on now.

'Hi Mum. What's new?'

Thought I'd try for irony.

She smiles her placid smile, and sits down beside me on the bench. She picks up my hands, turns them over, and traces the scratches on my palms with her fingers.

'What's been going on, Christie?' she asks me.

She asks me!

I want to scream.

'You tell me, Mum.' I want to snatch my hands away, but don't. I'm trying to not cry. 'Tell me, Mum. What's been going on?'

'Where do I start?'

'Well, let's see? You've told me the beginning, then you told me the middle bit, so I suppose next comes the end.'

'Sarcasm doesn't suit you, Christie.' Her voice is soft, uncensored.

'What do you expect? All my life is a huge fat lie!'

Now I snatch my hands away.

'No, Christie. Your life is not a lie. We explained how it was, I thought you were okay with it?'

'Okay with it? What choice do I have? You and Dad brought me up as *your* child. The one and only Christie, how lucky I've always felt, the whole village marvelled at what wonderful parents you were! But all the time, you knew! You knew one day I'd have to deal with *this*!'

'We did our best.'

'Your best?' I hiss. 'You did your best? Well, okay, I was just about getting to grips with you *doing your best*, when all my childhood is put on display for the entire world to pour over!'

'Christie, please—'

'I presume you knew about *Evolution*?'

'Yes, but Madeline thought—'

'*Madeline thought*! Well yippity do!' I snarl.

'Madeline thought you needed to have your own identity, before she went public about you being her daughter.'

'I *have* my own identity! I'm me, Christina Anne Harris! Do you not think you gave me opportunities to explore myself over the years?'

'Yes but...' sighs Mum.

'It's one of the many things you drummed into me. "Know your own mind, Christie, don't follow the crowd, think for yourself, set your own moral standards and stick to them"! Should I go on?'

'It was out of my control, out of our control, we had managed to pacify Maddie with your career. But she's ambitious; she didn't want you to settle for being a teacher.'

'Settle for being a teacher! I haven't settled for being a teacher, Mum. I was born to be a teacher.' I thump my chest. 'It's in here, being a teacher is who I am.'

'I know that, Christie, but Maddie doesn't.'

'Well, I hope she's a fast learner!'

'This is why, why I've tried to keep you two apart so long. Madeline is driven. She always has a new idea, a new project, she has to be doing something all the time. I knew she'd make your life into a new mission.'

'And she has. Congratulations, mother, on your insight! But then, she is your daughter!'

'Yes, she is—'

I snort.

'... And I love her very much—'

Again, I snort.

'... Despite all her failings. We all have failings, me more than most, as you're apt at pointing out today—'

And again, I snort.

'... Fundamentally, Maddie is a good person. She does good things—'

'Not for me!'

'How many years did she encourage you with your art? How many, Christie?'

'That's different; she did that to gain access to my life! My life!'

'She could have done that at any time. She did it to help you, to give you a purpose, structure, something to work towards.'

'To make me more like her; with her projects and glittering career,' I sneer.

'She walked away from her glittering career. It wasn't enough. She realised she'd lost more than she could ever gain.'

'Too late. She realised too late!'

'She was the same age you are now, when she left her glittering career. Do you think you could make that choice?'

'We are completely different people.'

'She was born to act. You were born to teach. Could you walk away from teaching?'

I stare at her. How dare she ask me that question?

'Well, could you?' she pushes.

'Never; I will never give up my teaching!'

'Good. I hope you never do… But you see, Maddie gave up the two most precious things in her life. First, she gave up you. Then she gave up her acting because of you.' The bench sighs as Mum stands up. 'Think about it,' she tosses over her shoulder as she makes her way back to the house.

'Think about it,' I mutter under my breath. Why should I? Seems to me like Madeline is quite shite at doing things right.

Close Encounter

The intimacy shocks me to my core.

And here comes Madeline's number one admirer now, practically galloping towards me, with his practically, permanently-etched scowl on his forehead.

'Do you mind if I join you?' His tone indicates that he doesn't give a monkey's if I mind or not. Sure enough, he settles himself down in the spot Mum minutes before left.

I edge away from him, not far enough to spare myself a whiff of his zesty aftershave.

'Do you know what your mother is doing now?'

'Rushing round, getting ready for the lovely Madeline, I guess.'

'You're right,' he says mildly. 'She rushed in, and started gabbling on about defrosting chicken fillets, peeling potatoes, cutting vegetables. She's a marvel, isn't she?'

He doesn't give me chance to answer.

'Yes, she just gets on with it. Whatever is thrown at her, she just gets on with it. It's called displacement activity, Christie. As long as you are keeping your mind busy with one thing, you don't have to deal with the other.'

'She always likes to be busy.' I shift uneasily away from him.

'I've noticed it often with Anne,' he carries on, as if I haven't spoken. 'But today there's an added urgency about it.'

'Well, that'll be because *Madeline* is coming to stay,' I hiss. 'Everything must be perfect for *her*!'

A hot, bubbling feeling surges up through my body, a feeling I'm struggling to put a name to. One I've never experienced before.

Jealousy!

'So, I asked her,' again he carries on as if I haven't said a word. 'I said "Anne, slow down, what's the matter?". And she said, "Christie and I have just had a full and frank exchange of opinions about how things are". By that, I assume you've had a row?'

He turns his body to face me, our knees touch. His jaw is tight, and the sinews in his neck protrude. His eyes challenge mine. 'Well, Christie? Care to enlighten me?' he asks softly, dangerously.

'It's none of your business.' I shrug, trying to ignore the goose bumps on my arms, and the rush of blood to my ears.

He smiles. 'Oh, Christie, you have much to learn about me!'

'Really? Do you suppose I have any desire, to learn anything about you? You flatter yourself Miles, you really do.' I can feel the heat of a flush creeping up my chest to my neck.

'Whether you have any *desire* to learn anything about me, is irrelevant, Christie. Like it or not, I'm here to stay.' Resting back, he folds his arms across his chest. 'So?'

'So, mind your own business,' I snap.

He stands up, arms still folded, and bends forward so his nose nearly touches mine. 'Listen, and listen good, I will explain this very simply, so that even you can understand. I have known Madeline and your parents for many years. All they have ever shown me, is kindness and respect… So, if anyone wishes them harm, let's just say, they'll have me to answer to.'

'Are you threatening me?' My eyes must be like saucers.

'I'm explaining how it is.'

'All I want, is to be left alone! My life has been turned upside down, through no fault of my own, and you, you come out here accusing me of wishing my mum harm!'

'You've upset her!'

'I'm upset!' Why doesn't he get it? A single tear slides from my eye. 'Is anyone jumping to my defence?' I shake my head. Turn away from him, before more tears escape.

The bench groans as he slumps back down. He peers round at my face, and passes me a hanky.

I snatch it from him.

No grace.

Blow my nose. 'Hay fever,' I lie.

'If I've added to that upset, then I'm sorry. We all want what's best for you; including me.'

'If that were true, why all this?'

'Your life has always been charmed, Christie. You have no idea what it's like for some people.'

I cross my arms, look into the distance. Right now, I don't care what life is like for other people, my own is enough. I can hear the distant hum of traffic from the main road, birds chirping merrily and trees sway elegantly in the breeze. Everything normal is going on about me.

But I feel arhhh. I want to explode, scream and shout. I want to hit out, and destroy. I want to rip off my skin, and give myself even more physical pain, to match the turmoil inside, so that everyone can see my pain exposed.

Miles sighs. 'Right now, Christie, you have an opportunity to find out who you really are.'

My cheeks hurt from clenching my jaw. 'I know who I am,' I say very slowly.

'You know who you are when you are surrounded by good things, good people. When it's easy to make good choices—'

My fingers dig into my arms, I keep my mouth tight shut because if I speak, I can't ever put the words back.

'... Like today. Do you care how much you've upset your mum? Are you going to leave her fretting about you? Does she deserve to suffer, just because you're suffering?'

My fingernails dig deeper into my arms, hurting me now.

'... So, who are you? Are you the caring, compassionate, cheerful Christie, everyone sees every day? Or, deep down, are you selfish, spoilt and spiteful? Who are you, Christie?'

'*She knew* I'd have to deal with all this! *She knew*, and never gave me a clue my life was so mixed up. Didn't prepare me!'

'She's spent twenty-four years preparing you.'

'Not for this charade!' I fling my arm up in the air.

'It's not a charade, *this is reality*. It's what the rest of us deal with every day.'

'Okay, so it's normal to find out your mum is your grandmother, and your real mum is a national treasure, who everyone seemingly adores?'

'It's normal to have to deal with everyday hassles.'

'Believe me, *Miles*, this is more than an everyday hassle!'

'Yes, yes, it is. This is you having to independently deal with your own dilemma, which incidentally, your mum, dad and Madeline have been dealing with for years.'

'They created it!'

Miles sighs and shakes his head. 'Can you imagine, what it must have been like, for each of them to make the choices they made? And stick with them.'

I don't want to think about any of them! This is about me. 'Well Madeline did very nicely out of it! Madeline De-Muir, the flawless charity worker, quintessential English rose, whose heart is as pure as driven snow, the darling of Hollywood.'

'Do not mistake Maddie Harris, for Madeline De-Muir! I work for Madeline De-Muir, but Maddie is my friend, the real deal.'

'They're the same person!'

'No.' He shakes his head; a flop of black hair falls forward; he scrapes it back into place and smiles. 'No. Maddie is the flawed Madeline, she's a rare English rose, she's the most passionate person I have ever met, and most certainly not, remotely the darling of Hollywood.'

'And I should care, because?'

'For you, Christie, she's prepared to expose her flaws and her mistakes. For you, she's prepared to risk losing the public's adoration. Because of you, she's passionate for young people to be given the chance to shine. Because of you, she left acting behind.'

'How very commendable. Maybe she should get a medal! How about, she could have been a single mum and surrounded me with love, and then maybe she'd have earned my respect.' The pain of her rejection pours spite into my heart.

'She can't change the past.'

'But she's trying to change my future. *My future.*' I shake my head. Dab at my drippy nose.

'You're a talented artist, Christie. She couldn't stand back and let you waste that talent.'

I'm exhausted with this argument, can scarcely raise my voice above a whisper. 'It isn't wasted, it's shared. I'm a teacher, and teachers share their talents.'

'Madeline wanted you to have the chance to become successful, a real artist.'

I shake my head; he doesn't get it. 'I am a real artist. I could have made the choice to submit work to galleries myself. She took that choice from me.'

'She knows you better than that. She knew you'd never risk being rejected.'

The grass tickles my ankles as I walk away from him. The garden promises to be beautiful through the summer; it's a relaxed mum and dad kind of garden. Just enough lawn to mow, not too much. Deep swaggering borders filled with perennials and shrubs, just enough to weed, not too much. A rickety bench and a bird table. A washing line with an old wooden prop. They probably love it already!

I assume Madeline bought this house for them. She chose well. It has charm.

I feel sick. With envy? Regret? I wonder if I'll get to spend much time here now. Already, I feel like an outsider.

Seems like Madeline has all the bases covered. Mum and Dad have the return of their prodigal child; Miles is her dutiful and adoring PA, and to rank up the attention, she's got a sodding broken ankle!

Well they're all welcome to each other!

'Christie?' Miles has slunk up behind me. 'Do you think she was right?'

'What?'

'Was Madeline right? Would you ever have risked being turned down?'

'Well…' I offer a tight smile. 'I guess we'll never know now, will we?'

'I guess not, but for what it's worth, I think she knows you better than you'd like to admit.'

I turn and look at him fully. A pitying smile is pulling at his lips, his hands are casually hooked in his pockets, and his face is tilted to one side as he squints against the sun. And again, the urge to slap his arrogant face is unbearable. 'Do you think I care what you think? You don't even know me!'

He shuffles, and looks towards the kitchen where Mum is at the window, head down, probably peeling potatoes. 'Did you really trip up?'

His change of subject catches me off guard. He lifts my chin with the crook of his forefinger. I go to slap his hand away, and he catches my hand in his. 'Play nice, Christie, your mother's watching.'

I look up, and Mum waves on cue. Miles lifts my hands, palms up, and examines the grazes. I watch, as the pulse in my exposed wrist quickens.

'So, was it a trip, or did you decide to drown your sorrows with your two budding alcoholic friends, and end up having a drunken fall?' He begins to trace the scratches on my hand.

The intimacy shocks me to my core.

'They look quite deep,' he continues.

I snatch my hand away, but can still feel the traces of his fingertips. 'My friends are far from alcoholics; they only drink socially.'

'If that's what you like to think.'

'So, I take it you haven't spoken to the lovely Mrs Price today?'

'No?' He frowns.

'Perhaps you should.' I raise my brows, and catch the confusion in his eyes.

'Mrs Price knows only to contact me in cases of emergency.'

'Mustn't have been an emergency then!'

'What happened?' Again, he picks up my hand.

'Bunty Hargreaves happened!' I snatch my hand back.

'Bunty Hargreaves did this?'

'Bunty Hargreaves decided she'd figured out who Christie is. She got it wrong; she thought it was Trudy. As we were leaving, she started taking our photos.'

'I told everyone no pictures!' snaps Miles.

'Obviously, she didn't take any notice of you.'

Miles mutters something under his breath. 'And?'

'And Trudy objected to having her photo taken, physically, by snatching Bunty's phone. I tripped getting out of the car. Trudy was livid; I wanted to stop her from—'

'Getting herself into trouble.' Miles nods. 'I see. So, did Mrs Price sort it all out? She should have let me know.'

'She let us clean ourselves up, and sorted us some clean clothes out. And then she...' I feel the colour drain from my face as the memory of the car journey seeps back.

'Then she what? What did she do?' coaxes Miles.

'She drove us home.' My words are hushed, solemn.

'You let her drive you home? The woman's not safe!'

'I know.'

'She used to do rally driving!'

'I know.'

'She's a demon behind the wheel.'

'I know.'

'She doesn't understand the concept of traffic lights and roundabouts.'

'I know.'

'So why did you let her drive you home?'

'I didn't know.'

Miles drops his head into his hands. His shoulders start to shudder, and he shakes his head. He covers his eyes with one hand, then forces his other fist into his mouth. A howl escapes. He drops his hand down. Tears stream down his crumpled face. 'I'm… Sorry… I… Can't… Help… It…' he splutters between gasps. The air is filled with the most resounding belly laugh I have ever heard.

He's laughing at me!

I turn on my heel, and walk back towards the house, the sound of Miles roaring with laughter still echoing in my ears.

Out of the Frying Pan

Trust the Trolls to jolly things along!

Mum's not in the kitchen. Pans line up along the counter, sliced potatoes in the first, green beans in the second, carrots and turnip in the next, the last one has a Snicker and a note:

Christie, peace offering,
knew you'd peep in all the pans.
Mum x

It does look tempting, I've only had soup, but if I eat it, it's kind of like accepting what she's said to me makes sense. I don't want to eat it! I want to throw it at the wall, or stamp on it, or, even more nastily, hand it back to her.

I click the kettle on, make myself a coffee, sit down, peel the wrapper halfway down the bar and dunk it into my coffee, one, two, three, four, five, the bar melts into my mouth, sooo good! Chocolate dribbles down my chin.

'Looks like you're enjoying that!'

'Dad!'

'Don't sound so surprised, I do live here!' He drops a kiss on the top of my head and sits down opposite me. 'Now, what have you been up to? Your mum says you've been falling over, and I can see you've grazed your face. Have those two friends of yours been leading you astray again with some of that horrid vodka?'

'Sadly not, it wouldn't have hurt as much if I'd been drunk. I tripped getting out of Trudy's car, and landed fully face down.'

'Ouch.' Dad scrunches up his face.

'Then Suzi opened her car door, hit me on the back of my head, and knocked me back down again!' I moan.

'Double ouch,' says Dad. 'Was she by any chance tipsy?'

'As a toad, but racked with guilt today.'

'And rightly so! You young ones, I don't know.'

'Oh, I think you do.'

'And Mum says the two of you have had words.' Dad spears me with his piercing eyes.

'You could say that.' I force the last bit of Snicker into my mouth. It doesn't taste as good as the first bite, has lost its appeal. I gulp it down without savouring the taste, and swallow. I can feel its progress to my stomach.

All of a sudden, the fight has gone out of me. I know all of this isn't just Mum's fault, if any of it, but it's like I want to punish her for how I feel. And I know she's been the best Mum ever. I'll admit it to myself, I'm making her suffer because she isn't making this go away. Until now, I didn't think there was anything she couldn't sort out. Somehow, ridiculously, I know, it feels like she's let me down, even though deep down I know she never could.

'What would you say?' he asks.

I close my eyes. What would I say? Think, think, she deserves for me to snap and snarl after what I've been through. I rest my elbows on the table and cover my face with my hands... Still not managing to be invisible. 'To be honest Dad, I don't know what to say.'

'She's very upset.'

'So am I.'

'And more than a little disappointed.'

'Me too.' Tears wet the palms of my hands. 'I'm disappointed.'

In both of us.

I hear Dad moving towards me, feel his embrace. I want to fall into his comfortable bear hug like I usually do, but my body won't relax, a shudder and a sob escapes.

'Oh, Christie.' His voice is hoarse. 'None of us wanted to cause you all this pain.'

'But you all have.' I wipe my nose on the already well-used hanky Miles gave me. 'You knew, Dad. You knew, and now all my life is a lie.'

'No, it's not a lie, all your memories are exactly the same. What has changed is the way you're cross-referencing them with what has happened.' He squeezes my shoulders. 'You'll always be my daugh—'

'Don't say it!' I pull away from him. 'I'm not! Am I?'

'You are, Christie! In my heart, I have never known you as anything else. I couldn't love you any more if...'

'If I were your own child?'

'Okay then! If that's what you want. Yes, if you were my *own* child. Does that make it better, Christie?' he demands quietly.

Looking at him, I can see the hurt carved on his face, somehow it feels more profound than with Mum. 'It makes it the truth!'

'We are all God's—'

'Don't! Don't start with God, don't start with God now my life is a lie! Start with the truth.'

'The truth, is, we did our best.'

'Really?' I find his simple truth hard to take.

'It was a difficult time for each of us.' Dad sits in the chair beside me, resting his arms on the table, as if still reaching to make a connection with me.

I turn, look him in the eyes. 'Was it the best for me? Did you do your best for *me*, or for *Madeline*?' That's the truth I need.

'We did our best for both of you. Maddie was sixteen, just a child, it would have been...' Dad wipes his hand across his face. 'She did love you; she does love you.'

'Well that's reassuring!'

'We just wanted to give her a chance at acting, we honestly didn't think she'd become the star she did. If she'd not been given that chance, well, she would have probably ended up resenting you. And that would have been no life, for either of you.'

'So, you'd no intention of keeping me?' Bile rises in my throat; I swallow it down. 'You thought she'd come back after—'

'We thought—'

'You thought she'd have her little adventure at drama school, then come back and...' I can't say it. I can't say "take me back".

'I couldn't understand.' Dad shakes his head.

'Why she didn't want me?' There, I'd said it. The words I'd dreaded hearing. She didn't want me. Both Dad's hands grip mine on the table. Tears sting my eyes. The comfort of those familiar strong hands around mine is hard to resist. I drop my head and rest it on my forearms. I can't bear for him to see my tears, but can't give up the comfort of his reassuring touch.

'Christie, I'm sorry, I couldn't understand her. Couldn't believe she'd just go off.'

'Leaving me with Mum and you.' I raise my head, and look at him now. Can see the pain of history imprinted on his face.

'I couldn't understand how she could leave you... Broke my heart that she could.' He shakes his head and looks away. 'Maddie got her part in *The Fallen*, and that was it.'

'The rest is history, I know.' I can't keep the bitterness from my voice. I just can't.

'We knew then, we knew she'd never put you first, we already couldn't have given you back even if she'd wanted us to. We had it all made legal. Maddie was more than willing to sign you over to us; we couldn't risk your life being made into a pantomime.'

'You mean, like it has been now?'

'Christie, you were so precious to us, *because* of how we'd been with Maddie. In a way she made us better parents for you. You don't know it, Christie, but you're strong.'

'Ha.' The hollow sound echoes round the kitchen. An echo of the emptiness inside of me.

'You've no idea, but you really are.' He grips my hands harder, gives them a shake. 'We made sure of it, like I keep saying, we did our best. *You* are *our best*.'

'I know I'm behaving like a spoilt brat, but I can't seem to stop being angry. I feel let down by all of you, and it's eating away at me. I hate feeling this lost, out of control. Why am I being so pathetic? Dad?'

'Because for the first time, you're not sure what's going to happen next. Like you keep saying, we've all known for years. Until now, you've just been trundling along. Now, Christie, now is *your* time to shine, to let everyone see what an amazing person you are.'

'I hardly feel amazing. Look at me, Dad, I'm a crumbling wreck. She didn't want me, and you had no choice.'

'We had a choice. We made it. We chose you. If anything, you should feel more loved because of that.' Even though he smiles his reassurance, I can see the strain on his face.

Even though I didn't start this whole chaotic charade, I know I'm adding to that strain.

Slowly, without warning, guilt begins to seep into my soul. I turn away from him, unable to witness the wounds I'm inflicting on this noble man. 'Dad, you should have told me the truth.'

'When?' He shrugs. 'When should we have told you? When you were seven, or twelve, or sixteen, eighteen or twenty-one? When do you think you'd have coped with it better than you are doing now?'

My throat is so tight I can hardly talk. 'I don't know. Anytime but now.' I look out of the window. Blue sky with fluffy white clouds slowly moving eastwards. The world just going on as normal. 'I wish things were different.'

He suddenly looks old, tired. 'It will get better, once you meet Maddie.'

'I don't want to meet her!' I yank my hands away from his, and clutch them to my chest.

'It's not just about what you want. Madeline could have forced it at any time.'

'And she would have been slated in the press.'

'I'm sure Miles would have packaged it, in such a compassionate way, as to have people sympathising over her lost years with you.'

'I can't believe I'm hearing this from you, Dad! She didn't want me!'

'But she does now. Look, Christie, I'm trying to help you, and if you won't meet her halfway, you'll end up being the one who is vilified in the press.'

'How, when I've done nothing wrong?'

'Maddie has put a lot of work into launching *Evolution*, and you're likely to become an in-demand artist because of that.'

'So, I'd be the ungrateful brat.'

'Something like that.' Dad nods.

Unbelievable. 'And you and Mum would let that happen?'

'We wouldn't be able to stop it.' He really does look old, defeated. She's done this to him, my dad, my rock, crumbling, just like me. His fingers are linked together resting on the table, he's probably praying, praying we sort this mess out.

The fight drains from me, my body feels limp. 'I have no choice, have I, Dad?'

His face softens. 'You do have some choices. You're smart and you're strong, Christie. This has all been sprung on you.'

'Everything is spinning out of control, out of my control.' Closing my eyes, I rest my head on the cool table. I'm talking to my dad, and it's hard to accept, that actually, he isn't my *real* dad. I know somewhere out there is probably Madeline's first love, maybe her only one. He obviously didn't hang about to meet me. Another rejection, but at least I don't have to meet that one face to face.

Only a few days ago I was happily looking forward to a relaxing break from school, not a care in the world, and here I am stuck in the middle of a family reshuffle. *The Jeremy Kyle Show* would have had a field day.

Dad stands and moves beside me, rests his hand on my shoulder, I lift my head to look at him. 'Well, Christie, *you* decide what outcome *you* want from this situation, then work your way back to where we are now.'

'And figure out what steps I need to take to make it happen.' This is a strategy Dad has talked me through many times over the years, to tackle situations I thought beyond my ability to deal with. None as complex as this.

Dad allows himself a half-smile. 'Good girl, Christie, you remember. What else should you aim for?'

'A win-win solution,' I reply.

'For all of us. Okay, so, what is the first step?'

'Ask myself what I want,' I parrot from the voice in my head.

'And then?'

'Consider what everyone else wants.'

'And then?' He raises his brows and tilts his head.

'Make it happen.'

'Simple!' He slaps the table.

'Maybe not that simple.'

'But definitely achievable. I feel better already, knew you'd sort it out, my girl! Right, I'm off to find your mother to tell her the good news.' And off he goes, probably to bring Mum up to speed.

From tears and tantrums to tactics in about two minutes. The way he turns things round is unbelievable. I could almost eat another Snicker; except my coffee is cold, and Mum only gave me one. I click the kettle on again and start rummaging through cupboards, now I've decided I want chocolate nothing else will do. I hear footsteps, probably Dad coming back.

'Dad, do you know if Mum's got any chocolate stashed?' I look up, feel the blood drain from my face as I see Miles. 'Oh, it's you.'

'Try behind the biscuit tin,' he says, and nods towards the cupboard he got the biscuits from earlier. 'I think I spotted a stockpile there.'

I manage to mutter, 'Thank you.' I find Mum's chocolate stash. Miles empties my cold coffee away and rinses the mug. He then takes over making my drink, adding his own mug to the counter, a tad too close to mine for comfort. 'Is this what you do for Madeline, make coffee all day.'

Oh, why does he make me such a bitch?

'Some days, yes, other times it's all work, work, and more work. Coffee two?' He sounds so upbeat. I feel like slapping him like Dad slapped the table.

I nod. He turns back towards the counter; he doesn't look bad from behind. Why I'm bothering to look, I have no idea, because his personality is abysmal. He turns back towards me, and catches me ogling his butt. A ghost of a smile flickers over his face. Why can one look from his smug face turn my insides to jelly? He puts both mugs onto the table.

'I don't mind if you dunk your Snicker, I know it's a habit of yours.'

I feel myself blush.

He casually pulls out a chair and sits down opposite me with a full-on smirk. 'There's not much I don't know about you.'

'You think?'

'And what I don't know, I'm sure I'll enjoy finding out.' He starts rapping a tuneless beat with his fingers on the table.

'Don't be too sure!' I snap.

Back in bitch mode. Again.

'I'm enjoying it already.' He leans back in his chair and folds his arms. 'Figuring out what makes you tick, what makes you blush.'

Two can play at that game. 'I wonder, Miles, how you'll feel when Madeline and I are reconciled?'

'I'll be pleased with a job well done.' He stretches his arms up, then casually links his fingers behind his head, resting back in his chair.

'Really? How long have you been working towards this reunion? How much time and effort have you put in? Are you not just a tiny bit worried, that when Madeline and I get together, you'll not be needed?'

'Good try, but you'll need to do better than that.'

Now his foot is randomly tapping away. He doesn't take his eyes off me as he sips his coffee, mine is left untouched and I'm itching to have my Snicker.

He nods toward my coffee. 'Go ahead, dunk it, I know you want to.'

'No, I'll save it for later. Actually, I think I'm going to go home, to my friends.'

He leans towards me. 'I thought you might like to make some plans about *Evolution*.'

'No, you and Madeline can do that. I want to go home and make some plans of my own.' I slip the Snicker bar into my pocket; I might like that later. I pour the coffee away, wash the mug, dry it and put it away. I do not want him accusing me of leaving a mess. 'Do you know what, Miles? A holiday sounds like a good idea to me.' I stalk out of the kitchen and walk slap bang into Dad.

'Whoa, where are you off to in such a hurry?' he asks.

'On holiday!' I wink at him to include him in the tease.

'Anywhere nice?'

'Don't know yet, but I'll send you a postcard.'

'Christie, you can't just go off. Not now!' says Miles from the kitchen doorway.

I turn, look at him and smile. 'I think you'll find I can do whatever I want.' It feels nice to have the upper hand for the very first time, and I'm going to savour it. I turn away, towards Dad. 'Is Mum still upstairs?'

'She is.'

'Mum!' I holler up to her. 'I'm going back home, you've enough to do looking after Madeline.'

'Wait! Wait!' Mum bounds down the stairs as fast as any lady in her sixties can. 'But I've sorted a room out for you now!'

'Another time, Mum, I'm sorry for—'

'Being a stroppy little madam?' Mum fills in.

'Well, yes… No.' Why am I sorry? 'I'm sorry for upsetting you, you're a good Mum. Actually, you're the best.' I lean forward, her cheek feels soft to my kiss. 'But I need to go, so bye for now. See you, Dad.'

I nod towards Miles, don't bother to waste words on him, pick up my bag and walk out the front door. I pull the door closed behind me, don't want spectators.

But still, how brave am I?

I pull out my mobile and phone Suzi as I walk down the drive. Come on, come on, answer!

'Hi, Suzi, are you fit to drive?'

'Possibly. Just about, why?'

'I'm desperate to get away from here.'

'You've only just got there, what's happened?' I can hear the impatience in her voice.

'Long story, short on time. Will you come, quickly?'

'On my way. But you'd better fill me in on all the details on the way home. Byeeee.'

'Bye.' The phone disconnects.

It's not a particularly busy road, but I feel slightly on show stood on the kerb with my overnight bag slung at my feet. I must look like I've been turfed out!

I peep back towards the house. No one is looking; I suppose I could wait inside the grounds, behind a shrub or something, hidden from the house and the road.

I sling my bag over my shoulder nonchalantly, and then tiptoe onto the gravel drive and dart behind a Flowering Blackcurrant bush, unseen, I think. I'm not sure how long it's going to take Suzi to get here, maybe fifteen minutes. I might as well make myself comfy. Patting down my bag on the ground, I sit on it.

Oh, and I've got my Snicker too!

It won't be the same without hot coffee to dunk it in, but still. I unwrap it, try to make it last, by sucking it. It's not as good as dunking obviously, but not too bad. The trouble is, the bit you're hold of starts to melt inside the wrapper. I stuff the last piece in my mouth, and let it ooze about. Yum, all gone, may as well lick the wrapper, as I'm all alone. I do hate waste, especially chocolate.

A car scrunches on the drive, it must be Suzi. She must have driven lickety-split. I don't want her knocking on the door; I'll just stick my head out and…

Oh no no no no no! It's not Suzi, unless she's nicked a Daimler. It must be, oh no can't be. A driver gets out.

He opens the passenger door, leans in, helps the occupant out, and...Shit, steadies her on crutches!

Madeline.

My mouth goes dry, and my stomach feels hollow, despite the two Snickers I've eaten in the last half an hour. I'm so glad I got out of there when I did, or I'd be trapped now. The driver knocks on the front door, I peer through the bush as best as I can; it's a bit prickly this close. Miles appears and dashes forward to help Madeline.

'Where is she?' I hear Madeline ask.

'She's gone, you've missed her.'

'What do you mean gone!' she squeaks. 'I left as soon as you phoned, did she know I was on my way?'

He shakes his head. 'No, she thought you were coming later.'

'Oh, Miles, I just wanted to meet her.'

I'm shocked at how needy she sounds, almost the total opposite of her screen persona.

'You will,' soothes Miles. I'm transfixed by his clear devotion to her.

'But when? I've been waiting years...'

Her vulnerability is palpable, and the fear of being discovered is overtaken by my curiosity. I strain to hear them clearly.

'Soon, Maddie, be patient for a little while longer. She's skittish.'

'Skittish? She's not a bloody pony, Miles! Sorry, sorry, I just want her to like me.'

'And she will.' Again, the soothing tones. 'Everyone does. Come on, let's get you inside before anyone recognizes you.'

I've got sunshine in my pocket blasts from my phone, I snatch it from my pocket and disconnect Suzi's flashing name.

Trust the Trolls to jolly things along!

'Actually, Madeline, maybe you're in time after all.'

I close my eyes and groan.

'There you are, Christie. How fortunate, Madeline and I were just talking about you.'

'I heard.' I risk a peep. He looks just as smug as he sounds.

'I'm not sure what you've been doing behind this bush, but the sunshine in your pocket gave you away.' He reaches out, and plucks a twig from my hair. 'But perhaps now is a good time to come out.'

'Why, when I've been having a perfectly good time in here on my own?'

'I can see. You've managed to get chocolate all over your face.'

'Oh...'

'Quite.' He passes me another hanky.

I snatch it from him.

Level of grace... Zero.

'Do you know, finding you here, like this, has made my day?'

'*Regrettably, Miles,* I cannot say the same.' I hiss, rubbing at my face.

'Come on, might as well get it over with.' He pulls me up, and picks up my bag so I can't sit back down, then turns to walk back to the house.

'I'm not ready,' I scarcely whisper the words.

He turns back to me. Is that sympathy? 'She only wants to meet you, come on, how bad can it be?'

Does he really want to know? I'm dizzy with a million things spinning around my head. My hands are shaking, I feel sick. It feels like the ground is moving. I feel sick, and hot, and my feet will not move.

'Christie.' He reaches out and catches my hand; our eyes meet. 'Just say "hello", I'll help Madeline inside, by then your taxi should have arrived, and you can escape, okay?'

I nod, and swallow.

'Good.' He leads me out from behind the bush.

'Christie!' Madeline is beaming ear to ear. She starts to make her way awkwardly towards us, her lack of practice on crutches evident with every step, as she drags them through the gravel.

'Hello.' It sounds like a croak; my throat is so tight. I'd forgot Miles is holding my hand, until he squeezes it.

'I have waited so long! And look at you two, getting along so well already. It's like a dream.' Her voice sounds breathless. She lunges the short remaining distance, and clinches me in a bear hug; her full weight on me, crutches clanging to the ground at either side.

Miles steps forward. 'Steady, Maddie,' he says, half lifting her weight from me. 'Christie's had an accident too, don't want the two of you on the ground.'

I disentangle myself, stoop to pick up the crutches and pass them back to her. She takes them from me, and settles her weight between them. Her eyes never leave my face, it's like she's trying to read my mind. I feel heat rising up my chest.

'Your photos don't do you justice; you are so pretty.'

'And you are much younger than I remember, Auntie Maddie.'

'Touché, but I think, from now on, simply Maddie will do.'

'Maddie, okay.' I nod. I am strong. I am smart. I can do this... 'Maddie, I need to figure out how I feel about this situation before I get swept along with...' I scrunch up my face. 'You, actually.' *I've got sunshine in my pocket* blasts out again. 'Excuse me, but I need to get this... Hi Suzi.'

'Turn around,' she whispers. I turn and there she is, halfway out of her car, one foot in, one on the kerb. 'Is that Madeline?'

'Yes. Of course, I know you're in a hurry, I'm coming.'

'No, no! I want to meet her!'

'Honestly, one second, Suzi.' I hang up, and wave her back in the car. Thankfully she does get back in. I turn back to Madeline and Miles, cross my fingers behind my back, and force an overbright smile. 'Sorry, got to dash, Suzi's in a mega rush, hot date, I think. Bye.' Snatching up my bag, I turn and scurry towards my getaway car.

'Oh, right, bye then.' Madeline sounds deflated.

'See you later,' adds Miles.

I wave with my free hand without turning back or answering, and prepare to meet the wrath of Suzi.

Escape?

"I wonder if they share a room."

I get in the car, plonk my bag down and wait. Suzi starts the engine and sets off. The relief of escaping Madeline and Miles far outweighs the trauma of dealing with a seriously miffed Suzi.

After the fiasco of a drunken Suzi yesterday, I feel she ought to cut me some slack.

Not a word.

Silence stretches out between us. I knew she'd want to meet Madeline De-Muir at some point. She's been a fan for years, but I'm not ready. Not ready to let my best friend defect to the other side.

Maybe she will anyway. The sting of her silence feeds my self-doubt.

'Thank you for coming,' I mumble. I notice a slight acknowledgement. Vaguely encouraged, I flounder on. 'And I'm sorry, I know you want to meet her, but she'd only just arrived, and I've only just met her. I don't know how to deal with all this. And I don't want you to like her better than you like me, and now you're not talking to me, and it's not fair.' I end with a gulp, my throat tight, as once again tears threaten.

Suzi indicates, slows the car, mounts the kerb in a very Mrs Price way, stops and switches on her hazard lights. Turning to me, she fixes me with one of her scary looks.

She says nothing.

Waits.

She is very good at this! A tactic she's learned from her mum, I think. Her theory is, if she waits long enough, she'll get a confession. So, wish me luck.

'I'm sorry, Suzi; I've had an awful day. When I got to Mum and Dad's, I found Mum and Miles having a cosy chat.' I pause for effect. I can tell Suzi wants to interrogate me, because she is still gripping the steering wheel.

I risk carrying on. 'Apparently, Maddie had some kind of accident, and has broken her ankle. Miles arranged for her to come to stay at Mum and Dad's house, until she can get about a bit better.' Again, I pause for effect. 'I had a sharp exchange of words with Mum.' I close my eyes to try and banish the memory.

'What about?' Suzi's curiosity gets the better of her. 'You two never argue.'

'About *darling Madeline*, and how she's ruined my life! Then Miles Hepworth, another blight in my life, took it upon himself to lecture me.'

Suzi releases her grip on the steering wheel, and turns towards me. 'What about?'

'About how I'd upset Mum. Apparently, he, Mum, Dad and Maddie are best buddies.'

'Nooo?' squeaks Suzi, eyes wide.

'They all go on holiday together! Can you believe it?' A knot begins to tighten in my stomach.

'No! Well… That explains why your Mum and Dad have encouraged you to come away with me and Trudy.'

'Doesn't it just!' That nasty feeling is bubbling inside me again. 'So that they can all play happy families without me!'

Suzi's eyes widen even more. 'I wonder if they share a room.'

'What are you on about?'

'Madeline and Miles! I wonder if they share a room, on holiday.'

'I don't know! I don't care!'

Oh, I think I do!

The knot tightens even more.

'But with your dad being a vicar, they aren't married.'

'Su-zi! Shut up!'

'Only saying.'

'Well don't!' I heave a great sigh. 'I'm trying to tell you what's happened *today*.'

'I know but…'

'Shh!' I carry on, while my patience lasts. 'Miles gives me a lecture about what kind of person I am. And makes me cry…' I remember.

'The pig.'

'Exactly. And then he *assumes* all these scratches came from me falling over drunk.'

'How rude!'

'Precisely, he even referred to you and Trudy as trainee alcoholics!'

'Well, he's gone right down in my estimation, that's for sure! The nerve of him,' says saint Suzi, who only likes the odd drink.

'So, I put him straight on that. Oh, and then I told him about that crazy woman driving us home.'

'Don't! She was something else.'

'And do you know what he said?'

'Go on.'

'Nothing! He just howled with laughter!' I huff. 'So, I just left him there, chewing on his fist. Next Dad had words with me,' I gabble on, eager to fully commit Suzi to camp Christie.

'What did he say?'

'Much the same as Miles, but with more tact. And he doesn't know about our near-death experience in the car with the mad Mrs Price… So, he didn't do the hysterical laughter thing.'

'It wasn't funny.'

'I know.'

'So, what about your dad, he usually comes up with practical advice?'

'He did, that's why I phoned for you.'

'He told you to leave!'

'No, he told me to think about what I really want out of this situation, work out what everyone else wants, then make it happen. And to do that, I need to have some space. I knew Madeline would be arriving at some point… I needed to leave before she arrived.'

'But you didn't quite make it!'

'Ohhh, I did. I was in the garden hiding behind a Flowering Blackcurrant bush when she arrived. I was at quite a safe distance… Close enough to see and hear what was going on, but not be seen and heard myself… Until, that is, you phoned the first time.'

'You didn't answer.'

'Funny that! I was too busy being escorted out from behind that bush by the ever-helpful Miles, with a very apt musical accompaniment, to go with my troll hair.' I point to my tufty hair.

'Oh, ha ha, sorry. Slightly embarrassing for you then.'

'You could say that. So, the first time I meet Madeline De-Muir, I'm being dragged from behind a bush, by Miles, with twigs in my hair and chocolate smeared over my face. And all you want is—'

'An intro. Sorry… But it did look like you were already relaxed with each other, Miles was holding your hand! What's all that about?'

I grit my teeth. 'He was making sure I didn't make a bid for freedom! So, when you phoned the second time…' I shrug.

'You escaped.'

'Bingo.'

Suzi's shoulders finally relax as she slumps back in her seat, all her indignation evaporates. She nods her head once, as if she's just made an important decision, clicks off the hazards, and off we go.

'It's time you start being the one making all the choices. If Madeline wants you to play happy families, she needs to play by your rules.'

'Just what I wanted to hear. On my side, then?'

'Only since we were three years old… You do know, Trudy is going to want to kill someone?'

I look at Suzi, and smile. 'Oh well, never mind.' The thought of Trudy in a righteous rant is *very* satisfying. Maybe everything will turn out fine after all. 'We can always go and visit her in prison.'

Commando

On my hands and knees.

Back at home, with my feet tucked up on the sofa, and a mug of coffee clutched between my hands, I am happy to bask in the glow of Trudy's fury.

'That man,' she utters, 'is infuriating, and I'm none too pleased with your parents for letting him infiltrate their home and family.'

'It is their home,' I point out mildly. Now I'm in *my own home* I can afford to be a little magnanimous. 'So, it's up to them who they choose to let in.'

'But didn't you say, you thought Madeline bought it for them?' asks Trudy.

'Yes but…' I start, and then I remember! 'She bought this for me too! I'll have to move out! We'll all have to move out!' Panic seizes me as I clamber off my comfy sofa, trying not to slosh coffee everywhere.

'Sit down!' barks Trudy.

She really is fearsome. I do as I'm told without a second thought. 'I have no money! What am I going to do?'

Trudy manoeuvres herself to face me full-on. 'First of all, you're going to stop panicking! This house belongs to you. Your mum took you to the solicitors to have the deeds signed over to you, I remember you going. It was gifted to you from your Great Aunt Maddie, who we now know is Madeline.'

'I know it *actually* belongs to me, but *ethically* it belongs to her. I don't want her to have even more of a hold over me.'

'Christie, ethics don't come into it, and if they did, with what she's put you through, she wouldn't have a leg to stand on.'

'She has just broken her ankle,' chips in Suzi.

'She's probably done that on purpose to get sympathy!' snaps Trudy. 'It changes nothing.'

The doorbell rings, we all look at each other.

I frown. 'Are either of you two expecting anyone?'

'Nope,' says Trudy. 'We're both still in recovery mode.'

'Can we just pretend we're out?' I suggest hopefully.

'It's worth a try,' says Suzi in a low voice.

We all keep quiet and still. 'The trouble is,' I whisper, 'the two cars on the drive are a bit of a giveaway.'

'We could have gone on a walk,' says Suzi. 'Or to the pub.'

The doorbell rings again, slightly longer than last time.

'Persistent, whoever they are,' says Trudy. 'I'll go; I'll say we're all suffering from the plague or something.'

'It could be Nigel though!' says Suzi. 'If it is, let him in!'

'No! He's only just dropped me off a couple of hours ago! I'll have to hide.'

Bang, bang, bang!

'I'm on my way!' barks Trudy. 'Honestly, the cheek of them.' I hear Trudy open the door with a brisk, 'Hello, and what do you think you're doing here?' I can't make out anything the other person is saying, just a low rumbling male voice.

'It could be Nigel,' Suzi whispers hopefully. She's too keen to be in with a chance.

'Well I'm out of here,' I say quietly. I roll off the sofa, and start making my way towards the kitchen on my hands and knees. Not quite commando style, but with a degree of stealth befitting my age and current recent physical limitations. I manage to nudge open the kitchen door with my elbow.

'Are you looking for something down there, or, let me guess, trying to make another daring escape?' croons Miles.

I can hear the laughter in his voice.

Now I have a couple of options here...

I can say, yes, I'm looking for something. Of course, he won't believe me. Or, I can say yes, I'm making another daring escape. And that, of course, he would believe. Or, I can simply ignore him, and carry on making my escape. Choice made, I continue on my hands and knees out of the room. Obviously now I've been seen, I no longer need to hunch down quite so painfully.

In the kitchen, I crawl up onto a chair, dust myself down, drop my head into my hands, and groan. I try my best to disregard the howls of male laughter coming from the other room. I slump, with the little dignity I can muster at the table, and wait. I know one of them will come in; I just hope it's not him!

And what is he doing here anyway? It's not as if anyone wants him here, both Trudy and Suzi are hacked off with him. He's got more layers than an onion, and the superpower to make me cry. I need to rise above my rancour and ignite my inner resolve. I'm just not sure if I can with that man, I'd probably explode.

Trudy comes in and sits down opposite me. 'He says he comes in peace. Doesn't want to talk about the family situation, because he knows it is all still very raw. But he says he does need to discuss *Evolution* with you. Can you manage that? I think he'd appreciate your cooperation.'

'I'd appreciate him leaving me *alone.*'

'Then the sooner you sort out what you are prepared to do, the better.'

She's "Miss Reasonable" all of a sudden! Two minutes ago, she wanted him to suffer a slow and painful death. He must've clicked on his charm button. 'I haven't had time to think yet, have I?'

Trudy places her hands flat on the table, her matt-mocha manicure at odds with the distressed pine. She leans forward. 'Look, Christie, you need to get up to speed, pronto! This is your chance to take the advantage.'

'How do you work that out? He's in control of everything.'

'I assume Madeline has been pulling all the strings up until now. Miles has been following her plan of action. She's out of action, so you pull the strings.'

'I don't think—'

'Well start! He's Madeline's right-hand man, he is used to being told what to do by a woman. So how about you start telling him what to do, and see what happens.'

'He won't listen to me. He's too… I don't know?'

'Confident?'

'Bolshie, obstinate, pig-headed.'

'And you're being wholly reasonable? Come on, Christie, step up to the mark!'

'I don't know how!'

She flings her arms up in the air, and tosses her head back. 'Then wing it. I have to do it every day at work, surrounded by men who resent my status. Listen, if you act the part, they believe it… He'll believe it.'

'Trudy… He has just watched me crawl, *crawl* on my hands and knees out of the room.'

'So, you'll catch him off guard.' She plants her hands on her hips. 'He won't expect you to come out all composed and competent.'

'I'd need to get changed out of these clothes, they're too…'

'Casual, I agree. Perhaps you should wear your interview suit.'

'Isn't that a bit much?'

'You want him to sit up and take notice, pretend you're interviewing him. Actually, in a way you are. Now those two have done all the donkey work with the gallery, you could tout for an agent. That would irritate them!'

'You forget, Madeline owns all my art.'

'You've stacks of it in the attic.' Trudy waves her arm in the general direction of the stairs. 'Anyway, you can use this to springboard you to wherever you want to be.'

'Year 7C, I want to be with 7C, and work with them until they become 11C.'

'Then tell him, but please have a bit of fun talking about agents too, make him sweat.'

'I bet he's never sweat in his life.'

'Then it's time he started. Go out the back door, and back in through the front so he doesn't see you. Get changed and slap on some make-up. I'll bring you a coffee upstairs while you're getting ready. Take your time, make him wait. And think what you're going to say.'

Okay here goes. I'm changed into a pair of smart pants and plain white T-shirt. I've added some lippy, blusher and mascara, and brushed my hair into an *ish* style... Well, no twigs anyway.

'That bra will have to go!' Trudy ambushes me on the landing.

'What do you mean "have to go"! It's white.'

'Lose the bra! You need to start playing dirty... They have! Come on, Christie, live dangerously.'

Trudy lunges for me, shoves her hands up my back, unhooks my bra, snags it at one shoulder, pulls it down my arm, and then pulls it completely out the other side.

Clearly, she has hidden talents in the bra department. She's now spinning it round on her forefinger like a hula hoop. I look down at my tiny boobs, now only just making an appearance. Trudy is smirking.

'Give it back!' I hiss. 'I look about twelve without it.'

'No, you don't. You look confident, self-assured. You look like a woman who knows she's sexy.' She pouts, and blows me a kiss.

'And since I'm none of those, I'll have my bra back please.'

'He won't be able to concentrate on what you're saying. He'll promise you anything you ask for.'

I do my best glare. 'Or I'll just go and put another one on. Probably purple.'

'How about we meet halfway, leave the bra off, and drape one of your arty scarf things round your neck. It'll send him mad trying to tell if you've got a bra on or not.'

'Now you're making him sound about twelve.'

'The male of the species, rarely mature beyond the mental age of twelve when testosterone kicks in.' Trudy pings the bra in the general direction of my bedroom. 'And it's down to us females to take the advantage.'

'Okay, okay, I bow to your superior knowledge. I'll go and find a scarf. But if he laughs at me one more time today, I will probably kill him, and that will be your fault, so you'll be an accessory!'

'He won't laugh.'

I snatch up my bra on my way back to my room, sling it on the bed and grab the first scarf I see. Trudy follows me, and arranges the scarf in what I hope is an alluring fashion.

'And remember, he's used to doing as he's told. Must be, he's been with Madeline for years.'

'I hope you're right.'

'Send Suzi out to make drinks. Don't let her interfere; she is, after all, Madeline's number one fan.'

'So, Miles will rate highly in her estimations. Gotcha.'

'Go knock him dead!'

Tempted…

Reviews

Grappling round his ankles

Hobbling down the stairs, I try not to think about escaping out of the front door. In the lounge, Suzi and Miles are stood in front of the mantelpiece with their backs to me. They're looking at a caricature I did of us three girls.

'Yes, I know,' says Suzi, 'she did it as a memento of our detox week. Can you see we've all got revolting looking drinks, and bowls of brown rice?'

'It's very quirky; do you think she knows how good she is?'

'Probably not.'

'I predict she's going to become very collectable, very quickly. That charming caricature will be worth a small fortune in a couple of weeks.'

'We'd never sell it!'

'I didn't think you would, she's lucky to have such good friends. You know, she should really have a studio.'

'Oh, I know. She spends hours cooped up in that nasty little attic, it's a wonder she hasn't got rickets, lack of vitamin D, sunlight deficiency,' coos Suzi.

Miles nods.

I think now is a good time to interrupt their little tête-à-tête. 'Well thank you, Nurse Suzi.' I cross my arms and raise an eyebrow as they both swivel round to look at me. 'Nice to know how concerned you are for my health.'

Suzi flushes, not used to being caught out gossiping.

I tilt my head. 'Maybe you could dig out that smoothie maker; I'm sure Miles would love to sample one of your specials...'

'Didn't hear you come in,' mutters Suzi. 'Wouldn't you rather have some juice?'

'Yes please, juice would be lovely, but don't let Miles miss out on one of your health drinks just because I'm being boring.'

Suzi shuffles from the room, and I feel like a complete bitch, but I can't go after her, it would spoil the ploy.

'A little unkind... On both counts,' says Miles. He doesn't look happy.

What a shame. 'Whatever,' I say, and gesture towards the sofa. 'Care to sit down? I'm eager to get this over and done with.'

'You make it sound like a visit to the dentist.'

'No, much worse than that, my dentist is rather dishy.' I remain standing, I have picked up some tricks over the years. Miles pulls out some newspapers from his briefcase. Odd that he'd keep them there, they're all folded unevenly.

'Okay, to business. These papers carry the initial reviews for *Evolution*. As you can see, you've only managed a show in four.'

'Excuse me! What do you mean, *I've only managed a show in four!* Surely, you mean, *you've* only managed it! All I did was turn up!'

'That is precisely my point, all you did was turn up. Nobody felt a buzz about meeting you, because nobody knew you were there!'

'Sarah McBride figured it out.'

'Yes.' Miles shuffles the papers. 'Here we are, in the Independently Art. Seems she's taken a liking to you. Here, take a look.' He passes the folded paper to me. It has two short paragraphs boxed in red marker.

> Today I've had the pleasure of being one of a select few to be invited to a preview of a remarkable exhibition, Evolution, by Christie Harris. What an absolute treat! The name says it all; we are lured into being guests in the life of this young artist, as she evolves from the age of eight years, to the present time, a span of sixteen years.
>
> We witness innocence and charm, move on to teenage angst and unrequited love, and then again to wit and whimsical wisdom! Her work is funny, warm, poignant, self-deprecating, and wholly unaware of the remarkable flair it embodies. What's more, I happened to stumble upon the artist herself. Watch this space, a star is born, methinks. Not to be missed.

I scan it a second time, and unravel the paper. Yes, it is the Independently Art! And it's a good, very good critique, except the bit about, oh here it is, unrequited love. Hope Trudy's brother doesn't figure that one out.

'Well, what do you think?' asks Miles.

'It's a good review, like you said, it seems Sarah McBride has taken a liking to me.'

'So, you did let her know who you are then.'

'She sussed me out while she was quizzing me about one of the pictures.'

'That's Sarah for you, she has an instinct when it comes to artists, can pick one out at fifty paces.' He shrugs. 'She was impressed by your work, and that bodes well.'

'And the rest?'

'Here, look at what Timothy Grey has to say.' He passes me another newspaper, again folded with red marker boxing off a review.

> From a clumsy start into a promising display, Evolution, by Christie Harris lives up to its name. The artist bravely shows off work that other less daring souls would hide away. None of us enjoy those first faltering steps into the limelight, especially when we know our imperfections are exposed for the public to devour. Bravo, Ms Harris, a masterclass in how to disarm the most venomous critics; I look forward to making your acquaintance.

'He says my work is clumsy!'

'No, he says a clumsy start, you were eight, what do you expect?'

'I expect to be judged as an eight-year-old should be, given encouragement and then pointed in the right direction.'

'Ah yes, but you aren't eight anymore, so, Mr Grey is quite right to treat you as an adult.'

'But it's cruel.'

'No, it's honest. Your work is, as Mr Grey points out, on public display, and therefore open to public scrutiny.'

'Not by my own choice!'

'Timothy Grey doesn't know that, and actually gives you the credit for bravery, which should belong to your backer.'

'You mean Madeline.'

'She has invested time, effort, and money. She's yanked a few influential strings to get some credible art critics to Chippington to view your work.'

'I didn't ask her to.'

'But she did it anyway.'

'I wish she hadn't.'

'We digress… Let's stick to what I'm here to do, and that is move forward with *Evolution*. So, the next review, here it is.' Miles hands me another folded newspaper. 'I don't think you met this one, James Butterworth?'

I shake my head, take the paper from Miles.

> A beautifully executed display set in sympathetic surroundings. Evolution, by Christie Harris is about to take the mainstream art world by storm. Refreshingly honest, simple sketches build, to produce an exquisite display of childhood and beyond. Not known for its artistic talents, on this occasion Chippington is well worth a visit… Or wait a while, for I'm confident we shall soon see Christie Harris in a gallery near you.

'So, what do you think?' Miles raises his eyebrows.

'I hope my work lives up to the hype.'

'It does. So now you've seen these initial reviews, you should feel more confident swinging into full PR mode. I'm sure I don't need to tell you that art is its own ambassador, but a little schmoozing goes a long way in the popularity stakes.' Miles returns the papers to his briefcase.

'Hold on, I thought you said I had four shows, you've only shown me three.'

'Oh, the other is only a couple of lines, hardly worth looking at.' Miles clicks his briefcase shut.

'But, since it's here, I may as well read it.'

'I've put it away now.' Miles settles his briefcase down.

'You know, Miles, I get the feeling you don't want me to read the last review.' Maybe it's just too awful.

'Not at all, it just seems a waste of time, that's all; let's get on with planning.'

'Not until I've read that review.'

'Christie, it's not worth bothering about.'

'I'll be the judge of that! Now, hand it over.' I hold out my hand, like I do when confiscating an illicit item from a teenager. And wait.

Miles doesn't move a muscle. I lunge for the briefcase, and end up grappling round his ankles. Miles holds fast to the darned case, as if his life depends on it.

'Let go! This is private property!'

'It's a newspaper!'

'It's my newspaper!'

'Don't be so childish.'

'You're the one trying to wrestle a briefcase from me! Christie, please.'

'Here we are, refreshments. Christie! What are you doing down there? Get up! You're embarrassing yourself!' splutters Suzi.

'He won't show me one of the reviews… It must be really bad.'

'It's not in a reputable newspaper.'

'All the more reason to read it. That's the sort of paper most people read!'

Suzi nods. 'Christie does have a point there, Miles. It can't be that bad.'

'All I'm trying to do here, is be objective. Reading an ill-informed, factually incorrect review will do nothing to move *Evolution* forward. It may even make you decide not to be further involved with the entire project.'

That bad?

'Miles, Christie is much more resilient than you seem to think—'

Thank you, Suzi

'…She's had to deal with that teacher, the one the kids call Slimy Sloan. He's a real pain.'

'Ah, yes, I remember…'

'Always on her case over something or other; does it get her down? No, water off a ducks back—'

Well actually…

'But… Madeline told me—' starts Miles.

'Look!' I snap. 'Can I see the review, or do we call it a day?' I glare at him. I do not want Miles discussing with Suzi, my alleged "private correspondence" to Auntie Maddie. He shouldn't even know about it. It's not on!

'Fine, you win, but it just… Here.' He clicks open his briefcase and passes me the newspaper. 'It is rubbish, utter rubbish!' He reluctantly leaves go of it.

> Well, well, well, what have we here? Evolution, by the so-called Christie Harris, is an indulgence too far! Of course, parents want to see their offspring do well, but really, should they use their influence to launch the career of

a quite mediocre talent, (I use the word "talent" in its loosest form)? In the long run it can only lead to tears before bedtime!

I have met Lord and Lady X on many occasions. If they believe their dear daughter has any artistic skills, why, oh why did they not simply ask my opinion, before lavishing time and money on a purely futile venture.

Lucky for them, I am not so crass as to name them in a national newspaper, after all, their private embarrassment will surely be enough to bear. Then again, watch this space. Yours, as ever, Bunty H.

'Bunty Hargreaves,' I croak, as the now familiar knot tightens in my stomach.

Suzi thrusts two drinks at Miles, one of which contains a revolting slushy mixture about the same shade of green as my face. The other, the same shade as Suzi's face. Hope it's *Vimto*. She takes the newspaper from my hand, and begins to read.

'The cow,' mutters Suzi eventually, looking to me. 'Christie, it's just spiteful drivel because Trudy had a go at her.'

'She said it's mediocre.'

Miles shrugs dramatically. 'What can I say? She's delusional. Everyone else thinks it's brilliant. Bunty Hargreaves is the Slimy Sloan of the supplement section. Nobody takes her seriously.'

'Mediocre…' I repeat.

'I've already contacted the newspaper in question, and explained Bunty has made an error of judgement.'

'An error of judgement. About her critique, or about my identity?'

'Both,' says Miles. 'When you explained how you came about all your scratches, it all started to make sense. Bunty must have been mad as a wasp, having her phone snatched off her. The only way she could outdo her fellow columnists, was to sensationalise the situation.'

'But it's very close to the truth. Madeline has used her influence to get me recognition.'

'Maybe, but you weren't party to it. And, crucially, your work is remarkable.'

'Remarkable?'

'Yes, remarkable. Anyway, as she's made such an openly hostile attack on your work, others will clamour to see it.'

'You mean, she's done me a favour?'

'Exactly,' says Miles. 'Can we get on? Which of these two drinks is mine?' He holds up the two glasses.

'The green one!' Suzi and I say together.

Fraya-Froo

I am not getting changed!

Trudy preens. Suzi shuffles. I can barely look at myself in the bedroom mirror. 'I look like... What do I look like? I can't believe Miles talked me into this re-launch. And you were no help, simpering like a love-struck teen.'

Suzi shrugs, not the least bit concerned about my predicament.

Well thanks for that Suzi!

I glare at Trudy. 'And you were no better, "Little-Miss-Whip-Your-Bra-Off"! Trudy... What am I wearing? I can't bear to look in the mirror again... My eyes might start to bleed!' I risk a glance down, multicoloured silk wafts about my legs.

'It's a *Fraya-Froo*. She's an up-and-coming designer. Basically, it's a jigsaw jumpsuit, the *Jigjump*. There's a whole range, the *Fleurjump*, the *Skyjump*, the *Petaljump*—'

'I wish she'd go and take a running jump into the nearest river,' I say.

'Oh, there is a *Riverjump*!'

'Trudy! It's hideous! Suzi, back me up here! Please!'

'Well, it is quite loud—'

'Quite loud!' I squeal.

Suzi grimaces. 'And if I'm honest, I don't think I could ever bring myself to wear it.'

'Thank you.'

'Not even for a bet.'

'Girls,' says Trudy, 'you are both missing the point entirely! *Fraya-Froo* is a brand-new label, Christie is a brand-new artist. By wearing a *Fraya-Froo*, you, Christie, will, one, give her some great exposure, two, gain an instant cutting-edge image, and three...' Trudy screws up her nose.

'Show the world I have no style?'

'And three, have other designers clamouring over each other to give you freebies.'

'Trudy, I know you're probably right on all three points, but it's just not me. And if I'm standing in front of people, with my whole life exposed for their scrutiny, I need to be honest enough to be me. Let them actually judge the real me... Because once everyone finds out I'm Madeline's daughter... I'll never get that chance again.' My eyes smart as I hold in the tears. 'I'll be—'

'You'll always be Christie Harris,' says Trudy softly. 'Now get out of that gruesome pantomime outfit, and into something *Christiefied*. Come on, we haven't got all day!'

Relief floods through me. I shove them both out of my bedroom before Trudy changes her mind. I swing open my wardrobe doors and inspect the mayhem. I whip off the *Jigjump* and sling it onto the bed.

Skinny jeans, I think, I've got the bum for them, and... I let my hand trail over the sweep of random oversized jumpers. This cornflower blue one with, yep, my Elmo T-shirt underneath, just in case it gets overheated in the gallery. I dress as quickly as I can; a pair of white pumps finishes off my outfit.

Done.

Just being in my own comfy clothes, makes me feel slightly more relaxed. The thoughts of meeting all those critics again kept me awake half the night. Lucky for me, Trudy is a whiz with all thing's beauty, and has somehow hidden the sacks of potatoes hanging under my eyes.

'Okay, here I come,' I holler, and wander down to the lounge. Miles is sat on the sofa between Suzi and Trudy. 'Oh, I didn't hear you arrive.'

'I'd been outside for ten minutes. Doesn't anybody ever answer the door in this house?' Miles stands when I enter the room. 'You're looking very—'

'I am *not* getting changed!'

'No, no, you look lovely. Fresh, you're going to blow them away!' He laughs. 'You know, I had an awful feeling you were going to come in like an overdressed peacock, but you're just you.'

Suzi and Trudy exchange glances.

'I'd rather people enjoy the gallery, than gawp at me. It's better if I just blend in.' *So* glad I managed to ditch the *Fraya-Froo*, I'd never have lived it down.

'Shall we get off then?' Miles gestures towards the door. 'We can all go together if you like, Suzi, Trudy?'

'Good idea,' simpers Suzi. 'I'll just get my bag.'

I notice the frosty look Trudy aims at Suzi. 'Actually, I've an early start tomorrow, so, I'll drive myself. You two get off, I can bring Suzi. Give you a chance to go over the last-minute details.'

'Good idea, come on then, Christie. There *are* a couple of things we need to discuss.'

Just what I need, more alone time with Miles. I follow him towards the door, then turn and give Trudy my meanest glare. She returns it with a sweet smile, and blows me a kiss. One day, I will repay the favour.

I'm pleasantly surprised to see a classic Jag parked at the front. Not flash, just understated class. Miles unlocks the passenger door with a key! And opens it for me...

'This is very classy,' I say, settling into the leather clad seat of his car. I love the smell of polished leather; not sure what that says about me.

'Nice isn't it? It's Madeline's; she lets me borrow it for special occasions.'

'Oh.' It would be hers, wouldn't it? The engine purrs, and we're off. Miles smoothly works his way up through the gears, and settles at a steady speed.

He starts tapping a random beat with his fingers on the steering wheel. 'Today, you are going to make them love you.'

'Most people usually just tolerate me, or humour me,' I say, and immediately think of Mr Sloan with his beady eyes and pulsing neck vein. I close my eyes and put him in his chicken suit so he can't intimidate me, fluffy yellow feathers, orange beak, overstuffed tail. That's better. I open my eyes and look ahead.

'Well today, all that is going to change.'

'Whatever.' I risk a sneaky glance at him, not sneaky enough because he smiles. His hands are slung casually on the steering wheel, and his fingers are still tapping an irregular beat. Very irritating, I doubt he even knows he's doing it.

'If I give you the formula, you have to promise to keep it a secret.'

'Pardon?'

'The formula! The formula for making people love you.' His smile spreads into a grin. I can't help but stare, his face is transformed.

A flutter starts in my chest. 'You are joking, right?'

We slow to a stop at traffic lights, and Miles turns to look at me with only the ghost of the smile remaining.

'It's no joke. It's not the truly, madly, deeply love. It's the superficial, wow, isn't she amazing, love. The sort celebrities clamour for.'

'I'm not a celebrity.'

'You will be.'

'Let's give the fortune telling a miss, shall we?' I say. 'And stop drumming your fingers!'

The finger drumming stops. 'Okay. Do you want the formula, or are you going to wing it?'

Probably best to humour him. I roll my eyes. 'So, what is it?' Anything to keep my mind off this re-launch will do. The lights change, and we're off again.

Miles glances at me. 'The first and hardest bit, you've already done, I'm impressed. That is, don't try to be someone you're not. Well done, you are wearing the kind of clothes you always wear, not too much make-up, casual pumps, and your hair is its usual fluffy self—'

'It's not fluffy! It's curly!'

'Fluffy, curly, same thing.' I can tell he's trying his best not to smirk. Failing.

'Strange you have this mystical formula to make people love you, and yet, still you manage to irritate me half to death.'

'Like I said, it's not the truly, madly, deeply… That takes a different route… Second, you need to be as absolutely honest as you can be, without, and this is important, not offending or upsetting people.'

'That's just good manners,' I say, everyone knows that.

'Without revealing too much about yourself. Which leads nicely to number three.' He nods, as if trying to secure this knowledge in his own well of wisdom.

'Have you always been so good at maths?' Starting to lose interest now.

'Hold back, make yourself an enigma; set people the puzzle. Let them glimpse only the edges of your secrets.'

Maybe I should have worn the *Jigjump* after all, now that is a puzzle. I fiddle with the edge of my jumper. I don't want people prying into my life, especially now. I'm struggling to come to terms with the whole Madeline De-Muir thing. I'm beginning to think becoming a recluse has its advantages, then I really would be an enigma. 'I'd rather, they didn't even assume I have any secrets.'

'Everyone has secrets… And four…' he carries on, clearly, either not picking up on my anxiety, or ignoring it. 'Eye contact and smile. Make the person you are talking to, think they are, to you, at that moment, the most important person in the room.'

'If I spend all day trying to remember all that, I'll probably end up with a nervous twitch.' Maybe they'll take pity on me.

Miles smiles, his fingers have started their random rhythm again. He must know how irritating it is. I stick my fingers in my ears. 'Will you stop drumming your fingers? The urge to sing la-la -la at the top of my lungs, to drown out that tuneless beat, is sending me batty!'

'Sorry, it's one of my many endearing habits.' Again, the smile, but he does stop drumming his fingers.

I gaze out of the window. Fields make way for rural villages, Wilton, Clover Beck and Brock Beck all pass by in a blur. The last of the open landscape disappears as we cross over the river into the large market town of Chippington. The tall spire of St. Mary's Church, and the backdrop of several old mill chimney stacks, dominate the skyline.

Miles negotiates the myriad of streets with ease, thankfully still no drumming fingers. After a maze of side streets, and lefts and rights we're back at the converted Mill. The *Evolution* banner, still proud and bold, sets my heart racing at what I'm about to face.

My critics.

If I'm honest, I suppose I've always wanted recognition for my work. I would never have chosen to show what is on display inside the mill right now. In my mind, I would have a complete body of work, which holds no tight emotional bonds to me. The work behind those walls is my life, or a huge chunk of it, and I'm terrified how I'm going to be judged.

'You okay?' asks Miles.

'Think so.' I lie so blatantly!

'Good, let's get to it then.'

We get out of the car, and Miles locks it manually, classics do have some disadvantage. As we walk across the gravel yard, the back door to the Mill swings open, and there stands Mrs Price.

The first hurdle of many.

'Oh, my dear girl,' she says, as she's squishing my face between her none too gentle hands, 'you're looking much better than I thought you would—'

Gee, thanks!

'... White as a sheet you were—'

Ummmm, I wonder why? You're driving, perhaps?

'... Let's get you safe inside. That Bunty Hargreaves has a lot to answer for, I'm surprised Miles invited her back today.'

'What!' I swing to face Miles. 'You didn't tell me you'd invited her!'

'Very good PR for us. Heaps of humble pie for her.'

'If Trudy sees her, the only kind of pie Bunty will manage, will be through a straw.'

'Trudy's cool with it.'

'You're sure about that, because?' I raise my well-practiced and manicured brow.

'Oh yes, we had a little chat while you were getting ready.'

'And?'

'And we all have reputations to maintain.'

'You blackmailed her!'

'I merely pointed out, that it was beneficial to all parties to preserve a veneer of mutual respect.'

'Mutual respect?'

'Yes.'

'Bullshit.'

'Exactly! That is why it is just a veneer; and I'm expecting you to go along with this mutual respect. In fact, I want you to make her feel so guilty about the way she's misrepresented you—'

'Lied about me.'

'Diplomacy, please... That she'll be on side when she discovers the actual truth, otherwise...'

'She'll dig up everything she can about me.'

'And Madeline. Don't forget, she was only sixteen when she had you.'

How can I forget that?

Once again, it's all about his precious Madeline. I'm sick of her name already. How am I ever going to manage to get along with her, knowing what she's done? And the way Miles is always on her side, is very unsettling. 'So, you want me to be sweetness and light?'

'I want you to be yourself, and pretend you are meeting Bunty Hargreaves for the first time. Give her a fresh start.'

'A fresh start? Like nothing's ever happened?'

'Exactly, you never know, a fresh start might be all she needs.'

'Whatever.'

'Christie, we all make mistakes sometimes.'

'Even you?'

His eyes crinkle at the sides, as a wide grin spreads across his face. 'I know! Hard to believe, but even me sometimes.'

'Well for all our sakes, I hope this isn't one of those times.'

'I don't make them very often, if that helps.' I nod towards Mrs Price, who is busy now stacking flyers. 'She isn't a mistake; she is in many ways awesome; even her driving when you're not a passenger...'

'Hmmm.'

'Mrs Price, could you remind me of the revised schedule for today?'

'There are only two revisions, firstly Frankie will not be talking about the *Keep*-a-Key charity, apparently a...' Mrs Price shuffles some papers. 'Where is it, oh yes, a Sarah McBride has his little speech on her Dictaphone. She's going to do something independently in one of the nationals about him and the charity. The other is you'll be introducing Christie as herself.'

'I don't have to say anything do I?' I ask.

'I'll just do a bit of background on you.' Miles looks at me as if I'm a terrified child. Very close.

'What will you say?'

'Local teacher from Little Upton, always loved art, always encouraged by a distant aunt to follow her artistic dream, vague. And then I will ask you to open the exhibition, all you need to say is something like, "I formally declare *Evolution* open". And then just mingle. Okay?'

'Sounds simple.'

'It is, so don't overthink it, you'll be fine.'

Meet and Greet

"Up a tree, actually!"

The hair on the back of my neck is prickling. Feels like I'm in a life or death situation. My hands are quivering, eyelids twitching, and my throat feels like I've just swallowed a brick. I'm not entirely convinced it's just because I'm stood in front of this hushed crowd.

Miles.

I can feel the heat radiating from his hand as it rests in the small of my back. His other hand is across the front of my body, and loosely clasping my fingers, "a casual, yet seemingly intimate poise", is how he blagged me into agreeing to this staged entrance.

A tad too intimate for my liking.

He keeps giving my trembling hand a gentle squeeze every now and then. It's his prompt for us to exchange smiles and eye contact, "Let's show them we're a good team". He's waffling on about the impact each new picture has had on him over the last few years. He's weaving in the background info about working with the *Keep-a-Key* team, to bring my art to the public's attention, blah-de-blah-de-blah, on and on.

'So now, here she is, my good friend, Christie Harris.'

Miles releases my hand, and gives me a gentle push forward. A ripple of applause fills the foyer. Whoops and whistles from Trudy and Suzi ease my tension slightly, making me smile. I feel a blush rush over my cheeks.

'Hi there, everyone.' My hand makes an involuntary wave. WHY??? 'So, thank you all for coming today. It's good to see my friends are here to support me, Trudy, Suzi. Some of you are here for a second time, so, thank you, Sarah, Bunty...' I scan the room. 'Oh, and Mr Grey, good of you, to all come back.' I rub my sweaty palms together, try to smile but my lips stick to my teeth. 'I'm not used to talking in public to grown-ups, so, sorry for being haphazard. I will be wandering about if anyone wants to talk to me later.' I try a smile again. 'So, feel free, but first I suppose I must open the exhibition.' I glance at the expectant faces. Deep breath. 'I declare *Evolution* officially open. Enjoy.'

Genteel applause, is accompanied by Trudy and Suzi's rock festival frolics, earning them both amused looks.

Can't take them anywhere.

'Well done,' whispers Miles. Goosebumps prickle down my spine. 'Just enough, not too much.'

Oh Miles... Not enough, and way, way, way too much...

'Don't worry, I'll chaperone Tru 'n' Su. Off you go, mingle, and it might be a nice gesture if you mingle with the ever-charming Bunty Hargreaves first. Get it out of the way.'

I search the room for her frosty features. She's hovering over *Score* like a vulture about to pick at a carcass. Typical! I try to look casual as I saunter towards her, swallowing frantically behind my smile.

'How kind of you to give me a second chance,' I say, when I reach her side. My smile is glued on waiting for her response. She merely nods, so I continue, 'I've got to admit, I'm rather embarrassed by this one.'

'What's his name?' she demands.

'I'd rather not say, he's from my youth.'

'You're still a youth.' She looks me up and down, and I can feel my face burning. 'I guess he's your first lover.'

'Goodness me, no!' I splutter in horror. 'No; just, he was just someone I had a crush on, that's all, it was a long time ago.'

'By the colour of your face, I'd say you've still got a crush on him, can't say I blame you, he's a bit of a hunk.'

'Artistic licence, he's just a family friend, so it's going to be awkward when he finds out about this.' I point to the exquisitely defined torso of Simon in my painting.

Bunty lets out a low cackle, then examines Simon closely with her beady eyes. 'You know, he looks quite like the Drummond girl over there.' My eyes follow her line of vision to where Trudy is standing. 'So, I'm assuming it's one of her brothers... Let me see, which one?'

'It was just one of those teenage things years ago, long forgotten, he never knew.'

'So, the poor lad never found out then, I'm sure he'll be flattered, when he does…'

'Please don't!'

'What, dig and delve? Surely you know dear, it's what we do; we trawl through other people's lives and pick out a living for ourselves. But luckily for you, I've just had my wrists slapped for overstepping the mark, so I'll leave it for someone else to pick up on.'

'Thank you.' I bite my lip.

She turns to face me; steel eyes bore into mine. 'A piece of advice.' I nod, unable to break eye contact with her. Her eyes scan the gallery. 'Do not trust them, any of them.'

'I'll try to remember that,' I say, trying to match her gravity. Not easy, when I'm eager to escape so I can go and lock Trudy in a cupboard until everyone has left.

'You're alright, despite being one of his pet projects.' Bunty gestures towards Miles. 'You've got courage, I'll give you that, after the roasting I gave you.' She twists her mouth into the semblance of a smile.

'You too.'

'I'll give you that,' says Bunty, narrowing her eyes. 'Now I suggest you trot along, and make pretend friends with the other scavengers.'

I scurry away and head directly for Trudy, who appropriately, is holding court in front of *Trudy Takes a Tumble.* A hand catches my sleeve.

'Well, well, well, if it's not the elusive Christie Harris.' Timothy Grey! Oh dear… 'Or should I call you Anne?' he purrs.

'Oh, hello again, Mr Grey.'

'Timothy, please.' He lifts my hand to his lips, and presses a kiss to the inside of my wrists.

YUK.

'Timothy.' I drag my hands away as gently as I can, look into his eyes and smile. 'How generous of you to come back for a second viewing.'

'Couldn't resist meeting the artist herself.'

'Here I am.' I shrug, with what I hope is a cute smile.

'So, now I've got you.' He secures his arm around my back, and starts steering me back towards *Score.* 'How about you tell me all about this young Adonis?'

'What is there to tell?' I say. 'Just a family friend.'

'You seem to have a lot of those.' He nods towards Miles. 'So, tell me, was he another of your lovers?'

'No! What is it with you all?' I gasp. 'And what do you mean, another?' My voice rises to a squeak.

'Come on now, it's obvious to everyone that you and Miles have a thing going on.'

'No! We haven't, we've only just, you know...' I nearly said met! Pull yourself together girl, or he's going to tie you in knots.

'Only just?' quizzes Timothy.

'Can I trust you?' I whisper.

Timothy's eyes widen. 'What a question! Of course, you can my dear. What's troubling you?'

You, you creep

'Miles is a friend of the family, of very close family actually, but, we don't always get on.' If I keep it as close to the truth as I can, he's more likely to support me after my exposé.

'And?'

'And just before *Evolution* got off the ground,' I whisper, 'we all had, let's call it a difference of opinion.'

'All?'

'Some family, and their close friend.' I glance across to Miles. He is going to kill me

'Miles being the close friend.'

'It's delicate,' I edge.

'I see.'

I hope not. 'So, please, not a word.'

'Your secret's safe with me, however, this young man here.' He points towards sexy, shirtless Simon. 'He was more than just a family friend?'

'I couldn't possibly say.'

Sarah McBride's bosom bounds into view, and heading towards it, I make my escape. 'Christie, dearest, how could you?' she says winking. 'Deceived us all with that innocent Anne act. Come and tell me what your game is.' Sarah links her arm in mine.

Relieved, I'm happy to relax a little in her presence. 'Oh, what a tangled web we weave, when first we practice to deceive,' I mutter.

'Yes indeed, my dear, so now we'll have the truth, the whole truth and nothing but the...' she says. 'Christie, my dear, what on earth is the matter?'

I feel the single tear snaking its way down the side of my face.

'Come on, let's get you out of here.' Sarah manoeuvres me out of the gallery.

The cool air bites my damp face. Away from prying eyes I slump against the wall, and make no attempt to stop the waterfall of tears. Sarah makes no bid to comfort me, she just watches. A bungle of tissues are pressed into my hand, and I blow my nose noisily. I look at Sarah. Her jolly round face has lost its warmth; her face is stern, eyes harsh.

'Are you finished?' she asks; her tone flat. I nod. 'Okay. I don't know what all that was about, I do know there is a room full of people looking for you.' She picks up both my hands, and turns them over, palms up. 'These hands are talented, and at the moment, those people in there are interested in you, and your talent. Don't blow it.'

'It's all a bit much.'

'Sift through your insecurities another time girl! Today, now, you need to be in control.' I nod, goosebumps prickle my arms. 'I told you the first time we met, that you'd better have pluck, and you'd better!' I nod franticly, eager to appease her. 'I have seen too many destroyed by that lot, I'd rather not see it happen to you.' She closes her eyes. I'm half tempted to make a run for it, except she's still holding my hands. 'I am trying to protect you.' She sighs loudly.

'I'm sorry,' I mutter.

'Do not let any of us see any weakness.'

'I won't.' I draw my hands from Sarah's grip. All I want is to get away from her. 'You're frightening me.'

She steps away from me, embarrassed, shocked? I can't tell. My tears stop, and Sarah appears almost to be the jolly Sarah I first met. I can feel the emotional distance she's opened up between us; it's just a mask, she's back to being the reporter. The critic. 'I don't want you to waste this chance, I like you. But too many people blow it. And even more don't even get the chance in the first place. You need to shape your own future, don't ever forget that. Right now, you have a choice. A biggie. You can either scurry off into obscurity, or get back in there, and make people remember your name.'

'I'm not going to waste this opportunity, honestly, everything's moving so fast.'

'How so?' She looks me over. I can see the speculation in her eyes. 'This has been months in the planning.'

If I'd have known about this months ago, I'd have emigrated.

She frowns. 'Surely you must have had time to adjust to all this, be excited about it?'

And so, how well can I trust Sarah? At this stage, probably not too much. 'I just got swept along with it.'

'Miles?' she asks.

I nod, if that's what she wants to think.

She nods. 'I've known Miles for eons, way back when he was first establishing himself as Madeline De-

Muir's right-hand man. He was hardly a man to be honest, fresh out of university, but that's by the by. What I do know about Miles, is that he does nothing without Madeline's approval, or backing. And this reeks of Madeline.' She gestures towards the *Evolution* banner. Her words are left hanging in the space between us; I can almost taste her anticipation. 'You have met her, I take it?'

'Briefly.' At last, a shred of honestly. I'm beginning to think she has a built-in lie detector.

'Now, there's a woman who had it all.'

'To be honest,' – and I am – 'I don't know her. I've heard about her, but that's second-hand.'

'Most things are. I interviewed her once. Twice actually.'

'Oh…' Please don't love her too much.

'The first time she'd just landed the part of Rose, in *An English Rose*. She was so vibrant and full of promise. Then off she went to Hollywood, an innocent—'

Hardly innocent!

'… I know it sounds corny, but I described her as a golden rose in full bloom. She was the darling of the industry. But when she came home, she'd lost her sparkle. She was burnt out, still a beautiful creature, but without emotion.'

'It really is interesting, but I've got to get back.'

'It seems, we have Miles to thank for her edging back towards the limelight—'

Typical.

'… He made tentative contact with a select few charities, got her involved. She became patron of a couple. I did think she was going to try to make a comeback.'

'Look, I had better make a comeback myself, before someone comes looking for me.'

'Of course, she could be using you to haul herself back into the limelight.' Sarah nods for me to go, her lips curve into a sweet smile. I head towards the back entrance, so I can freshen up before going back into the gallery. I keep my head down. The gravel crunches under my feet, I can feel the stones through my pumps. I around the corner, and walk straight into Miles.

I can tell he's been waiting for me, listening. His stance is casual. One shoulder resting against the rough brick wall, his arms folded across his chest.

His face, not so casual.

Here we go then.

'Having a nice little chat with your new best friend?' he challenges.

'She's not my new best friend.'

'I know, I was being sarcastic.'

'And I know she's a critic, a journalist. We were just passing the time.'

'So why the blotchy eyes?'

'Overthinking. I needed to get out of there.'

'You should have come and found me.'

'Why?'

'Because it's my job to look after you.'

I shake my head. 'Well, you were busy, but luckily, Sarah came to the rescue.'

'Again, she's a journalist...'

'So, I should have stood there, in tears and waited for you to come running.'

'No... Surely Suzi or Trudy would have been a better choice.'

'Probably, but they were both enjoying the exhibition.'

He lets out a deep breath, hoists himself away from the wall, and gestures towards the service entrance of the mill. 'Sorry I let you down, I'll keep closer in future.'

'No need. You didn't let me down; I wasn't depending on you.'

'Madeline requires me to look after you.'

'So, you let Madeline down.' I try to walk past him, but he catches my arm.

'I'm sure you don't need reminding, but you have Madeline to thank for this project.'

'Thank?' I pull my arm from his grasp. 'I don't think so.'

I head back inside, hear him follow. I go directly to the restroom and splash my face with cool water. I still look flushed, but no longer blotchy. I take a moment, open the door slowly, and check that Miles isn't waiting for me. Can't see him. I ease my way out into the corridor and make a dash for the exhibition.

As soon as I step back into the gallery, Miles falls into step beside me.

He smiles. 'So, shall we talk about the charming Sarah tonight, over dinner?'

'No, no need to talk about her at all.'

'Christie, I'm no fool; but more importantly, neither is she. She can sniff out a story at fifty paces. And whether you like it or not, you are one hell of a story.'

'And whether you like it or not, I will be talking to her at some point. Don't worry, I'll run it by you first.'

Miles takes my hand and links it onto his arm. He leans in close. 'All our stories need to be more than airtight. They need to be prytight and bombproof. So, I'll pick you up at eight, and we'll discuss this away from wagging ears.'

'Fine.' Just what I need, time alone with him. I remove my hand from his arm.

'Good, now that's settled, time for more mingling.'

The atmosphere feels relaxed. Sarah is back, and looks to be well established in conversation. Trudy and Suzi appear to be still basking in all of their newfound fame, and not missing me at all. So, all is well on planet *Evolution*.

Miles catches my hand, again, and links our fingers. My fingers curl of their own accord around his. My heart does a flippity flop, I wish he wouldn't touch me; I wish I didn't want him to. I'm trying to smile, but I probably look more like one of those teeth-baring chimps off the telly.

'Relax, Christie, everything is going great today. Come on.' Miles leads me across the gallery, back to *Score*. A smart middle-aged man in a checked bow tie is scrutinizing it.

'Alan, I'd like to introduce you to Christie Harris.'

Alan's head thrusts forwards and nods as he pommels my hand. 'Well hello there, Christie Harris, I'm Alan Devine. Great exhibition, well done.' He nods towards *Score*. 'This chappie here, does he have any idea how famous he's about to become?'

'Umm, no. As far as I know, he doesn't…'

'He's in for a big surprise then! Were you hiding behind a tree?'

'Up a tree, actually!' I laugh. 'Although I do hide behind bushes sometimes.' Why did I say that?

'Rather a lot,' says Miles.

'Sounds interesting,' says Alan.

'I like to rely on tried and tested methods. And, though I do say so myself, I am rather good at hiding in bushes.'

'Do you have any particular preference; in bushes I mean?' Alan Devine is very easy to like.

'Oh no, any bush will do, obviously the larger the better. On the last occasion it was a Flowering Blackcurrant bush, and it was rather spikey. If I'd had the choice... I would have chosen a Laurel. Sometimes you have to go with what you've got.'

'Indeed, and did you remain undetected?'

'Until her mobile rang, and then I found her.' Miles grins, as he lifts my hand and kisses the back of it. I can feel the heat of my immediate flush, burning my cheeks.

'You were hiding from Miles?'

'Sort of,' I say.

'The plot thickens.' Alan and Miles exchange knowing looks. 'So, back to *Score*.'

'Yes, I had a crush on him, no he doesn't know, yet, and,' – oh, well – 'see that lady over there?' I point at Trudy, and he nods. 'It's her brother. So, shit, fan, hit, I've a feeling I'm going to need to find some bushes to hide in.'

Both Alan and Miles laugh.

'No... That isn't a joke. Really!'

Not a Date

"... my boobs will fall out."

'It's not a date!'

Trudy raises her chin a notch. 'Okay, Christie. *You* keep telling yourself that.'

'Look, Miles just wants to go over what I'm intending to tell Sarah McBride. He's not interested in me, just Madeline's precious reputation.'

Trudy looks me over. As usual, she's dressed me up in a low-cut, skin-tight dress that just about shows every curve I haven't got.

I frown. 'If I lean forward in this, my boobs will fall out.'

She smirks. 'You haven't got any boobs!'

'Exactly! So how embarrassing will that be? No, Trudy, I'm just going to wear jeans and a top, maybe a dressy top. I don't want him getting the wrong idea.' Because if he ever finds out that I do find him slightly attractive, he'll get his own way with everything. As will Madeline

'Christie, you look great. And, so what if he thinks you fancy him? Use it to your advantage.'

I let out a deep sigh. I've got to tell her, here goes. 'Do you remember a couple of weeks ago, when I told you and Suzi about that bloke I really liked?'

'Oh yes, the mystery man? The one you said was a bit of a dish?'

'Yep, the mystery man.'

'And?'

'I told you I'd seen him a couple of times near Mum and Dad's. But then, just before school broke up last week, he was sat in his car across from school. He was on his mobile.'

'I see. You think it must be fate. You don't want to lead Miles on, because you're holding out for the mystery man to reappear.'

'Trudy, no.'

'He's probably married, with three kids and a mortgage. But if you want to let your imagination run wild, go ahead. Better still, I could track him down, and bring him to your door.'

'No need.'

'Good—'

'He'll be coming to my door tonight anyway.'

'You've got a date with him?'

'I keep telling you… It's not a date.' I watch Trudy's face as the penny drops. It goes from wonder to mirth in a split second. 'It's not funny. If Miles finds out I've always fancied him, he'll get all his own way, use it to his advantage. Then I'll stand no chance with Madeline.'

Trudy plonks herself down on my bed, covers her face with her hands and starts to massage her temples. Her usual deep-thinking position. Good.

I sit down next to her, then flop back to lie on the bed with my arms dangling over the edge. 'What am I going to do? Come on, Trudy think. I get goosebumps every time he touches me, and I've got to stop myself from jumping away from him, in case he guesses what I'm thinking.'

'And what are you thinking?' Trudy uncovers her face, turns to look at me, her eyes scrutinizing mine.

'Do you remember those raunchy books we used to read when we were teenagers?'

She grins. 'I still read them... In between trying to live them out! Go on.'

'Well, roll them all into one awesomely raunchy fantasy, and you'll be about halfway there.'

'But what about Miles? Not the fantasy Miles, the real one. The one whose job it is to reconcile you and Madeline.'

'Honestly?'

'Honestly.'

'Okay here goes...' I say, and hold up my hand to tick off pointers. 'First of all, he's loyal, he's proved that with Madeline. Second, he's protective, again, proved that with Madeline. Third, he has a wicked sense of humour, the Mrs Price incident? He had to almost eat his fist to stop himself from exploding into hysterics. Next, he's considerate; when I came face to face with Madeline for the first time, he let me escape. Then he's caring, he's lovely with my mum, now I've run out of fingers...' Trudy flops back and rolls towards me. 'What?' I roll over and prop my head on my hands. 'Just tell me.'

Trudy is looking at me, the same way she did when she found out I'd had a teenage crush on her brother. Horror and something else. 'Go on, Christie, what else is Miles?'

'I've run out of fingers, and you look a bit pale. Are you ill?' I bite my bottom lip. 'Trudy?'

'What else?'

'He looks at me. Properly at me. Like he can see inside, and knows my secrets. He probably does, if Madeline has let him read my letters.'

'And?'

'He's beautiful,' I admit.

'He has that scar under his eye.' Trudy's words are gentle, honest.

'I know. It makes him more beautiful to me. I've sketched him, from memory. Trudy, he is beautiful. He gets these tiny little crinkles at the side of his eyes when he's about to laugh, or trying not to, as if he can't wait to have fun. And his hair, I know you don't like Hugh Grant, but Miles' hair flops forward just like his. And when we met him together at the gallery, remember that first time, with Frankie and Mickey, I thought he was really horrible to the kids, but he's kind of like that strict teacher at school, that all the kids grumble about, but really love.'

'Enough!' Trudy points to the door. 'Go and make yourself a cup of tea, make mine a vodka and black. You've got a *date* tonight, and I need to think.'

There's no point arguing with her! I haul myself up off the bed, slip my dressing gown on over the skinny dress, and go down to the kitchen. It's almost seven now, Miles is picking me up at eight. I hope Trudy manages to do some fast thinking. I make my cup of tea automatically. No blackcurrant for Trudy's vodka, it'll have to be Vimto and vodka. Again.

Trudy stalks into the kitchen, and nods towards the table. 'Sit, Christie. I wish you'd told me sooner! This is serious!'

I sit down, and slide her tumbler of vodka across the table to her, like they do in westerns. She takes a gulp, and then sits down opposite me.

'Sorry, it's Vimto again,' I say.

'I know, never mind. Are you ready for this?'

'Just get on with it, Trudy, I'm in knots.'

'No, you're not in knots. You're in love.'

'I can't be! He's Madeline's.'

'Maybe it's infatuation, but probably not. And he isn't Madeline's. He only works for her. What you need to do, is find out about him, and why he's so loyal to Madeline. From my point of view, the only reason you haven't pounced on him yet, is because he's loyal to her. Find out why.'

'So, what should I do? Question him?'

'Flirt with him, get him to lower his guard, find out who he is.'

'And then what?'

Trudy picks up her drink, downs it, stands, leans over the table, ruffles my hair and winks. 'If it were me, I'd *devour* the man... But you, kiddo, you're on your own.' She walks out of the kitchen.

'But Trudy! Wait, what should I wear?' I shout after her.

'Whatever the hell you want! If he fancies you, you'll look good in anything... Or nothing... I'm sure you'll figure it out... Without a diagram,' she shouts back.

'Trudy! Wait!'

Oh great, I'm on my own. I make my way back up to my bedroom, which still looks like a clothes bomb exploded. I pick through the discarded heap. Nothing. I'm almost temped to put my Elmo T-shirt back on, that would show him how uninterested I am. I look in the wardrobe and settle for skinny cropped jeans, yet again, but with a cream floaty blouse. Considering my artistic bent, I'm rubbish at picking outfits.

I slap on more make-up than usual, not hard really, and try to tame my messy mop of hair. All too soon I hear the door bell, and Trudy's cheery voice welcoming Miles in. They're in the hallway as I walk down the stairs. Trudy's smile is fixed. Miles looks smart in a suit, no tie. His shirt has the top two buttons open.

'You look lovely, as usual, Christie,' he says.

'Thanks,' I mutter.

'Well, you two enjoy yourselves.' Trudy practically pushes us out of the front door. 'I won't wait up.'

'She never does,' I say, and look over my shoulder to give Trudy my "help me" look. She blows me a kiss, and waves.

Well yes, that'll help!

Miles opens the car door for me... Like a proper date? I'm so confused!

He smiles as he gets in the car and starts the ignition. 'I've booked a table at Santus, I know you like Italian.'

'It's always good there, they do amazing sticky toffee puddings.'

'Your favourite.'

I nod, I'm sure I haven't told him that. Madeline. Or Mum, or Dad, or I'm paranoid. Why does it have to be him? I look out of the window as field after field of regimented green crops whiz by. If only my life were that ordered. In less than ten minutes we're at the restaurant, and neither of us has spoken a word since leaving the house.

'Are you okay?' asks Miles.

'Yes, just tired, it's been a busy week.'

'For both of us.' He smiles assuredly. 'I think the sooner we sort this out the better, don't you?'

I nod, and get out of the car. This isn't a date, it's an essential meeting. One where Miles is going to try and talk me out of letting Sarah McBride interview me. I need to be on my guard, and make Miles lower his.

Miles walks beside me; I turn and beam my brightest smile at him.

'Look, Miles, I know this is just work for you.' I walk my fingers up his chest – always works for Trudy – 'But, shall we at least try to enjoy each other's company?' Again, I offer a big smile.

'Sounds good to me. I always enjoy your company anyway.' He looks down at my hand now lying flat on his chest.

'Well played,' I say in a teasing way. I am so rubbish at this flirting malarkey! 'So, I take it Madeline is paying for tonight?'

'In a way, I'll claim it as expenses.'

'Then I'll eat lots.'

'You always do.'

'Cheeky!' I attempt to flutter my eyelashes.

'You don't need to try so hard, Christie. I prefer the real you.'

I let my hand drop away from him. 'This might be the real me.'

'I don't think so.'

I look at him, no sign of a crinkle at the sides of his eyes… All business tonight. Oh well… I shrug and walk ahead of him, the burn of rejection flares through me.

Inside we are shown to our table, the waiter gives us our menus. I make out to read it, but I've already decided. Medium steak, fries, no starter. Not even Italian, shame on me. Let's get it over with. The waiter takes our order and hurries off to bring our drinks, hardly exotic, two sparkling spring waters. Clear heads, for clear thoughts.

'I've spoken to Madeline; she thinks it could be useful for you to go ahead with the Sarah McBride interview.'

'I'm going ahead with it anyway.'

'I know, I had already pointed that out to her. But what Madeline thinks… What she would like, if you are in agreement, is a double bill.'

'What do you mean?'

'What she's hoping for, is a double whammy. Your interview pre-recorded, explaining how Madeline's team have supported you. Obviously, at this point, it's important to keep your true identity under wraps. Madeline will gently release that within her own interview… However, just in case anybody gets an inkling of your relationship, your interview is to remain absolutely top secret, with the exception of Madeline's team.'

Ha! Does she really expect me to go along with that? 'By, Madeline's team, you mean you.'

'And her interviewer.'

'And who will that be?'

'Monty, Monty Mitten. She's known him for years, and he's the only one she'll trust to not destroy her. He'll be sympathetic.'

'To me, or to her?'

'To both of you. He's smart, and he's good at his job.'

'I watched their last interview, he seemed to treat Madeline gently.'

'He respects her right to privacy, and I suppose is flattered by the kudos the exclusivity gives him. He's clever enough to dance round the questions the public want him to ask, and wise enough to know when to back off.'

'Like when he questioned her about your relationship with each other?'

Miles offers a tight smile. 'Exactly. Madeline will reluctantly reveal her relationship with you—'

Oh, you might like to think so… That bombshell, is mine to drop!

'… So, Christie, does that sound reasonable?'

I sigh. 'I suppose, yes, that sounds reasonable.'

'So, we've cracked it before the main course.' Miles smiles properly now, his hair does its floppy thing, his eyes crinkle.

My stomach does a flip, but I can't let my traitorous flipping stomach control me. I close my eyes briefly. Give me strength to take charge of this situation, before I make a complete fool of myself. Miles is resting back in his chair now; he takes a sip of his water. His hand curls around the glass reminding me of his hand being curled around mine… And the impromptu kiss he placed on the back of it. Again, my tummy flips. I need to get on with it, before I completely lose my nerve.

I lick my lips. 'So, Miles, what's in it for you?'

He shifts in his chair. His face loses its animated appeal, is void of expression and emotion. Hard. Unlike I've seen it before. 'What do you mean?'

'What do you get out of this, besides a free meal?' I say. I can't quite look him in the eye, so start to straighten the cutlery.

'I get the satisfaction of knowing I've done my job well. I know that you will be, to the best of my ability, treated fairly in the press. I know Madeline's reputation will be held together. She'll take a knock in the popularity stakes, but ultimately, she'll be one step closer to getting what she wants.'

'And what is that?' I pick up my glass, and take a sip of the cold water, feel its icy progress to my stomach.

'Surely you know?'

I put my glass down. 'Tell me.' It sounds harsher than I intended it to.

'She wants you.'

'She'll never have me. I'm a grown woman, not the baby she abandoned.' I feel the tell-tale prickle of tears, look away briefly blinking rapidly to disperse them.

Miles sits forward, and looks around the restaurant, I presume to check if anyone's listening. 'She didn't abandon you.' His tone is low and measured. 'She did what she thought was right at the time. She knows she can't turn back the clock, she wants to get to know you.'

'She knows every little thing about me. *Ev-er-y-thing*. She's made sure of it.' And now the familiar bite of betrayal gnaws at me, chomping through my calm demeanour. The pain of my nails digging into my palms, offers scant distraction.

'She wants your forgiveness. She knows she has to earn it, give her the chance, Christie.'

I shake my head. 'Why, why should I?'

'Because you're a good person, and she's a good person, and you're both hurting. And I'm not saying it's going to be painless for both of you… But think of your parents stuck between the two of you…'

Now that's a low blow I wasn't expecting! 'That is not fair, Miles! It's not my doing.'

'But it could be your undoing. You could make it right—'

I could make it right? He sits there and puts that burden on me, like I haven't got enough to deal with at the moment.

'… Come on, agree, in principle at least to the double exposé, and let's enjoy our meal. The rest will probably pan out in time.'

The waiter sets our plates before us.

'Okay, Miles, one condition.' Our eyes lock.

Although he's still smiling, I didn't miss the unease, which, just for a split second flashed in his eyes. 'And what condition is that?'

'You. Why are you so loyal to Madeline? Why do you always defend her?'

'That's easy, it's my job.' He relaxes back in his seat.

I carefully remove the napkin from my lap, place it on the table beside my plate, and make to stand up and leave. With my hands resting on the table I lean very close to Miles, I do not want him to miss a word. 'There is no point in me being here, Miles. If you think you can pacify me with a throwaway line like that... I have spent a lifetime living, what is basically a lie. No more, Miles. From now on, I'm questioning everything and everybody... If you want to go back to Madeline with this sorted, I expect more than that.' I stand up. 'I deserve more than that.'

An unnatural hush settles around us.

'Wait!' He half stands and makes a grab for my hand still resting on the table. 'Sit down, please... I'll explain, but it's complicated.'

I ease back into my chair, and even though the only person I can see is Miles, I know everybody else's eyes are on us. The hush is replaced by an energetic buzz of conversation, and I'm sure we are central to most of that buzz. I replace the napkin on my lap, and try to rein in some calm by taking deep breaths. I'm not sure I really want to know what hold Madeline has over Miles. But I do know, that I need to know.

'Most things are complicated, Miles. But your loyalty toward Madeline, has nothing to do with working for her. One thing I do know, is that loyalty is earned.'

He shuffles uneasily in his seat. All of a sudden, that usual confident, and totally in control man before me, appears vulnerable. 'I've never told anyone.'

'So, the choice is yours.' I can still feel the people around looking at us. My steak smells delicious, but I can sacrifice it. 'You can carry on the rest of your life, and tell no one, and I'll walk away, or you can tell me, and earn brownie points with Madeline for getting me to agree to this exposé. Look, Miles, I need to know if *I* can trust you, and why.'

'Okay.' Miles shakes his head. 'I'll explain it all to you. But please, tell no one else, not Trudy, not Suzi.'

I nod my agreement.

Miles lowers his gaze. 'It started with me. I was kind of the first *Keep-a-Key* kid.'

The conversation in the restaurant is back to normal. I'm sure one or two folk are still taking sneaky looks our way. I wonder if any of them have noticed Miles' ashen face. I don't think he'd risk lying to me now, but it sounds too farfetched to believe.

I narrow my eyes. 'What do you mean? The charity has only been going for a couple of years, and you must be at least late twenties.'

'I'm thirty... It's a tricky truth... Long, long ago, in the dark ages... They were dark ages for me anyway, my mum left us. By us, I mean me and my dad. She was unstable, unreliable, and she probably thought she was doing me a favour. She drank too much.' He shrugs.

'I'm sorry.'

'It happens. It's not your fault. I was fourteen, knew everything, so I thought. Smart ass at school, too smart to pay attention in class, not smart enough to keep my mouth shut at home. Dad did his best, but I was out of

206

control, lashing out because I was hurting... He was handy, with his fists.' Miles touches the scar on his face. 'He didn't mean to, didn't want to be that person, he just couldn't cope with me... With no help.'

I let out the breath, I didn't know I was holding. 'Sounds like hell... For both of you...'

'I know it was for me. I was always getting into bits of bother, with the police. This one night, I was almost seventeen and up to no good as usual. They took me home, laid it on thick, gave me a good talking to... Anyway, when they left, Dad just exploded. Told me to get out, he didn't want to ever see my face again... And he hasn't.'

Our meals sit between us, untouched.

'Harsh.'

Miles looks down, straightens his cutlery. 'He did me a favour. He would probably have ended up killing me, or me him. I'd grabbed some money, was okay for a couple of nights, slept on friend's sofas, that kind of thing. But I needed to get away. So, I started walking. Walked for weeks. I looked older than my years, did bits of jobs on farms for food, money, or a bed for the night. Eventually I ended up in Ashwood, the posh end of Chippington. Someone had taken a disliking to me, and I was nursing a few cuts and bruises.'

'I can't even imagine living like that.'

Miles looks me in the eyes, lets out a quiet mirthless laugh. 'I was surviving. It was still, kind of an adventure.' Miles rests his chin on his hand, glances away, then focuses on some distant vision. 'I was scrunched up in a church porch keeping warm, or hiding. It was late, after eleven. It was cold, I was hungry and sore. This woman came and sat in the porch. I don't think she even saw me at first. She was muttering away to herself. I thought she was probably a bit la-la. Then she started talking to me, and she seemed a bit posh, kind. I thought she might give me some money if I gave her a sob story. So, she got a potted history of what had happened to me.'

'Madeline?' I guess.

'Madeline, only she didn't give me any money, hasn't, ever, actually. She took me home, fed me. One of her famous dribbling bacon butties, gave me a bed for the night. Before I woke up the next morning, she'd bought me new clothes and lined up a job interview for me at one of the market gardeners.'

'Fast worker.'

'That's Madeline. I wouldn't tell her my name, and when she asked where I'd come from, I just said I'd travelled for miles. She called me Miles. And it's been my name ever since. Later on, when I trusted her, I told her my real name... I changed it to Miles Hepworth when I was eighteen.'

'So, your dad couldn't trace you?'

'I doubt he'd want to. No, just so I could have a real chance at being the person Madeline thought I could be. She said, "Miles, no one is on the scrap heap at sixteen." And she's right. She turned my life around; in the same way she's turning around the lives of the other *Keep-a-Key* kids.'

'So, she really is a saint.'

'Ha, if only. At first, she was like a woman possessed. Made me go to night school to do my GCSE's. Then browbeat me into going to college and university. Told me I owed it to her for harbouring a minor. Said that I'd be wasting my life, if I didn't make something of myself, after all the hard work she'd put in, to reform me! So here I am, apparently reformed, and making something of myself... I hope.' His gaze returns to me.

I can read the vulnerability still lingering in his eyes; eyes which are usually assured and confident. I offer a small smile, resist the urge to reach out and touch his hand. 'I'm sure she's very proud of you.' Somehow the words don't ring true. And I can tell by the look on Miles' face that he thinks so too. 'Not proud, pleased with you, pleased for you. I don't know…'

'I think she still sees me as a work in progress.' He nods. 'And I always will be; we all are... She would give anything to be part of your life, Christie.'

'I've already worked that out for myself.' I look away.

'Can you not see, in a weird way, it's because of you, she goes so far out of her comfort zone to help kids?'

'Miles, honestly… I don't want to hear it. I get it now. I get why you are her most loyal supporter. But please, please don't expect me to play happy families. Madeline might know everything there is to know about me, but everything I know about her, is second hand. And she sounds wonderful, she does great work, helps lots of kids…' I shrug, raise my eyes to his.

'But?'

'I agree to do the interviews the way Madeline wants. I'm sure you'll be put in charge of organising that, so good luck. I'll keep your secret, Miles. And I respect your loyalty to Madeline. I hope we can be friends, you and I.'

'Me too.' Miles gestures to the untouched food between us. 'Lost your appetite?'

I nod. Miles gets the bill, and we leave. The silence in the car on the way back home is as deafening as it was on our way out. My stomach churns. I can't decide if it's with hunger, nerves, or both. I risk a glance at Miles. His eyes are fixed on the road, his face tense, emotional shutters closed. His fingers aren't drumming their usual random beat on the steering wheel.

For some reason I miss it.

I need to be away from him. Need time to process; time to weave the Miles I was getting to know, with the Miles, Madeline already knows.

The Miles she helped create.

This night hasn't been what either of us expected. I think he regrets revealing so much of himself. I'm glad he has. Glad at least to know why Madeline is so precious to him. I can't compete with her.

Won't.

She will always be the one he looks up to. I'm not going to set myself up for that fall. No matter how brave and vulnerable and beautiful he is. That particular fall would probably kill me.

The car stops outside my home, and Miles turns to me and offers a half-hearted smile. 'Good night, Christie. I'll start making the appropriate arrangements first thing tomorrow. I'll be in touch.' He starts to open his car door.

'Don't get out, I can manage myself, thank you.' My crisp words sound harsher than I intend, but I can't risk him seeing me fall apart.

I reach out and cup his scarred cheek with my hand, and look into his questioning eyes. Hope he can't see the longing in mine. Without thinking, I lean forward and brush a kiss on his lips, scarcely touching him at all, enough to send a jolt of regret through my entire body. I get out of the car without uttering a word, and walk towards the front door. I don't look back. Silent tears escape.

Too late.

Trudy is right.

I love him.

Paint Away the Heartache

He looks amused.

I close my bedroom door quietly behind me. I don't want Trudy or Suzi to see me like this. Luckily, I think neither of them heard me come in. I can wallow peacefully here. I curl up in a ball on the bed, and force out my tears. My stomach feels hollow, cramps as I hug myself.

I want to howl like a wounded wolf, instead silent sobs scream into my duvet. Thank God he doesn't know how I feel about him.

Will never know.

He will always belong to Madeline. But tonight, I will give myself permission to acknowledge the truth. Let myself grieve for losing him, before I've fully accepted my true feelings for him.

I love Miles.

Why couldn't it be someone like Nigel, with his easy smile and predictable nature? Someone easy to love, whose past isn't tangled with Madeline.

But Miles is easy to love.

Too easy.

So easy to love, I did it without even knowing. And now I do know, I've got to stop. I've got to pretend my only interest in him is professional.

I peel off my clothes, add them to the mound behind the door. I drag on my ragged painting garb. Head along the landing towards the little stairs to the attic, as quietly as I can. I need to paint.

Suzi nudges her head out of her bedroom. 'Thought you'd gone out with the marvellous Miles... Christie! What's the matter?' Suzi darts from her room, catches my arm. 'What's happened?'

I close my eyes and shake my head. 'Nothing,' I mutter, I can't say the words. 'I'm okay.'

'Trudy, are you awake!' barks Suzi at full pitch. 'Miles has upset Christie... Again!'

Trudy joins us on the landing, her skinny silk kimono, a stark contrast to Suzi's *Me to You* fleecy dressing gown, and my paint-splattered T-shirt and joggers. I look up to meet Trudy's questioning eyes.

I shake my head. 'He's not who I thought he was.'

'Go and paint,' says Trudy.

Suzi scowls. 'What's happened?'

'I don't know,' says Trudy. 'I think Christie needs to work that out for herself, and she does that best by painting, alone... So, let's leave her to it, okay?'

Suzi touches my arm. 'Do you want me to sit with you?'

I shake my head and carry on up the stairs to the attic. I push open the door, close my eyes, and breathe in the magical mix of aromas, soothing and enticing, promising relief. I open my eyes and see if I can spot the booby traps I set last time I was in here. No idea, I squat down and crawl under my desk. Cobwebs and a pine cone. And a knitting needle, and what? Green, gloopy and smelly, it can only be *Swarfega*; Suzi hasn't been in, or she would have cleaned it up!

I select an A3 cold press paper, secure it to my easel. Brushes, lint, pallet and water; I mix hues, colour. Closing my eyes, I bring the image of Miles sat across from me tonight. All the emotional elements of his personality drawn on his face. Each facet only hinting at revealing a hidden past. A past he wants to keep hidden, a past steeped in Madeline and misery.

His face is strong, solid jaw with a slight dimple, even and high cheek bones. Eyes of depth and emotion. Raven hair always threatening to tumble forward over his forehead. A scar. A face which conveys confidence. Expects respect. Is loved.

I open my eyes and look at the blank paper. My stomach rumbles, I pull out a Snicker from my desk drawer, eat without tasting. All my senses centre towards the task ahead.

Okay, Christina Anne Harris, if you are an artist, make art.

I toss the chocolate wrapper in the general direction of the bin, stretch my arms above my head, roll my shoulders, and begin.

First, I paint in the background, next I block in the colour. I stand back, close my eyes and bring Miles into my mind's eye. Stepping back to my easel, selecting a broad brush I start marking out his outline. Stepping back often, checking detail and proportion. I start making tentative strokes with a fine brush… Soon they are bolder and more confident, almost taking on Miles' persona. I work all night like a woman possessed, constantly assessing, adding texture and depth. Each brush stroke, a symbol of my love for him.

Eventually, the essence of satisfaction begins to seep into me. I finish by dry brushing before the urge to alter any part of his image strikes. As the first light of morning streaks through the skylight illuminating the portrait, I see the face of the man I would happily see every morning for the rest of my life.

Miles.

There's a hint of amusement in his eyes. The slight tug of a smile on his lips. His hair is threatening to fall over his forehead. A scar, well healed, but not concealed, a stark reminder of what he has left behind, and who rescued him.

The urge to reach out and trace his face swamps me. I will when the paint is fully dry, I know I will.

I don't know at what point I decided it, but it was sometime during my frantic painting hours… This will be my final painting for Madeline. For Auntie Maddie. I can't torture myself by seeing him every day, out of reach. I might be the artist, but Miles is Madeline's masterpiece.

I rest back on my chair, close my eyes.

An insistent tapping on the door disturbs my peace. 'Christie, are you still in there?' says Trudy. 'I've brought you coffee, can I come in?'

I must have made some kind of positive sound, because the door swings open and she's in before I've even had the chance to cover my work.

'Don't cover it.' She settles the mug of coffee into my hands. Stands behind me, and places a hand on each of my shoulders, rolls her thumbs to unknot my muscles. After a couple of minutes, she stops and rests her chin on the top of my head. I know she's trying to see Miles through my eyes.

'You're right, Christie, he is beautiful.'

'I know.' I can feel a prickly tickle in my nose, the warning that tears are about to fall.

'So, do you want to talk about what happened?'

I reach for a piece of lint to dab my dripping nose. I nod, not sure what to say.

'If you'd rather not…' offers Trudy.

'No, I think I have to. I'm not sure where to start.'

'Something neutral, the interview, did you sort out a way forward?'

'Yes, me and Madeline, we're both doing our own interview; hers will be immediately after mine. Mine will be pre-recorded, and top secret until it is broadcast. Hers will be live, and I presume she'll respond to what I've said. She's going to tell the world.' My words sound flat.

'And you're happy with that?'

'Happy?' I shrug. 'I can't outmanoeuvre her, and she knows it. The best I can do, is play her at her own game, try to get some sympathy without sticking the knife in. I've not told Miles, but I'm going to let slip in my interview that Madeline's my birth mother… I need to be careful; I've got Mum and Dad to consider in all this.'

'She's a manipulative cow.'

'She's Madeline De-Muir, and my mother.'

'And a manipulative cow.'

'I think, honestly Trudy, she does regret what she did.'

'She didn't have to make it all so public,' says Trudy.

'It is, what it is.'

'And what of Miles?'

I swallow, and close my eyes.

And what of Miles?

I open my eyes to see him looking back at me.

And what about you Miles? 'I think it's best for me to forget about Miles.'

'But!' Trudy gestures towards the painting before us. 'It's plain to see what he means to you.'

'It's plain for *you* to see, because you know me. Anyway, it doesn't matter what I think of him, it's what he thinks of Madeline...'

'And what does he think of her?'

'It's complicated.'

'Try me.'

'He's in awe of all her charity work. Probably has some hero worship going on, I can't compete. I'm just me.'

'So, she does a bit of charity work. That doesn't make her a saint.'

'It does to Miles. He'd do anything for her. It's better for me to keep everything professional, and leave them to it.'

'And this will be what, a reminder of what could have been?'

'It's my final work for Auntie Maddie. He'll always belong to her.'

Trudy moves next to me, her hand finds mine, and she gives it a squeeze. It acts as a trigger to my tears, I put my untouched coffee down, shake my head. She puts her arms around me and just holds me tight. 'Shh, come on, if it's meant to be, it will be.'

'No, there's too much happened between us.'

'The only thing standing between you, is Madeline, and I doubt Miles even knows it. Sometimes, Christie, it's worth the risk to get what you want.'

'I've never been one for risks.'

'Says the girl who set the church on fire.'

'That was an accident.' I half smile.

'I know, but you saw a way to heat up the church, and you made it happen.'

'I nearly burnt the entire church down!'

'No... Well okay, there was a lot of smoke, and you caused significant damage to the boiler house.'

'And could have killed off half the congregation.'

'Ha! They're indestructible... The point is, the church got a new heating system. You achieved your goal.'

'Point taken, but this is different.'

'Why? Because it's something for yourself?'

'No.' I gulp. 'Because he might not want me. I might be nothing more than a project.'

Trudy steps back and looks at me. She passes me more lint for my nose, and runs each of her thumbs under my eyes to push away the tears. She smiles.

'What?' I say.

'If Miles doesn't love every ounce of you, then he's the biggest fool this side of the Pennines. And as we both know, there's lots of worthy competition for that title.'

'Is it worth the risk of making a fool of myself, or making things even more complicated with Madeline?'

'Only you know the answer to that. But if it were me, then, hell yes!'

'Says the brave and the bold Lady Prudence Drummond!'

'I've only ever been Trudy, to the brave and the bold Christie Harris!' Trudy's face becomes serious again. 'Think about it.'

The flap-flap of Suzi's slippers on the stairs jolts me into action. I lunge forwards to drag a sheet over my painting.

Trudy catches my hand. 'Let her see. We've never had secrets, us three.'

'Cooeee...' Suzi's head pops through the open door. 'Is this a private party or can anyone...' She stops, mouth open, eyes agog. 'Oh… My… Word!' Trudy rolls in her lips to stop herself from laughing. I look heavenward. 'How long have you been—'

'I've been painting all night,' I say.

'No, how long…' Suzi wags her finger at me, narrows her eyes. 'Exactly how long, have you been in love with him, Christie?'

'All night.'

Suzi's face is like The London Eye on New Year's Eve. 'Oh, really?'

'She's only just realised.'

'Okay.'

'He's the mystery man I kept bumping into.' I explain.

Suzi nods. 'I see. He looks amused.'

'I'm sure he will be, if he ever finds out,' I say.

'Very wise, to play it cool, Christie, let him do all the running.'

Trudy shakes her head. 'He's a slow starter, on account of being handcuffed to the starting post by Madeline.'

'Madeline won't let him date you?' blusters Suzi. 'That's twisted, who does she think she is?'

'It's complicated,' I say. 'I'm sure she lets Miles date whoever he wants.'

'I'm going to *Google* him, what's his last name? Hepworth isn't it?' Suzi whips her mobile out of her dressing gown pocket. 'Let's see what—'

'Suzi, don't bother. It doesn't make any difference.'

'He might bat for the other side for all you know!' Suzi carries on tapping away.

'And I might not want the hassle of a boyfriend, with all my new-found fame.' I lie.

'I hadn't thought of that, but…' Suzi examines her screen. 'It's not coming up with anything anyway, other than Madeline De-Muir.'

Trudy grins. 'So, there we are, Madeline must keep him far too busy to fraternise with members of any sex, and I'm sure Christie can depend on us two to be discreet?'

'That goes without saying,' says Suzi.

Trudy suppresses a snort. 'Anyway, you haven't signed it yet. Do that, and once it's dried, I'll take it to your usual place to be framed.'

'No! I want it to go somewhere else, somewhere they don't know me. There's a picture framing shop on Vine Street in Driftwood Sands, take it there. I've heard they'll sometimes do it while you wait, if they're not busy; for a price. Please, if it's not too much trouble.'

'What's the hurry?'

'It marks the end. I want this charade with Madeline over, the sooner the better.'

'Get it signed,' says Trudy.

I select a fine brush and roll the bristles between my fingers, I dip it into the crimson paint on my pallet, and scrawl *Christie* under Miles' handsome face. I'm almost tempted to add "The end".

'All yours, Trudy. I'm off to bed.' I stand up, rinse my brushes, and do something I thought I'd never be able to do. I leave the two of them alone in my attic, no booby traps.

Glow White Knickers

... swooning like a Victorian lady.

Suzi is in mothering mode. My bedroom floor has been liberated from the mounds of washing. T-shirts, joggers and jeans are on the line. My glow white knickers are lined up respectfully along the landing radiator.

Suzi no longer allows underwear to go on the downstairs radiators. What seems like a lifetime ago, when I was going out with Nigel, he called to pick me up, and rows of Suzi's knickers covered the lounge radiators. Suzi was mortified, and ever since, knickers only ever go upstairs. Suzi instigated an underwear embargo downstairs, so that no one ever needs to suffer that embarrassment again. I do love her, but I wish she'd loosen up a bit.

She's been busy in the kitchen too, there's a cottage pie in the oven, and peeping under a tea towel, I discover an apple crumble waiting to be reheated. I can hear the hum and occasional crash of the hoover, as she's making her way round the house. The whiff of Dettol surface cleaner present in every room, is proof of a sustained attack on germs and grime. Suzi's way of keeping the world at bay.

I bring the washing in, fold it as neatly as I can, and take it upstairs, (it won't be up to Suzi's high standard). She's dragging the hoover out of my bedroom, has a healthy flush, and her usually perfect bob is skew-whiff.

'Thanks, Suzi, you didn't need to.'

'Oh, I think I did,' she says, holding up a carrier bag. 'The contents of this bag confirm you're back on your chocolate, Pepsi and occasional banana diet.'

'I have to eat when I can!' I try to defend myself. Suzi shakes her head in mock disgust. 'I'll make us both a cup of coffee,' I offer.

I dash downstairs as Trudy is coming in; she's carrying a large package wrapped in brown paper under her arm.

'You'd better make that three, I'm gasping. Why is it, that when I go to Driftwood Sands, the world and his mother goes too?'

'School holidays,' I say.

'Fine day,' shouts Suzi, bumping the hoover down the stairs. 'Is that what I think it is?'

'Yep.' Trudy puts the package down on the kitchen counter.

I try not to look at it. 'Thank you, Trudy, for taking it. How does it look in the frame?'

Trudy grins. 'It looks complete, and oh so obvious! I browbeat a man of about eighty-five into working at the speed of light to get it done. I had to bribe him with tickets to see Peter Kay at the Old Palace!'

'You had tickets to see Peter Kay?' asks Suzi.

'I went and bought him two tickets while he was framing Miles, you numpty!'

'He's awesome. Mum and Dad have seen him five times!' says Suzi.

Trudy's eyes twinkle. 'So, Christie, shall I unwrap Miles, or shall you?'

I pick up the package and lay it flat on the table. I can feel the frame beneath the thick brown paper. It's fastened with course jute string tied in a double bow knot. I pull the outer knot loose, and slowly pull open the bow. Smoothing the string aside, I find the edge of the brown paper, take a deep breath and peel it back to reveal Miles. A natural wooden frame complements his unnaturally beautiful face. He looks even more amused than I remember. I look away unable to speak.

'I think,' says Suzi, 'this is your best ever.' She gives me a quick squeeze.

I feel them both watching me. I pick up the portrait, hold it at arm's length. Remembering the frantic brush strokes of last night, I close my eyes and burn the image into my memory. I open my eyes, and lay the portrait back on top of the brown wrapping paper.

'I think you might be right,' says Trudy. 'Christie's poured her heart out.' She does what I long to, she traces her finger over Miles' face, from his brow to his chin, and then back up to his scar. 'I wonder how he got it.'

I shrug my shoulders, not sure if it was really a question aimed at me. My fingers flutter to my neck as I feel the familiar lump building in my throat, try to swallow it away. I don't want to remember his secrets, his past. They drag me closer to him. Bind him to my soul. I close my eyes, remember the scant kiss of last night. Wish for once, I'd been bold enough to drag him into my arms and—

'Boys will be boys, I suppose!' says Trudy. 'Both of my brothers spent half their school holidays in casualty. Mum used to say she needed a siren on the Range Rover!'

'I once stood on a nail,' says Suzi. 'It hurt too!'

'It would,' I say, thinking of Miles' hurt. My fingers instinctively following the same trail Trudy's had, over his brow, his cheek, his chin, and then back to that scar. It must remind him every day of what he's left

Kathleen Clunan

behind. I can almost see the frightened boy scrunched up in that church porch, hiding and alone. I can't even imagine what it must feel like to be totally alone.

I swallow back tears again. I fold the brown paper back over his face; stroke it down like a blanket over a baby. I tie the string into a neat single bow, a double knot would be too final. Place it back on the counter. I can see their concern as I face my friends, my forced smile warning them to leave those questions unasked.

'Tea should be ready now,' says Suzi heading towards the oven.

Trudy dusts her hands. 'I'll just go and have a wash; I always feel grubby when I've been shopping.'

'And I'll set the table,' I mutter.

Suzi rummages in the cupboard, and pulls out a tin of mushy peas. 'Ta da!' she says. 'Got to have mushy peas with cottage pie.' She puts them in a bowl and into the microwave. 'And ta da!' she says whipping the tea towel from over the apple crumble.

'I'd already peeped, but cream or custard?'

'Whatever you fancy, we've got both.'

'Look who I found lurking on the doorstep,' says Trudy, leading Miles into the kitchen.

'Let me guess, just passing?' says Suzi.

'No, a peace offering,' he says, holding forward a tin foil container. 'It's sticky toffee pudding. You missed out last night, thought it would make up for...'

Instinctively I move towards Miles, as I try for a casual smile. It's hard not to grin like a Cheshire cat, with all these butterflies flitting about my stomach. I feel hyperaware of every sensation gushing through my body. I need to savour these moments...I know, soon enough, they'll be replaced by the dull ache of emptiness. So, I'll enjoy them while I can, practise a bit of mindfulness and live in the moment.

Merely smiling, I say, 'Thanks, but you didn't need to.' Our eyes lock. I feel his scrutiny as keenly as I feel my own heart breaking. He makes to take back the pudding with a light-heartedness I can only pretend to match. 'On the other hand, it would be rude not to accept, since you've clearly made the effort.'

As I take the pudding from him our fingers touch, a spark of recognition triggers my blush. I put my head down and turn away from him to put the pudding in the fridge.

'What, you're not going to have it?' he splutters.

I turn back around and catch his eyes sparkling with jest. 'Suzi has made an apple crumble.'

He's wearing jeans and a rugby shirt. I've never seen him in casuals before, they suit his lean physique. I can't take my eyes off him; I'm just stood gawping, and he's grinning back. I can't help remembering the kiss of last night. I shouldn't have done it. Or, I should have done more...

Suzi claps her hands. 'Snap out of it you two! Miles, you're just in time to join us for tea; cottage pie,' the microwave pings, 'and mushy peas.'

'Sounds like an offer I can't refuse... If nobody minds?' His eyes still hold mine. 'I have made some progress in moving things forward with the interviews, I could fill you in with the details later, if you like?'

I shrug. 'Okay, but let's not talk about it until we've eaten.' I get out another knife, fork and spoon, and set his place between Suzi and Trudy, opposite me. Suzi places our meals onto the table as we all sit down.

'This is delicious,' says Miles. 'Christie's mum always says Christie would have starved to death if it weren't for you, Suzi.'

'Not true!' says Trudy. 'Christie always has a stash of chocolate, and if that does ever run out, she always has an emergency packet or two of chocolate digestives.'

'Says the vodka and Vimto queen,' I splutter, grabbing a chance to take the attention away from me.

'Can't say I've ever had that combination,' says Miles.

Suzi flashes him a smile. 'And since you're driving, you won't be having it tonight.'

And so, the banter continues, until four plates sit empty on the table. I rest back in my chair and pat my rounded tum, watching the three of them chatting easily with each other.

Like real friends.

Or family.

It could be like this. This natural. This easy. This perfect. Tears well up, I quickly collect up the plates and busy myself washing up. Their comfortable voices in the background, soaking into my reservoir of memories of Miles. Memories I'll be able to draw on later.

'You okay?' asks Suzi.

'Oh!' I drop a plate back into the sink.

'Sorry, didn't mean to startle you. Only you usually *don't* wash up,' she whispers. She picks up a tea towel and starts to dry the plates. 'And we do have a dishwasher.'

'Just putting some space between us. I'm fine.' I offer a half-hearted smile.

'I hope you two are talking about apple crumble,' says Trudy, 'because I have saved room for it.'

'Cream or custard?' Suzi lifts the steaming dessert from the oven.

Trudy raises a brow. 'What do you fancy, Miles?' she asks, her tone playful.

'Surprise me,' he says.

'Cream it is, ladies,' decides Trudy.

We eat our desserts accompanied by the same banter enjoyed during our meal. I feel like an observer almost. I join in the conversations when I need to, but feel like I'm hovering on the edge, not quite belonging. Stupid really, none of them would be here but for me. Both Trudy and Suzi seem completely at ease with him. I'm the one who is jittery. Can't let my guard down, even though last night, he did.

'Well that was lovely, Suzi, thank you, and not at all expected,' says Miles. Suzi flushes at his complement. 'Christie?'

'Yes?'

'Sorry to spoil the fun, but can we have a word about the arrangements being made for the interviews?'

'Oh, yes.' I'd forgotten why he'd called round. It wasn't to see me. 'Are you okay if we go through into the other room, don't want to bore these two with the details?' They'd both notice how frazzled I am about the whole thing. Knowing Miles' history, is going to make it impossible to be totally candid with Sarah McBride.

Miles nods. 'Ladies.' He holds out my chair, and then opens the door to the lounge. Over my shoulder I see Trudy patting her hand on her heart, and Suzi fluttering her eyelashes dramatically and swooning like a Victorian lady. It almost makes me smile. If only... If only it could be that way.

Miles sits in the same armchair he sat in when I grappled with him for Bunty's review. I try to banish the thought. This room is already laced with memories of Miles. The early evening sun bathes us in a soft golden hue. I sit at the farthest end of the sofa.

There will be no grappling tonight.

'Right then. I've had a very busy time of it, but I think I've just about gotten all of our ducks in a row. There are a few details you will need to decide on, but we'll sort those later.'

I nod for him to carry on.

'Because Madeline will only allow Monty to interview her, and she's adamant it will be a live broadcast, there is only one shot at it. Saturday twenty-fifth—'

'But that's this weekend!' I splutter. 'I go back to school on the twenty-seventh! No, it's too soon.'

He gets up and joins me on the sofa. 'Calm down, listen. I know you must feel like it's being sprung on you, but, and this is a big but, the sooner all this is out in the open, the sooner you can get back to normal.'

My head spins at the thought of ever being normal again. 'Miles, I doubt my life will ever be normal again, thanks to...' A surge of energy rockets through my body as he places his hand on mine.

'I know that it must feel like that now, but trust me, it will settle back to a new kind of normal.' I shake my head, try to drag my hand from under his, he doesn't let go. Instead, he continues, 'Because of her broken ankle, Madeline has begged Monty to interview her at home. She argued, that since it would be a personally revealing interview, it would be more intimate to do it there. Thankfully, Monty has agreed.'

'I'm sure Madeline is used to getting her own way,' I mutter.

'So that opens up the same option to you.'

'What, you mean have Sarah come here?'

'Think about it… It'd give you the girl next door appeal, and, hopefully you'd be more at ease. I must say, Sarah is chomping at the bit, and is perfectly happy to go with whatever you decide. Don't worry, wherever it takes place, I will be there to support you.' He gives my hand a squeeze.

'Will all of the interview be shown, or will it be edited?' I ask. 'I mean, what if I'm a bumbling mess?'

'You won't be, like I said, I'll be here to support you. Sarah has got twenty-seven minutes to fill, and I would say, at least half of that will be the background information she's collecting right now. Over the next two days I am allowing her and her film crew one hundred percent access to the gallery, your artwork, and whoever happens to be viewing it. So, the comments she is making to camera over the next two days can't be changed, and her angle is of course, your work.'

'She's not going to be best pleased when she finds out you've tricked her!'

'I haven't tricked her, Christie. I have *freed* her to make an absolutely honest appraisal of your work, unbiased or tainted by her opinion of Madeline.'

'I'm not sure she'll see it like that.'

'Maybe not, but she's astute enough to know that she is in a unique position, and also, that her interview with you will be pivotal as to how the public sees you.

As she already likes you, I'm sure she'll be eager to promote your profile, after all, it's going to elevate hers.'

'Okay.' I manage to prise my hand away from his. Stand up and walk over to the window, offering him the view of my back.

'Christie, she likes you. She sussed you out at the gallery the first time she met you. You chose her to do your first interview. She's going to be like the cat who got the cream after she sees Maddie's interview, and discovers Madeline is your mother. She'll be fluffing her feathers for months over her good fortune.'

Oh, dear! Sarah's going to find out much sooner than you think! 'But what if Madeline's reputation is ruined?'

'I think I know Monty well enough to say, he won't let that happen to her, or your parents. Also, Sarah has interviewed Maddie herself years ago, and I get the impression she's always liked to solve a mystery. Sarah will no doubt dig out her old interview, make another documentary by weaving a story through time. Get a second bite at the cherry, so to speak.'

'You think she'll be pragmatic over Madeline being my mother?'

'Absolutely. She's not that much older than Madeline, and I'm sure she can empathise. On the one hand, Sarah is as honest as anyone can be in her line of work, on the other; she'll not set anyone up for a fall. You chose well, Christie... But remember she is remarkable at seeing past the words you say.'

I nod, she won't need to, because I'm going to tell her who Madeline is!

I notice our front garden is in need of a good weeding. Suzi usually galvanises me and Trudy into doing something out there. I've often thought dandelions as pretty as a flower, and certainly tougher. My thoughts drift back to Sarah, 'She should have been an artist, she sees people through their emotions.'

'Use that to your advantage.' I turn to look at him, as I rest back against the windowsill. 'Let her interview you in your studio.'

'Oh, I'm sure she'd love it there! Miles! It's crammed with all sorts, there'd be no room; and besides, it's private.'

'I'm sure Suzi would help tidy, and Sarah would love to be the first to see your studio. Like I said earlier, it would give you that girl next door appeal, if you were seen struggling away in a tatty attic.'

'Hold on! I didn't say it was tatty!'

'Sorry, Cinders.' Miles laugh is deep and infectious. He puts his hands over his face, then takes them away, and looks at me seriously. 'I'm trying to make it as easy as possible for you, okay?'

I nod.

What else can I do? He's breaking my heart.

Pluck Required

... presenting him like a prize stallion.

Exhausted, I flop down on the sofa. Even though Suzi is still shuffling about upstairs in her bedroom, I refuse to feel guilty. I only had a handful of days to sort out three years of clutter in my attic studio.

It has taken all of them.

My two best buddies have been on hand in the evenings, helping heave a few boxes down the narrow stairs.

Ah, yes…And the supremely buff Simon has been on hand day and night to obey my every command. Trudy, honestly, is lucky to still be alive after presenting her sumptuous brother as a gift. I can feel the flutter of a blush creeping up my chest remembering how Trudy thrust him through the door, presenting him like a prize stallion. To say it was awkward, is something of an understatement! But, then, Simon being the consummate gentleman he is – apparently – proceeded dutifully helping his kid sister's best friend sorting out her attic.

Initially.

But, every time Miles came around to the house, Simon took on the persona of a lovestruck teen, following me about, and generally being a pain in the ass. This has made it near impossible to have any alone time with Miles. In theory a good thing.

In practice…

Very frustrating!

However, keeping me focused on the job in hand. All our bedrooms have been gifted boxes of all sorts of weird and wonderful things to keep safe until after Sarah's interview.

Suzi is mortified. Her Laura Ashley décor, has been tarnished by boxes of "junk". And now the dreaded day is here, all she is bothered about, is bedroom inspections.

In the world of Suzi, hygiene and order is of the highest priority. Her mother, a leading member of "The Little Upton Mafia" (WI), has done a sterling job of making Suzi examine every aspect of her life for signs of imperfection. Throughout Suzi's life, her mum has picked her to pieces, regardless of who was listening. At the age of twelve, Suzi made a pledge to be perfect, if only in her mother's eyes. So far, she's done a fantastic job. She only truly lets her guard down with me and Trudy, which is a shame, because she really can be very funny and mischievous. If her mother found out about the shenanigans at the gallery, Suzi's life would be hell.

Which brings us back to Suzi guarding her usually pristine bedroom from any media type, who might potentially expose it as a dump. I'm sure what those media types are going to learn about me is a tad more newsworthy, than Suzi Stapleton's bombsite of a bedroom.

Trudy passes me a cup of coffee and joins me on the sofa. 'You okay?'

'Think so.' I shrug. 'Thanks for protecting my stuff. I know Suzi would have chucked it out if she could.' I've stashed some boxes in my car boot, to save them from a trip to the tip.

Trudy turns to face me. 'She can be a bit clinical, but... Anyway, how are you feeling about the interview?'

I pull a face. I've tried not to think about it. 'I don't know, one minute I think I've got everything under control, the next I'm panicking about being sued by Madeline.'

'She can't do that; it was her idea. You'll be fine once you get into it. If you can manage a class of thirty teenage rebels, I'm sure you can manage one middle-aged dear, and a film crew.'

'Thanks for that.' I sigh.

That middle-aged dear, is supervising two cameramen, a lighting chappie, and a sound technician up in my attic as we speak. Last time I looked; they were all stricken with fear. The producer, who looks to be about fourteen, is wandering about with a mobile pressed to his ear, a tablet clutched in his hand and a scowl on his brow.

I can hear Suzi pacing the landing. She's been guarding all the bedrooms since they first arrived. I can say with certainty, the attic is the only sterile and tidy room in the entire house. Even the bathroom has had some unorthodox additions. A family of Toby Jugs reside on the windowsill, housing a selection of toothbrushes, an unsuspecting Easter Island replica statue is now a spare toilet roll holder, and a mosaic plant pot hosts a half-dead cactus. No doubt, in the fullness of time, these could all become valuable collectables, Christie Harris originals.

And what of Miles?

No idea!

So much for guiding me through this!

Oh, I know I'm being oversensitive, on account of doing my best to not be in love with the man... But honestly! The level of neglect today is helping *too* much. I'd feel much better wallowing in self-pity with Miles pandering to my every whim. Simon really was beginning to grate... Especially since, it became apparent he'd only put on his 100-watt devotion while Miles was about... Almost as if someone – Trudy – had briefed him.

Men!

For the last three days, Miles has been texting and popping in to see how I'm getting on fifty times a day, (well 2 or 3, maybe 4). And now that Simon is safely away, Miles is nowhere to be found.

Typical.

Only the absolute fear of having strangers in my sacred attic, has pushed me into making it as impersonal as I dare. That dear old lady up there now, is as sharp as they come. The less she has to pick up on, the better I feel. I've done all I can to prepare for this interview.

And now, now I've about half an hour of free time to immerse myself in the anguish of my self-denial... Miles is nowhere to be seen.

'Sorry, sorry, sorry!

Speak of the devil.

Trudy stands up. 'I'll leave you, to get on with...' She gives me a wink. 'Whatevs.' And off she goes.

Miles sits down in Trudy's place, and leans in close; the subtle aroma of his aftershave invades my senses. I can feel my heart slamming into my ribs, and my pulse quicken. For a split second I think he's going to kiss me. 'Mrs Price has had a run in with one of the kids, I had to do damage limitation, on both parts,' he whispers.

'Oh.' I manage. Maybe it would be better if he weren't here to scramble my senses.

He leans slightly away, fixes his gaze on my face. 'So, how's it going, everything under control?'

'I think so, I've been keeping out of everyone's way.' I do my best to sound relaxed, but my voice is all high-pitched and squeaky.

'No Simon, today?'

'Not today.'

Miles smiles, nods. 'I suppose Sarah has everyone jumping to attention.'

'She's very…' I turn, swivel towards the door, and put my finger over my lips. Miles frowns, I shake my head. I can hear her making her way down the stairs slowly, and quietly. I know it's her, the swish of her beads gives her away. Suzi says I've got ears like a bat. 'Oh yes, Miles, she's very efficient,' I say, loud enough for her to hear, while turning back towards Miles.

'That she is.' Miles grins, catching on. 'One of the best about. Lucky to get her.'

Sarah stomps down the last three steps and bounds into the lounge. 'Ah, there you are, thought you'd deserted the poor gal,' she declares. 'Look at her, she's like a rabbit caught in headlights.'

Miles is up on his feet, and giving Sarah air kisses. 'Couldn't be helped, but I'm sure you know I'm not the deserting kind of bloke. Certainly not if I have you to answer to.'

Sarah studies him, and snorts. She's obviously immune to his charm. 'I'm expecting you to be on your best behaviour, Miles Hepworth. Unlike the rest of the female population…' She gives me a pointed look, 'I'm unimpressed by mere lip service. I'll go back and wait in the studio while you give Christie her last-minute coaching.'

'She doesn't need any coaching,' he replies as she waddles out of the room. He shakes his head. 'Can you believe her? Just be yourself, Christie, and everyone will be enthralled.'

'I hope you're right. No last instructions?' I ask.

'Like I said, you'll be great. After all, I've already given you my foolproof way to make people fall in love with you.'

'Ah yes, but I've forgotten.'

'Come on, Sarah's waiting, and I for one am already in her bad books.' Miles takes the stairs two at a time.

I don't.

Madeline is not going to be happy when she learns I've given away the secret she's kept for twenty-four years. Especially, after I'm sure Miles assured her, I'd be a good little puppet, and do as she requested.

Not even sure I can go through with it now.

My legs are rooted like tree trunks, my belly churning like a washing machine full of bolts and my heart tries to beat its way out of my chest. I'm keeping my hands clasped together, stopping them from trembling. Suzi offers me a nervous smile as I pass her maintaining her bedroom guard.

'I take it we're going up there,' says Miles.

I nod. He's up there in no time, clanking about. I can hear him chatting to the others. Trudy's head appears in the attic doorway, grinning like a demented Cheshire cat. She waves excitedly for me to join them.

Suzi continues resting on her doorframe.

She takes her guarding very seriously.

Tilting her head, she asks, 'Have you decided what you're going to say yet?'

'No, I'm just going to be as honest as I can.' My chin gives way to a wobble, I try to rein it back under control by clamping my lips together. Blinking rapidly, I banish the threatening tears. I cannot go up there like this!

Suzi steps forward, and envelops me in a wholesome hug. Her simple show of support bolsters my resolve, but triggers another threat of tears. I feel our synergy, try to absorb strength from her, knowing she's willing it to me. 'You'll be fine.'

'Thank you,' I whisper. 'I really needed that.'

'Well for what it's worth, I think you're the bravest person I know. Everything that's happened... Well, it would have sent most people running for the hills.'

'Have I still got time?'

She shakes her head, and points to the attic. 'Afraid not, go!' She pulls her hair into two mini pigtails at the side of her head, and sticks her tongue out, making me laugh. 'Christie... Just go and be you!'

I doubt I could love this girl any more than I do right now.

The third step groans under my weight, it always does, as if to say "not you again". I usually answer it back, "and what if it is?", but not today. Today it's a relief to have its protestation. I'm tempted to loiter and force another groan.

Sarah hurries me into the attic with arms, scarves and boobs waving. 'Ah, here you are. Everything has been set up. Trudy, bless her, has been acting as your body double for our lighting chappie...' Trudy takes a bow. 'And the cameras are fixed, one will be trained on you, the other I. As you can see, it's rather cosy, but I'm sure you knew it would be, since it's your studio.

Anything else, anything else, anything else?' Sarah scratches her chin. 'Oh, Miles has stipulated no longer than twenty minutes of filming, rather stingy I think, but hay ho.'

Miles steps towards Sarah. 'I'm sure that will be plenty of time, after all you are excellent at seeking out the extraordinary in people. And Christie herself would not want this to drag on all day.'

Sarah gives him a scathing look. 'So, Christie, if you'll settle yourself on your stool, it *is* the one you use when you are painting, yes?'

'Usually, sometimes I stand up.'

'Well, as long as you keep sitting down today, dearie, that's it.'

Miles steps between me and the camera; bends down and crosses my ankles. He puts his hand in the small of my back, and gently pushes it forward. Next, he puts his forefinger under my chin, and lifts it about two inches. He nods, eyes dancing, he leans forward. 'Knees together, even in jeans.'

'Very familiar, Mr Hepworth,' notes Sarah.

'Good luck, Christie.' He leans in again, and his lips are brushing my ears, sending quivers through my body. 'Remember, don't reveal your true relationship with Maddie. Sarah is a canny one, she's bound to try and quiz you about it.' He leans out again and nods, his face no longer animated, has a haunted expression.

I can feel my face flush in readiness for the secret I'm about to spill. This is excruciating. A premeditated act to sabotage Madeline's plans, after an implied promise of silence.

'Places, everyone, step back, Mr Hepworth.' The producer claps his hands. 'Chop-chop.' His mobile and tablet are nowhere to be seen. Neither are his manners. 'I'm expecting this to be one take. If either of you *do* need a break, raise a hand and we'll cut.'

Sarah shuffles her ample behind into her chair, and smiles for the camera. Her bounteous breasts are buried behind layers of scarves, I do hope they don't become too animated. Her hands rest gracefully on her lap. She is poised, and oddly elegant in an ecliptic kind of way. The urge to grab a sketch pad and pencil overcomes me.

'Excuse me,' I say. 'Could I get out a pad, I think it might make for a more relaxed mood.'

'If you think it would help.' The producer snaps. 'Don't move. You can get it.' He points to Trudy. She raises a brow, but rummages in my desk drawer and finds an A5 pad and passes it to me.

'And a pencil, sharp please,' I say. It takes her a moment, but she passes me one.

'Okay, step away, Miss,' the producer says. 'All ready? Good.' He whips out a clapboard. 'On my count, three, two, one, take one, action.'

Snap!

Arrhhh, nearly had my nose off! I didn't know they actually still did that.

'Hello, I'm Sarah McBride, and I feel very honoured to be invited here, to the attic studio of Christie Harris. Hello, Christie.'

'Hello.' I glance at my pad, and my hand starts guiding my pencil over the paper.

Sarah's eyes twinkle. 'I'm sure some of you are aware of Christie's explosion onto the art world scene. Although this is not remarkable in itself, Christie's work is. And that is because of the meticulous attention to detail, not only of her work, but of the evolution of her progress from an early age. So, Christie, how did it all start?'

'I have always loved to sketch and paint, and am lucky to have parents who have given me the freedom and support to do it.' My pencil is moving frantically over the paper.

'But I notice that your work is only chronicled from the age of eight. What changed when you were eight?'

I close my eyes for a second, and remember my dear old Auntie Maddie. I miss her. And that red sports car, which has for years – if I'd ever been honest with myself – bugged me for being so out of character for an old dear.

'You're smiling, Christie, want to share?'

'When I was young, my very old, and very dear Auntie, used to visit. She was for a while, always bobbing round, she took a great deal of time to delve into my soul.'

'How so?'

'She was always asking about my friends, what I did, what I liked, hated. I suppose she was just curious about how I spent my time. On the last time I remember her visiting, she asked me what I wanted to be when I grew up.'

'And you said?'

'More than anything in the world, I wanted to be an artist. So, she set me a challenge, to prove my determination, and that was to send her two pieces of artwork every half-term.'

'And I believe the artwork in the exhibition *Evolution,* is the sum of all that work.'

'Yes, yes, it is.'

Sarah nods her encouragement, and looks for all the world, a sweet old dear, herself. 'Had it not been for your Auntie, do you think you would have been so unwavering with your artwork?'

'Never!' I laugh. 'The thought of letting her down used to keep me awake at night. Still does.'

'You still send it to her?'

'Oh yes, in fact my latest piece is waiting downstairs. I'm going to deliver it later.'

'So why does it keep you awake at night?'

I pull a face. Why does it? Why? 'I suppose when someone expects the best from you, you only ever try to give them your best. If she'd have said, send me a painting whenever you feel like it, I might have only sent her a couple, and then got bored.'

'So, you started sending her paintings, and then what?'

'She started writing back, encouraging me. She always made a point of asking for the story behind the work at first. And I remember her saying the work should tell her the story. I think that is when I started to push myself.' I glance down at the sketch my hand is creating, almost of its own will.

'So, had it not been for her, you might have even given up?'

My pencil stops. Looking down at my pad I try to process this question. Sarah is coming along nicely. Would I have given up? I look back at Sarah. 'I think I might have wavered, but being creative is part of who I am. The *Evolution* exhibition defines me as an individual. Every facet of my personality is etched out for anyone to see. It's personal. The shape of the person I am now, has been composed by who I've been while I've been growing up.' I shrug. 'But I suppose that's true of everyone.' I try to search out

Miles, but the lighting is too strong for me to see beyond it.

'My, that's a profound statement from one so young! I can tell you are trying to see your friends who are here with us today. Have they also been supportive over the years?'

'Oh, yes, although they were both surprised to be on public display!'

'You didn't tell them?'

'They hadn't seen all of the pictures, and it didn't occur to me that they'd ever see them.' I tap my lips with my pencil. Shut up, Christie!

'But surely, when you started to put the exhibition together, you must have thought about it then.'

I look down at my pad. Sarah really is coming along nicely. I'll show her at the end of the interview. I tap my lips with the pencil again, and look directly at Sarah. I wonder if she can feel the vibes coming from me, if her intuition is that good. Wonder if she can see my heart pounding under my Elmo T-shirt. 'I didn't take any part in the planning of the exhibition… Actually, I didn't even know anything about it, until that first day I met you.'

There, I've made the first admission, the rest should be easier.

'Let me get this clear.' I can see Sarah mentally regrouping. 'You didn't even know about *Evolution*?'

'That's right. In fact, you, and the other art critics knew about it before me.' I'm gripped by the same feelings now as I was then. I shuffle on my stool. Try to shift the queasy tummy and internal quiver.

Sarah sits bolt upright in her seat, and her bosom swings to life. 'So, excuse me, but I'm having a problem piecing this together. You didn't know, or participate in *any* of the preparation for *Evolution*, beyond it being your art in the exhibition.'

'That is correct.'

I can almost see her mind scrambling for facts, and snippets from our previous encounters. An almost unperceivable smile tugs at the side of her lips. I think she's made some connections. Surprised it's taken her this long. Her eyes lock with mine briefly, then she talks directly to the camera. 'The *Evolution* exhibition is housed in an old mill which has been redeveloped with the *Keep-a-Key* charity.' Then back to me. 'Of course, you know that, Christie.'

'Yes, I do, that's right. You interviewed one of the teenagers helped by that charity, didn't you?' I try to stave off the more probing questions.

'I did. The charity's founder, is Madeline De-Muir. She's quite a philanthropist. I remember asking you last time we met, if you had ever met her yourself, and you said you had, briefly.'

'That's right.'

Here we go. My queasy tummy is gripped by an iron fist.

'Forgive me, but could it be possible, for your Auntie and Madeline De-Muir to be one and the same person?'

If I can capture the look of excitement on her face. Her eyes are positively electric, her jowl is quivering. She leans forwards in her chair. The various fabrics of her scarves clamour for attention; beneath them her bosom oscillates.

'Christie?'

'Yes.' I clear my throat, and my thoughts. 'They are one and the same.'

'Okay.' Sarah rests back in her chair. Her breasts back under control. She's studying me. 'Is this something you have always known, or is this too, something you have only recently found out?'

Cunning.

'It's something I have known for a little while,' I answer honestly, vaguely.

'And, how did you find out?' Sarah shakes her head. 'It must have been quite a shock.'

'It was, although when I look back, my Auntie... Auntie Maddie, was always cloaked in mystery. She appeared to be an old lady, but she drove a red sports car.' I shrug. 'My painting, *The Long Farewell*, was painted from memory, my final childhood meeting with her.'

'I remember the way you were looking at it in the gallery when we first met, with longing?'

'Yes, I suppose I was. We have an odd kind of relationship,' I muse. 'She used to send me hurried postcards from exotic parts of the world, then sometimes rambling five-page letters packed with all sorts of things. I always looked forward to hearing from her.'

'You must have felt like it was a very special relationship.'

'Yes. As we never actually saw each other, I felt able to tell her anything and everything about my life.' At last some of the anxiety is ebbing away.

'All your secrets?'

'All my secrets, yes. All my worries, and my hopes, and all the icky teenage stuff we've all stressed about.'

'Your relationship was that close?'

I nod, hold her gaze.

'So, I wonder, why she kept her identity a secret from you.'

'I don't know, honestly. I have it on good authority it was to protect me, and that is as much as I know.' I look away, try again to seek out Miles' face behind the lighting. I've got to hold on to the facts as long as I can. I hope no one can see me shaking.

'So, when you discovered Madeline had organised an exhibition of all your artwork, how did you feel?'

My pencil stops scribbling, and I look at Sarah. I can tell she knows her question is distressing to me. Her expression is one of compassion not cruelty; that alone prompts me to answer. 'My work is, as I said earlier, an expression of who I am, and how I got to be me. And yes, initially I did feel like I personally was on display. I felt exposed, vulnerable. I felt like she'd taken advantage of me. Betrayed my trust. But Auntie Maddie was part of how I became who I am. Someone asked me a question, a question I would never have asked myself...'

'And that was?'

'Would I have ever been brave enough to risk exhibiting my work? Risk bad reviews, failure. And I know, deep down, I'm not brave at all. I'm not the kind of person who thrives on adventure, so I would never have fulfilled my ambition of becoming an artist. Not ever. I'm a happy trundler, I trundle along, and if I come up against a huge problem in my way, I go around it, rather than try to tackle it.'

So now the whole world knows I'm a coward. And still my hand is guiding the pencil across the paper.

'So, now, how do you feel about Madeline taking the bold step to exhibit your work?'

I can tell Sarah is trying to gauge my current relationship with Madeline. 'I wish I'd had more time to get used to the idea of all this.' I wave my pencil in all directions, aiming to include all my intruders. 'And although I doubt that I could have improved on *Evolution* in any way, I still would have liked to have had the chance to work with the *Keep-a-Key* team; they're a great bunch.'

'So, would you say you've forgiven her?' Sarah tilts her head, searches my soul.

'For what?' I scrunch up my face, very attractive I'm sure. For a moment there, I forgot she doesn't know Madeline is my long-lost mother

'For taking things into her own hands.'

I offer what I hope is an indulgent smile, maybe folk will forget my scrunched-up face. 'In her own way, she feels like she's finished what she started. After all, had she not prompted me to put some effort and discipline into my art, who knows what I'd be doing now?'

I know I wouldn't be sat here trying to smile and look normal, that's for sure. I am smiling my best smile at Sarah, but I've a feeling she's unravelling the truth. Every time I've met her, it's like she can strip back my words, and sense what's going on behind them. She's like that old-fashioned TV detective, Columbo, who always has just one more question.

'I wonder, it does seem odd that someone of Madeline De-Muir's calibre, would select one little girl, and strive to mentor her over almost two decades.'

Here we go, so Sarah might just have put two and two together and made the magical four.

'As you said yourself, she is renowned for her philanthropist endeavours.' I wave my hand, and dart a look at the camera.

'Have you not wondered why, of all the little girls, in all the villages, in all of England, why you? And why the charade?'

My heart is pounding so hard in my chest, I'm sure it can be seen. My mouth is dry, and my pencil has lost its will to sketch. I look directly into the camera focused on me, and then to the set of Sarah's face.

She knows.

Her eyes are telling me she won't push me. I know this look well; it's the look Dad gives me. A look of expectation. There will be no cajoling, no pressure, just the expectation that I will make the right choice, because it's the right thing to do.

I look down at the almost completed sketch. Slowly, I close up my pad and clasp it with my pencil in my lap. Forcing myself not to raise my hand for a break is almost killing me. If I don't say it now, it will be up to Madeline to offer her story first.

I look up at Sarah. Her eyes are like pools of pure compassion, and I regret closing my pad. She reaches across and brushes my arm with her hand. The tender gesture is almost my undoing. I swallow back the tears as I feel them forming.

'Take your time, dear, we are all friends here,' she says.

'Madeline is my biological mother.' The hushed words seem to speak themselves. 'I never knew.'

'You've only just found out?' Sarah asks almost reverently.

'Only just.'

It feels like a lifetime ago.

'It must have been a shock.'

'It was.' I bite the inside of my cheek.

'Would you like to take a moment?'

'No.' I shake my head; I can feel a single tear trickle down the side of my nose.

'Okay.' She nods and looks to camera. 'I'm sure we can all see this is not easy for Christie to talk about.' She looks back at me. 'It seems, Christie, if you met with Madeline alias Auntie Maddie as a child, your parents must have known that she was your natural mother. Is that right?'

'Yes.'

'And I also assume they were aware of your correspondence.' The lilt in her voice is calming.

I nod. 'Yes, they encouraged it.'

'They must have had a great deal of confidence that Madeline wouldn't reveal her own identity to you.'

'I believe it was agreed my childhood would not be disrupted, so they each had faith in each other. My parents trusted Madeline to keep a respectful distance. And Madeline trusted my parents to give me a stable, loving upbringing.'

'And you've had a stable and loving upbringing?'

I can hardly see for the tears in my eyes, I dash them away with the back of my hand. I hope this waterproof mascara really is. I raise my chin. 'My parents are the best.' I attempt a smile. 'Mum and Dad are my heroes.'

'Go on.'

'Dad is a vicar, and without fail sees the best in people. He's shrewd, and funny and honest. He sees beyond people's imperfections, he acknowledges we all have them, but then looks past them. I could always get away with bits and pieces with Mum... But Dad, he always saw through my master plans. Put me right, even before I went wrong.'

'Sounds like you didn't get away with too much.'

'I got up to all sorts… But you're right, I got away with nothing. Almost every week his sermons included one of my many gaffes.'

'That must have been embarrassing.'

'He didn't do it to embarrass me… He did it to prepare me for the real world. For this… I was a vicar's daughter in a rural village. Everyone knew me, and I think, to some degree I was cushioned from the harshness that is everyday life for most kids. He wanted me to be an orange not a peach.'

'I've not heard that before, what does it mean, exactly?'

'Well, peaches bruise very easily, and then go rotten quickly. An orange has a tough skin; you've got to dig a bit to get under that skin, and it only goes rotten if the skin is broken, or if it rests next to something else rotten. Basically, peaches might look good, but they don't do as well as oranges in the long run.'

'I like that. So, your dad tried to toughen you up?'

'In his own unique way, yes.'

'And your mum?'

'Mum is just Mum. She is amazing, the one who is always there when I need her. She makes everybody else's life run smoothly. She doesn't make things happen, but she makes sure everything and everyone are in place, to make it happen.'

'So, she's never the one to get the credit or stand in the limelight?'

I shake my head. 'She'd never want it. Happy to take a back seat.' An image of Mum in one of her mumsy cardigans makes me smile.

'Do you think, that could be, because she knew one day, Madeline would step in to take the limelight from her?'

'No, she's just happy away from fuss.'

'All of this now must be difficult for her to cope with.'

'She doesn't like me being upset. I think she maybe regrets not telling me sooner about who my biological mother is. She says there never seemed to be a right time. When everything settles down, she'll be much happier.'

'I'm sure she will. I'm sure it must be hard for her to let you go.'

I laugh as a fresh batch of tears swell in my eyes. 'She'll never let me go! She's my mum. How can a lifetime of memories change? I doubt I'll ever meet anyone who's as much on my side as she's always been. I love her to pieces, even though I can be a complete pain… Sorry, Mum.'

Sarah nods. 'So why now? Why has Madeline done this now?'

'Madeline wants to have a proper relationship with me, not just letters and paintings.'

'And she's used *Evolution*, as a way to entice you away from your parents?' Sarah frowns.

'Oh no; she's no intention of coming between me and my parents. Couldn't if she tried. She wants me to have a chance at being recognised as an artist in my own right, and not as Madeline De-Muir's daughter.'

'She wants you to have credibility,' says Sarah. 'That seems to be very noble.'

'Yes.'

'And refreshing, in the celebrity world of "me, me, me".'

'I know,' I say, I really hope my face looks like I'm grateful. Life would be so much simpler if Madeline were an out-and-out bitch. The more I find out about her, the more I have to admit to myself, the only

250

mistake she made was to give me away. Only one mistake, but a huge one; and she's been trying to recover from it ever since.

'She must have been what? Just sixteen when she had you. A child herself in many ways.'

'Yes.'

'It must have been a terrible decision for a young girl to have to make, to give up a baby.'

'I'm sorry, Sarah.' I close my eyes. 'I'm not comfortable speculating about the emotions of someone else.' I open my eyes. Sarah looks relaxed, in control. I feel in knots.

'Yes, of course, but I'm sure people will be interested to know what your feelings are about that.'

'I'm sure they are, but I'm not prepared to risk damaging a new kind of relationship with Madeline, simply to satisfy other people's curiosity.'

Sarah smiles and her eyes twinkle. I re-open my sketch pad, my urge to capture her twinkle takes over as my pencil glides over the page.

'You are very wise,' Sarah allows. 'So, what do you think the future holds for you now?'

'Good question. Three weeks ago, I could have answered with absolute certainty. Now I only seem to be able to think short term.' I close my eyes, and instantly an image of Miles jumps into my mind; I scrunch my eyes to banish it. I try instead to think of 7C, remember having to blast their papier-mâché maracas with a hairdryer to get them dry.... Chantelle, Dexter and the rest of my GCSE group, Mr Sloan. I open my eyes.

'So how about short term?'

'I'm eager to get back to school, and to guiding my GCSE pupils through their upcoming exams.'

'Do you expect to be treated any differently, now that everyone knows you're Madeline De-Muir's daughter?'

'It'll probably be a one-day wonder. I'd like to think people will be pleased I have an art exhibition, especially my pupils. But no, I don't think I'll be treated any differently.'

'And you plan to continue teaching?'

'I think I'll always teach. I'm as much a teacher as I am an artist. Luckily, I can do both.'

'Well you seem to be very confident of where your future lays, career-wise... What about your family, friends, relationships, boyfriends?'

'I can't see it making any difference to my friends. It hasn't so far, and I don't have a boyfriend.'

Sara nods, makes a slight shrug of her shoulders. 'It's surely bound to have an effect with your parents.'

'They have always had my best interests at heart. I can't imagine anything changing that. They will help Madeline and me ease into getting to know each other properly.'

'They must be very generous people, to help rebuild your ties with Madeline; I imagine most adoptive parents might feel threatened.'

'They are very generous. Also, they hold Madeline in very high regard.'

'Do you suspect that is because of her celebrity?'

Here goes...

One last blast of truth...

I take a deep breath. 'No... I think it is because she has kept her distance for all these years... But mostly, it's because she is *their* natural daughter.' I raise my hand to signal an end to my inquisition. I look down at the sketch of Sarah, and then pass it to her. 'I'd like you to keep this as a reminder of today. And thank you.'

'Christie, you are full of revelations! I thank you for your time.'

I incline my head in acceptance, and Sarah then looks to camera.

'And during this interview, Christie has been sketching me. May I show everyone?' I nod, and Sarah holds my pad up. 'Christie Harris truly is a gem.'

'Cut!' Shouts the director, and slams the clapboard.

'Christie Harris,' cackles Sarah, 'you're an absolute gem!'

Tied Up

Offering us both a nugget of hope.

The weight of this brown paper package tied up with string, is making my legs go numb. My decision to take Madeline this final piece of work, immediately after my interview, holds me captive.

I can hear them up in the attic, bickering on at each other. Not the cameramen. Not the lighting chappie. No, they were smart enough to sign the confidentiality form, and leave quick sharp.

It sounds like Sarah's signed, but the weasel of a producer keeps barking on about ratings and media hype. Miles is having none of it. I keep hearing a rant from said producer, followed by the level tone of Miles' voice.

Given I've told all about dearest Madeline, I'm surprised at just how calm Miles is staying. I've stolen Madeline's chance of a coy confession to the world…

Not a lot she can do about it…

And by spending more time here, Miles is putting off telling her. I don't blame him!

And here I am, trapped by my good manners. I want to go and give this painting to Madeline… Get this over with… Before Miles tells her about my revelation!

Yep…

One hundred percent coward!

But how can I leave without saying thank you to Sarah? She allowed me a swift escape, and was discerning with her questions. And what Sarah chooses to be included from the gallery, in the half-hour special, is up to her... And that producer!

I've been rolling this jute string between my fingers and thumb for so long, I've got friction burns. The temptation to untie the bow, and take a peek at Miles, is gnawing at my resolve. Knowing my luck, he'd walk in.

'I'm not happy about this!' shouts the producer, as he bounds down the stairs. 'This is my production, and you've gagged me.'

'You were well aware of the conditions before you came here,' says Miles. His progress down the stairs is more leisurely.

'But that was before I found out who she is!' He casts me a menacing glare as he reaches the lounge door.

'Exactly, so now you know *who* she is, I suggest you start thanking your lucky stars. You and Sarah have only a limited time to work on the final edit, and get a copy back to me before Friday lunch. A copy needs to get to Monty's production team ASAP. Tick-tock, time's a-wastin'.'

The house vibrates as the front door slams.

'Problems?' I ask.

'No, he's just rattled because he didn't get his own way.' Miles leans against the door frame, arms folded, a satisfied smirk settles on his face.

'You enjoyed that!'

'He deserved it. He should be rubbing his hands in glee, not complaining...' Miles frowns, rubs his hand over his mouth and chin. 'You've put me in an awkward position, Christie, with Madeline. Thought we had a deal.'

I hold out my hands palm down. 'Look, I'm still shaking. It needed to come from me, Miles. She's been controlling everything.'

'You could have given me the heads up... I could have prepared Maddie. She's going to be upset—'

'Upset! Really? I've had no control over any of this... I needed to do this, have some input as to how this plays out. Not simply be a puppet... Can you blame me for—'

'No, Christie, I can't,' says Miles in a low voice. He lets out a long sigh, shrugs. 'It's done now, so...'

I look away from him. 'I'm going to see Madeline now, I'd appreciate it, if you'd wait until later to tell her about...'

He nods. 'Okay. It will give me time to figure out how to break it to her.' Again, he shrugs. 'Doing that sketch of Sarah was a masterstroke. Now everyone will be able to see what a fine artist you are. Maybe that will end up being the real talking point.'

'Hope so... Sarah has such character.'

'Somebody talking about me?' says Sarah. Miles backs out of the room to let Sarah through. 'Aha, Christie, so this is where you've been hiding, while our menfolk have been doing battle.'

'Yes, I'm a coward. But thank you Sarah, for not... For not tying me in knots. Even though I'm still shaking, I think you treated me gently.'

'Oh, you silly thing!' Sarah bustles over to me, and gives me an awkward hug over my brown paper package. 'Like I said, we're all friends together. And besides, you might just be the find of my career. Lucky me!'

'I hope you're right,' says Miles.

Sarah places her hand on Miles' arm. 'And, thank you, Miles.' She grins at me. 'He's getting your sketch of me, framed.'

'That's thoughtful,' I say.

'Is that by any chance a picture for Madeline?' asks Sarah, looking at the brown paper package.

'It is.'

'Any chance of a quick peep?'

'I painted it for Madeline, so I'll let her choose who she wants to see it. Sorry.'

'Oh well. I've got my own masterpiece, and much work to be done, thanks to you! So, I'll be on my way.'

Miles walks Sarah to the door. I tuck my precious package under my arm and follow them. Sarah is halfway down the drive by the time I've even reached the door.

'Not even going to let me have a peep at it?' asks Miles.

'You'll have to ask Madeline.'

'I understand.' Miles nods. 'I might catch up with you later then.'

'Not sure how long I'll be stopping at Mum and Dad's, but maybe.'

'You did well today.' Miles touches my elbow with his hand, leans in and brushes a scarce kiss on my cheek, hardly making contact at all. A jolt of yearning surges through my body. I snap away from him as if I've had an electric shock. He looks surprised, offended.

'I need to go.' I look down at my feet, and shuffle past him. 'Tell Suzi and Trudy I won't be late back.'

'Alright, bye then.'

Thankfully he doesn't follow me to the car; I wrestle my precious package onto the back seat.

The pleasant spring weather has everyone out and about. The roads are busy with lots of day trippers to Driftwood Sands. The journey to see my parents seems to last forever. I try to appreciate the lovely countryside as I'm travelling, it's not easy. I want to get this finished with.

I'm ready to say goodbye to Auntie Maddie.

Nowhere near ready to say hello to Madeline.

Mum is pottering in the front garden; the scrunch of gravel announces my arrival. She waves, trowel in one hand, weeds in the other. A smudge of dirt on her face, tells me she's been at it for ages, probably overdoing it. A displacement activity maybe?

'Oh, what a relief! I've been wanting to have a break for the last hour, but if either of those two sees me, I'll be roped into yet another game of scrabble!'

'It's lovely to see you too, Mum,' I say. Her tools patter to the ground and she rushes over and gives me a squeeze. She smells divine, she smells like Mum. Her hugs are the best Mum hugs in the world.

'How did it go, Christie?' She holds me at arm's length, her eyes searching.

'Okay.' I shrug. I'm not going to tell Mum about my revelation about Madeline in my interview… I'll leave that to the ever-resourceful Miles. 'I'm getting used to all the fuss. It's only going to get worse...' Oh, it really is.

'It'll pass, love. Things have a way of working out.' She offers a wistful smile.

'I know, that's why I'm here. I thought it would be better to at least have one proper conversation with Madeline, before the media stick their oar in.'

'Maddie thought so too, but she's anxious about what to expect from you, after you bolted from her the other day.'

I glance at the bush I hid behind, remembering Miles' amused expression as he found me. The same expression I've painted. A flutter of embarrassment feathers over me. I feel my cheeks flush and try to brush away the rush of goosebumps from my arms. 'It was too soon; I wasn't ready Mum. That's why I was trying to leave, remember. If Suzi had got here five minutes later, I would have escaped.'

Mum tilts her head, and clasps my hand. 'Are you sure you are up to it now? I can't imagine how you feel. I wish we could have found a better way.' I can hear the echoes of regret in her voice. Know I certainly haven't made it any easier.

'It's done. It can't be easy for you either. How are you and Dad?'

'Bored out of our minds! I know it sounds awful, but I'm almost glad Maddie's broken her ankle, because your dad has a captive scrabble opponent, and I can pretend to be too busy. He seems a bit lost, follows me round the house asking "What needs doing next?" every two minutes.'

'Poor Mum.' Poor Dad!

'So, I have to keep coming up with excuses to leave the house.'

'After all those years of complaining about him always being out.' I manage not to laugh. 'I suppose we could both escape; go to Driftwood Sands and walk along the prom.' I sound almost as desperate as Mum.

'After you've talked to Maddie, put you both out of your misery. She's in the back garden.'

'Playing scrabble?'

Mum nods then wanders over to her gardening things. 'I'll go and put the kettle on, send your dad in to give you and Maddie some time to talk in private.'

'Okay.' I reach into the car and get the package off the back seat; this at least should prompt our initial conversation. I walk around to the back garden.

Dad and Madeline are sat across from each other. The table between them holds the scrabble board, two letter stacks and the mini sack for letters. Dad is leaning back. He looks smug, probably winning as usual. Madeline's looking at the board, her chin resting on neatly folded hands.

Their closeness is palpable. The urge to turn and walk away is strong. I have to crush the wave of jealousy threatening to engulf me. He's my dad, but I have to remind myself, he was hers first.

It's like she has first dibs on everyone I love.

I shake my head, shake that thought away too.

Taking slow, steady steps towards them, I fix a smile on my face. They both turn and see me at the same time.

Dad is up on his feet, and embracing me in a bear hug before I've time to say hello. 'Look who the sunshine's brought out, I said it was going to be a beautiful day, didn't I, Maddie?'

Madeline nods, while she's awkwardly scrambling for her crutches.

'Don't get up,' I say. She looks alarmed. 'I'll join you, if you don't mind.'

'Pull up a pew,' says Dad, and laughs at his own little joke.

'Dad, I think Mum wanted you for something, inside,' I say.

'But we're halfway through a game... Oh, oh yes, better go and see what she wants me for.' He picks up the paper with their scores written on. 'I'd better take this with me.'

I sit down in the seat Dad has just vacated, glance at the letters on his letter tray. Madeline doesn't stand a chance at winning. I rest the package awkwardly on my lap.

'I'm glad you've come, after the other day,' says Madeline.

'I wasn't ready.' She nods. Waits. All my thoughts seem to have evaporated. I hold out the package to her. 'It's for you.'

'Thank you.' Her face lights up as she takes it from me. She holds it to her nose and takes a deep breath in. 'It smells of you, they always do.' She smells it again, and then rests it down over the top of the scrabble board... Covering her defeat.

'It's the last one.'

'Then I shall savour opening it.' Her eyes softly crease at the corners, her smile curbed. Her skin is smooth peaches and cream, and she has not a single line on her forehead. She doesn't look forty, not even close-up, nearer thirty than thirty-five. Nearer my sister than my mother. Her expression is giving nothing away, other than caution.

'Madeline, I want us to talk properly, before all the media get involved.'

'Maddie, please, Madeline sounds—'

'Okay, Maddie it is.'

'So, what do you want to know?'

'I want to understand why, why you left me, in your own words.'

Madeline looks down at her hands, then back up to me. 'I was young. I didn't feel like I belonged anywhere. I met a lad who was on one of Dad's famous youth programmes. He was a bit of a loner, a rebel in a quiet reserved kind of way. He had an inner confidence... Super good-looking, he was to me, anyway... And we just clicked, he made me feel like I was the centre of his life... All of a sudden, I was pregnant. Dad's job always kept us moving about. We moved before I dared to tell him about you... I couldn't risk him not loving me... Didn't trust he loved me enough... Stupid really.'

'He wouldn't have wanted me, would he?'

'I don't know, Christie. I was young, so was he.'

'At least you had a choice,' I say it like a challenge. For a moment she looks hurt. I'm glad. I want to hurt her. I'm hurt.

'I had a choice, yes. I don't know if it was the right choice I made, but neither do I know it was the wrong choice.' She shrugs. 'That's life. I can't go back and change it, and see how it would have worked out any other way.'

'Everything has worked out quite well for you.' My words are hushed, the spark of spite slashed by her calm reasoning. But then, she's had twenty-four years to marinate in her own perspective.

She sighs. 'It certainly looks that way. I was sixteen. I'd never even lived in one place for more than eighteen months in my entire life. The thought of committing the rest of my life to looking after another human being, was beyond terrifying. I'd always accepted being wherever Dad's job demanded. I was given a chance for the first time in my life, to go and be what I wanted to be. I didn't for a single moment expect anything remarkable to come from it.'

'Then what did you expect?'

'An adventure of my very own. I expected some excitement away from Mum and Dad. That's the real reason I changed my name, so I'd not be embarrassed by being connected to them. You know, have some freedom without the embarrassment of being a vicar's daughter… You must know how that feels. I only ever expected the occasional bit part. But then, within a year I was being treated like a star. And then Hollywood, I was eighteen. How many eighteen-year-olds do you think could resist that opportunity?'

'Did you ever intend to come back for me?'

She looks at me. Her hands reach out, resting on the table. I keep mine resting on my knees, clutch my jeans to hold them down.

She shakes her head. 'Not then. I was too drawn into this new exciting world with everyone hanging onto my every word. They warned me, Mum and Dad, said I was living in a make-believe world of happily ever after. I promised I'd let them keep you.' Again, she shakes her head, and briefly closes her eyes. 'They told me time wouldn't stand still while I was off doing what I wanted. As usual, they were right…'

'Do you regret it?' The words tumble out without thought.

'I wish I'd been strong enough, when I first came back… They'd wanted me to come home to you then. They said we could be a family together; you could be brought up as my younger sister. I couldn't…' She looks down at her hands, then back up to me. 'I couldn't have seen you every day, and not been your Mum. I was too broken, drained. I would have clung to you like a leech. Maybe two or three years down the line... But by then, it was too late to introduce a big sister to you. So, between us, we invented Auntie Maddie.'

'It worked very well, up until a couple of weeks ago,' I say.

'It was never enough.' The snag in her voice claws at my conscience. The noose around my feelings relaxes, as I sense the pain Madeline's honesty is causing her. And still somehow, I can't let go of the jabbering jumble of bitterness I'm nursing. Seeing her so close with my dad, taking my place, makes me rumble with resentment.

'You were good at Auntie Maddie, I loved you. Relied on you for good advice, craved your praise.' I surprise myself by resting one hand on the table... Allowing our hands to touch for a moment, offering us both a nugget of hope.

Madeline nods. 'I so wanted to be close to you; to be part of your life.'

'You have been, probably more than you realise.'

'And now, are you going to let me be part of your life?'

'I have no choice really, have I? What kind of life have Mum and Dad had to live, keeping our lives apart? They will always be my mum and dad, just like they've always been yours.'

'But we can move forwards?'

I purse my lips. 'As long as you know, it's only for their sake. They've earned a rest from all these theatrics.'

Madeline nods. The meagre crumbs of reconciliation hardly appear to satisfy her hunger for total acceptance. What does she expect? I know for sure Mum and Dad would have wholeheartedly welcomed her back all those years ago, she's their child.

But the more I think about how they've had to shield me from the truth, year after year, and the strain it must have put them under, the less I feel like yielding to Madeline's charm.

'About your father...' she says, tapping her finger on the edge of the scrabble board.

'Dad?' I frown.

'No, your natural father—'

She can't be serious!

'... He's likely to put two and two together. He's always known who I am. He might want to acknowledge you.'

I close my eyes. Cascades of panic rip at my already rocky composure. Is there no end to this nightmare? My instinct for self-preservation demands I escape. I open my eyes, and can't help the withering glare I give her. 'He might want to acknowledge me? This isn't some period drama on the BBC! And I'm not some babe in swaddling, who can be picked up or discarded at your whim. Whoever he is, I'm not prepared to go there Madeline...' All of my, until now, controlled bitterness is evident as I spit the words out. 'So, don't! He's your problem, not mine!'

I stand and walk away, my hands balled in tight fists. Electrical bolts feel to be thundering through my veins, every neuron in my brain is sparking at the same time firing my inner fury.

Cups rattle on a tea tray as Dad breaks into a trot to catch up to me. 'Christie, I've made us a nice cup of tea. Mum's got a Battenberg.'

Battenberg! Shove your Battenberg I want to scream. But it's not his fault. The bite of gravel through my thin pumps is a welcome discomfort, one I can live with. I yank open my car door with such force it swings open, and then crashes back into my legs. I hold in the shout of pain, embrace it as a welcome manifestation of my anger. 'Bloody car!' I hiss under my breath.

'Christie! Wait!'

This sight of Dad in his carpet slippers, desperately holding the tea tray before him like a peace offering, almost breaks my resolve. 'Please, Dad, I can't!' Angry tears spurt from my eyes, I swipe them away with the balls of my hands. Every negative emotion I've ever known, is alive, threatening to explode. I need to get away before my poisonous thoughts escape.

'I know.' He sets the tray down next to where Mum's abandoned gardening tools lie. He pushes my hair off my forehead and plants a kiss on the top of my head.

How come he's so good? Takes everything in his stride, absorbs the shockwaves. Surely, he feels as trapped as I do.

'Go. I'll say goodbye to Mum for you.'

Nodding a "thank you" biting back tears, unable to speak, I leave.

Shifting Grains of Sand

caught in an exotic dance ...

Driving home on autopilot, I'm gripping the steering wheel as if my life depends on it. Not even managing to hold in my tears. My lips are so taut, they're probably blue. Out of the corner of my eye, I notice the sign for the backroad up to Driftwood Sands. Dropping my speed, I turn right, to take what is laughingly called the shore road... The sea only ever a distant blur. The road soon narrows to a single track, sweeping on towards the seaside town stuck firmly in the middle of the last century.

I pull over and park up in one of the many lay-bys dotted along this stretch of road. Sand spilling from the dunes is forever shifting across the road, caught in an exotic dance with the ever-changing sea breeze. Resting my head back, I close my eyes.

I need to get all this Madeline mess into perspective. I look out across the lane to the marsh running down to the sea. But for the barbed wire fence, and avid bird watchers, I'd be running across that marsh, allowing my screams to echo with those of the gulls.

Getting out of the car, I grab my trusty hoody, and head for the dunes gulping in the fresh salty air. As I clamber up the track, loose dry sand oozes into my pumps weighing them down, slipping them off allows the cool sand to caress my feet. Gripping the reedy grass on either side of me, I hoist myself up the makeshift path. Spotting an already flattened clump of grass, smoothing out my hoody, I plonk myself down.

Now I can cry without being disturbed. Without prying eyes. Or concerned friends consoling. Or imposters judging. Without causing any more upset to Mum and Dad.

I rest back and look at the enormity of the sky, birds swirl and soar high, occasionally calling out to each other. The sky is where they belong, where they are free to be. Like me with a paint brush.

But thinking about it, even though it was Mum who first put a paint brush in my hand, it was Auntie Maddie who made me commit myself to art. She has always been a tenacious critic, and enduring champion.

I don't think I'd even be half sane if I couldn't paint. Every major junction of my life, including this one, has been accompanied by frantic painting or sketching. Even when I'm only mildly stressed, I doodle on whatever scrap of paper I can find.

Even now! I've snapped off a long stalk of grass and I'm tracing the outlines of the clouds, without it being a conscious decision. It's as much a part of me, as the air in my lungs. Each breath of air is different, but each refreshes my life. Just like all my doodles, sketches and paintings.

I wonder if Madeline regrets giving up acting. Mum said she gave it up for me, for my protection. Right now, it doesn't feel like it. If I was born to paint, then surely, I can try to be fair-minded enough to at least acknowledge Maddie was born to act. She was given a chance, and she took it. And then, she let it all go.

I doubt I could do that.

What about Dad? On his way to becoming a Bishop! Focused always on helping people, leading by example, gives up that path to tread a gentler one with

Kathleen Clunan

me in rural Little Upton. Now that's a change of gear from urban troubleshooting. He must have felt smothered by the layers of tradition woven into the fabric of Little Upton life.

And Mum, always in the background making everything run smoothly. Sorting out problems, making sure everyone had what they needed, to do what they were doing. Feeding us with food, which frankly, Jamie Oliver would be proud of. She's never taken the limelight, but without her, the whole shebang would've come tumbling down about us.

I can't count the number of times she hasn't *told* me I'm wrong, just shown me an alternative viewpoint. She's like one of those tribal guides in the Amazon, hacking down all the major obstacles in my path, leaving me only the smaller, more manageable ones to deal with. I wonder how many she's tackled for me with Madeline over the years.

I know I've got to get to grips with all this. All of them have made sacrifices for me.

But I just start getting over one revelation, then along comes another.

How did Madeline think I'd react to the possibility of some random bloke stepping forward to, as she says, "acknowledge" me? Why doesn't she go the whole way, and search him out for me on *Long lost family*? I'm sure she'd get a hit.

I can't even think about that now. I just wish everything was back how it used to be, normal. Mum, Dad and me, with the occasional letter from Auntie Maddie. My phone vibrates in my pocket, pulling it out, I see a message from Miles.

But then without all this…

I wouldn't have met Miles.

Flowers

"Somehow I doubt that, Miles."

Once again Miles is in my front room. My eyes follow his every movement. The tilt of his head, the scant furrow of a frown that lasts only a moment, the way he drags his hand absently through his hair.

His thoughts, as always are with Madeline. 'Yes, I know it *is* short notice,' he says into his mobile. 'I know, sorry, should I try another florist? They're for Madeline De-Muir. After two-thirty, but before four, the message? If you just write, "believe in yourself", you don't need to say who's sent them, she'll know.'

At least he doesn't know how I feel about him. It's like knives are being juggled in my stomach. I don't know why he isn't with her, today of all days. I doubt she's as confident about her interview tonight, as she's used to being. "Miss cool, calm and collected", must at least be worried about what her adoring public are going to make of my revelation.

'So, Christie...' Miles slips his mobile into his jacket pocket, and focuses his attention back to me. 'I hope you've got a master plan for keeping yourself busy today, otherwise I'll have to resort to Plan B.'

'I was hoping to go over some lessons for next term, but I don't think I'm going to be able to concentrate... Has Madeline gone back to her own house now?'

'I took her first thing this morning, Mrs Price did offer...' He lets his words hang, as a glint of mischief

270

dances in his eyes. My heart somersaults about my chest. 'I thought she'd be safer with me driving her home.'

Relief soars through me. The thought of seeing her again after my outburst, has kept me away from Mum and Dad's all week. 'I might go and see Mum and Dad then.'

'I take it, you don't want to bump into Maddie, then?'

I shake my head and a shiver snakes up through my body. I wipe my sweaty palms on my jeans.

'She's not that bad,' he says in a half-joking kind of way. Tilts his head to one side, and offers a smile. 'She's almost got over you telling all in your interview.'

Goosebumps cover my arms, I try to brush them away before he notices. All it takes is a smile from him, and I'm lost. It's not even as if that smile was fully for my benefit. It was, as usual, an appeal on Madeline's behalf. I bite the inside of my mouth to stop waspish words escaping and force a smile.

Miles continues, 'Try to see her through the words she's written to you over the years; because that's who she really is. Christie, you probably know her better than anyone.'

'Including you?' I challenge, annoyed by the knowledge it's jealousy prompting my words.

'Yes.'

He says it so casually, he could be saying yes to a coffee. And why can't he understand why I'm so... Whatever I am? 'Somehow I doubt that, Miles.'

His expression changes to something more complex, anger tinged with hurt, smothering me in guilt. He stalks away from me, turns and walks back. Standing too close, crowding my space. The spice of his aftershave, further stirs my awareness, like I even need that. I can feel his eyes scrutinizing me. I keep mine averted from him. Don't want him reading them. I feel the heat of my blush working its way up my body, feel the pounding of my heart high in my chest. Again, I wipe my sweaty palms on my jeans.

He raises my chin with his finger, and I swallow. My eyes drift to meet his, the pain in mine, mirrored in his. 'You know what she is to me. And I know, she's always held herself apart from everyone…Including me… Including your parents. The only person, the only one she has ever fully invested her emotions in, is you, Christie. So, don't. Do not drag my relationship with Maddie, between us. We've both got too much to lose.'

Without breaking eye contact, he slowly dips his head. I moisten my lips; know before his lips brush mine, he is going to kiss me. The tingle of anticipation heightens the sensations swirling through my body as we melt together. I close my eyes to hide the intensity of my feelings from him, but at the same time my traitorous body moulds to his. A myriad of sensations brought to life.

The longing for this to last forever, overtakes my rational thoughts as my fingers rove through his hair, pulling him closer, deeper. Suffocated by desire, I'm lost in the moment. Can feel the heat of his body, his heartbeat…

The vibration of his mobile phone brings me to my senses, and I pull away from him, before it makes a sound.

He looks at the screen, and disconnects the call. 'Look, I've got to go.'

'Summonsed?' I can't even savour his kisses, without her intruding.

'It was Mrs Price; she left a message earlier about the gallery. I need to check it out, okay?'

'Oh.' I bite my lip.

'She's probably being overcautious; she knows how much it means to Maddie for *Evolution* to be successful.'

Again, with Maddie.

Whether he knows it or not, we've both already lost. My throat tightens as I swallow back the hurt. Always her before me. 'It means a lot to me too. Most of my childhood is in that gallery. I don't think any of you understand, it's my life on display. My life. Those pictures are part of who I am.'

'I get it, Christie, honestly.' Miles drags his hand through his hair where moments ago, my own fingers roamed. He looks away, and then looks back at me. 'And that is why I'm going to see what the problem is. I understand. And believe me, you don't need to explain how each of those pictures holds a chunk of you. I can see it in them.'

My throat still feels tight, and I try to swallow the choking ache away. Miles looks so earnest; it's hard not to believe him. I nod my acceptance of his words, and he touches my elbow.

I sigh. 'Go on then, sort out whatever it is you need to.'

'I'll be back as soon as I can.'

'I might not be here.'

'Don't worry, I'll track you down! There's a favour I need to ask... But I need to sort this out first. Until later then...' He tucks my hair behind my ear, cups my cheek. His eyes search my face. He turns to leave.

'Bye,' I murmur, following him to the door to watch him. As soon as he's in his car, he's on his mobile.

I turn and go into the kitchen. I flick on the kettle to make myself a coffee. The house shudders as the front door slams with force.

'Sorry!' shouts Suzi. She waddles through into the kitchen, grappling with shopping bags, she dumps them in the middle of the table. 'Been shopping.'

'You don't say.' I try to laugh, but it comes out wrong. Suzi doesn't seem to notice, she's too busy riffling through her bags. 'I'll make you a coffee, give you chance to hide all the good stuff.'

'Thanks. I'm going to hide them in easy to find places anyway. I think I'm going to be having a chocolate week.' Suzi starts piling boxes on the counter next to the fridge-freezer.

'Good idea. Is that a cheesecake?' I spy an interesting array of desserts.

Suzi slaps another box on the counter. 'Yep! And another sticky toffee pudding, and a chocolate torte, oh and some éclairs.'

'I love a girl who thinks ahead. Are we celebrating something?'

'Yes, getting fat, but only for a week.'

'Okay, so how does a chippy dinner sound?' I ask.

'Sounds good, Trudy said she'd be back for half twelve, so we'd better make sure we get her some fish and chips. And is Miles coming back?'

'Oh, perhaps. I'm not sure what his plans are; he just popped in on his way to the gallery.'

Suzi smirks. 'Hardly on his way then. I'd better text him later.'

'You've got his number?'

'Oh, yes! He gave me and Trudy his business card… Thought you knew.'

A familiar blush starts rising in my cheeks. 'I didn't know. You phone him then. You'll be able to report back—'

'Christie! It's not like that...'

I sigh. 'I know, I'm a bit confused about how I'm feeling... He did actually, come to ask a favour of me.'

'And what favour would that be?'

'Don't know.' I wrinkle my nose and grimace. 'He got called away.'

Suzi's laughter howls through the house, her face is so scrunched up it looks like she's ninety. She drops down on a chair dramatically clutching her sides.

I tut. 'He did get called away... It was Mrs Price.'

Suzi flaps her arms and draws a deep breath, and then starts laughing all over again.

'What?' I ask, the beginnings of a smile threatening to escape. 'He *was* called away!'

Suzi covers her mouth with her hand and pinches her nose. Her squeaks still sneak out. She rubs her eyes on her sleeve, digs in her pocket for a hanky and blows her nose elephant style. 'I'm sorry,' she says between giggles, 'but you're both so obvious, it's embarrassing.'

'I wish I'd never told you about him! It's not funny.'

'I'm sorry. But it's entertaining seeing you try to act all coy and uninterested, when you are more than interested. And Miles making up strings of excuses to keep calling here.'

'They aren't excuses!'

'He's been here four times in the last three days.'

'Talking about the interviews, or the gallery!'

'You do both have mobiles.' Suzi is loving this, likes to be with all the action, as long as she isn't the centre of it. Close enough to catch the vibes, but not get burnt.

Safe in her self-contained security bubble. Right now, I wish I could be in there with her.

'It's all very complicated,' I say. Plonking myself down on a chair at the table. I drop my head into my hands. 'My head is scrambled with all this stuff going on.'

'Oh well, by this time tomorrow all the worrying will be over. Trudy has put herself in charge of filtering through the social media networks tonight, to scupper any unpleasantness.'

'Stop!' I raise my hand. 'I can't even think about it.'

It hadn't even occurred to me that I might attract trolls. The only trolls I've any real understanding of, are those other cute little things called Poppy and Branch. The real ones, who hide behind their online persona and destroy people's lives, are a total mystery to me. What kind of warped pleasure do they get? I don't think I can do this. I close my eyes and turn away from Suzi. I know she's only trying to help, but I think we both know I'm out of my depth.

'You don't need to think about it. Trudy has it all under control.'

'I really want to believe that, Suzi, but somehow, I think it's going to take more than Trudy and her trusty tablet, to turn the tide of public opinion.'

'Aha, but she's recruited a team of trusty technological taggers, bloggers, vloggers or whatever they're called.' Suzi scrunches her face up, the trauma of tech taking its toll.

'Really? Do we know them?'

'Ye-es,' says Suzi.

'Well, go on, who are they?' I've got a bad feeling about this.

'Just some whiz kids Trudy knows.'

'Trudy doesn't know any kids, whiz or otherwise.' Please no. I close my eyes as the realisation hits me. 'She's enlisted the kids from the gallery, hasn't she, Frankie and his crew?'

'It seemed like a good idea at the time.'

'But they're Madeline's kids! They'll be on her side! And if we're being completely honest, what chance has a group of disadvantaged teens got against trolls in cyberspace?'

'Trudy made them advantaged.'

'She's bribed them!'

'No!' Suzi shakes her head. 'She's simply provided them with the proper equipment for the job.'

'And that is?'

'Whatever the latest in mobile thingy whatsit technology is, that is what she's got them. I don't know what they're called, but the kids were well impressed.'

'I bet they were. And how does she intend to make sure they're all going to be monitoring the various tweets and whatnots tonight?'

'Well, this is the clever bit. Do you know when they have elections in America, and it shows on telly all the young political wannabes locked in offices, madly phoning and texting and generally drumming up support? Their only relief, when they're sent boxes of pizza and Starbucks. Trudy has set up a "Campaign Headquarters". Mrs Price has volunteered her front room, and her husband is going to be the pizza delivery boy.'

Could it be any worse? 'And does this not sound like a recipe for disaster to you?' I shake my head. What was Trudy thinking? 'I thought Mrs Price and Frankie have issues.'

'Whatever they are, they seem to have been set aside for the greater good. Mrs Price has assured Trudy, that she'll watch both the interviews with the kids, to make sure they know what it is all about.'

'Does *she* know what it's all about?'

'She will do after she's watched your interview.'

'And, I presume Miles knows all about this?'

'Trudy talked to him about it, before she approached everyone.'

'And he's okay with it?'

'Trudy said he ran it by Madeline first, but yep, he approves.'

I glare at her.

'What?'

'This is why!' I grind my teeth. 'I cannot let anything happen between him and me. "He ran it by Madeline first", he didn't run it by me! What am I, chopped liver?'

'It wasn't like that,' says Suzi.

'Well what was it like? Because from here, it looks like I'm the only one, out of the loop.'

'Trudy wanted to make sure you got some cyber backup, and like you said, she doesn't know any whiz kids. And since you had such a good rapport with Frankie and co, she thought it was a good idea.'

'So why did Miles have to "okay it" with Madeline, then, if he thought it was a good idea, tell me that!' I cross my arms firmly across my chest, steam must be spurting from my ears.

'Because, Christie,' explains Suzi, with exaggerated patience, 'Madeline has duty of care for those kids, being a teacher, you know that.'

I let out the breath I didn't know I was holding. Of course, duty of care, her kids, her responsibility, what was I thinking? It's all about her.

Suzi shrugs. 'And, obviously, it's his job to report back to her.'

'He will always put her first.' All the anger seeps out of me, I need to accept it, nothing can ever properly start with me and Miles.

'He works for her, Christie. He's just doing his job.'

'And calling here, sorting things out for the gallery and interviews, is his job too. Look Suzi, I can't let anything develop with him. How can I know if he's being overly friendly with me, because he likes me, or for the benefit of his job?'

'Because he calls here every chance he gets.'

'Just doing his job,' I reply.

'He could phone or email, he comes here to see you; he watches you.' Her words fall over me like feathers from a burst pillow.

I tilt my head to one side, unfold my arms, and rest back in the chair. What would Suzi say, if I told her that less than twenty minutes ago, I was in his arms? I touch my fingers to my mouth; trace the line of his kiss. My lips are alive with sensations, and tingle with the memory of his. Only a kiss. I can feel Suzi studying me.

'You don't need to pretend with me, I already know how you feel about him.' She touches my arm and offers a lopsided smile.

'I'm scared.' I didn't intend the words to be spoken aloud.

'Me too, scared he's going to steal my best friend away.'

'No one could ever do that, you know all of my secrets, remember?'

'I think Miles could, whisk you away to a glamorous celebrity lifestyle, with proper dinner parties, no knickers lined up along radiators.'

'Don't.' I half smile. I've never wanted that lifestyle, I'm not a social climber, I'm just average.

'With proper posh puddings, champagne. And what about poor old me? I'd just be left here rambling around with only Trudy to boss, and there'd be no fun in that.'

'Suzi, you've been bossing me for twenty years, you're never going to stop!' It suddenly dawns on me, how true that is. Trudy might be the best friend who rides shotgun, striding in and taking control, but Suzi with her tweaks, and occasional unfettered remarks has steered my path many times. Probably totally unaware. Like right now.

'I could always apply to be your housekeeper.' Suzi puts on a forlorn face and sighs. 'Mother would be so disappointed.'

'Suzi, seriously, everything's changing, and I have no control over any of it.'

'Christie Harris, for once in your life, just go with it. What is it you say to me? "Loosen up", well, now it's your turn. Enjoy the adventure.'

'He kissed me. Just before he left...' I trace my finger along my lips, remember the sensation.

'Well, it's not as if you've never been kissed before...'

'I've never been kissed like that before... He said we've not to let Madeline come between us, we've got too much to lose, and then he kissed me.'

'So, don't. Don't let Madeline come between you.'

'How can I not? He's bound to her in ways you don't know.'

'Then tell me.'

'I can't.' I shake my head.

'Whether you tell me or not, whatever it is that binds them, it sounds to me like Miles is ready to risk the consequences of breaking those ties.' Suzi shrugs.

And she's right, maybe that's what frightens me more than anything else. 'I don't know, Suzi.' Can I take that risk? If it all goes haywire between us, I've still got Mum and Dad and the ever-zealous Madeline.

He'll have nothing.

I don't think I can do that to him. Don't think I can risk him doing it to himself. The thought of the Miles, Madeline rescued all those years ago flits through my mind. Alone and afraid. I can't risk him going back to a solitary life. He needs my family as much as I do. Maybe even more, after all, I'll always have Suzi and Trudy.

Suzi scurries her fingers across the table, and gently prods my arm. 'I think Miles has already made that decision for himself. And what's more, from what I've seen of him, what Miles wants, Miles gets. Maybe, my little friend, this is not your decision to make...'

I close my eyes. A curled-up image of the teenaged Miles in the church porch dominates my thoughts. Opening my eyes, the chair screeches as I stand. I need to do something, anything.

Paint!

'I'm going upstairs to paint; I might be some time.'

I'm halfway out of the door before Suzi replies, 'Whatever happens, you'll always have your paintbrushes.'

Shadows

But it seems I was wrong.

I'd been too impatient to paint. Now I'm glad of it. The fragile and broken pencil strokes add to the vulnerable spirit of the image on my pad.

His knees are drawn up to his chest, baggy jeans clasped by weary arms, laces hang forlorn from well-worn trainers. His face is framed by unkempt hair, eyes are wide and alert, fearful. There's shading under his eye, a bruise or perhaps blood. There's a tear, or just a hint of one threatening to fall.

He's in a church porch, coiled on an uneven wooden bench. His jeans look too long for his legs. A crumpled paper bag rests at his feet.

A shadow can be made out on the wall at the back of him. The shadow of a woman.

Madeline's shadow.

It almost wasn't there, but it crept in when my guard was down. Good, I must always remember, that with Miles, there will always be Madeline's shadow.

I look away, watch the particles of dust highlighted by the sun streaming in from the skylight. I always thought that, when I fell in love, I'd be like an Amazonian, strong and able to fight off any challenge.

But it seems I was wrong.

I'm not saying I'm happy to walk away, but that's what I'm doing. I can't let Miles give up this life he's carved out for himself. He deserves to have a settled life after his unsettled childhood. Now I know what went before, what the future needs to be, becomes clear.

And it's not as if I'm never going to see him again. No doubt he'll still pop in to see Mum and Dad. He'll still be Madeline's PA. If I ever do get to popping round to see her, he'll be there too. Perhaps.

The intensity of the last couple of weeks has probably heightened our senses, thrust us together in a way that is overly charged with extreme emotions. Yes, that'll be it, extreme emotions. Don't know why I didn't realise sooner. I glance back at the hunched-up child in the church porch, and know I'll never stop loving him.

'Christie! Are you up there?' Trudy's voice cuts into my thoughts.

'Yes, what do you want?'

'I think you need a hearing test! I've shouted twice. Fish and chips,' she says slowly. 'Suzi's buttering some bread, how many slices?'

'Two, thanks.' I close my pad and put it in the top drawer of my desk underneath my official sketch pad, the one I let anyone see. Miles can rest there awhile, safe. I'll check on him later. I close the drawer, and look up towards the skylight. Bright sunlight streams in. Again, I watch tiny specks of dust floating in the air; they're at the mercy of their surroundings, just like me.

'It's going cold!' shouts Trudy.

I close the attic door and go down to the kitchen. Trudy, Suzi and Miles sit cosily at the table. A mountain of buttered bread waiting to be eaten sits in the middle. Open fish and chip wrappers sit eagerly on plates in front of each of them. Mine remains wrapped.

'Miles texted back…' says Suzi, mischief dancing in her eyes.

'Hello, again. Suzi did invite me.' Miles has the grace to look bashful, though he shoots the smirking Suzi a look.

'Tuck in,' I say, 'don't wait for me; I need to wash my hands.' By the time I sit down, the mountain of bread has been cut down to size.

Suzi has laid aside her knife and fork in favour of her fingers. 'Did you manage to get any painting done?' she asks, waving a chip in my general direction.

'No.' I shake my head. 'Just a bit of sketching.'

'Anything in particular?' she asks.

With a mouth full of chips, I nod, and then shrug.

'I like your sketches,' says Miles. 'They're full of character. The one of Sarah really catches her mischievous nature.'

'Thank you,' I mumble. 'Did you manage to sort out Mrs Price?'

'Oh, yes and no. There's been some graffiti at the back of the mill the other night. Mrs Price had *mistakenly* thought it could have been a couple of our kids. Anyway, we've looked at the CCTV together yesterday, and now she's satisfied it's none of ours.'

'It could have been Banksy,' says Trudy.

'Don't think so. There were three hooded people...'

'So, what's being done about it?' asks Suzi, all eyes.

'Well, Madeline pointed out it is an art gallery, so we've left the images; they're quite good. The police have been asked to keep an eye open for any trespassers. Not a lot we can do.'

Trudy shoots me a glance, then looks pointedly at Miles. 'Are they likely to try and get in?'

'Probably not; the mill is alarmed up to the hilt anyway.'

Suzi snorts, 'That wouldn't stop them if they wanted to damage Christie's exhibition. I don't know what she'd do if anything happened to her art.'

'No need to worry, Christie.' Miles reaches across the table and puts his hand on top of mine. 'I promise nothing is going to happen to any of it.'

'Miles, I know I gave them to Auntie Maddie to keep, but I didn't expect to feel as attached to them as I still do. And I know it sounds stupid, but seeing them all again brings all my memories alive. I remember every one.'

'Trust me. I won't let anything happen to them, okay?' His voice is soft and coaxing as if talking to a fearful child.

I'm not a child, still, I look away. Those pictures are a measure of my childhood. He probably thinks I'm oversensitive.

In my head, my pictures were only ever for Aunty Maddie. I imagined her sat waiting for them, warming gnarly hands by an open fire, and when they arrived, I thought of her having all the time in the world to pour over their every detail. Getting pleasure from me carving out time from my busy career to set aside simply for her.

I thought they'd be propped up on bookcases... Balanced on sideboards... Wedged behind heavy cut glass vases, because, surely somebody of Auntie Maddie's age wouldn't be hammering in picture hooks. Or have the services of a local handyman.

Or have an enticing PA called Miles.

I didn't think of a woman in her prime, whose delicate demeanour commands the adoration of an entire nation. Who, just because it seemed like a good idea at the time, could transform an old mill into an art gallery, and organise an exhibition? Who could empathise so effortlessly with disadvantaged young people, make them bacon butties and fairy cakes... Offer them hope?

Somebody who, in the midst of her own despair, had enough presence of mind, to recognise a kindred spirit. The courage to take on the challenge of turning the future of a young man's life around. Somebody who'd nurture him into the man he is today, strong, confident and competent.

So now, as Miles assures me my artwork is safe, I know I should trust him. There's just a niggle, Miles and Mrs Price seem to have invested a fair bit of time, trying to find out "who dunnit".

Trudy pats my arm. 'It was probably just kids short of something to do, they'll have forgotten about it by now.'

'Hope so,' I say. But I'm not convinced.

Suzi is nibbling her bottom lip. Always a sign of trouble pending. She looks at me, and offers only a weak smile. 'Miles... Christie said you wanted her to do you a favour.' There she goes, trying to change the subject.

'Ah, yes.' He takes his hand off mine, and coughs. 'It's a big one, but it will pay dividends.'

I raise an eyebrow. 'Sounds ominous.'

'I think.' Miles takes a deep breath. 'I think it would be very beneficial to both you and Madeline, if you could be involved in the interview with her tonight.'

'Absolutely not!' My chair crashing to the floor echoes my attitude. 'How can you ask that?' I hiss.

'Christie, please...' Miles is on his feet too. 'I don't mean being interviewed with her.'

'I should think not!' I turn to leave the room; I do not need to hear this; can't even believe he's asking. I'm sure Madeline must have filled him in with what happened last time we met.

Oh no! She might have even shown him the portrait, no wonder he kissed me, probably thinks he can have me eating out of his hand.

He catches my arm. 'Listen, please.' His voice is quiet, imploring. I bite the inside of my mouth; swallow back the bile rising in my throat. Half-turning toward him, I raise my chin an inch. 'Thank you,' he says. 'Tonight, your mum and dad are going to be at Maddie's house while she is being interviewed. Your mum thought Maddie might need some moral support. Anyway, the conversation they had, led into "how about you three come into the room at the end of the interview?" And your mum and dad agreed.'

'So, you thought I would too?' My voice sounds alien even to me.

'I thought you might consider it.' He gently squeezes my arm.

Turning to face him, I catch the concerned expressions of my friends; friends who are wise enough to stay out of it, and loyal enough to back me whatever I decide. My moral supporters. I swallow again.

'Why?' I speak softly. Shrug. 'Why should I be there?'

The warmth of his breath caresses my cheek as he lets out a low sigh, I can already feel my resolve starting to crumble. He looks at my lips, for a moment I think he's going to kiss me again. He looks away, and then back, searching me out. Slips his hand into mine.

'Christie, this could be…' he falters. I can see him mentally selecting his words carefully. 'I think this time, right now, could be a healing time for your family. It's been a long time.'

'It wasn't my fault,' I say, my voice hushed.

'I know.' Again, he squeezes my hand. 'I know it wasn't your fault, Christie.' Miles looks back towards Suzi and Trudy, our spectators. 'Excuse us please.'

I let him lead me back through the kitchen and outside into the garden. The sun is still fairly high in the sky, throwing out her rays of light to the greedy garden, and me, and Miles. The rambling wild roses already threaten to overwhelm the picket fence, and dog daisies dominate the unruly borders. The bird feeder needs filling. If Trudy ever catches that squirrel, it'll be a kebab.

It really is a lovely little garden. Through the winter months it always looks kind of sad and unloved. The Buddleia dies back particularly badly, its bare branches take on a sinister form from October to March. Only now, in spring does it start to offer a glimmer of life. All the perennials creep out almost unnoticed, cramming the flowerbeds and keeping the weeds at bay. By mid-June the boarders become a riot of blooms all competing for their place in the sun, attracting all sorts of insects for Trudy to bat away while she's sunbathing.

Oh, and in a few weeks, no doubt there'll be rounds of debates about whose turn it is to cut the grass, and should we get someone in to trim the hawthorn hedge at the back, even though, really, it's the farmer's responsibility. And ought one of us think about giving the shed a coat of wood preserver, in the hope that it won't completely rot away.

Miles leads me to the bench, it groans as I sit down, reminding me, that it too could do with some TLC. I rest back against the warm brick of the house. He steps back, and sits down on the grass, runs his fingers through it. He plucks a daisy from the ground and passes it to me.

'Beautiful isn't it?' he says, looking around the garden. 'I like outside, it's honest, no pretence. It is what it is.'

'Mum says that, "it is what it is".'

'I know. I stole it from her. She's a good mum, you're lucky.'

'I know.'

'And that's why, that's why it would be good if you could be there.'

I snort, and shake my head. 'For Mum? Bit of a low blow, Miles.'

'For all of you. I know Maddie, have known her for a long time, and your mum and dad. Your family has been apart for a long time.'

'Like I said, that isn't my fault.'

'I know, but believe it or not, you're the one who holds it together.'

'I don't think so.'

'Listen,' Miles speaks softly, 'I know each of you; and you are all warm and caring people, good people… The best I've ever met... Maddie and your parents are the closest thing to a proper family I've ever had.'

His expression is so intense, I have to look away. 'Sorry,' I mumble.

'Don't be, they've shown me what a family should be like. Not always happy with each other, and more often than not, disagreeing over the silliest things. Your dad and Maddie could bicker for England, your mum's like a referee. I can see how much you love your parents.'

'They should have told me sooner.'

'Maybe they should, that's something you are just going to have to talk to them about. That's something they all disagreed about. They all wanted to protect you, and that shows how much each of them loves you. And they love each other, even when they don't act like it. That's family, simple as.'

'My life was just fine until Madeline turned up.'

'Maddie didn't turn up... She's always been here... She has been waiting for you all those years. Does that sound like a selfish person to you? Because it sure as hell doesn't to me.' His voice is gentle, controlled.

I shake my head.

He drags his hand through his hair, and then leans forward. Crinkles appear at the corner of his eyes as he offers a weary smile. 'I don't know how you feel, can't know how you feel... But please, for all of you, meet Maddie halfway.'

I close my eyes. Please God help me.

Sunlight bathes my skin, and the warmth it brings seems to drain the fight from me. The seed of acceptance matures as I breathe in the fresh air, fragrant with the scents of spring flowers. I open my eyes. Miles is watching me. I don't know if the seed of acceptance will bloom into forgiveness, but I nod. 'Okay, I'll be there,' I whisper.

'I promise, you won't regret it.'

I hope I don't.

Compromised

The remains of a once-white lacy bra ...

The wrought iron gates swing open automatically, as Miles presses his fob. He drives through, and the gates close. Mature rhododendrons well into their crimson spring bloom line the short driveway, offering added privacy to Madeline's home. I almost gasp as the driveway opens out to reveal a beautifully proportioned house. Impressive conical stone steps lead to a double front door.

To one side of the house I notice Mum and Dad's car, dwarfed by two huge vans with satellite dishes on top. To the other, there's a ramshackle outhouse with a lean-to greenhouse.

Despite being minutes off the main road, it feels like we're in a country garden, a world away from all the hustle and bustle. I suppose if you've lived your life in the goldfish bowl of celebrity, an oasis of tranquillity is the best cure. And this certainly fits the bill.

The car rolls to a stop behind one of the vans. Miles turns off the engine, and he looks at his watch. 'You okay?' he asks.

Am I okay? He asks some stupid questions.

He isn't even looking at me, more concerned about the time. Clearly doesn't want to be late.

And no, I'm not okay!

He should be looking directly into my eyes, and at least pretend to be bothered. Now he's got his way, or rather, Madeline's way, about this interview, his charm has turned off all of a sudden. He hasn't even noticed I've not answered him yet.

His knuckles are white he's gripping the steering wheel so firmly, almost as if he's afraid to let go. And on the way here, there's been no random finger tapping. He must be more worried about Madeline's interview than mine, she is the main event, after all.

'Bit nervous. It looks very grand, imposing even.'

'It does, I remember how I felt the first time she brought me here. I'd thought houses like this only existed on TV. You'll soon feel at home…'

Somehow, I doubt that. But still I nod, and he smiles back, hopefully content with that. I open the car door.

He touches my arm. 'It's all going to be fine.'

Again, I smile. I must remember to do that when the camera is pointing at me.

'Coo-eeee,' sings Mum. 'We're all in the dining room. It's all very exciting isn't it? Maddie's front room looks like a television studio, and I've had my make-up done by a proper make-up girl.'

'Mum, you look stunning as ever, give us a twirl.'

Mum does a slow 360. She looks fab. She's wearing a seaside print skirt, coupled with an aqua twin set. Very Mum. She's obviously had her hair done, and I notice she's wearing the pearl earrings I bought her for Christmas.

'Oh Christie, I'm so glad you've decided to come.' She envelops me in a Mum hug, and even though she's had a mini makeover, thankfully she still smells of Mum.

'You look amazing.'

'Oh, thank you. I'm so nervous I could explode, and I'm not even going to say anything. Monty said, you know it's Monty Mitten?'

I nod.

'Well Monty said if it's okay with you, he just wants a tableau of us all at the end of the interview. Anyway, I'm sure he'll tell you, come on.' She catches my hand and leads me towards the steps.

'Oh, Christie!' mutters Mum, and pulls me closer. Dad stands in the doorway. 'Tell him he can't go on the telly in that cardigan!'

'Yes, I can.' Dad plants his hands defiantly in his cardigan pockets. 'What's wrong with it, you're wearing a cardigan.'

'Yes, but mine's new.'

'New! Well, mine is just like me, comfortable and well worn.'

'It's almost worn out!' huffs Mum.

'Exactly, just like me... Now that's sorted out, how are you, Christie? I do hope you're not going to succumb to the trappings of make-up and image.'

'Probably a little bit.'

'Well as long as it's just a little bit, I suppose I can cope with that.' He gives me a bear hug and leads me in. The hallway is bright and airy. Fresh flowers sit in a huge vase on a stone pedestal at the base of an elaborate staircase, their scent fills the air. Voices drift through, Monty and Madeline. 'Come and say hello, they're in the dining room. Chin up, Christie, you can do it.'

I can hear Mum and Miles behind, making no effort to join us. Mum is probably enlisting his help to get Dad to part with his cardigan.

I'm as nervous to meet Monty Mitten, as I am to meet Madeline again. He has that kind of reputation… He either loves you or hates you, and since Maddie is his favourite…

'Here she is,' says Dad.

'Well aren't you the gorgeous one! How lovely to meet you.' Monty glides out of his chair. He's wearing a purple shirt with black skinny jeans, pointy boots and a perceptive smile. His eyes cruise over me as he bows elaborately. Taking both my hands, he leans forward and air kisses each of my cheeks. He smells amazing, and his grip much stronger than I expected. He tilts his head to one side, and looks into my eyes. 'Madeline has told me so much about you.'

I'm taken aback by his intensity. 'Hello, it's lovely to meet you too.' I glance over to Madeline; she's struggling to stand up with her crutches. 'Please don't get up.'

'Hello, Christie.' She perches on the edge of her chair, holding out both her hands to me.

For a hug?

I manage to extract my hands from Monty's, and offer him a shrug of apology. Walking over to Madeline I take hold of each of her hands in mine, lean forward and plant a brief kiss on her cheek. 'Hello, Maddie.'

'Thank you for coming this evening. It's all a bit nerve-racking, but I know Monty is going to do a great job, for both of us.' I glance back at Monty, not sure if I'm expected to say anything.

Monty inclines his head. 'Shall I run through what we've got organised, d-harling girl?'

'Sounds like a plan,' I answer.

'Shall we?' He gestures towards a window seat set in a large bay. He waits for me to sit, and then sits down, leaving a wholesome distance between us. 'So, Madeline and I will watch your interview together in the lounge immediately before our filming begins. We've obviously watched it through a few times already. I must say, sweetie, how well you handled Sarah... She's a wily one... Everything is set up in the lounge for the live filming. Everyone else will be able to watch your interview in the snug, is that right?' He looks to Madeline, who nods.

He taps his lips with his forefinger, then continues, 'And then the fun will begin! Obviously, d-harling, you'll be watching it with Madeline's wonderful mum and dad.... Your mum and dad too, ha ha.' He flushes at his faux pas and clears his throat. 'So, at twenty-three minutes in, I'll start to wind things up. Some historic images of Madeline will be cut in, and some of yours from the gallery. During that time, you and your parents will be ushered into place...' He claps his hands and clasps them to his chest. 'For an historic family tableau...'

Madeline nods. 'We thought it would look quite natural, if you and Mum perch on opposite chair arms with Dad stood at the back, his arm resting on Mum's shoulder. What do you think?'

'Okay, that sounds okay.' I watch as she visibly relaxes. I want to ask why Miles will not be included...

But then, he isn't *family*.

'And it will then cut back to moi...' says Monty, briefly placing his hand on his chest. 'I'll do the final round-up, and then it will cut to you all around Madeline. And fade...' He sweeps his tanned hand downwards, and rests it on his knee.

'I'm hoping our united front will deflect some of the negative backlash,' says Madeline, more to Monty than to me.

'Madeline, Madeline, your public adore you... Clamour for your every word. People are far more open-minded than they used to be, sweetie. I wouldn't be surprised if you gain new devotees, most people admire honesty.'

A tatty terrier trundles into the room, his advance hampered by the remains of a once-white lacy bra hooked over his head and right paw. Despite this, he is holding his head high, and valiantly trying to look dignified. Madeline purses her lips and claps her hands, then points to the floor by her left foot. 'Terry! Heel,' she snaps.

The dog continues to tootle over to me, sniffs my outstretched hand, gives Monty an insolent glare then ambles over to Madeline. He has at least the grace to bow his head in submission.

'Terry! Have you been stealing again?' The dog lies down with his legs in the air, exposing his pink belly, and black paws. Maddie unravels the bra from Terry and holds it up for inspection. 'That's another for the bin! He's probably done a dozen circuits of the garden with that.'

Monty strolls over and tickles Terry's tummy. 'Isn't he adorable?' His smile fixed. Terry's back leg starts to sporadically shake, as if trying to scratch an itch. Monty stops and backs away.

'He's a common thief,' declares Maddie. 'I've lost count of the number of things he's stolen out of the washing basket... Half of them buried in the garden, the other half ripped to shreds like this. And it's his fault

I've a broken ankle!' She reaches down and tickles behind his ear. 'It's a good job I love you, little rascal.'

Monty sits down close to Madeline. 'Well, I'm sure when the time is right, Miles will put that broken ankle to good PR use, d-harling.'

On cue, Miles and Mum meander in, arms linked. Everyone, it seems, is very cosy, and I feel like a spare part.

Miles nods towards the discarded bra. 'I see Terry's been up to his usual tricks.'

Madeline sighs, and drops the bra on the sofa arm. 'It's just his nature.'

Dad stands up. 'So, are we all ready?' He picks up the bra, and stuffs it in his cardigan pocket.

From nowhere, it seems, a young woman with a tray of make-up swoops in on me. 'You okay if I just take the shine off?' Before waiting for an answer, she clasps my chin in a vice-like grip. I close my eyes and suffer the assault. Thankfully it lasts only a few seconds, so, either I already look fab, or expectations aren't that high.

'I think we are,' Monty answers for us all. 'Madeline, sweetie, we need to go through now, not long.'

'I'll just hoist myself up,' says Madeline.

Monty, Miles and Dad all rush forwards to help... My eyes automatically roll heavenwards.

'Thank you, thank you, thank you.' She balances delicately on her crutches. 'Must make sure these are out of shot while we're filming, don't want people thinking I'm looking for sympathy.'

That would never do!

I cannot believe it! Even on bloody crutches she's elegant! Her flowing wide-leg pants cover her pink plaster cast. She's wearing a loose chiffon caftan... No doubt it'll be precisely draped around her once she's seated again…

I really must try harder not to be a bitch… But it's very difficult. 'Good luck,' I muster as she's pampered out of the room.

Everyone follows, except me. I relax back in the window seat, close my eyes. I let out a sigh; it's so good to be alone. It's still light outside; I tilt my chin towards the window. Slipping off my pumps, I tuck my feet under me on the seat, rotate my shoulders in an attempt to shift the tension that's been there since all this began.

I can't believe I'm even here. If Miles hadn't given me that speech about "time for healing", I'd be at home getting blotto on vino or vodka, with friends. I'd be healing myself, not— I open my eyes. 'Oh! You scared the life out of me! How long have you been stood there?'

'Only a minute or two,' says Miles. He's resting on the door frame. He seems to do a lot of that. 'I didn't want to come in and disturb you.'

'And, you think standing there watching me, doesn't disturb me?'

'Does it?'

'Errrr yes!' I say. 'Put "not normal", and "behaviour" together, and you've got it.'

'Oh well, never mind.'

I can't help noticing the unicorns frolicking about and plucking at my heartstrings.

He smiles, and walks towards me. 'But you looked like you were either dozing, or deep in thought.'

'I was thinking *I'm not a celebrity, get me out of here.*'

'It'll be over before you know it,' he says. 'It's almost eight o'clock, your mum and dad are in the snug waiting to watch your interview… I was sent to get you.' He holds out his hand to help me up.

'I think I'll give it a miss. It was embarrassing enough doing the interview with Sarah. I'm not sure I can watch myself on TV… Mum and Dad will probably be embarrassed enough on my behalf.'

'I'm sure they're very proud of you.'

'Sure, they are.' Sure, they must be prouder of Madeline. I glance out of the window. 'I love this time of evening, everything seems still.'

'Enjoy it a while longer, I'll go and tell them you'll be in in a few minutes.'

'No. Tell them I'm getting some fresh air.' I slip my feet off the seat and back into my pumps. 'They'll understand. It's not as if every second of that interview isn't seared into my brain.'

'It wasn't that bad.'

'Maybe not for you. Anyway, tell them I'll be in in time for our family huddle.'

'Okay, will do.' He waits for me to leave the dining room first. 'Quickest way out is through the boot room, there.'

I escape in the direction I've been pointed. The air feels cool, much cooler than when I arrived less than half an hour ago. A shiver sneaks up, and shimmies through my body, I rub my hands over my arms.

The garden is made up of deep borders filled with perennials and shrubs all bursting with promise. The tinkle of water draws me to the far end of the garden. A small waterfall trickles into a pond strewn with water lilies closing up for the night. The fading sun sparkles on the ripples of water ebbing over the pond. I crouch down to get a closer look. I squint my eyes to make it into a magical hazy moment, like I used to do with Suzi and Trudy all those childhood years ago.

Evening birdsong accompanies the faint rumble of traffic in the distance. I could be anywhere. I wish I were anywhere but here... Back in fairyland maybe.

I look at my reflection in the water, distorted, like in the funhouse at Driftwood Sands with its wiggly mirrors. Just how I feel, all over the place, belonging nowhere. I hear a twig snap, look up to see Miles strolling across the lawn.

'If you're planning on drowning yourself,' says Miles with little concern, 'may I suggest either off the pier at Driftwood Sands or the boating lake, that pond is only two feet deep.'

'I'm not, but if I were, even I know it only takes a couple of inches of water to drown in,' I return.

'Mind if I keep you company?'

'Not at all,' I lie. 'It really is a lovely garden.'

'It sure is.' Miles sits down on the grass, stretching his legs out before him. 'Maddie spends hours out here. She's been going mad to get out since she broke her ankle. When I called round earlier, she was shuffling round on her bum pulling out weeds.'

'Not an image Madeline De-Muir's adoring public would expect.'

'She's Maddie here, not Madeline.'

'Ah, but Maddie manages to keep her hands beautifully manicured for Madeline's image,' I say.

'Gloves, she always wears gardening gloves. I've noticed your mum always does too.'

Touché. 'Any idea how Mr Mitten is going to maintain her reputation?'

'Mr Mitten is a master. He's going to go all out for the sympathy vote, but in such a cunningly clever way, not even Maddie will know it.' Miles smiles. 'And, even though we've managed to keep her ankle out of the press until now, tomorrow it will be news. Especially the bit about keeping her crutches out of shot, so as not to get the sympathy vote.'

'And you know this because?'

'Madeline De-Muir has an excellent PR team.'

'I thought you were the only team she needed.'

'I'm flattered, but I rely on a small network of excellent contacts who deal with the nitty-gritty. I just drip feed whatever I need out there.' He taps the side of his nose with his forefinger. 'Mostly top secret, I could tell you, but then I'd have to...'

'Yeah, yeah... I get it.'

'Obviously, I'd have to wait until after filming has finished...' His eyes crinkle.

'Ha-ha, I'm so glad you know you aren't funny,' I say.

Miles slaps his hand on his chest, and falls backwards onto the grass looking sorrowful. I bite the inside of my mouth to stop a traitorous giggle escaping, instead I let out a snort.

How ladylike, but I suppose the odd snort is better than hysteria.

Miles raises is head. 'How can you say such words, when my wit is world- renowned?' he says with feeling.

'I thought it was your modesty and charm.'

'Those too.' He nods solemnly.

'Two out of three ain't bad.'

Miles rolls over onto his front, elbows bent, propping his head on his hands. His expression serious as he looks at me.

I feel suddenly vulnerable, just from his expression I know he's reading my soul. Goosebumps creep up my neck and send shivers down my spine, at odds with the flush of my cheeks.

He raises his eyebrows. 'You think I'm charming?'

I shrug, lick my lips. 'I think you can be.'

'I've never been called charming before.' He gets slowly to his feet, and steps towards me. 'Am I being charming now?'

'Nooo! You're being too close,' I mutter, just as his lips brush over mine. My senses blast into overdrive, his hand slips around the back of my neck pulling me closer, deeper under his spell. I pull away, and rest my forehead on his shoulder. A myriad of emotions bubbling through me. 'Miles, no.'

'Don't hide from me.' He lifts my chin. 'You are so lovely, Christie.'

'Don't. Don't say things like that.' I try to shake myself away from his hold.

'But it's true, you are. And you don't even know the effect you have on everyone. On me.'

'Miles.' I close my eyes for a second. 'You and me, we can't, we can't be like this. Can't be anything more than what we are now.'

'And what are we now?'

'Friends.'

'Just friends?' He lets go of me, holds his arms stiffly by his sides. 'Okay, for now.'

'What do you mean?'

'What I mean, Christie…' he says, flinging his arm in the general direction of the house. 'When all this is done… You and I are going to have a serious talk about your future.'

'I know. I'm going to need to make some changes at school, but after a couple of weeks things will settle back—'

'I am not talking about your career, Christie!'

'Well then…' I take a deep calming breath. It doesn't work. 'I'd like to thank you for all your help and concern regarding my family.'

I sound like a fraud, even to myself. I hardly dare look at his face… Can't drag my gaze from it.

Miles shakes his head and lets out a snort, and then folds his arms firmly across his chest. 'Go on, I'm waiting.' An arrogant smile settles on his face, and I know he can tell he's got me rattled.

'I know it has been your job, but… I know… I'm sure we all know, how seriously you take your work.'

'My work?' Storm clouds gather in his eyes, and a deep frown splits his brow. 'This is not about work,' he growls. 'And let's just leave out the other people I love, because this is about you and me.'

It takes me a moment to process this information… Does he actually mean? 'Leave out the other people you love?'

'That's what I said.' His eyes don't leave my face.

'So, that means…' I can hardly bring myself to say it, 'It means…'

'It means I love you.'

I close my eyes, can feel my heart beat high in my chest, and those blasted unicorns are back doing their stuff. My hand automatically rises to cover my lips, to the memory of his kiss. For a moment I allow myself to dream of a lifetime with Miles.

In my mind's eye, I see us strolling through a meadow hand in hand; with two small children playing tag, a ditsy dog running ahead of us… But then, a shadow falls across the image. Madeline. I open my eyes to reality. 'No Miles.' I shake my head.

'What do you mean, no?'

'You don't know me, so how can you think you love me.'

'I don't know you!' He laughs, sarcasm spears through it. 'I have known you almost ten years.'

'How can you say that?'

'Because it's true! I know you inside out, Christie Harris. I have studied every picture you have ever sent to Maddie, been told about every letter!'

I cover my mouth. 'How could she, they were private!'

'I was jealous of you!'

'Pardon?'

'Always, you were all she ever talked about. You would have been maybe thirteen or fourteen and already so talented at art. I was a nineteen-year old big fat nothing. A nobody, going nowhere. Okay, so she set me on the path, college then Uni. But when I came home, it was still, always, Christie this, and Christie that.'

'What has that got to do with her showing you my paintings? They were just for her.'

'She had made you sound so perfect, one day I just exploded. Not proud of it... Madeline told me some of what you'd written in the letter you'd just sent her... she'd always shown me your work. But she said your letter was full of problems you were having with your friends, your teachers, your mum and dad. She said there was a fair bit of attitude in there. Actually, you were a bit of a madam...'

'Those letters were supposed to be private.' My voice croaks.

'And you laughed at yourself too. For the first time, I could see you as a normal person, not the super perfect icon Maddie portrayed. After that, before she'd let me see what work you'd sent her, she'd tell me some of what was in the letter first.'

'Every letter?'

'Every single one. I was home from my second year at Uni when you sent *Score*, and then it wasn't you I was jealous of, it was him.'

'I got over him,' I say, and for the first time, realise it's the truth.

'And I got over you. Messed about, dated, and then just buried myself in whatever project Maddie had me working on. To be honest, you were just Maddie's obsession.' He drags his hand through his hair, and shrugs.

'So, what's changed?' I say. 'Aren't I just her latest project?'

'At first I thought you could be. But then, the first time I saw you, you just walked into your mum's kitchen and flung your arms around her and started talking to her. You didn't let go.'

'I remember, I'd had a rotten day... Mr Sloan...'

'And you hadn't noticed me sitting at the table, and when you did, you were so defiantly bashful, but you still held her hand, you didn't let go.'

'She's my mum, she's my best friend, and you looked perfectly at home at the kitchen table, like you'd been there for hours.'

'I had... I was... Everything about you, felt so right. It scared me. After that, I was even more determined to keep you at arm's length, for my own sanity.'

'You're not doing very well at it,' I say.

'No, I'm not. And I've lost the battle trying to convince myself I don't love you. And I'm sorry... Tonight is not the night to dump all this on you.'

'You're right, it's not,' I say. As if I've slapped him, he turns his face away. 'It makes no difference, Miles. We aren't right together; it could never work.'

'You're wrong, Christie.'

'Maybe.' I shrug. 'Maybe I'm scared, or I'm just not prepared to take the risk.' I start walking back towards the house.

'That doesn't sound like something Christie Harris would ever admit.'

'I'm sorry... Sorry for not living up to your standard of who you think I am.'

I daren't look back. Continue to walk away. And darn the tears that threaten to fall. How can he make me feel like this tonight, knowing I've got to go and play happy families?

'Just for the record, this isn't over,' he says to my back.

I wish I could believe it.

I close the boot room door behind me, rest back on it, and drop my head into my hands. 'Why me? Why?'

All for One

... like an off-pisté skier ...

I edge my way into the snug. On the TV, it looks like Madeline's interview is starting to be wound up. Monty edges forward in his chair. 'I notice by your feet a package. Could that be what I think it is?'

Please no!

It is!

Madeline's coy smile lights up her eyes. 'It is; it's the last piece of work Christie has done for me. She hand-delivered it the other day, and I've been desperate to peep… But… I thought it might offer some insight to everyone, if they could see for themselves the effect her work has on me.'

'So, you haven't even had a sneaky peek?'

'No, and I'm very proud of myself for that! It's been torture.'

'Here, let me.' He reaches down and hands her the package. Madeline nods a thanks, and very slowly starts untying the string.

Why is this happening to me?

I wrap my arms tight around my stomach, I feel sick. Mum does one of her little tight smiles of excitement. Oh please, why?

Madeline opens up the paper, and looks at my portrait of Miles. She raises a hand to cover her mouth, her eyes wide with amazement. The camera zooms in, and a single tear drops to her cheek.

'Are you alright?'

Madeline shakes her head, and hugs the portrait. 'It's too precious. Oh, thank you, Christie, my angel.'

Monty looks directly into the camera. 'So, there we have it, too precious! And the way you're hugging it, Madeline, it looks like you're not going to share this one! But thank you for sharing your time with us, in this live broadcast. I give you, Madeline De-Muir... And now let's have a stroll down memory lane.'

The TV shows Madeline hugging the picture, then it cuts to one of her early appearances in *The Fallen*.

The snug door swings open.

'Okay, folks,' says a man I've never seen before. 'Time to join Madeline for the final shot.'

Dad stands up, but waits for me and Mum to leave the room first. 'I thought Miles would have come for us,' says Dad.

'Got called away,' says the man.

'Must have been important for him to miss this,' says Dad, as we're ushered into the lounge. Madeline tries to stand as we come in. She has rewrapped the portrait, but is still hugging it.

'Oh, Christie, thank you, it's lovely.'

'It's the last one,' I say with a shrug.

Mum and I perch, as directed on the chair arms, Dad at the back of Mum. The make-up girl takes Dad by surprise, managing to dust his face with powder before he flaps her away, next Mum, and then me. Madeline has a dust over too.

'Allow me.' Monty props the package by Madeline's feet.

I'm tempted to lift it out of the room.

'Places, we're back live in one minute,' says the assistant.

Monty sits down, and obliges the make-up girl by raising his chin while she attacks with the dusting powder.

'Didn't she do well?' says Monty. 'If you all give your shoulders a roll, you'll look more relaxed, it's only a camera crew.'

'Okay people, five, four...' The man holds up three fingers, two, one.

'So, there we have it. It's time for us to say goodbye, and as a special treat, I leave you with Madeline, and her family. Goodnight,' says Monty.

I pull my face into what will pass, hopefully, as a smile. Mum will probably look like a Cheshire cat, and Dad, well, I'll have to see when it's played back... He is still wearing his cardigan though. We sit for what seems like minutes, but the man counts down from ten on his fingers.

'And cut!' he says.

'Well done, everyone,' says Monty. 'I think that went really well. And not showing Christie's picture Madeline, was a masterstroke! Keeps everyone guessing.'

'It wasn't planned, I was going to turn it to show everyone how brilliant she is...'

'So, do I get to see it now?' asks Monty hopefully.

'Sorry,' she says. 'It really is too precious.'

'Oh well, I'll wait until next time,' he says with a chuckle.

'Girls,' Dad says, wrapping his arms around both me and Madeline. 'You were both awesome, well done.' He kisses the tops of our heads. Hers first. He wanders over and shakes Monty Mitten by the hand. Mum ruffles our hair, and then she goes over to Monty too, leaving me alone with Madeline.

She turns in the chair to face me. 'Oh, Christie, I can see.'

For a moment I scrunch my forehead bemused, of course she can see! But then I remember the portrait, and feel the now-familiar blush creeping up my neck.

'Oh,' I manage.

'You're in love with Miles.' Her voice is scarcely a whisper. She rests her hand on mine.

'Maybe.' I shrug. 'But it doesn't matter, nothing can come of it.'

'What do you mean, nothing can come of it? Doesn't he love you?' Her hushed voice takes on the tone of someone who's an authority in these things.

'He says he does,' I whisper.

'So, what's the problem?'

I look at her puzzled expression. She genuinely looks like she doesn't know.

She starts randomly patting my knee. 'Look, Christie, I know...' She rolls her eyes. 'Don't I know; he can be a complete pain in the ass sometimes. When he sets his mind to something, nothing can stop him... And sulk, he can sulk for England! But actually, and don't tell him I said so, he is one of the kindest souls I've ever met, and I love him to pieces.'

'I can't, and that's why. You love him. He's yours.' My throat closes, as I force out the words.

'Hold on!' She stops patting my knee. 'What do you mean, he's mine?'

'Madeline, it doesn't take a rocket scientist to see what is between the two of you. He hangs on your every word.'

'That's what I pay him to do! He works for me.'

'And the rest! He told me, Madeline! He told me all about being the first *Keep-a-Key* kid. So, you see, I know what you are to each other. You saved him.'

Madeline looks down at her hands. 'We saved each other. That's supposed to be just between me and Miles.'

'Like my letters were just supposed to be between you and me?'

'He told you that?'

'He's told me everything.'

'Then he really does love you. Where is he anyway, he should have been the one who brought you in.'

'We had words,' I say.

'You argued?' she asks. 'Tonight?'

'It was more a disagreement than an argument, neither of us raised our voice.'

'Suppressed discord, that's worse than an argument. I take it neither of you were satisfied with the outcome?'

'Suppose not,' I mutter. What is she, a mind reader? 'It's complicated.'

'Take it from one who knows, get it sorted out. Don't make the same mistake I made, or you'll live to regret it.' She offers a tight smile; it doesn't quite reach her eyes. 'Anyway, something must have sent him scurrying off, it's not like Miles to back off until he's got what he wants.' She pulls out a mobile from down the side of the chair. 'Surprise, surprise, one new voicemail from Miles.'

She taps the phone and holds it to her ear, the colour drains from her face. She tucks it in her pocket. 'There's been some kind of incident at the gallery, he's gone to sort it out. Quick, get my crutches please. Dad! Can you drive us to the gallery? I think there's trouble.'

'Not again!' Dad huffs.

Again?

Dad jingles his car keys. 'He should just leave it to the police.'

'They're the ones who notified him!' says Madeline. I can hear the anxiety creeping into her voice.

Then I remember the phone calls Miles got from Mrs Price. I pass Maddie her crutches as she starts hobbling away from me. Dad rushes from the room.

'Christie, you stay here,' says Mum, gripping my hand. 'I'm sure it'll be something and nothing.'

'It doesn't sound like something and nothing to me!'

'You won't be able to do anything,' insists Mum.

'And she will?' I point towards Madeline, who's halfway out the door like an off-pisté skier, her crutches grabbing frantically at the ground ahead of her.

'Stay!' Mum runs out the door to catch up to Dad, who's already striding across the drive.

'Wait for me!' I shout. Coils of fear add a panicky edge to my voice. 'Please!'

I can hear the engine running, and the tyres screeching on the drive. I sprint to the car gulping air, my chest tight. Yanking open the back door, I launch myself onto the seat next to Madeline, and slam the door behind me. My whole body is prickling with tension. The car jolts forwards slamming me into the back of the driver seat.

'Seatbelts!' barks Dad, as he swerves the car down the drive.

'Press the fob! Press the fob!' squeals Madeline, as we head towards the closed gates. The gates make their leisurely arc open, and Dad revs impatiently.

'Don't drive so fast!' says Mum. Thankfully the roads are quiet for a Saturday evening, and Dad's driving steadies under Mum's watchful eyes. 'Did anyone think to lock the house?'

'The film crew and Monty are still there,' says Madeline. 'What a mess.'

'Monty might still be there, but at least one of the television vans is following us,' says Dad.

I turn to look out of the back window, and see it, three cars back.

In the distance, I hear the sounds of sirens.

Mum looks over her shoulder to me and Madeline. 'It doesn't mean anything; there are always sirens on Saturday nights.' She exchanges a look with Dad.

My stomach is churning like a witch's cauldron. My mouth tastes like eye of newt and toe of frog. None of this seems real.

A police car is parked across the entrance to the street the gallery is on. Dad stops and opens his window to speak to the officer. I can't make out what they're saying, but I can smell smoke. I strain to see what's happening, but all I can make out is the flashing red and blue lights in the distance.

The gallery is on fire!

All my work! All my work!

How could Madeline be so stupid as to put all my work together in one place?

'Miles,' I whisper. 'Oh, please God, no. Where's Miles?' I open the car door, and empty the paltry contents of my stomach into the gutter, wipe my mouth on the hem of my top.

'There's no way we can get any closer,' says Dad calmly. 'The officer says there's no way. I'll try to find a safe place to park, and take it from there.'

'Didn't you ask him about Miles?' I plead.

'He's just a traffic cop, Christie, he won't know anything. Let's just stay calm.'

'There! Go down there!' shouts Madeline, lunging forwards and pointing towards a back alley.

Dad turns sharply, and the car bumps down the cobbled road until it reaches a brick wall.

'Now what are we going to do?' I hiss. 'It's a dead end!'

'Look up,' says Madeline.

I can just make out the top of the gallery. Pale puffs of smoke drift from the far side.

Madeline taps the side window. 'The other side of that wall is the rough end of the gallery carpark.'

'So, this is as close as we can get,' says Dad.

Madeline looks at me; her face appears haunted in the semi-darkness of the car. She grips my hand. 'We need to find out where Miles is.'

'He'll be with the police, surely,' says Mum.

'But we need to know...' Madeline squeezes my hand. 'If one of us could get over that wall, and talk to the police.'

Mum spins round in her seat. 'Don't be so... No! You can't want Christie to go.'

'Mum, I need to,' I say. An eerie calm settles over me.

'Christie, no!'

'Mum, I love him.'

Dad releases his grip on the steering wheel, and turns for the first time to look at me and Madeline. 'Christie, this is madness.'

'I need to do this, Dad.' My voice is low, weighed down by emotion.

Dad looks briefly heavenward. 'Is there anything I can say, or do, to stop you?'

I open my car door. 'No, Dad, I'm going.'

Deadly Serious

... finding a lifeless body ...

I let the car door swing shut, and get up close to the wall. It must be almost six feet high. I almost manage to clamp my fingers over the far side of the ledge, the coarse bricks dig into my palms as I try to get a grip. Attempting to scramble up the wall, dusty fragments crumble and fall as my feet struggle to find traction. I hear the others get out of the car. I rest my head on the cool brick.

I'll have to find another way in.

I feel Dad's hand on my shoulder. 'If I can get you over that wall, will you promise me solemnly, you won't do anything stupid?'

I turn and look into his worried eyes. 'I promise, Dad. I just want to make sure he's safe.'

Madeline pulls out her mobile, and starts tapping. I can hear the ring tone. 'He still isn't answering.'

'Keep trying, Maddie,' says Dad. 'Anne, Christie needs to know you're supporting her decision here...'

Mum's eyes search mine. 'If you promise to keep safe... Come here, be safe my angel.' She pulls me into a hug, sweeps my hair back out of my face, and looks like she's trying to memorise my every feature.

Dad nods. 'Okay, Christie, let's do this.'

Madeline pats my arm, I allow a semi-awkward embrace, and am taken aback at the tears I see in her eyes.

Madeline flutters delicate fingers under her eyes, expertly avoiding smudging her mascara. 'Phone us when you know for sure, and be careful… Love you.'

I offer a tight-lipped smile.

Dad pulls me close. 'Now, you've promised me you won't do anything silly.' He rests his hands on my head. 'Father, keep this child safe. Amen.'

'Amen,' I answer the shortest prayer I've ever heard him say.

I run my hand over the coarse bricks, feel a perverse pleasure at the smarting of my fingers.

Dad takes my hand in his. 'This side is not the problem, what you are going to land on at the other side, is. Hopefully, it's even ground.'

'It's probably not, but if I lower myself down, I should be okay.'

Dad nods. 'Yes, and if you can find the torch on your mobile, you'll be able to check it out first.'

'Good idea.' I pat my pocket.

Dad rests his back square against the wall, bends his knees, and makes a stirrup with his hands.

Mum steps forwards, and lifts my left foot into Dad's hands. 'I'm going to count to three… On three, I'm going to push you up by your bum, so you need to take a giant hop, okay? Then you need to straddle the wall with your right leg… Got it?'

'Okay.' I bend my right knee in preparation.

'Okay… On three… One… Two… Three!'

I hop up. Mum pushes me up with strength I didn't know she possessed. A split second later, while I still feel oddly weightless, Dad lifts me up by my foot resting in his hands.

'Straddle!' says Mum and Dad simultaneously.

I swing my right leg over and cling to uneven bricks on the top of the wall. I let out a breath I didn't know I was holding.

'Well done, Christie, you did it!' says Dad.

I laugh. 'We did it! If I didn't know you better, I'd think you've both done that many times before.'

'We did a bit of Bible smuggling in Russia during the eighties,' says Mum. 'Before Maddie came along.'

'M-u-u-u-m! And you tell me not to do anything silly. I can't believe you!'

'I didn't promise my parents I wouldn't do anything silly,' she says smugly. 'After all, why should I? I was married to a vicar.'

'Be careful,' says Dad, patting my dangling foot.

'Okay.' I get my mobile out, tap the torch on, and point it down to where I'm likely to land. Weeds, moss and clumps of grass form a border around the base of the wall. 'It looks okay.'

I look across the car park. I can make out two fire engines and a selection of police vehicles all with their lights flashing. Thankfully, I can't actually see any flames leaping from the gallery, but rather swirls of smoke from around the other side.

'Does there look to be anyone you can approach?' asks Dad.

'No, everyone looks to be at the other side of the building.'

'That's probably a good thing,' says Madeline. 'It means you can get closer before you're stopped.'

'I know… You keep trying to ring Miles. I might hear his mobile when I'm closer,' I say, not sure who I'm trying to convince.

'I will,' says Madeline.

'Here goes...' I drop myself face down on the top of the wall, and then pull up both my legs, so I'm led flat across the top. The cold bricks dig into my skin through my thin clothes. Twisting, I try to balance my body weight onto my elbows with my legs dangling. Tiny stones jab into my forearms. Edging my legs down the side of the wall I try to get a foothold by prodding the wall with my feet.

'Arrrrhhh!' My foot slips down, thrusting my body against the wall as a chunk of brick crumbles. Digging my nails into the bricks, I try to hold for a second longer, take a breath and drop...

'Humph!' My feet hit the soft ground. Instinctively I bend my knees and drop backwards onto my bum, curling my arms around me. Turning, I sink my hands into soft grass, a safe landing.

'Are you okay?' shouts Mum.

'Yes, soft landing on my bum.' I stand, and dust myself down. 'I'm going to make my way over to the gallery now... See you later.'

My mobile's torch gives enough light for me to make out where to walk on the uneven carpark. Everyone seems to be focusing on the other side of the building. I stride towards the gallery, each step hoping to bring me closer to finding Miles.

I'm close to the back door I first entered only a couple of weeks ago. The scrunch of gravel alerts me to someone coming. I run to the back door... Push it... Locked... Two firefighters, fully kitted out with breathing gear round the corner. I flatten myself against the door.

Stupid! Stupid! Stupid!

One of them runs towards me. My breathing quickens, as my eyes desperately dart about looking for an escape route... I'm cornered... Can't get away...

He's too close... I slide helpless to the ground, defeated. He grabs my arm, yanks me away from the door... Shouts... Two police officers run toward me, each taking one of my arms.

'What do you think you're doing? This building's on fire!' the first officer shouts. 'Come on, let's get you to safety.'

I turn to look back at the gallery as I'm hauled away. The ear-splitting thuds of a battering ram smashing into the gallery door, fills me with foreboding.

'I need to find someone!' I try to struggle free.

'Wait a minute,' says one of the officers looking at me. 'Is someone in there?'

'I don't know.' Tears well up in my eyes, as the horror of what danger Miles could be in overwhelms me.

'Have you seen someone go in?' asks the other officer.

'No, but—'

'Are you here with somebody else?' he asks.

'No, I'm on my own.'

'So, let me get this right. You haven't seen anyone going into the building.'

I shake my head; try to streak my hand under my running nose. 'No.'

He nods. 'And you are here on your own.'

'Yes.'

'Okay, that's all we need to know for now,' he says.

They both start steering me further away from where I need to be. I try to plant my heels into the ground, but they still keep walking, dragging me along.

'Stop!' I shout, and lift my feet off the ground, desperately try to wrestle my arms free. 'You don't understand!'

'You, young lady, are in enough trouble as it is, don't make it any worse.'

'I need to find Miles! Miles Hepworth!' They loosen their grip, and I slither to the floor. 'Humph.'

One of them holds out his hand, the other lifts me by the elbow. 'Do you know Mr Hepworth?'

'He's, he's a very close friend. We argued, and then he got called out here to this... And I don't know where he is, and he isn't answering his mobile. Please, I need to find him... Can you please, please help me?' My stomach turns, I cover my mouth with my hand.

The officers exchange looks. 'First things first, let's get you somewhere we can have a proper chat.'

'Is Miles here?' I ask.

'This way, Miss.'

The roadside is unrecognisable. The flashing lights from three engines and police vehicles create a kaleidoscope of colour. I'm led mute, to a police car. An officer is talking on his radio, he turns and nods. A solitary white ambulance is the only vehicle without lights blaring.

'Has somebody been hurt?' I whisper.

'That's not something we can discuss.'

The new officer turns towards me. 'I'm Chief Inspector Kent. Can you tell me your name please?'

'I'm Christie Harris, and I'm looking for Miles Hepworth, he came here after someone from the police contacted him.'

'Thank you, Miss Harris. I've just had notification from the constabulary, informing me to expect you to turn up at some point... Not a wise decision under the circumstances.'

'Please, I need to know where Miles is.'

'Mr Hepworth was here earlier, speaking with me about recent disturbances at the gallery. He became agitated, and left abruptly.'

'Where did he go?' I look about, where would he go?

'We are not sure of his whereabouts at the present time, although there was an unconfirmed report of someone entering the building.'

'He's in there?' I whisper.

'We don't know, Miss Harris. Like I said, it was an unconfirmed report. I'm sure Mr Hepworth is well aware of the dangers of entering a burning building. The fire is now under control, and firefighters with breathing apparatus are making a thorough search of the building.'

He could be dead. I raise my hand to my throat, panic surges through my veins, my skin prickles with agitation. What if he is? What then?

What if I never hear him laughing again. Or watch as the tell-tale crinkles start at the corners of his eyes. I start to shake; a shiver takes hold of me. I rub my arms, hug myself. I touch my fingers to my lips, to where only a couple of hours ago he kissed me. When I rejected his love. What if the unicorns never frolic again?

The Chief Inspector clears his throat. 'He might not even be in there; we are just taking precautions at this stage. If you would like to wait in the car with one of the officers until we have any news, you can do. Otherwise, I'm afraid I'll have to ask you to remain behind the cordon.'

'I'll wait here,' I say, rubbing my arms.

The ambulance remains still.

'Officer, please stay with Miss Harris,' says Chief Inspector Kent, his tone neutral.

'Miss Harris,' the officer says, 'you'll be warmer in the car.'

I follow him to the car, and sit down on the back seat. He nudges the door to close it. I jam my foot forwards to stop the door from fully closing... Instinct demanding I'm not trapped in here. He seems not to notice, and the car heaves as he sits in the front. Holding the door slightly open with the tips of my fingers, I ease my throbbing foot inside the car and rub it with my other foot.

'You'll warm up in no time,' he says.

'I'm okay.' I need to find Miles.

'The Chief's not best pleased... Someone's got a film crew here, they've probably got long lenses trained on us right now.'

'Oh.' I keep watching the ambulance. If he comes out, when he comes out, I want him to know, need to tell him how I really feel.

'Looks like we're in for a long night, keeping the public away until the building is safe and secure.'

'What will happen?'

'Once the fire is fully out, a specialist team will check if it's structurally sound. If it is, it will need to be boarded up to keep looters out. If not, the road here will need to remain closed, scaffolding put up, traffic diversions put in place, the—'

'Was it arson?'

'Can't say. Forensics will be in before the clean-up, probably on their way; they just love Saturday-night overtime.'

'Why would anyone do that?'

'I can't answer that one,' says the officer.

And then I remember the fire I started in Church all those years ago. How Dad took charge of the situation... How he rationalised my actions to the troubled congregation. Only now, do I fully understand the horror of what could have happened that Sunday. The danger I put everyone in.

My whole body feels hypersensitive. Resting my elbows on my knees I drop my head into my hands, my body violently shaking. I feel cold and sick and frightened.

What if all this is my fault?

What if this is payback for all the stupid things I've ever done? My stomach makes involuntary jerks as I'm racked with silent sobs. Wrapping my arms round my body, I attempt to hold myself still by pushing back against the car seat.

My mobile vibrates in my pocket. It's Madeline. 'Has he answered?'

'No, no, so I take it he's not there?' she whispers.

'No. He was, earlier...' My voice sounds odd.

'Where are you?' she asks.

'Sat in the back of a police car, they found me too close to the gallery.'

'Well sit tight, and if... When you find out where he is—'

'I'll phone.'

I slot my mobile back in my pocket, and keep my eyes focused on the ambulance. If the paramedics spring into action—

My mobile vibrates again.

'He's answered!'

'Where?' My head swivels to look around outside. 'Where is he?'

'I couldn't make out it out clearly, only the word "gallery", so he's in there!'

I smash the car door open and hit the ground running... A shout from the officer rings in my ears. Keeping my head low I sprint to the back of the building, I know the door has been rammed open. Please God, help me find him. I drown out the shouts and chaos about me. Need to find him.

I jump over the splintered door and into darkness. With no power the meagre emergency lighting offers only minimal help. The acrid smell of smoke attacks the back of my throat, my eyes smart. Blinking rapidly, I squint, trying to minimise the discomfort, cover my mouth with my hand.

'Miles! Miles!' I grope along the wall, feeling my way, trying to remember. Where would he go? Where would be safe? I click my mobile's torch on, push open a door. 'Miles, where are you?' I choke out.

I flash my torch about the room. Not here. Please God, I can't lose him. I follow my hand further into the building. Pushing open the next door, I recognise it as the room I sat in that first day. My torch flicks over the room.

'Miles! Where are you?'

Surely the firefighters will have checked out this room already... I turn to leave... A niggle stops me, I step into the room. Remember Suzi throwing up in the loos, me showering in my underwear.

This room has an annex to the side... I follow the wall round, where is it? My fingers feel along the smooth plastered wall, there! An alcove with a door! Moving forwards, I push the door open and listen.

I can hear his mobile ringing! 'Miles! Where are you?' I croak. His mobile stops ringing. 'Oh please! Miles, answer me! Where are you?'

Only the groans of the building answer. Fear roots me to the spot. I try to focus. The back of my throat feels like I've been drinking paint stripper, and my eyes and nose are streaming. The floorboards creak as I edge towards another door.

Tapping!

There it is again! I ease the door open, partly through fear of what I might find, and partly through fear of causing harm to whoever I might find.

My hand flies up to cover my mouth and I gasp at the sight of the lifeless heap in the middle of the room.

'No!' All the fight dies in me. I drop to the floor, scramble on my hands and knees to the mound. Tapping again. Turning back, I see him.

'Oh, thank you, God.' I clamber beside his crumpled body. Smother his head with kisses. 'Oh, thank God you're alive. I'm sorry.'

I feel oddly weightless as relief swamps me. Drained of all emotions other than love, and relief. I wipe my hand over my face, pushing away the tears.

'Christie,' he rasps. I feel him nod in my embrace. Taking turns at wiping smudges from his face and then the tears from my own face. I close my eyes and hold him close, not sure if I'm ever going to be able let him go again.

'Safe,' he murmurs.

'Yes, Miles, you're safe now. I'll get help.' I stroke his head, his brow furrows and he shakes his head. He tries to speak, but I can't make out what he's trying to say. His mobile starts to ring. He raises his hand and waves his fingers towards the heap in the middle of the room.

I shuffle across the floor on my bum, the thought of finding a lifeless body flits through my mind. It feels like an old dust sheet, I rummage in its folds to find his mobile.

'Got it!' I press to answer. 'I've got him Madeline. Get help. We're in the private annex near the back.'

'Thank God! How is he?' I look over to Miles slumped near the door.

'Alive.' I disconnect the call. I start to shuffle back to Miles; he shakes his head and points back to the dust sheet.

'Safe,' he croaks again.

I pull back the sheeting, and cover my mouth with my hand. I stare at the heap of paintings, haphazardly stacked together, my eyes and nose still streaming. I shake my head in disbelief. My pictures.

'Oh Miles, for these? You risked your life for these?'

'For you,' he rasps. 'They're all your life.'

'Oh Miles.' I scramble back to him, stroke his hair back off his forehead. 'I was wrong; they're just my journey so far. My journey before I met you.' I cover my mouth again with my hand, close my eyes trying to hold in the sobs. I nearly lost him for these…

Somewhere nearby, I can hear voices and feet clattering about.

'In here!' I shout as loud as my lungs and throat will allow. 'We're in here.' I start bashing my hands and feet on the wooden floor. The closer they sound the louder I stamp my feet.

A firefighter all but falls into the room.

Now we are safe…

Fastening breathing masks over our faces, the two firemen work steadily to secure Miles into a head and body restriction stretcher. Does he need it? Miles struggles to free his hands.

'Steady on, mate, it's for your own good.'

Miles grimaces, and rolls his eyes towards the mound of artwork he risked his life to save. As another firefighter lumbers in, light floods the room casting eerie shadows across the walls. He settles his hand round my arm, starts to lead me out towards the back of the gallery.

I turn to watch as Miles is manoeuvred through the door. The building groans in disapproval as we make our way back towards the smashed-in door. Uneven floors, and the giant dancing shadows hinder our progress.

Stepping out into the crisp night air, I let out a sigh of relief. A shiver runs through me. Again, I turn back to look at Miles, his face and clothing are streaked black. His knuckles blooded.

I could have lost him.

I wait for his stretcher to draw by my side, curl my little finger around his. A faint smile hovers over his lips. A surge of love gushes over me. Pulling off my mask, I bend forwards and brush back the flop of hair from his brow. Look into his eyes. The uncertainty hovering in their depths, almost crushes me.

Putting my mouth to his ear, I whisper, 'I love you, Miles Hepworth.' I rest my forehead gently on his. The relief of saying those words aloud, allows some of my guilt at rejecting him to ebb away. I feel an odd mixture of vulnerability and strength.

'Love you too, Christie Harris.' His broken voice spears my self-control.

Closing my eyes, I squeeze back the whimper threatening to escape. The smell and taste of embers all about, reminding me of how foolish I've been.

How could I have risked shattering our chance at happiness? Now he's safe, I allow myself to cry at my own stupidity.

I open my eyes as a flurry of green surrounds us. Paramedics take over from the firemen. A foil blanket is wrapped over my shoulders. I'm eased away from Miles and into a wheelchair, hurried towards the ambulance. From the corner of my eye I notice a commotion going on close to the police cordon.

Madeline is waving both her crutches in the air in a most un-De-Muir way. 'Christie! It's me! We'll meet you at the hospital! Okay?' she hollers.

I wave at her. Fight the urge to laugh out loud at how ridiculous she looks.

'Christie, don't worry, everything's going to work out fine!'

I bite my lip, wave back and nod.

I hope she's right.

Dawn

"What about Maddie?"

'Mum… Dad, go to him!' I look from one to the other. 'Honestly, I'm alright! And he's all on his own. Mum, please.'

Mum pats my knee, and stands up at last. 'Okay, if you're sure then.'

'Just go!'

Mum brushes a kiss on the top of my head. 'What about Maddie? She's still sat out there.'

I sigh. 'Like I've kept saying, she should have gone with Miles.'

'She won't go anywhere until she's seen you're alright.'

'I am… Okay, she can come in when you go. It's a stupid rule only letting two people in at a time anyway.'

Dad ruffles my hair. 'See you soon, munchkin. And try not to be such a grump, we've all a lot to be thankful for.' His grey pallor is at odds with his upbeat manner.

'I know.' My throat tightens. 'I just keep thinking what if?'

'Well don't, you're both safe.'

I nod, and they wave as they leave the room. The smell of disinfectant, and the blood-splattered screen do little to ease my anxieties. At least I know Miles has already been admitted, I think they've forgotten about me.

I could just leave. It's been hours.

Clunk, clunk, shuffle, clunk, clunk, shuffle. Here she comes... Actually, looking wretched! 'Oh, Christie, there you are, poor thing! How are you feeling?'

I shrug. 'I just want to get out of here. I'm fine, really.'

'I'm sure it won't be long now.'

'It's been hours, and you should have stayed with Miles. He'll have been all on his own all this time.' Nastily, I want to say "again..." But she already looks close to tears.

'Trudy and Suzi are in with him... I have no idea how Trudy managed to get them both past security. He isn't alone... I would never have left him alone...'

'How is he?'

'I shouldn't have let you go after him.' Madeline lowers her head, but not before I see her tear-laden eyes. She pulls a hankie from her sleeve and blows her nose noisily. Turns away from me to dab her eyes.

'You couldn't have stopped me.' I admit.

Madeline looks back to me, carefully made-up eyes attempt to mask earlier tears. Her composure, so beautifully executed for her audience, is now only a thin veil. Her eyes are drowning in sadness, longing. I can almost see the frightened teenager she once was, in their depths.

I reach across, touch her hand. 'Madeline, really, you couldn't have stopped me.'

'I could have tried.' She shrugs, sighs. 'I thought you'd tell the police that Miles was in the gallery, didn't expect you to go barging into a burning building—'

'I needed to find him. To tell him.' I bite my lip. Now it's my turn to look away, to hide the guilt in my eyes.

'Have you told him?' It's almost a whisper.

'Yeah... I have. I think deep down he knew already.'

'It's important to hear the words, Christie. To be honest enough to say them.'

'I know.' It's like talking to the ever-wise Auntie Maddie. 'It's complicated.'

'Because of me? Don't let it be.' She runs her fingers through her hair. 'Miles is a good man.'

'I know.' I bite my lip again.

At this rate I'll have no lips left.

'And you *do* love him, Christie, that's plain for me to see.'

I feel defenceless under her scrutiny. She knows all there is to know about me.

Madeline, taps her lips with her forefinger. 'I'll tell you something, something I've told no one before... I was sixteen, and thought I was *in love* with your father.'

'Really... Madeline! I don't want to hear about him. Honestly, this isn't the time!'

'Well, you need to hear it, whether you want to hear it or not... So, please... At sixteen, I was pregnant with you.' She touches her flat belly. 'I didn't have the nerve to tell my boyfriend, thought he'd tell me to...' She shrugs. 'I don't know what I thought he'd do. So, I didn't tell him, haven't... That's not the point... I really did love him, and I never told him. And now, all these years later, I've never been able to stop loving him... It's like a part of me is always missing, always longing... For him... Pathetic isn't it? I've loved him a lifetime... Your lifetime... And he doesn't even know!'

She holds her hands steady on her lap, her head is held high. At a glance anyone would think her in control, but her eyes plead for my understanding. The urge to sketch her makes my fingers twitch.

A sad smile lingers on her lips. 'You see, Christie, it was complicated...'

I meet her steady gaze, see the pain in her eyes. 'Must run in the family,' I say.

'Don't let it, Christie... Buck the trend. You mustn't let *our* relationship come between you and Miles. You and me... We'll sort out... It might take us time to get used to each other, but... You know, life can be very lonely, even when it's full of people.'

I nod, acknowledge her loneliness, feel sorry for her.

Almost.

She touches my hand. 'You both deserve more than that, everyone does.'

'How is he?'

'Miles? He has no broken bones, lots of minor cuts, burns, bruises. His hands are a mess... There are still some tests they want to run on his lung capacity, but on the whole, he's doing well. Oh, ranting about your pictures being left in the gallery. I cannot believe he risked his life for them.'

I can, he did it for me. 'I want to see him.'

'He'll most likely be sleeping.'

'I need to see him.'

Maddie sighs, but her eyes gleam with mischief. 'I suppose you expect me to help you break out of here, do you?'

'I think you owe me that much... Sorry... Sorry, just tell me which ward he's on. And if by any chance a doctor does happen to stray into here, tell him I've gone to the loo or something.'

'Ward 10, men's surgical. It was the only male ward with a free side room.'

'I'll find it.' I slip my pumps on, tiptoe to the doorway. I peer out to make sure no one is about, not that I've actually seen any medical staff in ages.

'Christie, you and me... We are alright, aren't we?'

The catch in her voice lowers my defences. 'I think we will be. You're just like my Auntie Maddie, and I love her.' I step out into the deserted corridor, turn back. 'On second thoughts, come with me.'

Her face is transformed by a spontaneous smile. She inhales a deep breath. As she breathes out an aura of peace radiates from her. She nods her head, eyes filled with gratitude, and gets to her feet.

The rhythm of clunk, clunk, shuffle, swings back into action.

We make steady progress through a maze of short corridors, which lead to the main aisle running the length of the hospital.

Reception is practically deserted. Madeline perches on a seat to catch her breath. My skin prickles, as I control the urge to hurry her along.

A row of abandoned wheelchairs looks mighty tempting... We could just borrow one. Maddie stands up, positions her crutches, and we're off... Clunk, clunk, shuffle, clunk, clunk, shuffle... The aisle stretches out, crisscrossed with other corridors leading off in all directions.

'Christie, do you know where we're going?'

'I have absolutely no idea. I'm sure we'll find our way.'

Huge glass windows allow the first glimmers of daylight to ambush the overhead lighting.

The night is behind us, and now, is the promise of a new dawn...